# RUSSIAN BEAUTY

# RUSSIAN BEAUTY

## VICTOR EROFEYEV

TRANSLATED BY
ANDREW REYNOLDS

VIKING

VIKING
Published by the Penguin Group
Penguin Books USA Inc., 375 Hudson Street, New York, New York 10014, U.S.A.
Penguin Books Ltd, 27 Wrights Lane, London W8 5TZ, England
Penguin Books Australia Ltd, Ringwood, Victoria, Australia
Penguin Books Canada Ltd, 10 Alcorn Avenue,
Toronto, Ontario, Canada M4V 3B2
Penguin Books (N.Z.) Ltd, 182–190 Wairau Road, Auckland 10, New Zealand

Penguin Books Ltd, Registered Offices: Harmondsworth, Middlesex, England

First American Edition
Published in 1993 by Viking Penguin, a division of Penguin Books USA Inc.

1 3 5 7 9 10 8 6 4 2

Originally published in Russian by Moskovski Rabochi in 1990 as Русская красавица.
Copyright © Victor Erofeyev, 1990. Published in French by Editions Albin Michel S.A. in
1990 under the title La Belle de Moscow. Copyright © Editions Albin Michel S.A., 1990.
First published in English in Great Britain by Hamish Hamilton Ltd. in 1992. In the United
States, portions of this book first appeared in Grand Street and Index on Censorship.

This edition published by arrangement with Editions Albin Michel S.A.

LIBRARY OF CONGRESS CATALOGING IN PUBLICATION DATA
Erofeyev, V. V. (Viktor V.)
[Russkaîa krasavitsa. English]
Russian beauty : a novel / Victor Erofeyev ; translated by Andrew
Reynolds.
p. cm.
ISBN 0-670-83606-0
I. Title.
PG3479.7.R58R8713 1993
891.73'44—dc20 92-31454

Printed in the United States of America
Set in Goudy Old Style
Designed by Katy Riegel

# MAIN CHARACTERS

*Irina/Ira Vladimirovna Tarakanova*—Russian Beauty
*Ksenya/Ksyusha Mochulskaya*, lover of Ira, now married to
    French dentist—such a rare gift of joy
*Vladimir Sergeyevich/V.S./Leonardik/Uncle Volodya*—a legend
    in his lifetime
*Zinaida Vasilievna*, wife of Vladimir Sergeyevich
*Anton/Antonchik*, son of Vladimir Sergeyevich
*Yegor* and *Lyusya*, erstwhile servants to Vladimir Sergeyevich
*Tikhon Makarovich*, Ira's grandfather
*Stanislav Albertovich Flavitsky*, gynecologist with proclivities
*Sergei* and *Nikolai Ivanovich*, twin journalists

OTHER WOMEN

*Margarita/Rituyla*
*Polina Nikanorovna*, Ira's direct boss at work collective
*Veronika*, deputy director of a laboratory—a witch as well
*Natasha*—God's little eater of raw greens
*Nina Chizh*, co-worker

PROTECTORS/ESCORTS/LOVERS/HANGERS-ON

*Vitasik Merzlyakov,* the six-day lover
*Viktor Kharitonych,* boss at work collective
*Dato Vissarionovich,* Georgian musician
*Yura Fyodorov*—widely known in small circles
*Boris Davydovich*—a Jewish Hercules
*Timofei*—also a man

# RUSSIAN BEAUTY

# ONE

W*ell?*
    No answer, as he plunged in up to the neck.
He crawled, wheezing and puffing. Crawling
proved a slippery business. He kept on bumping into taut
elastic objects in the dark: they rocked slightly, like untethered
airships, and gave way reluctantly, floating off to the side.
The thick wreathing smell was discouraging, but he steeled
himself and crawled forward, muttering Latin names specially
invoked to counteract the gloomy, predatory spell of this mysterious mansion, to endow these awkward movements with
the character of a scientific expedition.

Persistence, experience, and faith in medical Latin were
of considerable assistance. He slid successfully into the ravine
between the warm gurgling rocks, rocks reminiscent both of
wineskins filled with warm liquid and of mollusks, in that they
possessed really disgusting-looking crests, small cockscombs,
and tiny suckers, which didn't stop their chaotic motion for
a second, their wriggling on spindly little legs. And so, having
successfully negotiated the suckers, although he had been
forced to tear out several of them roots and all—the mollusks
started to ooze blood—he reached his goal and, brought to
the peak of excitement despite himself, raptly eyed the wide

1

expanse, staring in silence at the spectacular view lying before him:

IN A BROAD, SUN-CARESSED VALLEY, BERGAMOT TREES WERE BLOOMING WITH A TENDER LIGHT-BLUE BLOSSOM.

*Well? What are you doing down there? Hey!*

Stanislav Albertovich was radiant. Stanislav Albertovich threw himself upon me with slobbering kisses. *Congratulations! Congratulations!* He was deeply touched, the way only old men can be. To tell the truth, I was amazed by his reaction, although you could have knocked me over with a feather after this news, and black dots whirled before my eyes, but I kept myself in check, I didn't shout out in a mad voice, didn't try to hide, didn't crash into unconsciousness. I merely gripped the armrests and received the blow uncomplainingly and worthily, like a nun or a queen.

A needle of horror entered my heart. It started to shudder in its final melancholy, trembled, missed a beat, stopped. Sweat was streaming down my spine. As my legs waved in the air, I said farewell to life, which in this ill-starred year had ostentatiously turned its back on me, as if I had done something wrong. In turning its back on me, it had pointed out the road into backwoods and wastelands so impenetrable that the foot of man had left no imprint there, or if it had, it had been immediately swallowed up by the earth and disappeared without a trace.

I turned down the cotton ball soaked with smelling salts —no, thank you!—and looked at Stanislav Albertovich with undisguised suspicion. Why, when it came to it, was he so moved? What business was it of his? What a bastard! Do you think I've forgotten? I remember everything, Stanislav Albertovich, everything! I have a long memory, Stanislav Albertovich. I remember how I was the granny of Russian abortion and the little children born in bondage. . . . But I was shocked by his news and said nothing, accepting the blow of fate, even though the news was not unexpected, for I had recognized that aftertaste as soon as I woke up one morning, the unmistakable aftertaste, the earliest herald of alarm. And there had been a nagging pain down below, like on all the other occasions, when, smiling unconcernedly, I had thrown caution to the winds and got pregnant. But hope had kept my spirits up, because this was just not possible; they had all unanimously assured me, Never again. And in that choir of white doctors' smocks Stanislav Albertovich had been the first to spread his hands in a gesture of grief, the first to make himself a figure of compassion, but I smiled at him from the table—Don't snivel over me!—and joked about little children born in bondage, so that I had every reason to believe that this was indeed the case and therefore, laughing unconcernedly, had long since given up precautionary measures of various types: all those coils of theirs, pills, lemons, and bits of soap, to say nothing of all the other life belts. And he was not a bad physician, really. It would be hard to find his like again, despite his proclivities, which Ksyusha remarked on when she brought us together at the dawn of our friendship, before she was a Frenchwoman and before she rushed around in the dark in her bellowing pink automobile, but instead drove a canary-yellow little Zhiguli; it was in that car that she drove me to see Stanislav Albertovich, telling me along the way about certain of his proclivities, which, as Ksyusha noted, bring his female patients out of their depression. What's the point of turning him down, if from now on I'll be in need of him, even if he *is* a bastard! So I merely waved away the slobbering kisses and declined the smelling salts. But interpreting my weakness to his own advantage, and also to the advantage of the increase of human resources, he turned red and started crooning with tenderness, saying that this was a miracle such as had not been seen before. It might even be the time to organize a symposium and give a talk about what our playful one has brought forth, our naughty pussycat, but I say to him, Keep your hands off my pussycat! He withdraws his hand unhurriedly; he stands there laughing, and his cheeks quiver.

Oh, Stanislav Albertovich, what an indefatigable old goat you are! Don't you get bored, poking and poking from morning till evening? You've ruined your eyesight at your post, but still you don't relax, still you haven't sated your boyish curiosity, after spending a lifetime glued to that frosted window, ever since the first day you pressed yourself up against it! Okay, I said sternly, for starters let me climb down from this table of yours (and do you remember, Stanislav Albertovich, how I came to you the first time, on Ksyusha's recommendation, complaining of painful tears in my tissues, and you permitted yourself to feel my breasts with impunity, under cover of medical immunity? I was young then, cheerful . . . ), let me get down from this damn carousel that flies into a chamber of gloom and horror, there you are, and let me slip on, if you'll pardon me, my panties! Leave me alone! Oh, Stanislav Albertovich, only the grave will change the leopard's spots and make the hunchback straight, but I say to myself: The grave won't make the hunchback stand erect, this is a hopeless case, the hunchback will make the grave straight, and this is the reason why shivers creep down my body and there is a needle of horror in my heart, but I took myself in hand by pretending to concentrate on getting dressed.

Well, then, I say, that's more like it, now you *may* congratulate me. *Merci*, of course—only, strictly speaking, what exactly are these congratulations for? Don't you see? Don't you see? Since you, my child, are no longer a little girl, you must understand what a miracle you and I are witnessing together, despite all the scientific laws of infertility—which, I interrupt him, suited me just fine—in which, he retorts, I never believed and never will, seeing your "infertility" as the fruit of a stoical defense mechanism, child—but you're wrong to think that, Stanislav Albertovich, very wrong, and indeed if I were to tell you about all the nuances of this *miracle,* then you too would understand that this isn't an option, and instead of getting angry, you would demand, as a doctor, an immediate termination of this budding miracle, and this is the course of action on which, basically, I insist, which course, in accordance with my rights and desires, I shall follow, preferably with your help, my good Stanislav Albertovich.

As I understand it, the problem is the father. Is he, forgive me for asking, someone handicapped, an alcoholic? Worse, I answered laconically. Stanislav Albertovich was taken aback, his face acquiring a stupid expression before my very eyes, and he grew pensive. . . . "A Negro?" the doctor uttered at last. In spite of the chill in my soul, I started to guffaw, as if I were being tickled, although, to be honest, I'm not afraid of being tickled, or if I am afraid, it's just a tiny bit—I think it's more that I don't like it rather than that I am afraid, in contrast to Rituyla, who actually longs for it, takes a girlish pleasure in it, which I find incomprehensible. She is still young, Rituyla, and I look condescendingly at her squealing when I tickle her. Well, if someone wants to be tickled, why not? Rituyla will appear here soon. "Have you ever had a Negro?" Rituyla asked me. "No," I admitted honestly. I was always clean. But Rituyla was courted by Joel from Martinique. A Negro but, characteristically, with a French passport. Rituyla even used to give him blow jobs! But then he went away and sent a postcard from Martinique with a view of the lagoon and of shaggy-haired palm trees, and in it he wrote that he hadn't liked it in our country, because it was too cold and there were no

carnivals. Rituyla was very annoyed and called Joel an un-
grateful swine.

"No," I say to Stanislav Albertovich, "not a Negro.
Worse!"

"You can't get worse than that," says a perplexed Stanislav
Albertovich, but his curiosity is aroused. I didn't say anything.
He can't be relied upon. Okay, I said, let's end this conversation. He gave me a cigarette. Can I give you some advice,
child? I shrugged my shoulders, but he continued anyway.
You, of course, don't have to take my opinion into consideration, child. You are a celebrated woman, you have become
world-famous in the media. You have, it's quite understand-
able, friends, patrons, and advisers, so I understand this is a
slippery issue, and it's not for me, an old-fashioned man, about
to take full retirement and move to my country residence—
I didn't know that he had a country home and thought: Oh,
indeed, he must be a rich bastard; he's made a fortune on
women's tears and indispositions, and he smokes good cigarettes, the best brand—but where is the country residence?
In Kratovo! Ah! the Jews' enclave—I get it—Israel-on-the-
Moscow. He develops his thought further: It's not for me,
child, he says, to interfere in your wild and wonderful life,
certain features of which he'd had the unexpected opportunity—here he lowered his voice—to contemplate in a most
original little magazine—I raised my eyebrows coolly—a well-
guarded copy of a little magazine he respected very much. He
was filled with delight—these were his very words—the most
genuine rapture, although, thank God—he sighed noisily—
I've seen all sorts of things, and indeed not only I but a few
of my very closest friends felt like this, friends who thought
I was bragging when I told them that I had benefited from
you in this way from time to time, in a medical context, that
is. More than that: our boundless admiration went so far as

to cause certain involuntary incidents among our number, to which we were all forced to admit with embarrassment and pride, and it became clear to us that your charm, child, was far more effective than many foreign manifestations of this type, and since my friends are on occasion prone to generalize, they made the generalization that here too, in this area, reasoning in exclusively patriotic terms, we might well have a certain superiority.

In my mind's eye I vividly pictured this respected company, the type of men who wear suspenders and short beards, crowding around the table with their magnifying glasses to contemplate the glossy delicacy, who carried on her back a heavy cross! "Oh, Stanislav Albertovich, what nonsense you talk!" I said, more annoyed than flattered by his admission, though I was flattered too. "What the hell sort of fame is this! And where exactly is this wild and wonderful life of mine? You might as well know, Stanislav Albertovich, that as a result of this incident I live like the humblest church mouse, afraid to even wave her paw lest she be gobbled up!" "Sometime we'll learn to value beauty here too," Stanislav Albertovich said quietly, drumming thoughtfully on the table with his trained fingers and wondering why my beauty couldn't have been placed at the service of the fatherland, instead of being employed in quite the opposite direction, about which I now expressed my regret and hinted, as a precaution, that this direction could still change. "And indeed I would give up all this fame, all this noise and vanity," I exclaimed in a fit of temper, "for a quiet, cozy family life, sheltered by a husband, whose feet I would wash in a basin before going to bed!" "That's just what I'm saying," the old scoundrel answered joyfully. "Give birth to your baby and bathe it in a little tub, bring it up, it is yours, definitely have it, and its father will fade away, since that is what he deserves!" "You don't even know what you are pushing me toward," I said sadly, and decided to ask him point-blank, seeing as he was a specialist: "Stanislav Albertovich, do you remember my smell?"

He wavered slightly, he hesitated over his answer, for what I referred to was a fact discernible to anyone who wished to know. "What do you mean, child?" he asked in a false voice, as if he himself had not on a number of occasions praised my unique aroma, an aroma that had become legendary and was comparable only to the flowering of a bergamot tree, whereas, he liked to laugh, the variety of smells is amazing and often not to the bearer's credit, particularly when one is talking about marshy effusions or fried cod; he had also singled out Ksyusha's smell: the smell of a string of dried mushrooms sold in the market at a phenomenal price, which is a powerful smell and belongs to a woman with an intelligent and expressive face. . . . Ksyusha! Ksyusha! I write and feel you, yearning for that time when, on the beach in Koktebel, tearing your eyes away from a French novel, you looked at me with open curiosity, without a trace of rivalry, saluting my virtues. Women don't look at other women like that, and I was overwhelmed, I fell in love immediately, without any ulterior motives, with the words and objects surrounding her, I even fell in love with that red-and-white French paperback, which, as it turned out, after we had come together as lovers, never to part, gave a hint of our future separation, proving to be a distant peal of thunder and lightning, which totally unjustifiably would turn her into an international adventuress, all but a spy.

And sometimes, expatiated Stanislav Albertovich, one comes across the most interesting examples: "Are you listening, child? They smell of dill or, incidentally, of elderberry. . . . *Shes*," he corrects himself, using an archaic feminine form, "that's what they used to say." But I said, "What a lot of liars you all are! *Shes* have the same fragrance." I deliberately contradicted him, although with regard to the string of dried mushrooms he wasn't wrong, only Stanislav Albertovich's attempt to avoid the answer in that false voice was in vain, and when I pinned him down, yelling that surely he couldn't have missed that I had gone rotten, stank as if my innards were stuffed with rotting rags, then, with his back to the wall, Stanislav Albertovich admitted that in fact the changes had brought themselves to his attention, but after all, the bergamot couldn't flower forever; in time it brought forth fruit.

He was pleased with his unsuccessful witticism. I burst out crying right there, in the office, before the amazed Stanislav Albertovich, who of course knows all there is to know about women's tears; he is, moreover, my friend; he has, on more than one occasion, painlessly and without fuss freed me from the need to go to a lot of trouble. But then again, he is also my betrayer, who after his treachery apologized, waiting for me in the rain under a wide black umbrella on the opposite side of the street and hurling himself at me: "Forgive me, child, they forced me!" He tried to kiss my hand. "That's enough, Stanislav Albertovich! They didn't have to try too hard, apparently . . . leave me alone"—and I departed in a taxi for Granddaddy's, where there was also a performance. Stanislav Albertovich understands now that this is serious; his expression changes as he decides that it has nothing to do with a Negro, but is something totally impermissible; he's worried that he might come out of it badly again. I stop crying and set about calming him. He says he'll calm down if I am frank with him. Well, okay, you guessed it: a Negro! He doesn't believe this. "Well, I don't want to give birth, I don't want a child, not a boy, far less a girl, born to suffer, nor a frog, nor a pig—no one! Diapers, potties, sleepless nights. Brr! No, thanks!" "This, child, is your last chance." "So be it! I don't want to!" Thus I spoke.

Where's Rituyla? Where the devil is she? That's it! That's

it! Everything's settled. I'm getting baptized! Tomorrow I'll notify Father Veniamin. His eyes breathe grace, eyelashes down to his cheeks. But Stanislav Albertovich, when I said that I was planning to be baptized, asked: "Not as a Catholic, by any chance?" "What—are you a Catholic?" "I was at one time in my childhood," he says, "but now I'm nothing, even though a Pole has become Pope." Stanislav Albertovich is a Pole. He's from Lvov, though he has Jewish blood. "I don't understand—why aren't you in Poland?" "It just turned out that way. And you see, I don't know Polish." "Well, what sort of a Pole are you, then! My grandmother, for example, was a real Pole. No," I say, flapping my wide skirt like a wing, "no! I am Russian Orthodox, and I don't want to be christened because of some fashionable whim, which is why all *ours* at work have long since been christened and have had their children christened, in christening gowns obtained from Hamburg by mail order, but I am getting baptized as a matter of necessity. I feel, Stanislav Albertovich, a tormenting godforsakenness!" "Well, what is there to say?" says the doctor. "I understand your spiritual urges, only how is one to square them with . . . This isn't something very pleasing to God, you know." "How do you know?" He was surprised and says, "Sit down, child, for one more minute. Do you want another cigarette?" I say. "We're agreed in principle?" "Okay," he answers, "let's wait just two more weeks. Why hurry?"

Why? If he only knew that I'd become the arena for the struggle of higher powers!

And at this point Stanislav Albertovich, as if he'd picked up some vibes, asks whether it was true that I was connected with the death of V.S. "I," he says, "read a strange article in the paper, where, as I understood it, you were being talked about, child, under the heading 'Love,' signed by two authors, from which, however, I gathered only the fact that at the moment of V.S.'s death you were alone with him in his apartment. Have I got this right?" Yes, I answer, the article was pretty incomprehensible, and I myself couldn't make much sense of it, because the pretender brothers Ivanovich had set up a thick smoke screen, but, I answer, V.S. passed away with great dignity. "Yes"—he shakes his head—"they couldn't make head or tail of it at first, and set up a disgraceful inquiry. I was dragged in too . . . I'll tell you about it sometime. You're not angry with me, child?" Okay, I say, let bygones be bygones. . . . Yes—Stanislav Albertovich went all pensive— not every woman can boast that a whole epoch, in effect, has died on her breast. "Wait a minute!" he yells suddenly. "It's not his baby, by any chance?" and gives me a penetrating look, like someone with ESP, and although I do have a strong biofield, to be honest I'm embarrassed by his gaze, but he answers the question himself, without any prompting: "But what am I saying! When did he die? April? And now . . ." He looks through the window: sleet is falling, and we are reflected in the glass. "It wouldn't be a sin to bear a child by such a man," notes Stanislav Albertovich. "But I had some sort of aberration, child. Forgive me." "As if there are no other men!" I grin with dead lips. . . . Rituyla! Rituyla's come! Yippee! With a bottle of champagne! Let's drink, let's have a good time. . . .

# TWO

Rituyla asserts that I cried out during the night. This is quite possible, but I didn't hear anything. As proof, Rituyla shows me her hand, with scratches from my nails: "I barely escaped!" "It was probably nightmares from the champagne. But what was I shouting?" "Simply A-a-a-a . . . !"

I love Rituyla, but I struggle to keep silent. The official version: I am hiding from a certain guy. It contains a small amount of truth. The most terrible thing is precisely that I have to bury the secret within me, I can't share it with anyone. I'm afraid that they'll declare me insane, bind me, leave me to rot, burn me in a crematorium as a witch. Merzlyakov alone is bad enough. Merzlyakov, when I told him in the most general terms, in his horror had been about to extend the hand of old friendship. He took me, just to be on the safe side, to a church on the outskirts of Moscow, where he ordered me to pray. I prayed as well as I was able, with all my soul. I listed a whole pile of complaints before the icons and burst into tears, and then we drove to a restaurant. In the restaurant we had a small amount to drink, then left, and under the influence of my still fresh fear I invited Merzlyakov to spend the night with me and in this way recall our forgotten six-day love. But Merzlyakov

12

was fainthearted and declined, claiming that he would catch the devil only knows what sort of mystic syphilis. What a swine, eh? He insulted me deeply. I would have tossed him out of the house, but he was already pretty drunk. Instead we got totally drunk and couldn't help falling asleep.

Having tested the human reaction to my secret, I realized that it was better not to talk about it at all. But I have to say it's quite a burden to carry round. . . . My one and only, I'm telling you about certain events that have taken place. I admit that what has happened to me, although almost unprecedented as well as very disturbing, is not so extraordinary that it threatens to destroy the established order of things; it's just that one prefers to keep quiet about it, because the women think: why get involved? I have no intention of keeping silent; I've got nothing to lose, if only in the interests of science, because science might be able to offer an explanation, if I'm not carted straight off to a nuthouse. For I am categorically convinced that I haven't gone mad and that I'm not a witch, unlike Veronika, and she has Timofei as camouflage; and if it happened in the way it did happen, then there must have been reasons, about which I'll write separately.

I can of course write, but I can't help worrying about the fact that I don't know how; that is, I have no connection whatsoever with literature. It would be so much better if, for example, Sholokhov were to take up the writing of my story. I can just imagine how he would describe it, in a way that would make everyone's jaw drop, but he is very old, and in addition, they say, he has become such an alcoholic that he's even started spreading false rumors about himself, as if his works of genius were written not by him but by someone else entirely! No other living writers inspire my confidence, because what they write is boring and they all lie, either painting a pretty picture of the facts of our national life or, on the contrary, putting it down completely, like the gulag dissidents, who in their camps, V.S. reliably informed me, were well-known informers and deserters. It was not surprising that they went mad afterward, in contrast to Sholokhov, who wrote honestly about everything just as it was and therefore earned universal respect and even a private plane. More interesting and compassionate are the writings of foreign authors (with the exception, perhaps, of the Mongols), which are published frequently in the journal *Foreign Literature,* to which Viktor Kharitonych used to subscribe on my behalf. They are more successful than our writers in conveying psychology, and then of course it's more exciting to read about foreign life, because everything about our life is all too clear, what's the point of reading about it; I don't even want to see that rubbish in the cinema, it's a waste of time; but their writers sometimes rant on and on and produce such "transense" that you can't tell the end from the beginning, pure modernism, which weakens artistry, and it's unclear why they publish it. And in general, judging from my own experience, I must say that writers are a shallow bunch, and as men even shallower, and in spite of their impressive airs and leather jackets, they are always rather agitated, they fuss, and they come very quickly. I never wanted to marry a single one of them, even though several times the opportunity came up; there was even one director of a publishing house. He was relatively young, but with a completely skewed nervous system, and wanted to "dispossess and liquidate" everyone as if they were kulaks all over again. He particularly dreamed of dispossessing and liquidating the singer Alla Pugacheva. In his dreams he got positively hysterical. From modesty I let on that I was a helper in a kindergarten. This captivated him. But he wanted first to liquidate the kulak in me and only then to get married. I had to give him up. And many of these literary men married such sluts that it's really shameful.

It's not just that I want to astound science by providing this new information. Frankly, that doesn't worry me at all. It is time, finally, to put my own life in order. I don't plan to repent, though. Sometimes I strike myself as an unhappy and stupid woman whom life—in the form of that loud ugly mug Polina Nikanorovna—has disfigured, and nothing is left but to hang myself in my own bathroom, where an inhuman invention, a gas water heater, roars, never shutting up for a second, and sometimes, having let down my fluffy hair, I look at myself and say, "Wipe away your tears, Irina! Maybe you really *are* a new Joan of Arc. So you got shit scared and bailed out. So what? You weren't able to save Russia, but on the other hand you weren't afraid of taking a deadly risk for the sake of a dubious undertaking! Who else of your fellow Russian women could have done such a thing? Their greatest daring consists of establishing, in secret from their husbands, 'something on the side,' in the words of my mother, who rushed to Moscow to spray herself with my perfumes, and carrying on with him once or twice a week, on the way home from work, under the pretext of searching for goods in short supply. Who among them could have risked so beautifully and hopelessly as you!"

More than once I had sat down in a puddle wearing an evening dress, more than once I had covered myself with shame and been led away, but not from some dive, like a tart who works the railway station, but from the hall of the Conservatory, where during a premiere I bombarded a British orchestra with oranges as a result of the hopeless position I found myself in. No, Ira, you were not the least of women: men went mad from your beauty, you drank only champagne and received bouquets of flowers, like a soloist, from cosmonauts, ambassadors, and underworld millionaires.

The beautiful Carlos, the nephew of the president of a South American republic, made love to you on the table in his residence, forgetting his bony wife, and Volodya Vysotsky often winked at you from the stage when he came out to take his bows after *Hamlet*. There were others too, more basic models, there were also simple riffraff and base scoundrels, but only in comparison is a man's greatness to be seen! Really I loved only great men; from their faces shone the oily light of life and fame, before which I was powerless, all of me burned, though I was able to create miracles, and not without good reason did Leonardik call me the "genius of love," and he knew what was what. Indeed, all that love with him, however ominous and destructive it turned out to be for me, is it really possible to call it cheap? No, Ira, I say to myself, you're giving up too soon; your fate is not being decided in some insignificant office: six of the most fabulous beauties in America are following your story with fascination as, gazing at them, seeing them constantly on TV and in the movies, a million-man army of average Americans is jerking off, and once they gathered together—five white, one chocolate brown—in the fashionable Russian Tea Room in New York on Fifty-Seventh Street and, to the flash and hum of still and TV cameras, declared with one voice that I was not to be insulted, not touched, their sister who in her only fur coat, of fiery-red fox, had seemed a distant beggar woman, a Cinderella, a scarecrow lost in snows and misfortunes. I thought that together with the greeting they would send me some sort of present, if only a sheepskin coat, as a memento, which I wouldn't have accepted anyway out of pride, which I get from my great-grandmother, whom I resemble—I have her portrait above my bed—but they didn't send anything, didn't give out. "You should just spit on them!" said Rituyla, when we looked at the photograph showing them all linked in an embrace: five white, one chocolate brown. "They're all teeth and no tits!" growls Rituyla, jealous of my attachment to the American girls. "Kharitonych was right to curse them out!" she gloated. There is no love lost between Rituyla and foreign women, because foreign women claim the lion's share of foreign men. But she's very kind and affectionate toward me, like a billy goat. This is my second month at Rituyla's, in a state of constant agitation. I believe in the tender bonds of female friendship. Without them I would have perished utterly. "You'd be better off phoning your Gavleyev!" advises Rituyla. What about Gavleyev? He too had forsaken me. Oh, to hell with them—they've all become repulsive. But formerly I couldn't go three days without them, I was fragrant like a pale-blue bergamot orchard on a moonlit night, when the stars blaze out in the southern sky, and my Ksyusha is doing laps alongside in the waves. But the orchard has been trampled. Get baptized? And what if I can't? Because nothing on earth will make me confess to Father Veniamin! Everyone's conspiring against me! It was with good reason, good reason, that he inquired about Leonardik: how, so to speak, did he die. With pleasure I'll tell you, I shall answer from the heart, as I did to the investigators, who tormented me, then vindicated me, and if anyone should have been the chief mourner at the funeral, then I should have been, not her, or at any rate a reconciliation should have taken place, as fine as the one at the grave of the crushed Anna Karenina, where Karenin and Captain Vronsky made peace with tears in their eyes, because all are equal before death; but Zinaida Vasilievna couldn't summon up such magnanimity, and indeed where could that shit have started looking: not only was I thrown out on my ear, but her intrigues extended even further! She used all her widow's influence to wipe me out. And then there was my *running*. . . . Oh, why did I run?

If only they knew, the five white and the one chocolate brown, how bad things are for me now! Oh, how bad! But they couldn't help me now; nothing will help. No, that's not true! When I get christened in a few days, then we'll see! Then the radiant host of divine forces will rise up on my side, and if anyone dares to touch me—let him try! The offender's hand will shrivel, his legs will be paralyzed, his liver will be covered with a cancerous tumor. . . . Don't grieve, Ira, I tell myself, you're as alive as forty thousand cats! You have as many lives as forty thousand cats. . . . Yes, perhaps you really *are* a new Joan of Arc.

# THREE

I drank only champagne, without exception. Generally I drank little, not making it my daily bread, avoiding the common people's habit; I drank infrequently and little, and only champagne, nothing but dry champagne, and before drinking I would dip into the tall goblet the wire that stops the cork from popping like a car exhaust backfiring. Then the goblet foams and fizzes, and prickly bubbles, unbearable to the throat, fly up. And I preferred brut to all other champagne. O Brut! You are brutal, you are a gangster, you are Blok the mystical bird of prophecy! You are divine, Brut . . .

When there was no champagne, I would yield to persuasion and drink cognac, I would drink whatever was poured me, even Bulgarian vino, but that's not the point: I wanted understanding, but they got me deliberately drunk and with just one aim in mind, and I used to pretend I didn't suspect and would start to behave capriciously and despise everything. "I don't want Martell! I don't want your Courvoisier! I love Cointreau!" I would say with a triumphant smile, wanting to spite them all, and they would answer: "But that isn't cognac." "Why isn't it cognac? Can't cognac be orange?" They all guffaw. The expert is disgraced. "And don't treat me like I'm dumb!" "Okay, Grisha," they'll tell him, "shut up. Bring some

Cointreau." But Grisha doesn't have any Cointreau, and the effect isn't very impressive. "And once I was in a group where there was, just imagine, a baron, a real baron, gray-haired—right, Ksyush?" Ksyusha looks at me tenderly, like at a child who's up to mischief. "The owner of this cognac." "And what did he drink, this baron?" asks some lousy professor from Moscow's Lumumba University. "His own cognac?" No, the host answers him, winking, wounded by me, already hating me on account of the Cointreau, this—what's his name?—Grisha, whom Ksyusha and I had visited, having already done him a favor, you could say, merely by consenting to be there. "No," says Grisha, with irony, "that's the same as drinking your own urine!" "Oh, how witty," I say coldly. "So amusing, I don't think." And with horror I realize that they don't understand me here, that I am an alien at this festival of life, that I must drink, drink as quickly as possible, so as not to burst out crying, must learn some language or other, because the baron doesn't speak Russian, if only twenty words a day, but I'm so lazy, so lazy, I could infect an island the size of Iceland with my laziness, and ruin would set in in Iceland . . . ruination! But what do I care? I looked around to find Ksyusha, but instead of Ksyusha her shoes were lying on the floor, because they'd dragged Ksyusha off to the kitchen, attracted by her fantastic splendor, and she'd only just arrived in her pink car, in all her finery, dazzlingly well dressed, elegant, smart, arrived and said, "I can't live in Russia. I can't live without Russia. What am I to do, Sunny?"

She always called me Sunny, putting so much tenderness into this word! They'd taken her away barefooted into the kitchen. I went after her and see two "directors" from the Mosfilm studios are in a whirl around her, but she sits and drinks instant coffee apathetically. I say, "Ksyusha, let's get out of here! They don't understand us here, they're just trying to get us drunk." "Let's go, Sunny," she says to me. "Help me get up." The chaps in their suede jackets grab our hands and hold us back, invite us to dance. But I say, "Dance to what? To this old rubbish? Thanks but no thanks." I say, "It's no fun with you!" With difficulty we break free, but Grisha reels in the doorway and looks at us evilly as we hoist ourselves into the elevator. "Perhaps, girls, you'll change your minds? I've got a cantaloupe." But Ksyusha says, "Give us the melon. We'll bring it back tomorrow." Grisha blazed with anger at the insult, but we pressed the button and went down. "Not our type of people," I say, "not our caliber." And she answers, "How on earth did we end up here?"

We get into the pink car and think: What next? Ksyusha suggests going to Antonchik's. What's this Antonchik like? Won't we end up, I say, by losing out again? I never had enough time to get to know all her acquaintances, friends clustered around her like bunches of grapes. Well, how are things with you, I ask, in France? Pretty shitty, she answers. Ksyusha married a dentist, laughing that at least her teeth wouldn't ache anymore. This René had come to Moscow for a scientific conference, and she had filmed him for television; he brought his little hands together in the innocent pose of the Madonna. . . . Oh, Sunny, she would tell me, his shirt button had come undone, and I saw his belly button, edged with hair. My fate was sealed. She thought she would be able to work in television in France, because she'd known French since childhood and played the piano, as they did in the last century; but the Frenchman didn't allow it and put her on the outskirts of Paris, at the Fontainebleau railway station, where Napoleon is buried. But I won't go on about that: Ksyusha lived in a spacious home with a large pear orchard and wrote me heartrending letters. My tender Sunny, she would write, My husband René turned out to be, on closer acquaintance, a complete prick. For days on end he drills teeth, he measures out his time to the very last second, he pins his money to his pocket with a safety pin. In the evenings he reads *Le Monde* with a self-important expression and discusses the special path of Socialism with a French Face in bed. His touch and sterile smell remind me of a dentist's office, though his cock isn't like a drill and indeed it doesn't resemble anything reasonable at all. I've pigged out on pears and have chronic diarrhea. I get diarrhea too from the Russian expatriates around here. They are all slightly touched and mourn the fatherland all the time. It's pointless arguing with them: they are suspicious and clumsy. Have you read the Harvard speech? It's really embarrassing. I blushed for that old blockhead and found the old Party formula especially apt: "Thanks for yesterday's services, but pay for today's!"; but they decided that I was totally red. I have developed an Emma Bovary complex and have got myself a young truckdriver, but he's a bore too. . . .

In another letter she admitted that France is a rather beautiful country, that out of boredom she'd decided to travel, that Normandy was a real joy, only unfortunately there were fences everywhere, private property, and Frenchmen, unbearable people! What particularly shocks me is Parisian snobbery, she wrote; nobody says anything straight out, everyone creeps and says yes to everything, thoughts are useless, pure rhetoric and hot air! My husband and I were at one academician's. The academician gave René two fingers—can you imagine it?—instead of a handshake. René didn't lose his cool. He sat on the edge of an armchair with the sweetest expression on his face. . . . Where is that corrupt West? wrote Ksyusha. I can't see it for the life of me. They are all depressingly positive, and when they sin, they sin with such an awareness of the limits, with the reliability and thoroughness and ac-

curacy of a *charcutier* slicing bits of sausage or ham. Or the
way they drink vodka—tiny sips and no more than two glasses,
and then, from their awareness of having committed a sin,
they go around all pleased with themselves and even more
positive than before. I didn't believe her letters, I thought she
was playing the fool. My sole joy is masturbation, she wrote.
My thoughts are about you, my Sunny!

I decided that Ksyusha had an agenda of her own, that
she *needed* to write this way, and I continued to love Europe.
Oh, for example, what a man that gray-haired baron had been,
the one I'd seen in the restaurant of the Cosmos Hotel! But
Grisha had made up his mind that I was lying. I measured
Grisha with a withering look, the sort that men can't endure
without feeling their own insignificance. Oh, Grisha! Where
on earth did he come from with his weird idea about the
cantaloupe? "Ksyusha," I said, "hey, think, for goodness' sake,
we can't go anywhere, since you, Ksyusha, are totally pissed!"
"I don't give a damn," said Ksyusha. "In the last analysis, I'm
a Frenchwoman. What will they do to me?" She spent ages
trying to thrust the key into the ignition, and finally the car
let out a roar as if it was about to blow up. The snow was
coming down, and it was dark. "Ksyusha," I said, "let's take
a taxi!" "Just sit quiet and listen to some music," said Ksyusha,
and switched on the radio. A singer from Brazil, I don't remember her name, started to sing loudly, but with such a
warm voice it was as if she'd started singing just for Ksyusha
and me. I remembered Carlos. We embraced, clinging to each
other tightly. She in a fashionable wolf-fur coat—which destroyed the miserly reputation of the dentist, whom before the
wedding I hadn't even known, because Ksyusha, notwith-
standing our love, always led her separate life and admitted
no one into it, and I would take offense and try to be like
her—I in my old reddish fox, which Carlos, the president's

nephew, had given me, only Carlos was no longer in Moscow and perhaps no longer among the living, because the president had been overthrown and a junta of crooks had come to power. They had summoned Carlos from Moscow, and he had vanished, without writing me a single letter.

I don't know whether Carlos was a good ambassador, but I'm certain that he was a stunning lover! He turned his embassy into the trendiest place in Moscow. He was very progressive, and gritting their teeth, they didn't stop him. He was so progressive that he would go to receptions in a Zhiguli jeep, with his flag, striped like pajamas, attached to it, and without a chauffeur, but *I* knew that his garage contained a Mercedes, with shiny black sides, and at night we would hop in it whenever I felt like going for a ride. He equipped the basement as a nightclub. He bought endless quantities of food, booze, and cigarettes in the foreign-currency shop on Gruzinskaya Street and arranged sumptuous feasts. All intellectual Moscow used to go to them. There Bella Akhmadulina admitted to me—and these are her very words—that "you, child, are unspeakably good-looking." Carlos danced beautifully, but I danced even better, and he soon noticed this and valued it appropriately. I stayed with him as toward morning the last guests dispersed, and the militiaman saluted each of them in turn. "I am the ambassador," Carlos informed the militiaman who was guarding the private residence, and, holding in his hand a glass and a bottle of Moskovskaya vodka, continued, "and if you refuse, I'll take offense." The militiaman, out of fear of offending the ambassador of a foreign country, downed it without blinking. I stayed with Carlos, and it turned out he made love even better than he danced. We made love to classical music, and that night our bed was his enormous writing desk, with its small pile of books and papers on the far end, holding the ephemeral secrets of a banana republic, but he didn't have jet-black hair and eyes or a black stripe of a mustache promising brutality and the false ardor of oaths. His southern exterior was softened and restrained by that Oxford chic amidst which he had lived for many years as a student. I was not dealing with some hot upstart. He won me with his aristocratic calm, and I didn't believe Ksyusha.

Ksyusha had returned after a year, having dreamed up the pretext of a business trip to gather reproductions for an exhibition catalog. She was dressed so carelessly and impeccably that there was no need to examine the labels of her dresses, boots, sweaters, and nightgowns to know that they came from the most famous boutiques, not to mention the pink car, which everyone rushed to surround, but no sooner had she got out of her car, showered and changed after her long journey than she started to abuse her husband and, along with him, the pear orchard. Accustomed to understanding her from half a word, a hint, or even no words at all, just from looking into her matchless face, I felt disappointed; still I kept silent. But when, after all the fuss and presents—she always spoiled me —at last we went to bed, I asked for explanations. Can it really be, I thought, that Ksyusha has degenerated? No, I said to myself, I won't love her any the less for that; in fact, I shall forgive her everything and I won't contradict her. But you see, I didn't want just to forgive; I had also thought more than once how her escapade might fit me, her plan that she hadn't told me about until the wedding itself. She, yawning, said that it wasn't difficult to get used to good things, Sunny, but as soon as one had got used to them they stopped being good, and everything begins from zero again and one starts counting the losses. "What's this, nostalgia?" I asked. She protested weakly. "But you say 'losses.' " "Oh," she said, "let's leave it till tomorrow," and kissed me on the temple; but the following day she was indignant for another reason: during the night the windshield wipers from her pink auto had been swiped, while on the hood someone had scratched COCK in large letters. She swore, and this I understood. Standing beside her, I got a lot of pleasure from this. She made a telephone call to Fontainebleau and spent a long time twittering with the dentist. "Strange people," she explained. "No sooner have you got married than they demand a baby, like the Central Asians here. Disaster. He's so jealous too. . . ." "Stay here," I suggested. "What do you mean!" Ksyusha challenged. I didn't answer, and instead we started on a round of revelry and on the fourth night came upon Anton, who looked, Ksyusha noted, like a young Aleksei Tolstoy. "Is that good?" I asked, able to picture, to be honest, neither a young one nor an old one, but only the street of that name, with its parade of Party bigwigs. "It depends on your mood," said Ksyusha. "I met him in Paris." "What was he doing there?" "Screwing me." We traveled beyond the Moscow city limits. "Ksyusha!" I worried. "Where the hell are we going!" It was dark, but the snow wasn't falling heavily anymore.

At the Moscow border checkpoint, the traffic police stopped us. "Relax," said Ksyusha, and pulled her black knitted hat over her eyes. Winding down the window, Ksyusha greeted the inspector affectionately. She always managed to sweeten them up with disposable lighters, key rings, ballpoint pens, cigarettes, Swedish condoms, cassettes, chewing gum, and small calendars with naked women—these calendars make them wild, she exulted. Her glove compartment was crammed with this priceless rubbish. The inspector, frozen to a brown-and-raspberry color, saluted gallantly, asked us to take care on the roads, and last of all eyeballed us greedily. We drove on and were immediately surrounded by forest. "Now this is what's impossible in Europe," said Ksyusha in triumph. Then she was silent for a moment and added, "Savages."

She was inconsistent, my Ksyusha, both that evening and later. And the longer things went on, and the longer she lived there, the more inconsistent she became.

In a settlement of dachas, occasional lamps burned and occasional dogs barked, but the road had been cleared of snow in exemplary fashion. Along the way we had a drop more to drink and became totally exhausted. Ksyusha was laughing and grabbing my knees. We felt hot. Ksyusha blew her horn as loudly as if she were one of the locals. The dogs started yapping on all sides, but nobody came to open the gates for us. The clock in her car showed past two. I said nothing but swallowed some Martini for courage. Finally, the gates opened slightly, and in the gleam of the headlights we caught sight of a bearded type in a homemade black sheepskin. The bearded one examined the car sleepily but with unconcealed suspicion. This night watchman with eyes like a calf's was destined to play a role in my life, though I didn't suspect it at the time. Whether the watchman knew Ksyusha, or whether it was her car that made him respect her—whatever, having given it some thought, he let us through, and we drove into the estate, which seemed to be a large park. Ksyusha turned the wheel toward the house, its entrance illuminated, and we slid out of the car with its loud music. Ksyusha took several steps and fell drunkenly into a snowdrift. I rushed to help her. We lay in the snow and looked at the pine trees with their rustling tops. "What a high!" said Ksyusha, and laughed. I agreed, but amazed by the expanse of the house, I asked, "Ksyusha, where are we?" "In Russia!" she answered confidently. It was good in the snow, and we raised our legs, in sheer tights, and started to caper. A man wearing just a shirt came out onto the porch and, looking closely at us, shouted: "Ksyusha!" "Antonchik!" yelled Ksyusha. "We're taking snowbaths! Come and join us." "You'll catch colds, idiots!" Antonchik guffawed and ran to drag us out of the snowdrift. "Antonchik!" shouted Ksyusha, resisting, not wanting to get up. "Are you going to screw us or not!" "You bet!" answered Antonchik, his voice animated. "Well, let's go, then!" said Ksyusha, and stopped resisting. Anton lifted us by our arms and dragged us toward the porch. "Generally speaking, the verb *screw*," reasoned Ksyusha, now wet through from the snowbath, but beautiful in her black woolen hat, "lightens the heavy business of Russian fucking. . . ." I acknowledged in my gut that she was right, but I kept silent, being slightly embarrassed before an unknown man.

On the porch Anton introduced himself to me, after which we hurried into the well-heated house. Having thrown off our fur coats, we went through into the dining room, where people were sitting at the table and finishing supper, or perhaps they weren't sitting there and weren't finishing supper and there was no one there, because as a result of the heat and the new impressions, I was really out of it, just like Ksyusha, who couldn't remember anything, not even how we'd got there and how she'd talked with the border guard.

How to convey the condition when you switch off and start living in another dimension, having pawned yourself entirely, having accepted bail from a kind guardian, whom, however, you have never met! And sometimes you suddenly float up to the surface and are supported by the water and then go under water again and—goodbye! Thus, rising to the surface that night at various disconnected moments, I found myself in bed, and alongside me wallowed Ksyusha, her distorted face extended toward me, and she bit me so hard that I jumped and couldn't decide whether to object or to succumb; however, I was distracted by a more categorical presence, which pressed into my cheek and became hot. I grabbed it, at which it quivered and bent, and I said to it: Hello, chief

of the redskins! Kneeling on the bed and treating it with great
affection as a sign of greeting (and how!), I was amazed by
the fact, which was evidently the reason I'd come to the
surface, that a certain other chief was stuck into me from a
completely different direction, while Ksyusha, like the moon,
had risen from somewhere on the right. It seemed to me that
I had been surrounded, and I couldn't make head or tail of
it, since I'd been introduced on the porch to Anton alone—
surely he couldn't have split himself in two—however, I was
occupied, I had my hands and mouth full and could only moo
in astonishment, and Ksyusha too at last got impaled, but
instead of crawling off me, she pressed herself against me even
more firmly, and embracing, we were lifted into the air.
Gripped by arousal and passion and humped up doggy style,
we gained height and started galloping, our heads stretched
out, racing one another, laughing and shrieking: we galloped!
galloped through the air! And once more I switch off, and
memory sleeps—then suddenly pain and my cry. I had stepped
on a goblet and cut myself, and I pulled the sole of my foot
toward me. Ksyusha, like a dog, licked my wound, while I lay
on my back and moaned to an applauding hum . . . and once
again Ksyusha, with her lips bloody, like cherries, stupid and
dear, and I started crying with unbearable love for her—
against the background of a toppled giant, who, still gathering
his strength, was hanging gloomily and windlessly in the air,
a wet rag at half mast. But it's not part of Ksyusha's or my
principles to give up! I'm full of pity, like any woman. I perform
miracles and stupidities simultaneously.

Anton was standing in his dressing gown and playing with
a glass. Here, drink this! I raised myself on my elbow but fell
back again. I didn't have the strength to sit up. Anton sat
down beside me. I didn't like his chin—plump, small,
useless—and I turned to the window. On the windowsill

bloomed purple and white alpine violets, but there, beyond
—winter! The *fortochka!* Open the *fortochka!* Let's have some
air in here, I asked, and took a sip. It was champagne. I
downed it. He poured some more. I drained the glass once
more and lay down, gazing at the ceiling. "You were a genius,"
whispered Antonchik, smiling. The champagne was doing its
stuff: I was coming back to life. "You weren't bad yourself,"
I said in a weak voice, remembering with effort some sort of
game of doubles, split identities, and my flight with Ksyusha.
"But where is Ksyusha?" I said, worried at not being able to
find her. "She went off to Moscow this morning. She's got
things to do," explained Antonchik, confirming my admiration for Ksyusha, who, aided by willpower, could recover
quickly and step over into the life of the day.

After a sleepless night she would become even more self-
disciplined and effervescent, and only her swollen eyes might
arouse the suspicions of someone who knew what was what.
In both lives she remained herself, she never crumbled; she
combined skill with tenderness, with equal ardor giving herself
to night and to day, finding in each a peculiar charm. I recovered much more slowly, and the morning after would be
a complete write-off, particularly in winter, when it gets dark
by lunchtime and you only feel like sitting in a warm sweater
and gazing motionlessly, preferably into a fireplace, of which
there just happened to be an example in this miraculous dacha,
together with pictures, furniture made from Karelian birch, a
library, knickknacks, and rugs laying their heavy soft weight
on the parquet floors. "You were a star!" I said to Anton.
"Thanks for the mouthful of champagne," and he bent over
and kissed me, and I, after some hesitation, called him to me,
despite his chin: plump, small, useless.

When I had got myself together in the light-blue bathroom
with its nymph portrayed in tiles the whole length of the wall,

a nymph washing in a basin—and what's more, they had a
real Finnish sauna on the first floor—I carefully came downstairs, my head spinning slightly, which made everything seem
frail and transparent; but this feeling also has its highs. Anton
invited me to the table, held my chair, and smiled a somewhat
ravaged smile. The hors d'oeuvres scattered all around in vast
quantity didn't really attract me, but I was impressed by their
abundance. The tall, thin servant—the night watchman's
wife—was good-looking though rather goggle-eyed, and her
mouth was like a chicken's ass. She didn't realize the joke her
mouth made, and wore bright lipstick. The watchman himself
stuck half his face out of the kitchen, taking an interest in
my person, in order to discuss me afterward with his wife, and
I scowled at him, but Anton, being in that blissful state which
all men enjoy after they have demonstrated their abilities,
invited the watchman, whom he addressed with the familiar
"you," to drink a glass of vodka with him. The proposal induced theatrical alarm: the watchman clasped his hands emo-
tionally, his eyes started rolling, and he began to refuse,
looking anxious to be gone. Only the greatest vodka-lovers
refuse it in such a way, and I couldn't hold out any longer
and burst into laughter. The watchman's wife—also, it was
apparent, an expert at drinking—was the first to give in to
the entreaties. While they were being entertained, I examined
everything from the corner of my eye. This certainly wasn't
a plebeian home, and I regretted not having asked Ksyusha
about its owners, although the green toy soldiers, standard-
bearer at their head, arranged in a row on the fireplace told
me more than the wedding ring that he didn't wear. Borscht
was served. I was overjoyed at this oily hot borscht, which
breathed and steamed in a white tureen, that forgotten, barely
used item in a dinner service, the same sort of thing as ga-
loshes. How healing was this borscht! The blood rushed to

my face. No, there *are* bright moments in life, not just blizzards and twilight!

But that's not the point: at that moment, as the morning hangover started to disperse, as Anton, bringing his lemon-gray face close to me, with his elastic advertisement of a smile, uttered compliments, which spoke not only for his gallantry but also for his good breeding, as I was joyfully eating hot borscht and Anton was saying that while he'd met a lot of beautiful women, it was rare for one of these beauties to be beautiful in her sleep, because during sleep a beauty's face gets relaxed and grows ugly, on it appear the traces of an inerad-icable vulgarity and original sin, but on my sleeping face he had read only sincerity and beauty—at that moment, as the morning hangover vanished, a new door was flung open in my life, and through it, out of the December frost, with the firm step of a successful and famous man, walked Leonardik!

# FOUR

He entered to the peals of my laughter. I was laughing with my head thrown back, laughter expressing a happy doubt that I was beautiful and sincere, in that hung-over, postcoital state I had plunged into without coming to—that is, I'd moved from one switched-off state to another—but Antonchik, who later proved to be a rare shit indeed, turned to the door and said, "Oh, hi!" I looked around and saw *you*, Leonardik!

For me you didn't come out of the frost, or from the misted-up entrance hall, unfastening your driving gloves made of thin leather—because, in spite of yourself, you were an inveterate motorist. No, you came to me from the television screen, came in surrounded by the dark blue of the flickering box, in a cloud of unhurried words, you streamed from the world of art, in a garland of laurels and respect—only you were smaller than I had assumed, and a bit leaner than I had thought, but your face, capped by its silver head of hair, small reddish bald patches, barely visible part, shone with precisely that infallible light which indicates success in life, although in its depths, as I would later discover, a certain bewilderment was hidden.

Oh, if by that time I had not graduated from Ksyusha's school of good manners and deportment, if I had never had

Carlos with his Oxford chic, if I had never sat at table in the National Hotel with three ambassadors simultaneously, not including the Ethiopian chargé d'affaires, if I had not been friends with important people, including Gavleyev, and also with celebrities who were second-rate stars in comparison with you, I would have turned to stone on meeting you! But I was no longer that twenty-three-year-old fool who had fled to the Moscow she worshiped from her ancient native town, where, to tell the truth, there was nothing good, never has been and never will be.

I didn't jump up like a schoolgirl, I waited, not leaving my chair, I awaited his gaze and greeting, and this greeting —I swear it—already contained signs of interest, and not just the abstract politeness and humanity of an exceptional personality. "May I introduce you!" Anton shone, having observed all this, and he was introduced to me personally by name and patronymic, and his hand was offered. "And this," said Anton, and they admired my fragile neck, which rose from the lilac-patterned dress, slightly gypsy in style, although unmistakably elegant, a present from my betrayer Ksyusha, who had thrown me to Antonchik for a morning performance, to add a second helping of lovemaking, which men demand not so much from greed as out of the involuntary spiritual needs of a body that has had a rest. "And this," they admired, and V.S.'s somewhat dry profile softened, that profile of the holiday medallion, minted on the Victory days, which he would give at the first opportunity, before he forgot, to every old cow, although on the autographed photographs hanging in his office his profile melted a bit in the heightened temperature; however, it was clear from them all how strong-willed and shockheaded he'd been in his youth. Here Hemingway himself scrutinizes V.S. penetratingly, shaking his hand against the backdrop of a non-Russian southern town, and V.S. scrutinizes Hemingway just as vigilantly. "And who on earth is this old fogy?" "That is Dzhambul, a narrator of epic folk tales, legendary during his own lifetime, in the thirties." "I don't know him. . . . And this one, affectionate, with a little box in his hand?" "Kalinin. My first medal. And look here. At the front. With Rokossovsky." "And this?" "That's of no interest—some folk choir. . . ." "And do you have one with Stalin?" "Yes." He bends over, sticks his hand into the desk drawer; he protects it. "Look. In the Georgievsky Hall." "But where are you?" "See, in the left corner, behind Fadeyev and Cherkasov." "Oh, isn't he small!" "All great men were smaller than average," he says, slightly put out. "That means that you are great too!" He modestly laughs it off: "I think that they'll write in my obituary: 'Outstanding.' " And it was as if he'd seen his future reflected! In the obituary they wrote "Outstanding." "And this is Shostakovich and me." "Why does he look so furtive?" "Probably done something wrong." He became pensive over the photographs, laughed good-naturedly, turning to his shockheaded youth, and playing with something—he liked twisting something, anything, in his hands: a small box, a candy wrapper, a fork, my brooch, a lock of hair—"It wasn't difficult to do something wrong in those days," he added (he always considered me worthy of his addenda). "It so happened that I was also on the receiving end once. . . ." He grew thoughtful again, but not tormentingly, not worryingly, not cheerlessly, not irrevocably, the way all sorts of *shallows* grow thoughtful—this was how he classified the riffraff, chicken-brained people laying down the law left, right, and center, suffering from verbal diarrhea and a tendency toward unforgivable generalizations. But he didn't allow himself to use his medal to play noisy games: "Well, you know, like children, quarreling as they push coins around . . ." "Art must be constructive," he would growl, not maliciously but ironically. "And what do *they* know about our property?" He loved this little word, *property*, and used it in both a political and an everyday sense, and even a few very earthy matters he called lovingly, "my *private* property." I was always in the depth of my soul a patriot, and I used to say, "Imagine, my girlfriend, the wondrously fair Ksyusha, writes heartrending letters to me from Fontainebleau!" He listened to me in the most attentive way, pulling his earlobe—this was another of his habits. He had beautiful ears, thoroughbred; they didn't jut out, didn't bulge, his earlobes weren't joined to his cheeks, weren't pointed, they curved, captivating me and hinting at his musical nature. I noticed these ears right away, although ears are a redundant subject for conversation and there's no fashion for them—people aren't fussy: just give them a bosom and hips. People are great lovers of bosoms—I know from experience: a huge bosom is what matters. I agree it's not the least important consideration; I too resorted to comparisons, objectively awarding myself the victory: Just take, for example, those very photographs, and the Ivanoviches ask me, "To which photographs are you referring exactly?" "As if he had only been photographed with Hemingway!"—and I see I've hurt them to the quick. "Only," I say, "don't get it into your heads to search—seek and ye will not find; I'm no fool either." But people are wrong to honor the beauty of ears so little and pay such limited attention to them. An ingenious organ. Useful too. And on the medallion, I might add, highly visible. More obvious than eyes or eyebrows. In profile, that is. Though when the bosom epidemic started, I too immediately stopped wearing a bra, feeling proud, which induced in Polina a grimace of heartburn, and how often she ruined my nerves in connection with this: again and again! Sometimes she'd go wild the minute she caught sight of me. I complained to Ksyusha in Koktebel, and

Ksyusha quietly sidled up to me, on soft pillows, so as not to frighten me accidentally, not to scratch me with an importunate movement, for she could see that I didn't understand anything, that I was a simpleton, who had come there just to get up to some mischief and had appeared on the beach in a revealing little costume; she burned with shame on my behalf, my Ksyusha, she thought so highly of me! But Polina used to get hysterical, she just didn't want to hear; once she even threw a coat hanger at me, I almost lost an eye, as if it weren't enough that my father was one-eyed! It actually got to such a pitch that she yelled at the top of her voice: "Write out your resignation!" even though she had only the authority of being Viktor Kharitonych's plenipotentiary, Viktor Kharitonych, who valued and respected me and who was in addition my patron and would take a certain degree of risk, who used to permit me to be late or not come to work at all, to lead a relatively free life. But how she rejoiced, how malicious she was when the degree of risk was canceled, and hatred, like boiling water, had scalded my legs thoroughly, but I was still trying to stand firm, to hold myself well, as if one could get used to hatred. . . . You can never get used to it! However, until the last episode, there's no denying, Kharitonych protected me, made allowances for me, this and that: well, envy was part of our work collective; why all these privileges, and what's in it for you? Normally they spread all types of stories, but we didn't give them any grounds for suspicion, not in public! Although there were, of course, slips, from his side and not from mine! He just didn't like being sensible and risked a lot for my sake; he would crudely try to force me into his office, as if to say, We need to have a chat. I would answer with a refusal, he would grumble, Polina would rant and rave, but in fact he and I had thought up a plan—that I would transfer to the Bolshoi, take the role of the queen, you don't have to dance, the important thing here is posture and grace, the main thing the ability to bow one's head regally and cool oneself with a fan: all this is stored in one's genes, it is not difficult to develop it. In addition I was tempted by the fact that all the best dancers and even national stars dance at the queen's feet, thanks to which a simple spectator often falls victim to the illusion that the queen is the real star, so why not lead them up the garden path? The issue was already in part settled; in any event, certain preliminary steps had been taken and our network of connections set in motion, and see, I had the prospect of fooling not just provincials but audiences on our foreign tours. At that point Viktor Kharitonych suddenly came to and put on the brakes, fearing that if I broke loose from his patronage I would become unattainable, like the queen herself, and this psychological barrier proved impossible to overcome. He was stubborn, although he didn't bear grudges, and also was getting on in years, and anyway I didn't want to offend him; even if I had offended him, it wouldn't have been a major tragedy, he would have got over it and forgotten all about it: there were so many others to pick from, all everyone does is just sit and hope for such perks. He would have found consolation, nothing would have happened to him, but one's word is one's word—I hadn't hung on for nothing! And no sooner had I set about cautiously overcoming this psychological barrier, on the principle that a motionless stone gathers nothing at all, than I suddenly got involved in another, exclusively private side of my life, because my patience ran out in that area too. It began in the trajectory of that morning hangover, at the very minute when, laughing over a chance witticism, I had thrown back my head, and there he was, with an unspoken question, as if to say, And who is this? And this, answered Anton, taking his time over introducing me because, despite all his compliments, he was forgetful—but I am unprejudiced where men are concerned, on the principle that the important thing is for a man to be a good fellow. "Ira," I named myself casually, as if I'd picked a forget-me-not at the very edge of a swamp. "Yes, this is Ira," Anton echoed enthusiastically, though he really should have remembered this straightforward name, which Ksyusha had returned to me, though not without some wavering on my part, because once Viktor Kharitonych had started the ball rolling, everyone had called me with depressing vulgarity "Irena," and I'd even liked it. But Ksyusha had grabbed her head in despair: "Irena! That's as bad as going around in polyester!" I had taken offense and hung my head, since as a first-generation member of the intellectual classes, I had not learned how to distinguish a fake gem from a real one right away, and the years kept passing. All the rest sounded like a dithyramb. He said that to call me Ira was not to call me at all, because I was a genius of love, unsurpassed, divine, stunning! "Father!" Anton shouted irritably. "You won't believe it! This is really something!" He squinted his eyes and smoothed down his dressing gown—it had fallen open from his wild gestures—bought, to all appearances, in Paris, whither he could take himself as frequently as I could take myself to Tula, except what do I want with Tula.

Vladimir Sergeyevich said nothing but simply came up to the table, poured himself a glass of vodka, and drained it. A glum-looking maid in a white apron popped out of the kitchen and asked him if he wanted some lunch. He responded enthusiastically, as if he were really hungry, though some time later he confessed laughingly that he was full, since he had been visiting, but I hadn't realized and was amazed that, having sat down at the table, he refused everything except for a small piece of salmon. I watched him closely as he downed a second glass, though he didn't clink glasses with us but drank alone.

"It's cold today," he noted. "Minus twenty." "Cold," An-

ton answered wryly, and also downed his vodka. "But I love
winter," I said with a touch of defiance, although never in
my life have I felt any love for winter; I prefer any other
season. Vladimir Sergeyevich looked at me with slowly growing approval. "It's good," he said, "that you love the winter.
Every Russian should love winter." "Why should they?" asked
Anton. "Pushkin loved the winter," Vladimir Sergeyevich
explained. "Well, so what?" said Anton. "What's Pushkin got
to do with it? I don't like it! I hate it." "That means you're
no Russian," said Vladimir Sergeyevich. "What do you mean,
no Russian?" Anton said, astonished. "What am I, then, a
Jew or what?" "Jews also love the winter," said Vladimir Sergeyevich. "How can you fail to love such beauty?" he asked,
and gazed through the window.

Twilight was falling.

Vladimir Sergeyevich seemed rather severe, but I was
happy to be sitting at the same table with him and carrying
on a conversation. "You're not Ukrainian?" he asked me,
slightly disingenuously. "I'm a pure-blooded Russian," I answered, and continued: "It's good in winter. You can skate in
winter." "Do you like skating?" "I adore it!" "I really thought
you were Ukrainian," Vladimir Sergeyevich confessed. "No,
I'm Russian," I persuaded him. "Has Yegor cleared the skating
rink?" he asked Anton. "In winter we turn the tennis court
into a skating rink," he added for my benefit: even then
he considered me worthy of his addenda! "The devil only
knows!" said Anton. "And anyway I don't skate." "He's
cleared it," intervened the maid, taking away the plates.
"That's good," approved Vladimir Sergeyevich. "So you'll go
skate after dinner!" Vladimir Sergeyevich practically ordered
me, and I answered him with a grateful look, which was only
indirectly related to the skating rink, and he gave me a smile
that was hardly perceptible, and my smile was hardly percep-

tible to him, and he took a fork and started tapping it on the table, became pensive, turned to Anton, and started up a conversation about telephone calls, which was soon cut short when Anton revealed he had disconnected the telephone the previous day.

I lit a cigarette and held it in my outstretched hand, letting it be known that not only was I used to cultured manners but my hands were graced with particularly slender wrists. In the contest between noble beauty and perfect physical development I give the palm to nobility, and my ankles are slender too, but in truth, most of our men are peasants with simple tastes: bosoms and hips, that's what they go for, although I never allowed such creatures liberties. I was nowhere so alone as in the aggressive company of these vulgar people and would look sadly at the degraded faces in buses and suburban trains, in stadia and the cinemas' creaking rows. They need my ankles and wrists the way a dead man needs a bathhouse or a hole in the head! Bent and bowed by worries, they moved en masse, they slid in gray shadows by wine and vodka shops, and none of them understood the best thing about me, and I would take taxis and leave such lowlifes behind, even if I was down to my very last ruble. I started to despise them so much that I even got it into my head to save them. A Joan of Arc was always latent in me, and she finally awoke. My patience burst.

Well, so what? Nothing good, that's what. However, I must point out that I am still warm, I am still alive, though pregnant, though stuffed with a charge deadlier than an atom bomb. I am alive, I hide out at Rituyla's. The whole civilized world knows about me. But what significance does this have, if fear creeps in, particularly in the guise of rustles from under doors, the creak of the parquet, the fridge's rumbling, the shudder of its sides as it switches on in the middle of the night? Bastards! Bastards! Look what they've brought me to! And if there weren't Rituyla, her obedient and tender eyes, her thoughtful touches, removing if only for a minute my mortal disgrace, my undeserved horror, what would have remained for me other than a bathtub full of blood, a body slumped within it? But I have taken pity on her and won't entrust her with my secrets to the end. I also don't trust Stanislav Albertovich, but since he's offered to help, let's see him help! And you, Kharitonych, you are a shameless hardhearted specimen too, even though you formerly indulged me and I would sleep, have my full beauty sleep, till one or two o'clock, and then I would lie in a pine-scented foam bath, and a seven-ruble masseur would visit, so efficient (although Rituyla massages no worse than he) that beneath his hands I would achieve the final shudder. I never admitted this to him, and he also gave no sign of noticing, not crossing the bounds of common civility—he told me all the latest gossip about actresses and ballerinas and never once referred to my involuntary shudders. And yet, after all that has been between us, you, Kharitonych, call upon me to write a sharp reply to my defenders! No, my dear, write it yourself. And at the same time you beg me again and get understandably annoyed at the fact that what had recently been accessible has become distant and not yours! I laughed at you, bastard! What faces you made! How I laughed!

Coffee was served. The conversation became general and animated, but suddenly heavy female steps were heard, and into the dining room, where the conversation flowed so spontaneously—Vladimir Sergeyevich kept stealing looks at me, although he was a secretive person, taking his cue from classical models, quite different from Antonchik, who had sauce dripping out of his mouth and made too much noise to have deep feelings, while in compensation Vladimir Sergeyevich turned down dessert and seemed happy with our friendly conversation—into the dining room came the mistress of the house.

Full of premature indignation, and with an inflated sense of her own importance, she looked around the table and spied me, and it was as if she had suddenly become nauseated, even though I half rose to greet her, as one is supposed to, and honored her with my most submissive face and demeanor, but she looked at me, as at a bat! "Anton! And just who is this?" she screamed. "This is Ira." Anton made the introduction coolly, not noticing any ill feeling. "Do you want coffee?" "Don't you know that coffee's bad for me!" Everything was bad for her, this overfed turkey, this uneducated goose, who in high society passed as an educated woman, knowledgeable about art; and having surveyed me from head to toe, as if I had stolen the monogrammed family silver, which I hadn't even noticed, not having in my nature the slightest tendency toward materialism, she held on to a false impression of me and left the room. How could he live with her? What did he, a man of a deeply spiritual makeup and secret impulses toward liberation, have in common with this peevish old cow? I admit that in her youth, judging from a few tarnished photographs, while she was no beauty or even particularly pleasant to look at, she might nevertheless have been attractive, perhaps, by virtue of her erudition and her loyalty to her husband's ideals, and Vladimir Sergeyevich, naive and uncalculating, was hooked by this. However, the *dolce vita* in which she had vegetated had destroyed her completely. Not everyone is suited to an idle existence, although on the other hand, when I had become more intimate with Vladimir Sergeyevich, I guessed that she hadn't hit the jackpot with him either and, most likely, he had pretty heavily frayed the nerves of his Zinaida, more than once leaving traces of woe on her fresh and chubby little face, despite the fact that life in their country estate, where the only things missing were tame deer, would have seemed to an outside observer a symphony of joy in a major key, to resort to a musical analogy, music being my only delight in my afflictions. However, I never complained, I didn't lay down my arms, but sometimes, leaning out of someone's window in the region of the boulevards, where I had posed, just after arriving in Moscow, for the penurious artist Agafonov as a fairy for a children's book of fairy tales, I see: jangling streetcars, trees, roofs, and, in the distance, ponds, ponds, and from above people even look a bit happy—and nothing is needed; how good it would be to sit like this all day and, wrapped in a white sheet, watch the sunset. And I wished this creature widowhood and disgrace, even though I'm not evil. These she would receive in full measure. In the meantime the coffee has been drunk, the cognac has gone into the bloodstream, it is as if the hangover has never been. I want to go skating! "And how about you?" I ask him directly. He declined, but when he looked at me his look did not lack some ulterior meaning. Antonchik looks out for his own interests, invites me upstairs to sit in the leather armchairs, but I know what such invitations mean, and he says that he would love to have me stay awhile, except that Mother would misinterpret it, looking after the interests of the family, even though she doesn't get along well with her daughter-in-law, from which I draw the obvious conclusion that Anton is a *married man*—with a child! A good-for-nothing, a ship passing in the night, and I am planning to depart for Moscow, I leave my phone number without any enthusiasm, and suddenly a coincidence: Vladimir Sergeyevich is also going to Moscow and is prepared to give me a lift. I'm aware of the mutual vibes, but I don't hurry to congratulate myself. Nevertheless, Antonchik finally enticed me upstairs, where there were still various articles of my clothing scattered about, and I gave way: why make an enemy of him? But Antonchik showed himself to be unworthy of his dead father! Yes, yes, Antonchik, I write and I do not forgive. I feel pretty bad myself! At about

nine in the evening, Vladimir Sergeyevich and I left his hospitable home. The watchman, Yegor—who only pretended
that he was a watchman, as he oversaw the glorious life there
with his eyes wide open—obligingly played the part of a
flunky, as if under the ancien régime, wished us well on our
journey, flung open the gates, and stood rooted to the spot,
his beard sticking out; Zinaida, fortunately, didn't come out,
declaring that she had a migraine and was reading in bed—
this was what Antonchik informed me, kissing my hand as a
sign of gratitude. He was satisfied, the prick!

# FIVE

O h, Rituyla! Oh, well, snore away, don't mind my writing! We move on. Moscow comes closer. Moscow burns in the sky, between the pine trees and the fir trees, amidst a blaze of wildflowers: They'd wanted to deprive me of my place of residence, but I didn't give in, I got really mad. But then, on that evening, when Vladimir Sergeyevich, turning to look at me in dumb admiration, was approaching Moscow, everything was sleepy and mist hung over the meadows, the river ran, everything was romantic and flickered like a television screen. The villagers were getting ready for bed, old women quacked, the sleepy cattle lowered their heads to the water troughs and mooed, a peasant scrutinized his feet and scratched his chest. We traveled through all this. We almost went through fire and water, almost ended up flattened like a pancake before we had even approached some sort of understanding. This brought us closer together.

Vladimir Sergeyevich just couldn't make up his mind to do it; I saw this; nor could I bring myself to encourage him. But Moscow was getting closer, I was becoming anxious, I was in a real panic as he dragged out the time. Finally, he asked me, "Do you remember Pushkin's fairy tale in verse about the fisherman and the golden fish?" I did remember the tale, but only vaguely; I hadn't reread it for a long time. He asked me so sternly that I actually felt ill: what if he's testing how well educated I am? Perhaps he will force me to recite the whole tale by heart. There's no knowing what he might think up! I didn't know him at all then. And so I answered evasively: "Well, in general terms, of course. . . ." No, this is intolerable. I'll strangle her! I went over to Rituyla and turned her on her side. My stomach is tight, my breasts ache. Nausea. Okay, I won't do much today. Let's move on. "Remember, in this fairy tale," said Vladimir Sergeyevich, after a short silence, "the old fisherman asks the golden fish for favors." "He asks him for a new washtub!" I said, remembering. "Not just for that," Vladimir Sergeyevich objected, holding steadfastly to the wheel in his motoring gloves, and there was always a good aftershave wafting from him, but sometimes, in life, he was so indecisive! "On the whole," said Vladimir Sergeyevich, "in my opinion this old man was rather stupid. He lost his head, he asked for the wrong thing, and in the end the fish swam away. And so then, Irina . . ." I actually shuddered at the sound of my name. "Do you feel in yourself the strength and desire to become, for example, a golden fish?" A point-blank question. "I sometimes feel that . . . ," I answer vaguely, but I'm thinking: Perhaps he's planning to offer me money, to insult me; does he perhaps take me for someone else, for a whore? "Although," I add, "I'm not at all made of gold, and I have no acquisitive passion." "What do you take me for? Of course not!" he exclaims, startled. "I mean in the very highest sense!" "Well, if in the highest sense," I say, calmer, "then yes, I feel it." "Then," he says, "do you know what I would have asked you for if you had been the golden fish?" "I'm afraid I can guess," I answer. His face changes sharply. "Why," he says, "are you afraid? I"—he casts a sidelong glance at me—"am not terrifying. I"—he adds with bitterness—"have long stopped being terrifying—" "I understand." I nod. "I understand everything, but all the same it's terrifying. You are a celebrity, everyone knows you, I'm even afraid to take your hand." He cheers up. "Irina!" he says. "I'm captivated by your honesty." Now he lays his hand on my knee and squeezes it in a friendly manner. This squeeze leaves an indelible trace: I can feel it even now, despite the difficulties I have had to endure.

This was not the weak squeeze of an old profligate, although he was, of course, an old profligate, now ill from frequent excess, because, as he said, unlike most Russians, even though he himself was a Russian, he loved women more than he loved vodka, and he always liked a drink.

A real, *cool* profligate is able to conceal his depravity: he will pretend to be a comrade, a friend, not interested, actually not inclined that way at all, and such a profligate is dangerous and exciting for women, but ostentatious ones, with frenzied and decisive faces—those types are fools; and I find it amusing to watch the movement of their bodies. Vladimir Sergeyevich had achieved a high position in so many fields; he was very talented in all areas! But old age had got the upper hand. He was able, of course, to find various safety valves for himself, but he was powerless in the most important area and consequently much aggrieved. You didn't have to be particularly bright to guess this. He was so distressed that his grief was reflected even in the squeeze of the knee. He squeezed it with chagrin. Yet with dignity too. So I answered him! "Do you know what, Vladimir Sergeyevich? A golden fish can have her whims too." He met my words with reciprocal protestations: that he wouldn't leave debts unpaid, that I could rest assured on that score. "No," I said, "you don't understand me. It's just the way I am. I have to have love."

I read in his eyes a timid distrust, and this grated on me,

for I had always sought love. I wanted to love and be loved, but around me there were rarely worthy people, who in truth are few and far between. Where are they? Where? For a while now I've doubted the nobility and warmth of people. I've noted from my own experience: eighty percent of my far from numerous men, on laying down their weapons, would fall asleep without a single pang of conscience, having forgotten about me, and I would go to the bathroom to wash it out and off and to weep. The remaining twenty percent wouldn't fall asleep but would wait for my return and then seek other ways of bolstering their egos: smoking in bed, for example, preening themselves, showing off their biceps, telling jokes, discussing the failings of other women, complaining about certain negative features of their family and professional life; they'd ask for tit mags to amuse themselves, would have something to drink, watch sports on television, eat sandwiches, offer up their backs for stroking and purr, and then, with renewed strength, they'd be sucked into my embrace so that they could fall asleep like the other eighty percent, and I would go to the bathroom to wash it out and off and to weep.

I won't deny that there were exceptions. There was chic ambassador Carlos, whose gallantry led him to desire a woman's happiness. There was Arkasha, who loved me selflessly, despite the fact that he was an ordinary Ph.D. student in technical sciences, with a Zhiguli car that was falling apart, but his wife, as if out of spite, gave birth to twins, and he was forced to part with me. There was Dato, a Georgian pianist. He loves me even now, he would even today knock at the door of my apartment and in all likelihood is knocking, only I'm not there, and the light is out, and the shards I didn't sweep up are on the floor: I'm living at Rituyla's. She's snoring again. Whenever she drinks she snores. But Dato was a slave to Georgian habits, and though his parents loved me like a

daughter, they had to have a virgin for the wedding night!
Dato wept, his father wept, the procurator Vissarion—we all
wept; I wasn't a virgin. And guess what? He will come to me
after the wedding, twisting his hands in front of him, as they
do, and will say in the Caucasian way, "Let me fuck you!"
"No, I won't!" I'll answer. "Sleep with your artificial cherry:
you've been stitched up!" No, there were, of course, a number
of good men—my dressing table groans under the weight of
their trophies—and they excited me, I was always a sucker
when it came to enjoying myself, but Ksyusha is wise like a
cat and taught me to look at men with more detachment and
to depend on them only when it suited my own whims, and
my whim on that stifling evening of fantasy and wildflowers,
when Vladimir Sergeyevich and I were nearing that Moscow
reflected in the sky, knew no bounds. "Vladimir Sergeyevich,"
I said, "I'll bring about a miracle. I won't deny it: I'm a genius
of love. *But for this you will marry me!*"

You'll never believe what came over him! No, Ksyusha,
you won't believe it! He laughed so hard that we literally ran
off the road and hurtled toward the headlights of an approaching car. We were almost killed by his laughter, which
echoed with rapture and consternation. We barely avoided
the crash. The furious driver ran up to us, ready to fight from
mortal fear. But Vladimir Sergeyevich found the right words.
The driver shut up and calmed down. Vladimir Sergeyevich
was a strong personality. We stood parked on the roadside,
with the sound of the other car fading away. Vladimir Sergeyevich once again put his hand on my knee and once again
squeezed it, and he said starkly, "Fine."

Moscow burned in the sky. We kissed, a long-drawn-out
kiss. Heartfelt and innocent, the kiss ratified the agreement,
while, in her wide bed, that scum Zinaida Vasilievna
shuddered.

# SIX

Father Veniamin, a priest of pure and sincere soul, baptized me yesterday, in the afternoon, in the god-forsaken side chapel of the church entrusted to him. Delicately casting his eyes away from sin, he poured holy water over me, while a female assistant, old and as frail as a dandelion, with iron-capped teeth, tugged at the elastic of my underwear, so that the holy water could cool my pudenda and my shame.

Despite my pregnancy I looked like a girl, except that my breasts had become heavy and felt as if they belonged to someone else.

In a white dress with a narrow belt, in white tights and a little dark-blue scarf, I fluttered, winged, airy, affectionate, out of the church to greet the sun, the maples, and the beggars, to greet the graveyard crosses and wreaths and the black railings around the graves, the spirit of the meager autumn earth, the noise of trains rattling at one another. As a daughter of the Russian Orthodox Church and a humble novice, I declare an armistice in my trivial and unholy wars. I ask my enemies for forgiveness, and at the slightest provocation I resort to the advice of Father Veniamin, who emanates an intensity of agonized holiness from an earlier age. I don't wish anyone ill or feel reproachful; I myself shall remain pure, and if I do sin, still I'm closer now to God, regarding whom all my doubts are fast disappearing. Today I believe more than yesterday. Tomorrow, more than today!

Rituyla is envious. She has made up her mind to get baptized too, but I don't feel like acquainting her with Father Veniamin, because she isn't yet ripe for it. "Now the temptations may become particularly alluring," Father Veniamin confided to me with a sigh. "Battle with them. Fight them. Be vigilant!" "I understand!" I answered.

But Rituyla is wrong to be cross with me.

Lord! I don't know how to pray to You, forgive me, it's not my fault, no one taught me how, my life flowed far away from You, not toward that particular steppe, but a disaster has overtaken me, and I recognize that except for You, there is no one I can turn to. I don't know whether You are, or whether You are not, though it is more likely that You are than that You are not, because I so much want You to be for real. If there is no You, and I am praying into emptiness, why then have so many different people, Russians and foreigners, invalids and academicians, old women and younger men, always, from time immemorial, built churches, baptized children, painted icons, sung hymns? Can it be possible that all this should have been in vain? I refuse to believe that it is a total and utter swindle, a universal blindness, to be suddenly mocked and ridiculed!

Of course, You could well object that until I needed You I lived far from You, giving myself up to joys, to singing and dancing. But is this really bad? Should one really not sing or dance? Must one really never sin? You may say one mustn't! You may say that I didn't live by the rules, which are written down in the Gospel, but I didn't know them. And now? Am I to go to hell when I die and be tormented there for all eternity? If that is the case, then I have to say, what cruelty and injustice! If there is a hell, then it follows that there is no You! You use hell just to terrify us. Say I've guessed right! But if I am mistaken, and it does exist, then abolish it by an act of divine will, give the sinners an amnesty—many of them have been imprisoned for a long time—and tell us about this, and, altogether, stop hiding Your light under a bushel: why have You hidden for so many centuries, for it's because of this, You see, that people doubt and hate one another. Give us a sign!

You don't want to? You think we are unworthy? Then tell us, why are we here, why did You create us such bastards, Father? No, if You have created us thus, the question arises, what right do You have to take offense at us? We're not to blame; we want to live.

Abolish hell, Lord, abolish it today, this minute! And if You don't, I'll stop believing in You! And I'm asking this not just because I'm worried for myself but because we're all un-worthy of heaven, and it's precisely because we're unworthy that You should let us go there!

Or have You decided that I'm frightened of Leonardik? Of his visitations? Of course I'm afraid! That's why I'm living with Rituyla, who also wants to get baptized, but only to be fashion-able; she isn't ready, believe me! But even if I do fear him, then it's not because he's dreadful: I simply didn't expect to see him. He was not too dreadful, in fact, only those fingernails, but on the whole more affectionate than before, and I got confused, did lots of stupid things, and I'm frightened of him because I might not hold out and, I admit only to You, might agree to his offer. And what will this baby be, if I keep him? Answer me! Should I part with him or not? But is this not the only docu-ment that confirms my life outside any other life, that, apart from life, is the only confirmation that I am alive?

Wait, I still haven't decided anything, and I entreat You, if it is within Your powers, and everything is within Your powers, let him not come here for a while, forbid him, I entreat You, let me decide for myself, and remove this fear from me!

The prayer hasn't turned out very coherently, although I was never a troublemaker and never lumped married men into it, so don't offend me, because I can give as good as I get. I even hit Dato in the face when he got mixed up with a prostitute just to annoy me, although he fiercely denied it, as if they had never been in that compromising position on the couch, as if I hadn't seen them with my own eyes and wasn't prepared to forgive everything and throw the blame on that greasy-haired piece of trash, who had been creeping behind the stage curtains for ages, looking into his face and uttering empty words that were clearly aimed at one target alone, and I would warn Dato, Beware, I can be jealous! I won't permit it! I won't endure it! And he would try and talk his way out of it, baffled, and with that same baffled look gazed up at me from the scene of his crime, like the time when his father, Vissarion, caught me and him at it, when I was ironing his shirt for him, the fool—that's the stage our relationship had got to! I was ironing his shirt, and he pounced on me from behind, arriving through the stage door like some sort of snow leopard and slid into place! He stands and sings ditties in his musical voice, in English no less—he loved turning *chastushki* into English—and we roared with laughter, only no, that wasn't Dato: it was a boy called Volodechka, only my size but with a great technique, who engaged in commercial trans- actions with foreign countries, out of duty, not pleasure, and he and I were holidaying in Yalta, in a luxurious hotel, and an Englishman, the father of two English children, knocked at my room, number 537, and made a declaration of love to me, while his spouse was worrying below in the foreign- currency bar, but I didn't react at all, and at precisely this time Volodechka was planning to make a trip and asked me along, but I declined: so what! As an air hostess, I told him,

I had flown to so many different airports, I'd been to Somalia
and Madagascar, to Dakar and Tierra del Fuego, and I wanted
to spit on his invitation, and he could hardly have been surprised, he believed everything I told him, he too had passed
through Dakar, and now he was asking me to go with him to
Tunis: don't worry, everything there is like in white man's
land. I seriously considered accepting the invitation, even
though he was only my size and six years younger, but with
great technique, almost like Dato, only Dato liked moving
around more, biting and teasing me, and even when I had
arrived at the scene of the crime, where his noble ass was
gleaming rhythmically, he denied everything with baffled stupidity, even though I had grasped what was going on and had
invited the little worm to get lost!—"Well, I'm surprised
you're not ashamed, girl! Aren't you ashamed of yourself?"—
but she, not at all embarrassed, goes to the mirror to comb
out her greasy hair, tidies herself up, and chuckles, as Dato
and I had chuckled when the regional procurator of Georgia,
Daddy Vissarion, suddenly comes in and says in a bass voice,
"Uh-huh!" and I am ironing to the sound of music, because
my Dato was a soloist of international standing, always on
tour, and would carry my photo with him everywhere, the
one taken after I had visited a restaurant in Archangelskoye,
near Moscow, and I was crocked and my pose was captured
by a Polaroid, and I show it to him, I can't think why, and
he says, "And who's that?" and prods the person he doesn't
know, and this stranger has a sweet impotence depicted on
his face, as they always have in such a situation. "What bloody
business is it of yours?" I want to take it back, but he doesn't
give it up—"Let me look after it"—and it goes into his wallet,
"or else your mother will see it," and I didn't manage to snatch
it from him, and the photograph flew in planes and helicopters,
traveled around half the world, was in Somalia and Madagascar, in Dakar and Tierra del Fuego, was witness to the

plane crash of the century in Las Palmas, and I say casually,
An air hostess. Do you notice the way I walk? He notices.
That's how I went all around Yalta with him—and Daddy
Vissarion is at the door—Uh-huh!—and Dato fell silent, a
reserved person, though he's a Georgian, but they can sometimes be like that, I have observed this for myself, but as soon
as anything happens they reach for the knives! Although of
course not all of them, and when the little worm was leaving
and saying "Goodbye," as if nothing had happened—she
wasn't lacking in nerve—I was amazed: Well, I think, one
couldn't go much lower!—unwashed, but so shameless, I
turned Dato's back to her at a concert, and it seemed he hadn't
noticed her, but as soon as we had got into the car to drive
along Rustaveli Avenue, where the shops are open until midnight, I look: she is sitting in our car, and Dato is stretched
out in the middle, between two girls, like a gardener. "No,"
I say, "Dato, that's no good," but they're already kissing: she
kisses him on the lips and crawls over his trousers like a pubic
louse. "Look at me for a second, darling!" He was occupied
but turned around. I socked him in the kisser! He grabbed my
arms, held them: "What do you think you're doing?" I said,
"How can you put *that* on a par with me?" and I started biting!
He even shed a few tears, he felt so insulted and helpless,
nervous like so many musicians but up to all sorts of schemes:
no tearing up of the photograph, no howling—no, on the
contrary, he put it in his wallet and carried it all around the
world, and as soon as she was through the door he denied
everything. What do you mean, nothing went on? I was
stunned. But he started singing in English:

> Come, Marusiya, there's duck—
> We shall eat and we shall fuck!

Stop, Volodechka, I say. First earn the right to be vulgar. I
used to think that way, never swore at all, considered it showed
a lack of culture, but Ksyusha explained that when a word's
primordial meaning is acknowledged, this is a high! And the
only people who don't swear are teachers, who don't understand anything about getting high. True, my friend Ksyusha
wasn't wrong here either, but it's still a great mystery to me
why she bad-mouths the French so, and recently she was in
the U.S.A. and tells me, "There it's even worse—a totally
uncultured people, like ours, only a bit richer and very proud
of the fact that they are sincere. They say we are sincere like
no one else, and without any complexes whatever, but," she
claims, "there are too many sincere fools among them; it's a
real epidemic." If one is to believe her, she even breathed
easier as she flew back to Paris. "They're an awful little
people," she says, "the Americans. And as for their taste! You
can recognize them from the other end of the street in Paris,
and in the museums they're like monkeys, going around with
headphones." "What sort of headphones?" I don't like her
speeches, and the more they go on, the more I don't like
them! "You should spend some time standing in line," I say,
"run around to the druggist's, looking for some cotton balls,
or shop for boots," I say. "How d'ya feel about paying two
hundred rubles for them?" She gets angry. "I," she says, "never
stand in lines; I can survive without oranges, live on cheese!"
My turn comes; I'm bursting with anger: "Ksyusha, don't say
another word about the Americans! An obtuse nation doesn't
fly to the moon. But come on, tell me, what are these headphones?" "Well," she says, "it's the way they do things: you
visit the museum, you rent a cassette, the cassette chatters,
and you wear headphones." And so, she explains, the Americans waddle in single file from picture to picture, like clock-
work toys, with headphones. Their brows are furrowed, their

expressions stupid. The recorded guide orders them: One step
forward. They step. Approach the picture! They approach the
picture. Back! Two steps back! They move away. Now into
hall number three. They pass through hall number two, where
they don't examine anything, because they've been told to go
to hall three. Well, idiots or what? I took offense on their
behalf: I don't see anything contemptible here, I said, apart
from progress, and I myself would go around in these headphones, thankfully I still remember English from school and
can even sing *chastushki* in English:

Come Marusiya, there's duck . . .

Well, he asks her to come to him with a goose, a goose, you
understand, goose! We shall eat . . . well, that goose; "eat"
means to eat, and then—the Englishman stares, becomes
tense, he doesn't understand the humor, blinks, smiles politely, no sense of humor; however, I say, much depends on
the company: if the company doesn't mess it up, a *chastushka*
can be a work of high art, flowing from the sources of popular
life, because the life of the people, as I have found out to my
cost, is a contradictory phenomenon and one that has not
been totally eliminated. There are many good qualities, which
make me feel patriotic (I am a patriot), but there are of course
total disasters too. Jews, for example, say we are a slow-witted
people, that such sluggish people can't be found anywhere
else. Hold it! Our people are not very quick, particularly in
the countryside, where they live even worse than they have
to, although, on the other hand, if they were to live better,
to feed on mandarin oranges, walnuts, meat, what would be
the result? As was explained to me by the two brothers Ivanovich (they are journalists), the people have within themselves a limitless reservoir of natural wisdom, even if they are

stupid, but as soon as they stop drinking and living worse than they have to, they will lose their native wisdom and their other virtues, because the soul is made pure by abstinence! "True," I say. "In me, for example, there is no low materialism," and now, now that I have been baptized, I subscribe to this with both hands: an understanding people! But Ksyusha is mistaken about the Americans; they are also a good people, only we are a bit better! I speak as a native daughter of the Russian Orthodox Church and not as some sort of outcast. When I fell to my knees to pray, I looked at the icons and I didn't know what to say. Merzlyakov whispers to me: Pray! pray! I say, I am praying. But in fact I am only an embarrassment to the air in the church. Yet when the priest Venedikt appeared on my path, then gradually I started to discern beauty and to inhale the smells of the meager autumn earth, where the fallen leaves flutter down, preparing a yellow carpet under the feet: you walk along it, not belonging to yourself, the soul delights, a song rings in your ears, and as soon as they close off the capital from the provinces, hold a nonstop Olympics in Moscow, it will get even better, because as I can tell them from my own experience, they get spoiled otherwise and don't want to return, buying up all the goods, and for those who have some pretensions and are not total degenerates it's particularly harmful; the capital confuses and corrupts them. Get your entry visa for Moscow, and then you can enter, but if not, sit at home, don't make a fuss, otherwise you'll dream of Moscow each night. You'll even shout out sometimes in your sleep, only one night's journey from Moscow, and here's a significant fact: the train going there was overcrowded, no room, like in the metro, they sleep on the luggage racks, but on the return journey, in third class, I was often almost the only passenger. Nevertheless, the population in our town didn't decrease. I was married twice before I was twenty-three, both times because of my own stupidity, but that isn't the point: I traveled to Moscow to visit the theaters and the restaurants, to rest my soul, more and more often I visited Moscow, struck up some acquaintanceships, and the main thing was that my very own granddaddy lived in Moscow and—miraculously!—in a two-room apartment! Alone! Well, his wife had died, my grandmother, while I had to while away my life in total provincial nothingness. Not everyone, of course, has a granddad residing in Moscow, an old Stakhanovite, with weak health that demands care, but only his son, my dissolute daddy, was mad enough to give up his Moscow residence permit and get stuck for all eternity in our old town, to become scum in every sense of the word. I suspect him of a criminal past, which, by unwritten agreement, we never discuss in our family; it was no coincidence that Daddy turned out to be one-eyed, while his artificial eye was small and very unsuccessful, which was why they started teasing me in school in first grade, but Granddaddy prudently kept silent, and now Mother writes that he lies on his cot, immobilized by a stroke, perhaps he's died this very minute, how am I to know? I live at Rituyla's, though I'm fed up with being at Rituyla's, damn her! My mother too was always crafty, but when my father's past manifested itself in a brutally direct way—although because of my youth I suspected nothing, in my red schoolgirl's tie—I thought it was just his way of bringing me up, that it was punishment for my offenses and bad marks and was nothing unusual. I didn't catch on right away, I would never have caught on, I was ignorant, had no idea, but when everything was revealed to Mother through the fluttering curtain, when she came home unexpectedly and ran off immediately to report him to the militia, I thought: Well, now they'll definitely kill each other—they were yelling at each other so!—but my father was at one time a cabinetmaker, at least that's the family

legend, although I don't remember him ever holding so much
as a piece of mahogany in his hands.

Well, they didn't kill each other, they are living to this
very day, but Granddaddy—what about Granddaddy?—will
remain a luminous page. The stroke is serious, by the way.
And when Mother decided to come here, planning to emigrate
to Israel, hoping to skim off the cream my misfortune gave
rise to, she said that my father was totally out of it, he'd lost
his artificial eye for the umpteenth time and wasn't ordering
a new one. In any event, one can't exclude the possibility
that Daddy spent time in prison, for what I don't know, or
perhaps they only planned to put him away and he took off,
into the backwoods, and because of him, the one-eyed bastard,
I was teased right from first grade, they reduced me to tears,
and I was an unusually big girl for my age, with a foolish
expression, two pigtails and a bashful, lopsided smirk. I was
very shy, timid as a deer, I was embarrassed about undressing
in the girls' bathhouse, and in my soul I have remained the
same, only Moscow painted her layer of metropolitan gloss on
me, and how deeply I fell in love with Moscow!

I couldn't live without Moscow; it was as if I'd been
drugged. I tell you, I was delirious at nights, I frightened my
husband, particularly the second one, and he by the way was
something of a celebrity in our town: a football player. While
he was in the hospital with pneumonia, I was, as they say,
unfaithful to him. I would have been happier not to betray
him, but he himself had fanned such a fire inside me that
though I tried to hold out, I couldn't sit around chewing my
nails forever: instead of Moscow, I started to dream about
nothing but cocks, whole families of them, like agaric mushrooms. I would wake up in a sweat, dreadful! And the problem
wasn't so much that I was unfaithful to him but that I picked
the wrong person to be unfaithful with, from a rival team.

And he, of course, boasted about it to everyone. It's a small town; most of the houses are still made of wood, with an ancient winged emblem. The gossip made its way to my play-ground sportsman. He beat me up brutally, and it was a miracle I wasn't maimed for life, simply a miracle! I still bear a small scar on the bridge of my nose, a salute from the world of football.

The scar's okay—it adds piquancy—but I couldn't endure the insults. I fled to Moscow, to my grandfather's feet: let me look after you! Grandfather, with his strict views, was worried that I would start misbehaving. I swore on the health of my parents, and if I misled the old man, I really didn't mean to. And even now it isn't clear: who misled whom? Because of course Granddaddy didn't have to speak at the meeting; if he'd reported himself sick they wouldn't have dragged an old man there, and as for his claim that he was defending me, well, that's an old wives' tale, my late grandmother's. Well, to hell with him; but the moment Ksyusha and I lie down, embrace, I ask impulsively, "Well, and how's New York? The skyscrapers don't oppress the soul?" "No," she answers, "not one bit. On the contrary, a beautiful sight." Then I think: You're lying *all* the time, only I don't know why. But Grand-daddy makes his way barefoot across the Gulf of Finland. "Aren't you fed up," he says, "of wasting your time? Your loverboys are overloading the phone circuits!" He was my secretary and answered the calls, using the old-fashioned greet-ing: "Yes, I hear you!" And Carlos would phone, the Latin American ambassador. And Granddaddy would say to him: "Yes, I hear you!" And Leonardik also would dial the number, burning with love and languor, and Granddaddy: "Yes, I hear you!" He made all my telephone appointments, but he grum-bled a bit, he didn't understand pluralism, and now there he is, dying, or perhaps he has already died.

We lie there chatting while memories of Koktebel break

upon us like an ocean wave. Night bathing under the search-lights of the frontier guards: we bathed, swam on our backs, thrashed our arms through the sea, and when we came out of the water we were detained as Turkish spies, only Ksyusha, knowing what was what in espionage, crushed the soldiers by explaining, "We're not Muslims! Or can't you see that?" The toy soldiers gleamed in the lamplight and sniggered: "You're not actresses, by any chance? You're both so tall! You're not celebrities, are you?" Ksyusha, quick as a flash, says, "Celeb-rities!" The soldiers sniggered, and we ate watermelon, redder than red, and sat under a tent, and she was reading a French novel—she'd learned languages from childhood—while a pack of men followed us around: we despised them, we loved each other, it goes without saying. And Yurochka Fyodorov is mis-taken in asserting that I'm an enemy of culture, it's stupid for him to talk that way, because he has a bald patch in the place where I have bergamot trees rustling, where a rivulet babbles and there are fish with red fins—while all he has is a bald patch, scorched earth, and as far as culture is concerned, he's mistaken. I'm well read and I understand everything; even Ksyusha used to be amazed: where does it come from? Not without some cost, of course, because for a long time I couldn't wash away that smell of the ancient town with its winged emblem, however hard I washed, no matter what shampoos and perfumes I resorted to. I had only to sniff myself and got that putrid smell: household soap and mold. No, Yurochka, you wouldn't understand! And do you remember, I say, Ksyu-sha, how you and I discovered a great law, basing it on the observations we both had made? Do you remember? How could I forget, she says, Sunny, a great law and a just law, only not accessible to all. We shed a few tears and embraced, and we don't need anyone else. And then I tell her about Leonardik, about our agreement. She had known Leonardik from child-hood, had called him Uncle Volodya, because he was a friend

of her parents', she had played doctors and nurses with Antonchik from the age of four, and so for her he was simply
Uncle Volodya. Whereas, I say, it was at that time that I was
nearly killed, when a dump truck got stuck in the mud in our
street. Tractors arrived to pull it out, they pulled and they
pulled, while we kids watched them pulling. And suddenly a
cable snapped, like a guitar string, and started to whistle and
struck the little boy next to me, hit him in the temple, and
he fell, and I was right next to him, well, squatting half a
pace away from him, also interested in how they were pulling
it out, and how could you pull it out if it had stuck in the
mud right up to the cab? And I see the boy is lying there,
dying, and you, I say, were showing each other naughty bits
in the raspberry bushes, while your fathers were strolling com-
placently under the pine trees on a hot day, discussing world
problems, in canvas hats and summer suits, carrying on conversations about historical moments, about an article in the
paper and perspectives for the future, nodding their heads,
while the beautiful wives minced along behind, twittering
about clothes, except that the men's talk was not about world
affairs but most likely about getting laid. There were all sorts
of things, says Ksyusha, not necessarily getting laid, although
getting laid too, because Uncle Volodya was always a tomcat,
and my daddy too wasn't a saint, although he was very talented. So what about the boy? "He died," I say, "immediately.
They buried him. Then his loving mummy declares: 'It doesn't
matter. I'll have another one.' And she had another child,
but first she cried, grieving over him, clinging to him, not
giving him up, she pulled him out of the coffin, she wouldn't
let him go, she screamed and screamed, and then she gave
birth, a boy again, as alike as two peas, an identical suede-
head, with a blue-gray nape, like a dove, and I was alongside:
squatting." "But did they at least pull the dump truck out, or
is it still bogged down there?" We laugh, as if we hadn't parted,

as if she wasn't a Frenchwoman, as if she didn't travel around in a pink car, frightening people. "And what's happening with you and Uncle Volodya?" she says. "Is he going to marry you, or is he joking?" "It's not a joking matter!" I do complain, though: he's dragging it out, using his reputation as an excuse. "He and a surgeon once," she says, "a professor of pediatrics, I remember, contemplated screwing Siamese twins. Two heads, two necks, scarves on the necks, two hearts, four nipples, and then—one navel and one hole: everyone was after them, licking their lips; the girls were nine years old, they were kept away from everyone, a nanny was hired, they were pampered, attempts were made to get to them. 'If only,' the professor groaned, 'they live long enough, but they won't make it,' and it was true: the young girls checked out without reaching the age of consent." I, of course, memorize this, even if it is only a joke, and I ask Leonardik: "So why do you write about such very different matters? I read you," I say, "you were part of the national curriculum. I saw films too; they made me sick!" This was when we had started to quarrel. "What's new, then?" asks Ksyusha. "Have you resurrected his Lazarus? Or is it still hanging down to his knees, drooping grayly?" "Oh," I say, "what a bitch you are, Ksyusha!" "To hell with him!" she says. "He's repulsive!" "He's repulsive, René's repulsive—Ksyushenka, with you everyone's repulsive, but I think that everyone's beautiful in some way! For example, my Carlos, while his long-nosed wife was stuck at home in the motherland, he had a good time, he and I fucked on his desk, in the midst of his writing implements. 'You,' he used to say, 'are a rare woman, Irina; you can keep your legs in the shape of the letter Y!' Only he gets an unexpected summons home. What is it? A junta's taken power!" "I know," says Ksyusha. "Filthy crooks! They're even imprisoning the priests!" "Who?" "Why, the junta! Don't try to be clever, Sunny, marry Arkasha!" "Marry him! He's devoted to me, of course, like a dog, and his wife still puts up with him—I'm totally amazed at the woman—but what would I gain by marrying him? Just boredom." "Oh, Sunny, boredom's everywhere!" "That René—is he still a Socialist?" "What of it?" she says. "I'm a Socialist too, you know!" "Ksyusha," I say, "don't make me laugh! You . . . a Socialist?" But she doesn't laugh, she is serious, and her attitude to money is far from casual; she pins her money, her francs, together in wads. I see that things aren't so simple; as we entwine for what may be the last time, I think that perhaps when next she visits she will have changed totally, she will reject me, and who was it who taught me what an idyll could be? Who? It all started in Koktebel, in that very same Koktebel, by the same old Black Sea, in eastern Crimea, and I will never forget this, how she knelt before me, how solicitously she dried me with a towel after the night swims, and I'll carry this memory with me forever, I will never disavow it, even to some Nina Chizh, who doesn't even know where women piss from, because she asked me about this herself, and she's over thirty—how dare she insult me! But I suppress my hatred: I am a Christian, for a long time I've been drawn toward religion, I wore a crucifix, I thought for pleasure, but it turned out I was mistaken. That crucifix was sanctified with holy water, and the priest Valerian proclaimed me a martyr.

As for my first husband, let's just say that if I chanced to meet him in the street, I wouldn't recognize him, he's been totally effaced from my memory, and if you were to ask me, How long did you live with him? I would answer, Well, a month, maybe two at the most, but according to my passport, for two whole years! And now in the street I wouldn't recognize him. Not because I'm proud, not because I'm bluffing, but because I've simply forgotten: lived for two years, and have forgotten everything, even where he worked—forgotten. . . .

But I do remember the second: the football player! I was
savagely beaten for my enforced unfaithfulness, because things
had got so totally out of hand while he was coddling his
strained groin in the infirmary that once, seeing two stray dogs
licking each other's ears, I got all agitated and decided that
enough was enough. From now on things are going to be
different! The wind of old age is blowing in my face, and my
breasts stick out in different directions, like a goat's. Okay,
silly mother dearest, where can I go? Who needs me? No, this
is the end. The wind of old age is blowing smack in my kisser.

"And, Granddaddy, why," I say, "are you so shamelessly
plowing your way barefoot over the waters of the Gulf of
Finland? Tell me, for heaven's sake, where do you plan to go?
Surely you haven't got it into your head to make for Helsinki,
to stock up on junk? You see, the Finns are, they say, a shrewd
lot. Don't walk, Grandfather, over the waters of the Gulf of
Finland, don't frighten me before bedtime!" "No," answers
Granddaddy—and he just goes ahead proudly, heedlessly,
across the Gulf of Finland—"no, I wasn't planning to go to
Helsinki-Helsingfors, not to the flea market. I'm too old to
lie or pretend; I don't need anything, just a breath of fresh
air." "Watch out," I say. "They'll wing you, you old Stakhanovite, you'll sink to the bottom!" "It's time," he answers,
"for me to do some wandering along the Gulf of Finland, and
if they wing me it's no great tragedy if I go to the bottom."
"Well, Ksyusha," I say, "what a circus: Grandfather is strolling
across the Gulf of Finland, enjoying himself," but she snuggles
up against me and whimpers gently. Her hair is done in the
latest style. I must, I think, have mine done like that too; I
couldn't help it: I was a bit jealous, though what is there to
be jealous of? A person can be unhappy as a result of being
loaded or because of dire poverty—what's the difference!

When she lets herself go, there's no stopping her! "Look,"

she says, "I'm not a Muslim, though I do have Tatar blood, like all of us, sinners that we are!" And she and I stand in a path of moonlight, up to our knees in the Black Sea, holding hands, Moscow celebrities, stars of world cinema or bits of fluff, while the border guards examine us, and their trousers twitch at the wondrous sight. As soon as Ksyusha noticed, she gave a naughty scream: "Come on, boys, throw down those little machine guns, take off your uniforms; we'll have a nice swim together," but they answer as one in their southern Ukrainian accents: "We must stand by our posts." "Leave," commands Ksyusha, "your posts for a minute; far better to have a swim, get friendly." The border guards looked all around them, then they said, "We aren't allowed to swim, but it'll be okay to sit on the beach and have a cigarette." Well, out we came. The night is all stars, all around are cliffs, and the waves whisper. Nature creates the right mood. The boys couldn't stand it any longer, they threw off their heavy machine guns and led us to the rocks and there they laid us, the spies swimming from Turkey forgotten. The locks were off the state border. Afterward we all sat round and had a smoke. The young soldiers straightened their uniforms and loaded their weapons onto their shoulders. We parted friends. They went off to continue guarding the border, and we once again dive into the sea—plop! into the water!—and we swim along the moonlit path. "What do you think?" I say. "Have they got VD?" "You must be joking! Clean as a whistle!" She swims off. "Masturbators!"

But the next morning she scolds me: "Your bathing suit, Sunny, is awful, really common! Change it!" It's easy for her to talk: change it. For that revealing swimsuit with one strap I had paid . . . and she says change it. She didn't like vulgarity; she gave me her own: "Here, try it on." I learned a lot from her, although Ksyusha was not always right; she was wrong to offend Leonardik. "Well," she says, "tell me, how are you getting on with the old bastard? No." She makes a wry face. "Don't tell me!" "But why do you call him," I ask, perplexed, "an old bastard? He's not an old bastard at all. He's courteous, he knows how to romance a woman, helps you on with your coat at the right moment and holds your chair at the table. He suffers, of course, for his reputation, but in love he's like a young man: he sends roses to my home, and Granddaddy sniffs them." "But don't you find it repulsive with him?" I answer truthfully: "Not one bit!" She looks at me like a Frenchwoman. "You are," she says, "strange people." "Who's *we?*" She gives no answer, is silent; she's becoming degenerate before my very eyes, and no sooner has she arrived, stayed awhile, walked in freedom awhile, far from her dentist, than she's preparing to leave again. She gets hold of pressed caviar for presents and is given to cursing fascist juntas. Of course, they were wrong to kill Carlos, wrong to break off diplomatic relations and put a stop to his basement with its dances, although of course there was a sigh of relief when they boarded up the door: he'd really taken so many liberties! He refused to wear American jeans, never wore them: like Ksyusha, he had no time for America, he used to say it was a trashy, worthless country, but I couldn't care less: if trashy, then trashy; if a junta, then a junta!

I answer her candidly, from the heart, hiding nothing: "No, my dear Ksyusha, not one bit! He," I say, "is a great man! A dinosaur! And as for what he writes," I say, "it's not for us to judge; he looks from the state's point of view and sees further than us, whereas you and I lack depth. Yes," I say, "different horizons, far different from ours." She looks at me, shakes her head: "What strange people *you* are. Strange! Strange!"

# SEVEN

**T**he drawers are wide open. The yellow tights with their worn-out soles hang down. I am returning to my deserted house.

Here the flasks of perfume, the cut-glass stoppers, stand in a row, Diorissimo; they jostle for space: the mother-of-pearl vase with its dried forget-me-nots, cotton balls in various colors, lotions, tortoiseshell combs, the golden cartridges of lipstick. I still haven't swept away the shards since it happened, let them lie there, on the dressing-table mirror I write "Ira" with my finger, I start up my spluttering phonograph, frown, and write some more, and what is written is reflected in the mirror: Here the flasks of perfume, the cut-glass stoppers, stand in a row, Diorissimo . . .

Here is my belly. Soon it will be beyond hope. I will shout to him as soon as he dares to enter: "Here it is, my belly, here!" The mailbox is full of newspapers; they are Granddaddy's. A canvas, unframed, is attached to the wall with big nails: my great-grandmother. The portrait is an ancient one by an unknown artist, talented. My suitors, surprised, used to praise it: "Who's that?"

The bed is glorious. The bedspread is satin, heavy tassels. Merzlyakov, who once went with a tourist group to Poland, used to relate how ex-votos hang in gratitude, silver and gold, in their Catholic churches. Thank you, Jesus Christ, for curing my daughter of meningitis, or thanks to you I became a new person—thank you! There they are, he says, hanging in their churches, screwed to the walls, to the iconostases, to the columns, but how many such grateful ex-votos could one screw to your bed? I, said Merzlyakov, will affix one made of pure gold: *Dziekuje, Pani Irena!* He didn't. . . . That was when our six-day love was going on: for hours he and I look at ourselves in the dressing-table mirror; the poor man can no longer stand upright, he ejaculates blood, yet still he gazes, eagle-eyed, rapt—but what's the use? He stayed with his wife, an interpreter, started breeding, forgot about the ex-votos, got together with his old friends again, twice a year he'll drop in to drink tea, and it's not the same any longer, not the same at all, without its inspiration; it's as if I were with a completely different man.

Granddaddy will die, they won't allow me to keep this flat, it's too spacious. Grandfather served well and faithfully: but what have I done? I was given the brown envelope, as is the custom, kicked out on my ass, so that Viktor Kharitonych could write his rotten letter, all injured innocence, stick a stamp on it, and send it to my American champions, saying, Look, we haven't caused her any real harm, she decided to devote more time to her private life, as happens in our country too, although in percentage terms we have six times more working women than you have, and no representative of the weaker sex lays asphalt on the roads here, that's all lies. "You really ought to scribble a couple of lines yourself: for example, thanks for the concern, for the affection, but you really needn't have troubled yourselves . . ." "You can manage without me!" I answered, and thought: Perhaps it's really true that they won't touch me, after their article, for after all, if they've assumed it was all because of love, that means I've got an alibi. I keep quiet, I hide my furious resentment, I summon Ksyusha urgently from the settlement of Fontainebleau with its French railway service, but in a flash, they start pointing the way back to my native town, they're slinging me out. I proceed to make a thousand phone calls. There's a certain Shokhrat, who has been prominent in his time, an important man all over Central Asia; I wanted to sit out the siege at his place, to come to my senses: It's me, Shokhrat, I say with false cheer, and he and I used to fly around all those Samarkands of theirs and visit the Muslim shrines, holy places, only we didn't go any farther than the hotels, we stayed in the luxury suites: grand pianos, air-conditioning, select cantaloupes. They melted in the mouth.

I part with Margarita, my Rituyla, rather coolly, though, it goes without saying, perfectly amicably, and she's not going to prevent my leaving either. Margarita has acquired someone or other, despite all my embraces and services rendered; it doesn't matter, I think, you'll manage okay, you won't come to grief, because she simply hasn't got enough of a conscience. As if I had forgotten how you infected your Japanese, the wheeler-dealer, or how he flew away to Japan completely shattered, although you knew you were infected! And the next minute she's calling me to the bathhouse, as if there were nothing wrong with her; words failed me. That sort of thing's just not done, Rituyla, it's not nice. Only she thinks differently, and I don't really object: she got cured and stretched out her hand in friendship once more, we got friendly, but most likely she enjoyed our intimacy out of curiosity; there was no wild passion in her, not at all like my Ksyusha, who has more than enough for everyone! Sometimes Ksyusha would speed along Leninsky Prospect in her canary-yellow little Zhiguli, black upholstery, with her breasts quite naked, even though they have a definite flaw—one nipple sticks out, but the other doesn't seem able to manage it, asymmetrical, definitely unusual—not during the day, it's true, more like midnight, while the taxi drivers and the rest of the late-night public just gawked stupidly and rubbed their eyes.

But Veronika had told me, You will go further. And go further I did—and what do I mean, go: I *ran!* And I know Ksyusha would not have been capable of this: she is granted almost everything, but something like this is granted only to very rare beings. Veronika explained: "This isn't Ksyusha's domain; she has been allotted the theater and joys, but you, Ira—death!" "Stop this rubbish!" I say, but I don't look into her eyes: her gaze weighs on me, I can't endure it. On top of everything else, Veronika is a witch as well, with her bulging brow—plenty of ideas there—and it's odd, but if you see her in the metro, on the way to her laboratory: no looks to speak of, hair untidy, indistinguishable from everyone else, fat legs, and as for her clothes, better say nothing, not one man would spare her a glance—but if she looks at you, you tremble! When Ksyusha went away—and Veronika had loved Ksyusha, had found a joy in Ksyusha that we had forgotten—where, she asks, shall we find another such joy, where? We turned around: a total eclipse, as if we'd been poleaxed, and Ksyusha couldn't stand it, the rattlebrain and Veronika and I were left together, only it's impossible to make friends with her, she's from another world. But when she's in the metro: a woman like any other, with an advanced degree, going to play with chemicals. The deputy director of the laboratory. That's how it is.

But I'm like my grandmother, my great-grandmother—tell me I am, Granny! She hangs there, proud, indifferent. And so, pardon me, I'm not plebeian! How they all praised me: what ankles! what ankle bones! After prompting, however; otherwise, only Leonardik noticed of his own accord.

Ksyusha asks: have I raised his Lazarus? Well, I'm not going to boast, but I resurrected it, although the situation was tricky, he wasn't promising, and that's doubtless why he agreed to our pact and ratified it with a kiss, though he was cunning: he didn't believe in his potency, he was at his last gasp and in addition had been totally spoiled. He loved to list the ballerinas he had been with, swelling boastfully as he named them; he wanted to stun me, like a fish. But I knew my stuff; and when Ksyusha pestered me for details, I replied, "You don't really want to know the details about 'Uncle Volodya,' I won't tell you," but I did tell her, because of course I wanted to show off; I had resurrected him, to put it mildly! Well, and once I've resurrected him, I say to him, as if in jest, Now it's your turn, but not right away, naturally, let him enjoy everything to the full, and he came so gratefully, not as if he were an international genius but like his own man, and when he died, Granddaddy runs in with the paper, joyful with the news: Look who's dead! Do you think I don't know, you stupid old fool? He'd chosen his moment well: I had just come from *there*, I had had great difficulty persuading them to let me go, they barely left me alone, and am I to blame that I didn't know how to open the lock? That was no door but a portcullis. Wasn't I the one who called the ambulance? "When?" they ask. "At that point he still hadn't died, apparently," I say, but they say, "It's you! you! you!" "No!" I answer. "We were in love! I'm all shaken up," I say. "It was horrible: he died before my very eyes, not to put it more crudely." "And where do all the abrasions and the bruises on the body come from? You can't fool us!" they say. "No, thank you," I say, "I don't have to say anything, I'm shaken up as it is, and as far as his tastes are concerned, well, he, pardon me, liked it that way! Get it? No?" They get it, but they don't believe it; however, I notice that they've started using the polite "you" to me.

They're nervous. I say, "Phone Anton." Anton would be a witness, I hoped, but it didn't work out that way, though they did release me. But instead of a direct answer to my joke about his turn: "When are we going to the registry office?" he preferred to buy himself off with insignificant trifles, and thus it dragged on for a long time. I waited for him to get so hooked that he would have nowhere to go, the darling; he wouldn't go to Zinaida Vasilievna, that's for sure! And I think it's also a good idea to put Zinaida Vasilievna in the picture, because she is a woman given to hysterics, but here I miscalculated. Ksyusha was no friend either; it was not that she condemned me, she followed with interest from a distance: I wrote to her, she complained about my handwriting, I don't know why, she didn't like my handwriting, she said, Your slant is too sharp, ease up! So what? my handwriting's perfectly normal. . . . Only she wasn't a friend, because in all probability she didn't want me to be with her father's big buddy, but what could I do if he worshiped me—that, I say to them, is how it is. She never believed me, she couldn't allow such a possibility, but it turned out I was right, only Zinaida frustrated the plan. As soon as she found out, thirdhand, she said wearily, "Oh, let him fuck who he likes!" I had been thinking: She'll start squealing! But she says, Darling, do what you like. . . . I didn't expect such subtlety or wisdom from her, I was taken aback, but I thought: Just wait! And I started to play hard to get. He is patient. Granddaddy shouts, "Yes, I hear you!" I see he's on the phone. I say, "I'm not home!" "When will she be home?" "She won't be home!" and I had a special little list—I added to it—for my granddaddy, Tikhon Makarovich: Respond negatively to a certain Vladimir Sergeyevich, and he is only too happy to oblige, he would be delighted to respond negatively to them all, but don't try that with me, I'm not quite dead yet; they would phone, visit wearing their raspberry-colored jeans, scum, of course, and Granddaddy is in another room, like a marmot, he never pops out after ten o'clock, he'll watch TV and go to bed, well, of course, we're quieter when he's there, and for the summer he would go away completely, to his chicken coop—he'd been given a little patch of ground outside Moscow, he liked digging about in the earth. Suddenly he'll descend on me with red currants. Don't you want to try some red currants? You are a strange creature, not eating vitamins! I would thank him humbly: I had learned all the little words of gratitude; here Ksyusha had lifted all the filth from me, pressing me to her asymmetrical breasts as if I were Ophelia, and when she found out that I called him Leonardik, she roared with laughter.

I keep on playing hard to get, but when he does get to meet me, I say, "Take me to a restaurant or to the Philharmonic or to the theater; I want some culture!" He immediately goes sour, vacillates: "Why don't I buy you a car instead," he says. Buy me a car! No, thank you very much, I don't want it. I want to go to the theater. I used the formal "you" to him, right up to the end. I kept my distance, out of respect for his profile and for his achievements, and as soon as Ksyusha arrived to help, her first question, in the door, was: "What did he die of?" "What do you think?" I answer without hesitation. "Of ecstasy!"

I shall now affirm, taking as witness my great-grandmother, whose portrait I shall never sell: I'd rather hang myself in the bathroom—but can you really call it a bathroom? With its gas water heater, a mockery of modernity; on the other hand, there's always hot water. I shall now affirm—because we have royal blood, even though it went astray somewhere along the line and its circumstances are now a bit messy—my Leonardik died of ecstasy!

Placing my hand on my heart, I swear I didn't kill him. I

just drove him to a state of ecstasy. Beyond that he drove himself. . . . For you see, at this point they swooped on me, the pubic lice, the bloodsuckers, they went totally wild! What did I do to you! Why have you fastened on me? You are not worth my broken little finger! Look, there, my great-grandmother—she's a member of a long-established family of Russian gentry from Kalinin! There's her portrait, painted in oils! A supremely elegant woman, masses of charm, décolleté, a haughty mien, jewels. I'll sell everything, I'll go around the world begging, but I won't sell the portrait, though I freely admit that I haven't got a thing to live on, and if I eat caviar, it's only because it's part of the trophies I've received, the spoils of love, supplies are running out—caviar and cognac, that's the sum total of the presents you have given me, but I didn't give in, I started stringing him along even more furiously, and if it comes to that, then I never had more than ten lovers! But I shan't sell my great-grandmother! It's a memento. Rituyla says that we look like each other. Well, never mind Rituyla, I made my own comparison: I attached the portrait to the dressing-table mirror, stood next to it, and looked: the resemblance is indubitable, and the mien is also haughty, not of our time, and the necks are alike. Only she has less agitation in her face.

And you, Leonardik, you're a fine one, I must say! See how ugly everything's turned out. And now they're hassling me: "Why the bruises?" And what can I answer? Why should I be the one who suffers for your fantasies? On what grounds? Of course, I should like to keep your reputation intact, but I just don't like it when people yell at me! I'm not used to being treated that way, I was brought up differently, I wasn't raised like a peasant, and as for the presents, if you're so interested, as if they reflect the true worth of our love, then I'll say: a real miser. They were more bribes and promises than presents.

Arkasha, before the twins, gave me far better presents, robbing from his family, a real niggard he was, and what do I need a car for, when even without one I can always get where I want to by taxi, but they read extortion in these abrasions, and Zinaida Vasilievna says, "I know nothing about this, this is the first I've heard of it." She told a complete pack of lies. How could she fail to know? *Everyone* knew; I was always dying to go out in public, and if there were any objections, I started playing hard to get again: "No, she's not at home," and that's all; and he couldn't stand this, he'd hold out for a week, and then: "*Irishenka* dearest, get ready. I've got some tickets." He had grown attached to me and couldn't let go. . . . So I get all dressed up in a way that sets all the men sighing, but he says, "You ought to be a bit more modest; as soon as you lean over, people can see everything!" "Well, so what? Let them envy!" He didn't like this, though he tried to strut like a general and a turkey cock; acquaintances were encountered: "This," he says, "is Ira," he introduced me (he calls *this* an introduction), even though he didn't like it, he was happy to avoid doing so, but I stand out, everyone looked, Ksyusha used to give me such dresses, clearly not purchased with my salary. Thus a year passed by and a second started, and I got rather fed up, things hadn't progressed, although it's true he made various efforts to spice things up, sending Zinaida to a sanatorium in the south, or some other place. He invites me to his dacha. Yegor smiles, delighted for his master, but he too was a complex case when I got to know him better: it turned out that he wrote little plays, and Vladimir Sergeyevich paid him one hundred and fifty rubles a month, acted as his patron, and Yegor would whisper to me: "That's because he's hoping to save his neck thanks to me; he was the one who took me in." But his wife, the thin servant, she liked wine a lot and was unbelievably dense, because, Yegor would explain, he'd married too young, before he believed in himself, but Vladimir Sergeyevich, every time he gets a bit drunk, calls Yegor to him and says, "You, Yegor, take care! Don't write anything you shouldn't!" And Yegor immediately makes like a holy fool and starts fawning: "Of course not, of course not, Vladimir Sergeyevich. I shall always remember you, Vladimir Sergeyevich. . . ."

And yet, soon after his master's death, I meet him, he's spouting off. "I observed," he says, "his morals: he was, I can tell you, a real swine." In front of my new friends I put Yegor in his place, saying, "Shut up, you, don't flaunt your ingratitude for everyone to see." I realize that for them Vladimir Sergeyevich is not a real person but something rotten, which means that everything is permitted, blame it all on him; I didn't argue, I was wily, but if you look at it fairly, then Yegor was wrong to make his speeches, because Leonardik was an exceptional individual, and as for *what* he wrote, well, it shows that there was some need to write as he did. But Yegor made nasty comparisons: He glorified, he said, heroic deeds, when people got burned alive for the sake of a piece of straw belonging to the collective farm, but would he have allowed himself to be burned to death for the cause? Oh, no, I say, people are different: some have to die, and others have to compose songs about them, that's perfectly clear, and then this Yurochka Fyodorov, who from the very beginning thought of me as a spy from Vladimir Sergeyevich's dacha, starts to wonder whether I am an informer; usually I love people with inexplicable souls, but when such a question arises, I immediately feel sad.

He also unmasked my Ksyusha, though he had followed her around like a dog; he got a dossier together—there are lots of stories there—and as soon as Ksyusha walked in, smiling at everyone, he did her dirty, caused a scandal, although, strictly speaking, what right did he have? "You," he shouts, "are a dirty whore. People like you should be shot, dirty whores!" Ksyusha smiles, not understanding, but listening with interest, she even starts to laugh, not at all hysterically—I only saw her in hysterics after caresses: she couldn't stand it, and sometimes she would scream and then all of a sudden how she would yell, how she would start thumping! Well, real convulsions; you would put your hands on her face to quiet her: she would calm down, lie still, and afterward wouldn't remember anything, and indeed it's a sin to recall this, but I was staggered by the strength of her orgasms, it was pathological, even stronger than the organization of her intellectual's mind, although I too, on occasion, have yelled out, and if someone came prematurely I was ready to kill him, but Ksyusha—she'd go purple, she'd come so explosively, like one of Turgenev's heroines! Anyway, she just stands, smiles, and looks at Yurochka Fyodorov with a smile: "The poor boy! He's exhausted!" But he curses, his eyes grow bloodshot, he hates the world, and now he says: "So where, then, is your own dear sister, where's Lena-Alena, then, why don't you ever mention her?" Ksyusha shrugged; why should she bring her up? Things are bad enough for her, there at the dacha. And at this point I remember that Ksyusha's parents have a dacha, only she never visits, never spends time there. Sometimes, when her parents call, she'll go for an hour and immediately return; she never spends the night. And she hadn't told me anything about Lena-Alena either; I too listened carefully: what if something's been going on? You can expect anything from Ksyusha, but foul play? Yura Fyodorov was to be my escort, although I objected. But to no avail: Merzlyakov refused, out of fear, and the remaining friends, who were a bit older, were doubtful about my undertaking, it even embarrassed me to look at them, but I believed that I was Joan of Arc!

"No," says Yura Fyodorov, "you tell us, dirty whore, *why* your sister spends her whole life languishing at the dacha, with old women, spongers, why they carry out chamber pots full of her excrement winter and summer. . . ." I look; Ksyusha is pensive, doesn't answer: Well, I think, this is a scandal, and Ksyusha was always proud; if something wasn't quite right, she would get furious, she despised everything, but now she's silent, and the company is drunk, Yurka also, and when he is drunk he can be very rude, and he too used to get furious, although I was never with him, I must confess, not once. I didn't like him—all he had were theories, exposés, I, he says, am a one-woman man, but as soon as he got drunk he became a total bastard, everyone knew this, but all the same they used to invite him, and I too, on occasion, would summon him. I know in advance that he will twist his lips and snort and demonstrate his learning, but the way things turned out, whenever he was due somewhere it was like some sort of event, though as to what he did, and how, I didn't have a clue and didn't want to: well, widely known in narrow circles, and so what! And when they started to take an interest in, among other things, Yura's character, I answered, "The devil only knows! But he's a psychopath—that's certain!" And they were pleased with my answer, which was sincere, because no one's allowed to offend my Ksyusha. But all the same it was interesting, just from a human point of view, to know what my Ksyusha had done wrong. "Okay," says Ksyusha, looking the company over, and she wasn't a Frenchwoman then, she was still a good judge of people. "Okay," she says, "I'll tell you: I have a paralyzed sister, she's spent her whole life in bed, that's where the pots come in, and the spongers, and her mental backwardness. She lies quietly, whimpering, that explains the bedsores and other inconveniences. It would be better if she died, but you understand, there's no sign of her dying. . . ." "Don't try to tell us what to think," says Yura Fyodorov.

"They're all hip here, they see life as it is," although the company was nothing special—someone would come in, someone would leave, and this is happening in my apartment, without Granddaddy, he's working the earth, the old mole— in short, it's summer, Ksyusha and I, just the two of us, an idyll. "How can you live like you do, when your sister's condemned to a sickbed, has spent her entire life unable even to speak? How could anyone be capable of jumping with joy, when such tears flow? You're a dirty whore!" Ksyusha is still smiling, and says, "Perhaps I am living for both of us since she," she says, "has been granted such unhappiness, it's better to have one living corpse instead of two, better," she says, "to have a balance, and not sheer hell, darkness visible, which is dark enough." "Yes," says Yura, "I didn't expect that, to tell the truth—or more accurately, that's exactly what I did expect!" He gets up and makes a dramatic exit, I don't detain him, and the company is nothing special, a random selection, we sat, were silent for a bit, and then it's why don't we have a drink and something to eat. An hour later, Yurochka returns, apologizing for intruding upon someone else's secret. But Ksyusha is already quite tipsy, has turned her thoughts to something else, has sat down beside someone, and is chatting away. He barges in to make it up with her, and she was forgiving, and when almost everyone had gone Yurochka lingered, expecting a reward, and he wasn't mistaken, she went over to him, deserting I don't remember who, but it doesn't matter: I took an actor, she Yurochka, and she was soft as silk with him, she went all meek and obedient to his orders—no, that's wrong! I was with a *captain*, such an interesting captain—he told me he would soon become a cosmonaut. To be honest, I didn't give a damn, and we set about screwing, and Yurochka tormented Ksyusha till morning. And when in the morning my captain and Yurochka departed, mortal enemies for some reason, and went their separate ways in silence, throwing dirty looks at each other, I asked Ksyusha: "Was that a fairy tale, or is she really suffering?" "She suffers," she says. "She scratches the wall, makes strange noises, now she mews, a little later she laughs, and then she'll suddenly howl. I can't listen, I have to leave, but she's not likely to die soon, Mother's at her wits' end, and that," she says, "is the situation." I was curious to see her sister, to compare their faces; it's an interesting situation: one of them prances around while the other suffers in bed; take me, I say, to the dacha sometime—next time you go. "Certainly, Sunny! I have," she says, "no secrets from you, and the only reason I didn't tell you about my sister, you must understand, is that it's all so difficult. Look"—she smiles—"I live for two, and as to whether it's a sin to have fun when there's such a thing in the background, well, perhaps it's true that it's a sin. . . ."

She smiled and lit a cigarette, but she didn't take me there; whether it was a matter of chance or because I didn't remind her, Ksyusha didn't take me to see her family's shame, how they carried the chamber pots and how tears fell round the clock. She was proud. But to make up for this Rituyla is really annoying me, I'll be quite open about it, she is worrying me, she'll suddenly slip out of her skin, skinless, all veins and muscles on the outside, and up onto the windowsill, in order to slide down the pipe, and I know if she leaves she won't return. I grab her leg—I feel mucus. A slimy leg. She tries to tear loose, but in the end I get the better of her, catch her, pull her back in, and thus save her, for you see she could have been smashed to bits, the fool. And there's nothing I can share with her, apart from love: you are my wondrously beautiful stepdaughter! Oh, Rituyla, you could have perished . . . girlfriend! But not a minute had passed when—the telephone rings!

I creep up to the phone, all nervous, my hands shake as though I'd been caught stealing chickens, a bell ringing in the dead apartment, someone's putting through a toll call for my soul. I stand there, not knowing what to do; I'm frightened of answering, but my curiosity gets the better of me, I pick up the receiver but remain silent and listen attentively, let him speak first, and I feel: It's *him,* though why, in fact, by phone? But that's what I thought, and I keep silent. I hear, however, Rituyla's little voice, I breathe more easily. I, she says, will come over to see you, I've got a business proposal —a tender voice, as though the offense is well past. I rejoiced. Of course, my love!

Who can fathom the desires of a pregnant woman? I didn't suddenly crave herring or marinated cucumbers, but desires that had nothing of grace about them descended upon me: was it the dressing-table mirror acting on me, giving birth to strange images, or was it that fear was seeking an outlet?

I opened the liquor cabinet: a little bottle, half empty, the cognac Dato and I had drunk remained from the recent quarrel; I poured a glass and sat down, grew warm with what I had drunk, deserted by everyone in my twilight years, I had an Evening Chime, sweet, with a nut in it to help the drink down, but I'm still alive and warm—I look at myself: white skin, not sunburned, I could do with a trip to the south, riding a horse, you could only rent horses if you had really powerful contacts and pull, and Volodechka, who used to operate a happy trade with foreigners, only he wasn't a black marketeer—he was doing it for the fatherland—he got hold of a fast horse. I like riding, he provided everything, only he was rather small in size, but he urged me to come to Tunis, and he went into raptures over the way I walked, and then he went away, well, I will fly all around the world anyway, as a stewardess or with the prescription for foreign leave the doctor

will issue me—I'll look in on Fontainebleau, visit Ksyusha.
"Hello, Ksyusha!" She will be overjoyed, we'll sit down to
dinner with her dentist, we'll see how things are there, and
then to America, to my saviors, five white, one chocolate
brown, and we'll meet on the roof of a luxury hotel, open to
the winds, all sables and minks, and me in my moulting fox,
and beneath it emptiness and no me, because, I shall say, I,
girls, am drunk, put me to bed, don't touch me, or else I'll
be sick, I'm sorry . . . and because, I'm sorry . . . I got drunk
. . . I've found some more! Got drunk on liqueurs . . . and I
announce to everyone . . . just listen!

I'm going to give birth to a little monster, just for you,
and it will avenge me, like Hitler or some such monsters too,
I know, only the women kept quiet, so that they wouldn't be
burned, I've gathered that much! I'm not the first, that's what
the voice says to me, it prompts me, I'm not the first and not
the last. For vengeance! Don't you try wiping the floor with
me! I don't want to suffer for you, you suffer for yourselves,
suffer with all those ideas of yours, you are ass-lickers, and
you, my native people, but that's not the point, here's our
law, Ksyusha and I thought up a law and Ksyusha said that
humankind had never before thought up such a law and we
named it the Mochulskaya-Tarakanova law, it's a very important law, it unites everyone, I'll tell you later, you understand what I'm saying, but I'm going to give birth come
what may, wait with joy, what a present it will be for you,
out of love for you, for you all, what a . . . only I've gone to
sleep, bye-bye . . . I name my enemies . . . remember me . . .
have you understood me? . . . well, that's everything . . .
academic . . .

# EIGHT

**A**nd everything became pure, as if nature had put on white lace lingerie.

I was returning from Stanislav Albertovich through the first snowfall. He had greeted me like kin, hadn't made any advances; sensing the gravity of the occasion, he was severe and just kissed my hand; he was businesslike, as I was. He was satisfied. We agreed I should have the child. He promised his support. When all's said and done, I've always dreamed of having a baby. I shall nurse it. It will have tiny hands and feet. I shall cut its little nails. I feel my maternal instincts awakening. He was angry that I reeked of alcohol. I gave my word not to drink, because I don't really like it, it's against my principles, and I had got drunk by chance and everything I've written up to this point I revoke as total nonsense! *I erase and revoke all this nonsense!!!*

**Don't read any of the above!**

However, I came home and had a drink, because the decision was an important one. I don't confide in Rituyla, but yesterday Rituyla, undressing me, was surprised by my roundness and the smashed dressing-table mirror. I became faint, I didn't have time to answer, and in the morning, when she asked me once more, I answered evasively, but she's a suspicious one, all whys and wherefores, so I started tickling her—she was distracted and started squealing, and when she recovered it was too late, although, of course, murder will out. N.B. In the near future, underground tremors are promised, and if he is alive there and not dead as a duck . . .

I shall become a single parent and keep a close eye on things, and if anything happens, then I'll confide in science —why the hell not—and thus I shall give birth, inasmuch as nothing else is in prospect, and moreover, I'm categorically giving up drinking and I despise drunkenness to the bottom of the glass. However, I don't look upon my decision as my capitulation before Leonardik, who is for me, as previously, a traitor and a man who used me badly, because if he promised to fulfill the agreement, then he should have fulfilled it! Such a respected man shouldn't indulge in idle talk, a man whose obituary was supported by a black forest of signatures, and I tore the paper out of Granddaddy's hands and locked myself in the bathroom, sat in the warm water, and I read them and wept. I loved him even more for his obituary, printed in all the papers; his death was announced on TV too, in a gloom-laden voice, and all those signatures! I was stunned.

Of course I had known before, Leonardik, that you were famous, a legend in your lifetime, but when I read it I under-stood that we had lost a great man, one who had brought his talents to all the many things he did. I had known of you since childhood, and my new friends, with Yegor at their head, that Judas, carrying his betrayal on his tray, the minute the master died, they all rushed to expose you, saying that you were shit, but you aren't shit, you entered history, you were photographed with almost everyone, and even with me. We studied you in school, I was even forced to stay behind after school once because of you, to study you, that is, while all the others ran off for a swim before the storm broke, in the pond where at the beginning of the century the daughter of the landowner Glukhov had drowned, a young lady twenty-two years old, and from that day on, as gossip had it, no one had bathed there, out of superstition, and on the spot where the estate had been an empty patch of ground remained, around which they diligently planted evergreen trees, but to make up for this, in the town itself Glukhov had left a three-story building in an intricate style, and it is now our school, the one I went to.

Time will pass. Your dacha will be turned into a memorial museum, and visitors will brush up and down in their felt slippers, with their hands behind their backs, gliding over the parquet floors as if on ice, and your bed will be cordoned off with a silk ribbon, your bed made of Karelian birch, where you and I revived the withered Lazarus. The task was not simple, but your Irochka managed it, because she had given her word and wouldn't go back on it, and I can't even begin to understand why you didn't want to leave your wife: you yourself admitted that she was a clumsy old cow. . . . And what a wife I would have been for you, do you know! Oh, with me you would have lived in clover: you would still be here to this day, I would immediately have worked out who your enemies were, who was secretly ill disposed toward you, like Yegor, whom you sheltered and who shat all over you for his own sake, and moreover he's promised to write something about you that will be total slander. I told him, "Yegor! No sooner has your master's corpse grown cold than you can't wait to slander him. Fear God, Yegor!" And he swears that he's a believer. Such believers should be put against the wall! This is what I'll say to you all, and if anyone finds time to read Yegor's calumny, I beg them not to believe it, because it is all untrue. Vladimir Sergeyevich was a multifaceted man, the obituary wrote about that better than I can, and anyone can read the obituary in the papers, even in the farming paper; I cut it out.

I sat in the bath and cried, the tears kept flowing, despite the humiliation I had just endured, like the last martyr. Veronika was not wrong in her prophecy: for Ksyusha, joy, but you, Ira, are doomed to suffer torment! However, sitting in the bath, I remembered not only the bad things. Not only your dodges. Not only your deceit and your final refusal. I had pretended to assent to this refusal, or, more accurately, not so much assented but simply said I couldn't live without you, even in the smallest, most humble capacity, although your arguments sounded childish to me, and if you were afraid of being cuckolded, then, my God, for the sake of life with you I would have told all the others where to get off, and as for Ksyusha, for example, well, that doesn't count. That's totally different, that's the same as doing it yourself, only much better, because I know that once, on the tennis court, the power behind her serve made you suddenly realize that she had grown up, and you missed the ball, causing her papa a certain embarrassment, despite your friendship, and Ksyusha said, "Well, all right then, if you're worried, then I won't go *there* anymore. . . ." I remembered not only the bad things; there were happy days, when you strutted like a general, proud of your achievements and of your fantasies, which are rarely encountered in people of your generation, as you yourself used to say, and indeed you were probably unique, and if you were a miser, well, who is without foibles?

Meanwhile, on my part, I didn't deceive you, and as for dressing beautifully, that's not a crime yet, yet you didn't trust me, in which respect you were like lots of other men, who weren't great like you, although there were some good people, among them, Carlos, the Latin American ambassador, far more generous than you, and a foreigner to boot, and I could have married him long ago if I had so desired, because he was mad about me and would speed beneath my windows in his Mercedes and even— Oh! the door creaked . . . there I am, getting frightened. . . . No, I tell the truth: you were wrong to be jealous and to doubt me!

Except it's too late now. It was wrong to kiss me on that first evening and give me hope if you weren't serious about me, because although you didn't, as it happened, disgust me with your age and your impotency, since I understood what I was agreeing to and, besides, you had this aura of fame, still, when your hand fell on my breast I cringed slightly, to tell the truth. I *do* feel the difference in age, it's like with my grandfather, but no, this doesn't worry me, I could discern the man in you and I liked your élan very much, I wasn't squeamish. For your sake I was ready for anything and affectionate right from the start; you came to life from this, but instead of being grateful you suddenly feared for your reputation, although all great men get randy in their twilight years, make mistakes and let loose. Reputation! Reputation! Who would have dared touch your reputation?

This is what unbalanced me, led me on to dark thoughts about seeking consolation, for example, with Dato, who honored me by playing the piano for me alone, although on tour he played before audiences of thousands and he would show me programs and reviews that called him a new phenomenon, but you would glance back cautiously at your family and fidget; however, I don't remember only the bad things, and Ksyusha is my witness: when she arrived after your death, I was inconsolable, not only because those bastards had reduced me to such a state, that goes without saying, but also because you weren't there to defend me. As I say, I don't remember only

the bad things: I remember the happy days, when we went to
the dacha, had lunch, drank dry wine, you listened to me, to
my thoughts, which I spoke aloud, and your fantasies had also
started to attract me, but when a year had passed and a second
was drawing to a close, I was getting fed up, because time was
running out and the rumors were registering me as your possession. Dato had smelled a rat, but I burst out laughing. "Pure
friendship!" I convinced Dato. "I just know him through Ksyusha," and Dato's attitude, incidentally, is still respectful, although everything about you somehow faded after your death
and your name is rarely spoken, which means your enemies
are triumphant, and I weep.

I *don't* remember only the bad things, Leonardik! I loved
you, that's the truth, and that was the truth they wrote later,
though vaguely, to ensure that no one would guess, though
the Ivanoviches said it was necessary to write in such a way
so no one would understand, to write it like a legal document.
And then Zinaida Vasilievna blew her top, went redder than
a boiled beet, deprived of her due by this article with the title
"Love!" And I won't let her mock me! I was triumphant. I
can't deny it. But I was sinking to the lower depths, and the
gas water heater was humming, and Granddaddy, the old
Stakhanovite, reminisced about you as a genius and a hero.
But I knew well the weaknesses of my genius with his cherished
fig leaf, his Order, which I didn't just play with but pinned
on myself with his permission; I would pin it on my T-shirt
and then throw myself in his arms, and he would laugh and
feel a swell of new energy, because he was always wanting
something out of the ordinary; or I would squeeze it between
my knees: "Seek, my beloved!" Or, when summer was approaching, he would decide to shave me: he would work up
a lather with the brush and, wearing his glasses and knitting
his brow solemnly, would shave me like a barber or a nurse,

only, of course, with greater care, because nurses at the clinic
scrape harshly, with a blunt razor blade, and then scream
frenziedly, "Well, which of you virgins is next?"—but I would
beat them to it, having spent some time admiring myself before
the dressing-table mirror, where amidst the prized perfumes I
would look like a little girl, and I didn't wear brassieres, for
which Polina Nikanorovna bore a grudge against me, as if she
needed a reason! And thank you, Kharitonych, he kept me
safe, and I didn't say a word to him about Leonardik, although
he loved gossip: Tell me, tell me more, he pumped me about
everything. But Leonardik saw me from the other side completely, although after the event he contrived to be jealous
of Antonchik's interest in me; I didn't give in, though; I went
on the offensive, and to Rituyla's suggestion, which she made
to me yesterday, I answer that I'll have to think about it,
because my money started to run out long ago. The example
of my incomparable Ksyusha rises before my eyes, but then
again, with her of course it wasn't for the sake of a single
kopeck! She's well-off, the Mochulsky family is famous, and
her papa was friendly, incidentally, with Vladimir Sergeyevich. They would stroll beneath the pine trees and sit down
to play chess after dinner, yawning and humming couplets,
to help them think. Whereas she did it simply to get high,
and she would get these highs (there were occasions) just by
stepping out, nonchalantly, on Manezh Square, with her big-
eared spaniel. I couldn't believe it, but she invited me, for a
laugh, except I couldn't bring myself to do it. But why? I
willingly got involved in other incidents, and Ksyusha and I
will have something to remember, two silky grannies, but it
wasn't so much that I felt ashamed as that it seemed not very
becoming somehow, and indeed Ksyusha didn't insist: "If you
don't want to, that's fine, I'll go with my spaniel." Veronika,
however, couldn't stand men as a matter of principle, she

didn't consider them human because they were not aesthetically pleasing, she didn't like, you see, the fact that they have balls dangling there, for example—ugh! how awful! We argued, but you can't argue with her, and when she got angry, she would say, as if she were joking, "Your beaver, Irina, is bigger than your brainbox," which was upsetting, but a witch is a witch!

And when Ksyusha was peddling her pussy around the architecture I adore, amidst infinite tulips, I admitted defeat: I wouldn't have dared! Fearing one moment my Polina Nikanorovna, the next moment one of the militiamen, who would look expectantly up my skirt and wait for me to slip, so as to make fun of the mommy longlegs—and always dreading to be sent back to where the football player still plays, and time stands still, despite my betrayal with a rival in a new pale-blue nylon jacket, which I liked so much! I couldn't resist touching it, which resulted in a wild provincial affair, when in the evening chill he threw his jacket over my shoulders and beneath us our shallow brown river ran and children waded, catching crayfish in their nets as the sun was setting, while my second husband lingered in the hospital with a temporary injury to that part of him for which, thanks to him and to his cost, I'd acquired a permanent taste; I was viciously beaten with a bicycle pump. And as for the fact that my first husband is totally out of the picture, well, there's a dose of injustice here too: if he hadn't given Irochka shelter, hadn't concealed her from her parents, then what would have become of the little girl, and would she have ever seen Ksyusha— that's a question, although Leonardik didn't get much amusement from society, and a sense of grievance welled up in me. In what ways am I worse than Zinaida, whom he parades through the foyers and banqueting halls, with diamonds in her old ears? Is it really the case that they wouldn't have understood him? They always went out of their way to meet him, in everything! And he scintillated, and I was the only one allowed to tease him, and if there were bruises and abrasions on the body afterward, well, he thought this up under my guidance; I had an instinct for guessing his penultimate whim, and Lazarus rose!

We hurled ourselves into embraces, hastened to celebrate the triumph, I helped him, with a tongue-wetted finger, to relieve his suffering, and so he came and, having come, said, wiping his face, which was radiant, "Hey, my genius of love! Hey, my goddess!" And I am lying on my back as if nothing had happened, and he tenderly concerns himself with pleasuring me; like perhaps no one else of that hard generation, which had passed through glory and death, he was a victim of his own success, and when everything had been completed, he felt like hymning this molehill into a mountain, because his creative soul had been enlarged, like his liver, and he also loved big tits (like all of them from the hard generation). But I sat in the bath and wept, reading so many good things! He was vigorous in his efforts to please me, and I played along: I breathed faster and faster, I moaned, but bitterness was welling inside me, and I didn't need a car, and even if he had given me one, I would have smashed it right up, like an egg!

I didn't want a car, I wanted happiness, and the reason I was friendly with Kharitonych was that I'd wanted to dance the role of the queen, or, to be accurate, not dance exactly, more stroll up and down, but at times a grander dream would creep into my mind, a dream Ksyusha saluted: to walk down through the orchestra pit and step out into the auditorium as queen, showering them all with my favor and grace, my generosity, my goodness! I could have done it too, echoing my dashing predecessor in the field of culture: a riot's a riot, but if it's for a noble aim, then may my motherland prosper! I am a patriot! Ksyusha went numb with delight, she adored the exuberance of my dreams, she said, I believe! I believe! And I thought I just needed Leonardik to help me ascend, and this was why, at the slightest provocation, I played hard to get and grumbled and ran away. And everything collapsed, my cavalier's temperament suffered from a lack of breadth, he was preoccupied with urgent antlike business, was full of the importance of his own face. I could see right through him, but the dream was stronger: He and I are walking up the staircase, white marble, with bigwigs all around us, and the sweet priest Venedikt marries us and wishes us happiness and the motherland prosperity, and I too! I want to make a gift of my modest happiness to the cause of common harmony, only I mean to cut down somewhat on the number of folk songs and dances, because they are *so* tedious, but to make up for it I'd want such well-being to prevail that a massed throng of bigwigs would march with torches around the festive squares of the capital, while I—the picture of modesty—stand surrounded by my devoted acolytes. I look and rejoice with the shameless Ksyusha, that hussy, always ready to piss on anything from her unforgettable pussy, which I adore! I'm going mad! There isn't another like it! I die! I weep! Yes, my joy was boundless, I would sometimes overflow with tears, I would be carried away and then weep once more—such visions! Except that Leonardik was timid, my good little boy, he would hold out his hands, but not a word about the treaty, and I would say to him, Take care! Your heart will act up! and he would answer, "Don't you treat me like an old man! I've still got some arrows in my quiver!"

I remembered this, but time was contracting, deception expanding, and dreams dimming. Shortly afterward he sends me an invitation, which I had been demanding from him, having found out that an English orchestra was to visit and that Britten was in the program. Well, Britten or not, an important occasion; I want to go! For the umpteenth time he is beset by doubts, uses his indecision as an excuse, saying that many people he knows will be there, they'll misinterpret it, and rumors will spread. "You'd be better off with your granddad." With Granddad! Ha ha! No, I think, that's enough insults. "Am I a golden fish or not?" "Golden!" he answers. "My golden one! Fairest of them all! Only please don't!" Well, here's something, I think, my lover's getting obstinate. No, I think, if you don't go with me to the Britten, I'll become merciless. He gave in, foreseeing total disaster; I was implacable, and he'd become incapable of living without me. He tries to make the best of it: "Oh, all right, then, let's go!" I put on my dress like a flame and step out on the porch; I stand there, impregnable, unapproachable, we set off, he is in a state of fear and trembling because of the dress, he's mumbling, reputation, he says, reputation, you know, I mustn't. I have a reputation as a serious man who hymns heroic deeds and labor, but you are all dolled up and your bosom's bare, to say the least, he says, how about some sort of shawl, and I say, Please be so good as to tell me what it is you're afraid of! You're stronger than any of them, they quail before you, but you are frightened of them, and even if I was stark naked, as long as I was with you they'd salute us and let us into any embassy! No, no, he says, anything but that! He was a master, but still he was afraid, such was their upbringing then; now they're all dying off, alone, they receive their pensions, they used to be able to get hold of anything, as long as they made no fuss, they hid the cognac in the dumbwaiter, away from uninvited guests, and sat in their cars behind drawn curtains, betraying the poverty of their feelings, and Ksyusha's papa, who is also a public figure, lectured her when she was a student, saying, "If you're going to fuck, make sure you fuck quietly!"

That then was the setup. I didn't like it, but what choice did I have?

We drive up to the entrance, the lights are shining, it is as if my dream has come true, and we enter, the whole auditorium is expecting the English orchestra, flags along the walls, excitement, beauty, we take up our places in the director's box, my darling is gallant, he nods his head to the greetings all around, I sense the looks and I hold up my chin, like a lady, the English orchestra is tuning up, they are soon to play, a conductor of Japanese air and appearance enters, there is a storm of applause—and they're off! I close my eyes. "Divine!" I inform him, leaning toward him. "Such bliss!" "I'm glad," he answers, but, I sense, somewhat coolly. He's all wound up and can't relax, he's miserable, he's willing it to finish, he sighs furtively, he'd prefer to go to the dacha; over the fence there, he's his own boss, but here that Japanese without a stick calls the tunes. I think: They use sticks for eating rice, and that's why he is controlling the orchestra without one. I whisper this, he gets the joke, but our neighbors shush us; as soon as the intermission comes I say, "Take me to the buffet for ice cream," but he says, "We're better off sitting here, I've had a hard day, no strength left, I'm still under the spell of the music and don't want the bustle of the buffet," and I say, "Oh, please, let's go!" He says nervously, "You go; as it is, everyone's staring at us!" "Oh, to hell with you!" I turn and leave, he gladly gives me a twenty-five-ruble note just to go away. I go out as if in disgrace, I stand in the line, looking like thunder, people all around are exchanging opinions, speaking highly of the conductor. I agree with them, but I keep silent, alien and superfluous in this line; my turn comes at last, and I say, "Open a bottle of champagne for me, and can I please have five kilos of oranges." The answer: "We'll open your champagne, but we won't give you so many oranges;

this isn't the market, you know." I realize that they are de-
riding me. People laugh—she's come to an English concert
to stock up, like in some sort of comic strip—except that I
have a different plan; I couldn't care less about the oranges.
"I'm afraid you don't understand," I say. "I don't need them
myself; they're for the director's box." They thought a bit,
had a confab, and served me. At this point Ksyusha would
interrupt me, roaring with laughter: Why on earth did you
buy so many? From malice, I answer, from pure, unadulterated,
undisguised malice. I was thinking I would return to the director's box with five kilos of oranges, like the last of the
philistines; if he's so pathetically afraid for his reputation, let
him groan, and as for the champagne—I take a glass, as is
the custom, and before the third bell had called us back I had
drunk the whole bottle, under the gaze of the amazed public
having a snack with their beer and discussing the merits of
the scuzzy Japanese. And the minute I finish the whole bottle,
before the third bell, not a single drop left, I return to the
director's box, which was full of distinguished people, unknown to me but, I note, known to my cowardly cavalier—
I burst into the director's box with five kilos of citrus and
create, it stands to reason, the expected effect. Vladimir Sergeyevich's expression changes, and he whispers furiously, "Are
you feeling all right, Irina!" I answer, "Never felt better," and
breathe champagne over him. "What," he says, "do you need
this pile of oranges for?" "I love oranges," I answer, "haven't
you noticed?" He looks at me and says, somewhat baffled,
"Have you been drinking?" "So what, isn't it allowed?" "Of
course," he says, "but we'd better go home; there's nothing
for us here." His speech appears calm, he knew how to keep
a rein on himself, the good old school, I notice, but underneath, I see, is total bewilderment, like jelly, I even start to
feel a tiny bit sorry for him, but I dig my heels in. "No!" I

say loudly. "I want to hear Britten, and, darling," I say, "don't you worry, everything will be perfectly all right!" He went white, and his expression was so eloquent that I understood: The End, and Britten will be our funeral anthem, they will sing the requiem to our love—those were my feelings, although I'd had a bit to drink and was a wonderful shade of red. Leonardik is also silent, pale, but still a very nice-looking old man, if you regard him from the side. And me with my oranges. I sit, the conductor walks onstage once more, stormy applause, I also, naturally, applaud, but strictly speaking, why should I? My love has vanished, an end to my dreams, and I will never be my predecessor, and as soon as they started to play I felt totally downhearted, the wind of old age blew in my ears, the champagne took hold of me, I wanted to cry from these blues in a minor key and all this obscenity, from all those married men who treated me like an airhead, not asking after the needs of my soul but just sniffing the bergamot air, they sniffed and went mad and crammed me with caviar, caviar, caviar. They lured me with promises of luxury apartments and cars, but in fact only gave presents of perfume, perfume, perfume, and looked furtively at their watches, boasting, boasting, boasting all the time, each in his own way, promiscuously: one of his fame, another of his money, another of his genius, another of the fact that he despised everything, so would you kindly therefore take notice of him and respect him, in this time of double-entry bookkeeping, the mocking Ksyusha joked, she who scorned such people both in Paris, the nonexistent city because it doesn't exist and Ksyusha, after getting into her pink auto, would vanish into emptiness, and here, on our hard native soil, because, she considered, every career is full of adventures, of zigzags and mean tricks, one's as bad as the other. All this she hated but couldn't live without; she would return for a laugh, and then she would go away again, and would return again, and I'm supposed to sit still and hold my tongue! But Ksyusha says in answer to this, "Let's leave together!" "I'm sorry, but I'm afraid I'm having an affair." "Who with? Antosha? Forget it! That's not serious!" "No!" I answer. "Go higher! With Vladimir Sergeyevich, your godfather, the laureate!" "I'm not going to congratulate you," and Ksyusha frowns. "Why? He is a prominent man after all. He won't humiliate me." That's what I thought then, and I look: he sits there pale, ready to tear me limb from limb, to pay off his debts and not phone anymore, despite the fact that he's attached to me and, he sighs, he finds it difficult to live without me. And I argue from a position of strength: "Excuse me," I say, "but what about our agreement?" "And what about the oranges?" he asks wrathfully. "What have the oranges to do with it?" That's how we quarreled at that fateful meeting, but things hadn't got as far as that yet. I'm sitting at the Britten concert, I like it very much, I'm in rapture, I've turned red, I'm listening: "Yes! Very excellent!" The only problem is the person in the next seat, Vladimir Sergeyevich, who has withdrawn into himself and is ruining my life.

Because I always felt like a shy schoolgirl with stumpy pigtails, I never knew how to be rude to people, even the weak and defenseless, whom it's not difficult to insult, but I didn't like it when I was treated like a slut, when they fattened me up and demanded beauty, because I value myself highly and my beauty is not subject to their power. The only person who has the right to judge me is a woman more beautiful than I, and men have no right at all to judge, but only to admire, and as far as beauty is concerned, I've never met anyone more beautiful than myself. "What about Ksyusha?" they'll ask. Let's examine this. Ksyusha, of course, is a knockout, I don't deny; she has, let us say, no flaws, although what often happens is that a beauty's face surmounts a back covered with blackheads,

I've seen lots like that and felt disappointed. Ksyusha un-doubtedly is beautiful, but I am a *beauty*. I am a genius of pure beauty, that's what everyone called me, quoting Pushkin, and Vladimir Sergeyevich also used to say, "You are a genius of pure beauty!"—that is, *unsullied,* a beauty not of the gutter, a noble beauty, you can't tear your eyes away from it! Thus spoke Carlos the ambassador and the Central Asian Shokhrat, but when I phoned him and asked, "Do you know who this is, Shokhrat?" he answered without any humor and clicked his tongue in the receiver. I understood everything at once: "Well, until better times, Shokhrat!" but I'm almost crying. "Until better times!" answers Shokhrat, a big man in Central Asia, he and I flew from one republic to another together, we ate trout, and he read Akhmatova and Omar Khayyám to me, taking pride in my beauty—high-class, not gutter! "Until bet-ter times!" repeats Shokhrat, and tuts, as eastern people do when betrayed in their deepest feelings. But Flavitsky, Stan-islav Albertovich, turned out in the final analysis to be a friend: Well, why should he care, one asks, that I should give birth? What's the point? But he is anxious, he phones, he invites me for consultations, and when Rituyla informs me about her proposition, not suitable for discussion over the phone, I go to see him: "Won't it cause harm?" Because I was afraid that it could threaten the life of an unborn infant, that the Armenian might let himself go and make a hole in the skull. "That's impossible," Dr. Flavitsky reassures me, "only, child, take a bit more care, after all it's a unique case," even though he'd earlier said that I would never give birth, and I had smiled at him, pleased as Punch with this state of affairs, only during the nights I had grieved a bit, and Ksyusha had also said, "I don't want to!" But the dentist has been pressing her for God knows how many years, and Ksyusha's pussy is having kittens, amazed by his request: "Well, as bad as Central

Asians!" And at this point my heart can't stand it any longer: it explodes. I grab an orange from the bag and throw it! A hit! a second! and I'm off! I'm off! The oranges fly at the Japanese villain and on to his English brothers, on to the violinists and cellists, dressed in tails—take that!—and I start hurling them, and my famous and heroic cavalier, by now as white as a ghost, flings himself at me, but I push away his old bones and keep them flying, onward! at Britten, at his scandalous symphony, until the music dies away into the silence of the grave, and ushers burst into the box like three fat dogs, old hags who carry the programs close to their chests. I pepper them with oranges, and I find it all very funny, but silence and a high-class public reign in the hall, and everyone in the box has recoiled from me, and I'm battling the ushers. "Don't rip my dress," I shout, "with your filthy hands! How dare you!" And I struggle in the director's box, like a red rag, and the Japanese turns around in my direction with interest, and all the English do the same, but then strong and desperate men of some kind rush into our box and hold out their hands to make me stop. However, they don't want the English to witness any violence, they are seeking an amicable agreement, they are trying to coax me away, waiting until they can get me outside, the playing of the national anthems before the start of the concert must not have been in vain, but I think: To hell with you all, I shall fight. They act like real gentlemen, they see that I'm sitting next to Vladimir Sergeyevich himself and think: What if that's how it's supposed to be? Maybe the order's been given to rain oranges down on English music from all sides. This was what Ksyusha concluded, hearing the story and very impressed by the confusion. "See," she said, "you, Sunny, turned out to be bolder than me! I wouldn't have risked that—at the English! That's neat!"

It probably should be added that Yura Fyodorov, on hearing of this, broke off his friendship with me on the grounds that it was an insult to culture, he decided that it was cultural terrorism and that ignorance was deeply rooted in my soul, but all I can say is, "Tell him to fuck off!" And just imagine, I met this Yura in the company of my new friends and he starts to bad-mouth me, even though by that time I was the object of universal notoriety. As for him: "You, scum, who are you?" And he was ashamed because I'd had the last word as a martyr for an idea. But at that moment Vladimir Sergeyevich sees that they are twisting my arms and treating me rudely, dragging me out into the corridor, and there too a crowd of people is waiting to catch sight of me and tear me to pieces, some in tailcoats, but beasts are beasts! And then Vladimir Sergeyevich, my cavalier, says to the staff gathered there "Ma-a-ake way!" And everyone, I must say, starts to make way, and Zinaida Vasilievna says that she didn't know about me! Everyone knew, but she didn't know! For everyone learned about this episode, even people who had never worn tails, and Vladimir Sergeyevich, my Leonardik, waved his small hand and says, "Make way!"

They made way, despite the militia and the hullabaloo at the doors. I wanted to take the oranges with me, but the paper bag was ripped from my hands, and they started to roll and immediately got squashed by men's clumsy feet. Vladimir Sergeyevich grabbed me roughly by the wrist and dragged me toward the staircase, where a bunch of inquisitive people were hanging over the banisters; in the hall the music was silent, and he said to the manager, who wanted to tell him off about his companion, "You'd be better off continuing the concert!" And the manager, conceding that Vladimir Sergeyevich was right, ran to calm the Japanese, and the Japanese calmed down quickly; in any event, Britten was once more hovering over the arches when we went out through the stage door. Britten was reinstated, but my head had started to throb from the music, and I could hardly see, my head was aching so!

# NINE

We roll along slowly. We are silent for a long time. We are a hearse.

Well, I think, he'll murder me. He's got the right.

His white profile is distant; he's upset. "Well, did you get what you wanted?" "No!" I answer; I am afraid of his anger and I'm also in rapture: he's a savior, he could have let me be torn to bits, yet here we are, riding along. "And what next?" asks Ksyusha. What next? Next he says, "I hope you understand that this is the end, that this is," he says, "final," but still he drives on, not tossing me out on the street. I am silent, I listen, migraine, oranges flying past my eyes, the amazed Japanese, who looks askance at my performance, startled by foreign customs, or else he sensed something unpleasant, a violation of his rights, but Britten once more hovers over the arches, and I have retained all my rights. "You understand," he says, "that this is the end of our agreement!" My jaw dropped. Aha! Well, I think, very clever. The bastard! I didn't expect it. Neither Ksyusha nor I. A subtle thinker, he'd made distinctions, and I, it emerges, am back where I started from, next to the broken tub, and I poke the dusty dressing-table mirror with my finger: the end of our agreement!

But the start of everything else! I move into another category, I am deprived of the status of a golden fish, I have become, it seems, a piece of cheap trade. I open my mouth wide: I gaze in amazement at the noble profile, we travel farther, and he's even glad, as if a weight has been lifted from his shoulders, and Zinaida Vasilievna exults exceedingly on hearing the news. Rejoice, marauder, rejoice! But you will cry later, when you follow the coffin of a great man along a path you have not trodden before, and in the cold dacha you'll come to blows about the partition of the estate with Antonchik, who is speeding to the funeral either from Oslo or from Madrid, because the boy has got himself fixed up very nicely. He'd pretended to be my admirer, but I'd been wise to him right away: a real louse. Before Vladimir Sergeyevich, however, I bow my head: a great man! But I was upset by the relief I saw on his pale face. He'd wriggled out of it! The whole deal had cost him very little, his hands smell of car leather, and he's taking me home, where Granddaddy, having passed the evening with the television, sleeps the sleep of the just Stakhanovite and loyal old soldier, he sleeps and couldn't care less that his favorite granddaughter is being thrown out to walk the streets right in front of his house, and in parting is being wished "Good night!" Well, then I howled my fill, pulled myself together, came home, entered the apartment, oranges are rolling under my feet, people in tails gesticulate and foam at the mouth and shout in evil voices, and the Japanese conductor eats cold lumpy rice with his baton, except it's not rice but boiled kasha, as if the war had ended yesterday, lying in bed, the slant-eyed one looks on cunningly, and oranges roll underfoot, and Timofei whirls round between my knees and sniffs my skirt, sensing a kindred spirit, and I say to Veronika, "Don't cry for me! Don't cry!" And she starts to weep, she starts to weep, although she is a witch and a bitch, and she

is very crafty, because she didn't allow men near her, and only
Timofei was in favor with her, and Timofei says, "Oh, well
. . . what's the difference." A kindred spirit all the same, and
he spins around, has a sniff at the skirt, I see he's really
enjoying it! "Well," I say to Veronika, "your Timofei's a real
cock hound." I stroke his ear, tousle him, and Timofei bares
his teeth, laughs. Only I'd come to her with an ulterior
motive—I'd come to seek advice and to get her blessing, and
she said in a weak voice, "There's no harm in trying. But,
Ira, don't you touch Timofei." "And Ksyusha?" I try to get
an answer. "And Ksyusha?" She keeps silent. A break in the
conversation, and I hadn't elicited the secret, she won't give
it away, and Ksyusha also didn't say a word, not once did she
let the cat out of the bag, regardless of our friendship, and
Timofei looks at her commandingly, as if she's his property.
And this means that my girlfriends have duped me here too,
I note to myself, although there's no evidence, but nevertheless I had been refused point-blank, and Timofei and I felt
badly used. I came with nothing and went away with what I
came with, and Leonardik prides himself on the spat, using
it to his own advantage, having wished me a good night alone
with the dressing-table mirror. And I rushed to the telephone,
in order to alert the whole honorable company, except it was
late, and I hear in the receiver pips and angry awakened voices
making their excuses, it's late, well, okay, and I remain one-
on-one with the mirror, but that can be fun. I lie there like
a young girl and moan, painstakingly tracing out monograms
and patterns, in my mind's eye returning to my town all alone,
but it was Moscow I adored, I couldn't get enough of Moscow,
and I moaned, seeking comfort in this solitary trifle but a trifle
that is dear to me and something I can call my own, yet it
didn't prove possible to forget everything, and as soon as I
came to and stopped singing, I saw: night, and in the sky an

uneasy wind, the clouds bunched up into storm clouds, the shadows from the full moon on the bedspread, and my arms and legs stick out in the mirror, and between them hovers an abandoned face. And I made up my mind that night, I withdrew into myself and understood everything, because he won't leave me but will just twist me and bend me to his will, so that everything goes according to his desires, both at the dacha and here, in the splendid apartment, and I suddenly saw myself as its owner, pressing my cheek up against the furniture of Karelian birch. Rejoice, Zinaida Vasilievna! Tonight you can sleep soundly, but the news has spread, and in the morning —but is it like that? The oranges rolled and rolled and finally hit their target, I didn't have long to wait, and while I was giving out false denials left and right, keeping the open secret, the phone rings and Granddaddy, like a trained parrot, rushes to answer it and shouts, "Yes, I hear you!" and to me, covering the receiver with the palm of his hand, "Are you home or not?" "At home! At home!" I run out of the bathroom, forgetting to fasten my dressing gown, and Granddaddy is like Father Venedikt, he gets embarrassed, hiding his eyes while the old woman pours the jets of water down past the elastic, the streams of holy water. I didn't look after myself during those two weeks, which seemed to stretch, to spread out into half a year, my defenses were down, I lived a river nympho's life, swimming from one bath to another, embarrassing my Cupids with their chubby faces, lemurs, a head of the motor repair bureau, for example, who used to phone from bed in the mornings to give his subordinates a roasting—horrible memories. But Ksyusha was far away, Rituyla was treating her disease, realizing the wheeler-dealer suspected the worst, pus on panties, discharge on lips: he flew home, and the Japanese had conquered the whole earth, so that Ksyusha cursed and swore, calling the Paris she lived in a Japanese city, and I stepped up to the telephone meekly: "Who's that? Hello?" I listen: Leonardik's voice is hesitant; the deceased didn't like the telephone, suspected it of endless shortcomings, and he would muffle the phone with a pillow when he called, but I say to spite him, "Well, then, say that you love me! That you're burning with passion! Tell me how you'll carry me in your arms and fondle me and look after me!" He quickly broke in: "Wait, not now, don't call me by my name, I can't hear anything, I'm phoning from a booth, people are knocking on the glass with their kopecks," as if I had thrown oranges before the amazed public in vain, having overcome the cordons of militia, their numberless human chain, my numbness, everything. Our underground existence is over. A crime against his image. In the course of his life he'd gained, thank God, the valuable experience of being able to creep into every corner and up and down marble staircases, and bewilderment had lodged deep in his face. The boss, the master chef, would give his underbosses a roasting; these little dictators would roast the smaller fry, the smaller fry would grill their page boys. The boss would pull the blanket over himself, and the rest can freeze and die like dogs, and bewilderment took up residence in the crevices of his face, and his glorious life passes by in peace and quiet, but dislike of the telephone is just not practical nowadays, and it's not that I was missing him—I was just weary from carrying my dreams to full term and was amazed that he'd wriggled out of it, repaid my humble supplication, my unique art, with a petty rescue. Only this time I was in no mood to play hard to get, I didn't want to keep silent: I stand, I listen, water drips from me. Granddaddy has gone back to his room, unshaven, bewildered. He informs me that he'd like to and that Zinaida Vasilievna has gone away for treatment for her bladder, that he misses me and where have I been? I answer, "I haven't been anywhere, I drag out my life in loneliness, with a book, I've fallen in love with Blok." "With whom?" "Blok, you know! The poet. I've learned some poems by heart." He is silent, having already committed a sin against himself by dialing the number and starting to make up, but then I had always known it would end that way, but Ksyusha didn't believe me: "Did he really phone in person!" She couldn't do without me either, she would fly in all impatient, and I too, even though I was friendly with Rituyla, but Rituyla disturbed me with her pragmatism, she loved objects, particularly expensive objects, jewelry especially, she adored gems, and if the Japanese had returned, she wouldn't have come to me, I wouldn't have gone to live with her, and where could I have gone then, and though we were pleased with the success of our friendship, Ksyusha is Ksyusha is Ksyusha!

She wasn't scared by the intricacies of intellectual conversation, but she didn't have much time for brainy women, and I remember how quickly Natasha vanished, who was eager to strive for the joy of the common cause but was inevitably unmasked. "She"—Ksyusha nodded at a brainy woman—"is as cold as an Eskimo's ass or the legs of a cripple in some Kamchatkan church" (this must have been a veiled allusion to her little sister), and Natasha vanished soon after, together with her cumbersome clitoris, the butt of jokes for us real ladies; she swapped us for intellectual conversations, and when I met her amidst select company at the Béjart Ballet, one of her intellectual pleasures, I greeted her indifferently and walked past, I remained cool. But Ksyusha was totally different—not the thinking type, but unthinkable! And I believed in her and imitated her until the point when she threw up her arms in a gesture of despair: "You're something! To phone in person! After all those oranges . . ." "But you don't understand!" Here I smiled shyly. "He was bound to call. He'd

come to the conclusion that I'd given in and was sorry."
"Okay," I agreed, sedately, and he said, "Well, then, that's
marvelous!"

We agreed to meet at his place. No, I was far from coming
to a decision, I wanted to see how things would turn out, and
when he and I met in the bladder-free apartment he seemed
quite agitated, which was not his style; he complained that
his health was shaky, he wheezed: an old man with traces of
his former splendor was sitting before me, but no more than
that! "Ira!" he said, and led me into the nest of Karelian birch.
The windows of the apartment looked out onto a little square,
the doors gleamed with bronze handles, but the main door
was like a portcullis. "Ira!" he said sadly, complaining of his
indisposition. "Why didn't you phone me?" He was wearing
the same formal suit they buried him in, his favorite; it was
a trick of his: to wear his formal clothes at home for me! just
for me! I confessed that I had not believed there would be
any sequel, that I had considered it to be over once and for
all, and had reconciled myself to his decision. He sat tensely
in the armchair, as if it belonged to someone else. I knew
that he wasn't overjoyed that I had resigned myself to such
an outcome. "Ira," he said, "I just can't." I answered to the
effect that I couldn't either, and he smiled weakly, he actually
began to look radiant, he was revived by the fact that it was
the same for me, and he lit up. Except I was in no hurry to
be pleased about this; I understood the hidden agenda of his
proposal that we both give in and then everything could be
hunky-dory again, but why on earth should I give in? What
had I lost? Did I need his frantic embraces? His age spots the
size of peas? He *was* a gent, though! I kept silent. I merely
said, Me too, since I felt like saying that, Me too, and I said,
Me too, and he lit up! Then, growing bolder, Vladimir Sergeyevich told me how the incident with the oranges had

ended, how he'd put out that bonfire by pissing on it, and everything had turned out very nicely, all had ended well—only I didn't want everything to be smoothed over! I didn't want this. And I said, "Marry me." I said it just like that, with no nonsense, no warning or hint. "Marry me," and that was that. "You must understand," I said, "I'm tired of being on the shelf," but he was always frightened I would disgrace him, that people would gossip, to which I said, If I love, then I love selflessly. "You love me?" he asked, digging into the armchair like a bedbug: he was full of doubts, he was in agony, he was suffering and scared. I found him repulsive at that moment, and answered, saying, of course, how dare he ask me, or hadn't my despair been deep enough, just take for example those oranges. This, then, is how the dragged-out declaration of our feelings ended up, the final feelings of his twitching penis: I answered, "Yes, I love you." I didn't dissemble, I answered, "Yes." He answered me, "Yes!" I said, "You must marry me! I'm fed up with being on the shelf!"

# TEN

Even brainy women with clitorises the size and sensibility of a horse's weep as they look at their aging faces. Fading skin frightens their anxious imaginations. They too seek a commanding hand and voice, they too let themselves go in an orgy of debauchery, yet they always hear time at their backs, ticking like a taxi meter. That is why their eyes are so feverish, and their words, when they are a bit tipsy, are like a lament, as if there were a corpse in the next room, as if the trapped soul is unable to stand the moans and flies owl-like into the night. Even brainy women with horse clitorises the size of a finger fall into despair and, after they have shrieked to their heart's content in someone else's bed, get depressed.

I am alive. I visit Stanislav Albertovich and hardly smoke, I steer clear of men, and my future avenger knocks in my belly. I had no choice, and despite everything I haven't forgiven the insult, although I live like a true Christian, because I'm afraid. But not of you, Leonardik! I know that you'll come again, if you don't melt away, or rot away, deprived of your self, in the posthumous mists: I am prepared. And as for Viktor Kharitonych's visit yesterday, well, after all, that's my business, nothing extraordinary about it, I don't even consider it

112

worth mentioning, but he didn't hesitate to assert himself, and then he started asking what my plans were; he came with cognac and with perfume, and his vileness was reflected once more in the dressing-table mirror. I looked and thought: What is a man? What's the main thing about him?

My girlfriends weren't slow to criticize. Gathered together, we argued. Veronika was particularly malicious. She accused Ksyusha and me: "You curse them out, but you give them what they want like whores!" "What can one do if one feels like it?" Ksyusha smiled, taking the appeaser's role. Veronika doesn't like men as a race: neither their hairy bodies nor their souls, corrupted by male conceit. As far as the soul goes, I'm in agreement, but I liked it when they were hairy like bear cubs. Natasha was there too, full of all sorts of theories. Natasha said to us authoritatively that men need us less than we need them, but nature has so arranged things that we claim they are very much in need of us. Love flourishes on this lie. Rubbish! Veronika rejected this coldly. Timofei, he's also a man, Ksyusha noted in parenthesis. Timofei, thank God, is a race apart, snapped Veronika. "Girls," I said, "there's never enough warmth in a man! He's like an apartment house where the radiators give off hardly any heat: you can't get warm there." "It depends on who he is," said Natasha. "My husband radiates so much heat it makes you sick." One must admit, she argued, now that women have started to chase after men openly, that male heat emission, in general, has fallen appreciably. Ksyusha set about tickling her, so that her theories would vanish in laughter. We examined Natasha—a covering of prickly hair, breasts as sloppy as your shit after you've pigged out on fruit in the country—examined her and got dressed: thanks but no thanks!

And when Viktor Kharitonych was reflected in the mirror, I reminded him of his treachery and his interrogation of me,

about his sarcasm and his top-brass crudity. There were plenty
of things for us to recall together, to drink down with cognac,
but I myself remained as if untouched, as I'd positively disliked
all this, if one judges by the mirror, in which many things
had been reflected: Carlos, the Latin American ambassador,
the president's nephew, and my old friend and ex-lover Vitasik
Merzlyakov, who had run away to hide his head in the sand
like an ostrich, and even that cretin Stepan, who knocked
me over on the crossroads, bashing my thigh with all his might:
I crash to the pavement in deathly horror, and look, he's
standing above me, also scared to death, and he rocks backward and forward, a violation of every rule of the road. And
my new friends convinced me that Stepan had knocked me
over with malice aforethought and had only pretended to be
drunk. He didn't want to kill, only to cripple me. Because my
strength is in beauty—that's what they wrote in the papers
and that's also what Leonardik thought—he called me a genius
in this regard—I didn't argue, but I got angry: I was slightly
concussed. He begged me to forgive him, he'd been at a birthday party, and on my thigh there was a bruise the size of the
Black Sea and much the same shape—what an impact! He
whined, and offered money, and finally, having peered at me
in the middle of the night, fell in love. Whether he was
pretending, or whether he had fallen in love with his new
assignment, who knows? Although my new friends recalled
various similar stories and were convinced he had been ordered
to hurt me. Boris Davydovich offered the classic example of
the Jewish actor and the truck and also cited an instance when
one activist was hit on the head with a bottle: they all imagined
that people were trying to harm them; and Ksyusha uttered
the following words: "All their efforts are in vain. We can't
manage without a miracle."

And I remembered this. And when I had made up my

mind, I said to them: I have, it seems, the ability to suck up all the evil forces that have been spilled. I feel this vague strength inside me. Veronika, for her part, questions me about the rapist, and I answer that literally month in, month out this flight along the streets repeats itself, the same dirty entrance hall into the apartment house, the first steps on the staircase; I slip into a dark alcove, and he finally catches up with me: monstrous and magnificent! "Well, try, then!" says Veronika, but without any enthusiasm. She wasn't concerned with social problems, what's so marvelous about that? As if her Timofei were better than everyone! She'd found her imitation leather to replace real skin—and it was fur, stinking and repellent: the things you come across in the capital! I didn't approve, and if I helped her by inviting people to make things swing, then that was out of unselfishness, although Veronika was a sort of girlfriend; she was a good cook too— I especially remember her lemon pie. Timofei always got the biggest slice and rumbled under the table, totally ignored, as if he had not been a participant in the performance half an hour previously. I, at any event, was astounded by his little ways, his knack, and the guests too got aroused: they started encouraging and exciting one another; the hostess also demonstrated great art, and instead of a mirror, which wasn't to her taste, we the guests were the mirror, she took twenty-five rubles from each, from each couple, that is, and in the morning, having rushed breakfast and warned Timofei, "Don't howl!" she would set off for work, for the laboratory, and Timofei, the parasite, would stroll around the apartment, one foot in front of the other, as if he owned the place, would have a shower, stay by the telephone, and not bestow any particular favors on us, with the exception of me perhaps, because he'd grown accustomed to me and ate my food. I stroke him, slap his sides: clever fellow! and Veronika, I see, is looking with unremitting suspicion, she's jealous—and it's all okay, she always gets away with it, no one even informed. Just compare this with my suffering for no reason on account of my innocent love for Leonardik!

On the day of reconciliation, Leonardik was rewarded for his valor, and I didn't begrudge him, because I'd missed him and I was expecting a marriage proposal, but when he'd had his fill and decided that he'd fucked me good and proper, Vladimir Sergeyevich got all uppity again and several times actually compared himself with the great Tyutchev. Only he, he says, is going to portray a fatal love not in trochees but in the trenches, in a trenchant prose allegory. The action, as is the custom, takes place at the front, and I, it goes without saying, am a nurse. In general, explains Vladimir Sergeyevich, he's planning to immortalize me, he's gathering material and looks at me for a long time, examines me with narrowed eyes, memorizing those features that have caught his fancy: eyes the color of a sea wave, not quite green, not quite gray, enigmatic, a mischievous nurse, open to love, while he, a middle-aged wounded colonel, falls in love with her, watching as she, full of energy, laughs with the lieutenants. As a well-read woman with a taste for poetry, I knew that Tyutchev, for all his poems, didn't leave his wife, but Leonardik hints at the parallels: I write, he says, against the background of earth-shattering events from the last war; he shared his swan song in an interview with one literary newspaper. I endow the nurse-heroine with your almond-shaped eyes, he says. I pretend to be overjoyed, but in fact I grow quiet, because I see in this a final rejection, and I said to him that I can't see him anymore, for the very good reason that he's deceived me, and as for the oranges, that was hysterics. There is such a female thing: hysterics! And please don't try, darling, to make me change my mind, don't kiss my hand; I want to get married, to have children. And then he answers unexpectedly: "Well, okay, have it your way, we'll never see each other again, but I will portray you and will suffer as if you had died, I'll start traveling to a conference in Geneva and beyond, on to Mont Blanc, and I shall remember you and be depressed, and now, my dear, farewell, only look, before our parting, let's have one for the road, let us abandon ourselves to love, like that lonely colonel, discharging himself from the hospital as bombs were dropping, or else some other dreadful happenings, only the coquettish nurse perishes, he shoots her himself with his smoking revolver, because otherwise she'll be with the little lieutenants again, and this is more than he can endure, and so he will shoot her and explain it all as the result of military activities; such, he says, is the plot of the book, over which the whole country will burst into tears. Only I fear, he said, with a sweetly sinking heart, that they'll ban it (occasionally, after supper, he would dream of creating something forbidden), and the libretto for the opera is already ordered, and the fuss has already started in the film industry about who will write the screenplay. He stands above her, his legs apart, with a smoking revolver; nearby are the burning remains of a supply train, and in the sky delicate fighter planes fly west: a mixture of Tyutchev and the shockheaded colonel, he then departs to take Warsaw, or Prague, or Copenhagen, but remains morally unsullied, and he has a wife, a carbon copy of Zinaida Vasilievna, a shrew, his domestic cross, who spent the four prewar years black as night and with clouds hanging over her, but why, well, that's a mystery.

Zinaida Vasilievna Syrtsova-Lominadze.

"You are my last muse! Because of you I reach for the pen once more," he says, but he's reaching, not for the pen, but for me, and is all excited, and says that he wants me to show him no mercy, he wants to crawl on the floor and grovel at my feet, but I keep kicking him away and am ready to fight rather than give in to his demands, and he himself thrusts the belt into my hand and locks the front door still more securely, just in case. In a word, I see: the parting drama. It was not the first time, I must confess, that I'd tanned his hide and even found myself enjoying it, because he was an important person, a museum piece. I, he yells, am real shit, you won't find anyone worse in a month of Sundays! I don't lose my head at his yells, and I sock him in the face with great pleasure and shout: I couldn't give a damn that you're a bastard and a shit, that you disgraced and wiped out someone after the concert, without realizing you were covering yourself in shit too, I couldn't give a damn! You tricked *me*, you trampled *our* agreement underfoot, you didn't have the guts to marry me, you creep! He screams and is in ecstasy from the plain speaking, he loves it, and I think: It's a bad omen that you're cheering up so. Do you think I'm going to play hide-and-seek with you, a real Tyutchev! Naked and old, he crawls and sings my beauty's praises: You are beautiful, Irina, you are perfection, I am unworthy of you! I am an old shit-scared hypocrite!

I answer, "Shove it, asshole!"

He rolls around at my feet, trembles—you are my goddess and so on—but I whip him! whip his back! and I don't believe in his yells that much; those other times I had encouraged him to shout wildly: Shout for all you're worth, I would urge him. Spew all that grandeur out of you, and Lazarus will come alive, and he did come alive, and now, I see, he's coming to life slowly, slyly, a muddy drop of jism is quivering on the naughty fucker! I, he shouts in a heartrending cry, betrayed you, I am unworthy, but do me a final kindness: let me lick you from your toenails to your hair, with my lying and foul tongue. Let me lick you all over, Irina! and he chokes on his saliva. He pouts, puckers his lips, like a snout, with foam on his lips. Well, I think, I'll finish you off now! However you lie, you won't lie your way out this time! And I start scratching him, biting him, thrashing him, whipping him, flogging him, while he slobbers, all crimson, he gasps for breath and whispers, "For the last time, forgive me, Ira!"

This had at one time formed the basis of our alliance: he'd given himself license and I'd done the same. That is, I didn't find it boring either, and when you think about it, who else could have satisfied him after me? Leonardik would have come crawling back on his belly like a jackal or else become a killer, because with me he'd thrown aside all restraint.

He said as much afterward too, after he had come to me and scared me; he said: I felt a kindred soul in you from the start, you and I are like a bride and bridegroom. You are my unearthly bride! I let happiness slip through my fingers on earth. Gifted with talent, as everyone acknowledged, I gave it all to the service of the social structure and to my own tranquillity. I thought, I'll live my quiet life, I'll get by, but in the twilight of my life I found you, my bride, stripped off my gloves, stopped caring about everything else, and began to shout that I was a bastard! Other people, Irisha, consider themselves good to the bottom of their souls; I, to my justification, with these very eyes—and here he jabbed his eye with a misshapen fingernail, almost poking it out—with these very eyes I have seen much, too much; but I didn't touch the sores, because I love the people, that's the truth, a people slow to anger and quick to forgive, and it would be a mistake to disturb them, to stir them up!

I didn't memorize everything and didn't ask him to repeat things: I'm not a spy and not a seeker of confessions. One needs Natasha for that; she would have been equipped to worm out the secrets, except that he wouldn't have opened up to her, wouldn't have given her the time of day. Once, when

he wanted to see Rituyla, he said no at the last second; I had
described everything to him, how we would perform in front
of him, and he went wild with excitement, he demanded it,
he shouted—and then said no. "I don't need Rituyla," so
Rituyla stayed home, all dressed up and nowhere to go.

He bawls, and licks, licks and farts, he's all crimson and
he's breathing unevenly, and I say to him, "Well, give me a
go too." And I start sucking him! He starts to quiver, and I
think: Quiver, traitor! and he quivers all over, and contorts,
and begs me to let him take me in the old-fashioned missionary
way, his kisser bloody and bruises all over his back—I had
given him a real hiding—and having exhausted him, I let
him take me. He started to push in and out, like a youngster;
I was surprised. Come on, I shout, quicker! Don't slacken,
you old cockroach! He gets quicker and quicker! and I shout,
Yes! Do it to me! Oh, no-o-o-o-o . . . ! His chin drops, his
eyes come out of their sockets, as if a truck had run him over,
his cheeks shake, and he gallops! gallops! and he makes an
odd noise—and then suddenly he shoots his hot bitter old
man's semen into me! and he comes crashing down! What
wild howls of ecstasy! and I howl along with him, which hadn't
happened often. In fact, to tell the truth, this was the first
time it had happened properly, there'd always been a lot of
faking, and when he licked me, I was sometimes on the
brink—yes, there, there!—but the wave would fade away, I
was left with nothing, and I would get angry: "Oh, to hell
with you! Fool! If you don't know how to turn on the heat,
stay out of my kitchen!" But this time he was able to fire me,
he knew how to, it's just I was a little late, worrying about
him, so that he would believe in his little powers, which were
nothing to speak of, and he collapsed, and started snorting,
and bubbles came out of his mouth and nose, only I didn't
catch on at first, I was a bit stunned, and Ksyusha listens and
looks at me with her sharp little reddish-brown eyes, looks

now and again and is silent, and I'm silent in reply—there's
no proof, pure fantasies. When I recover I say, "Leonardik!
What's the matter with you?" and he snorts with an awful
wheeze, as if his innards have burst. It's time to call a doctor.
I want to get free, but he has become leaden and continues
to live only by inertia. I want to get out, and accidentally my
eyes meet his. He looks at me as if I'm a stranger, and then
I understood: He has no desire to die with me, because however you try to twist it, he didn't live with me; that's how I
interpreted it. That is, I don't know whether he would have
wanted to see Zinaida Vasilievna, perhaps he wouldn't have
wanted that either, or perhaps Antonchik? He looks at me
with a certain hatred, even, and is dying, I see, giving up the
ghost. I start slapping his cheeks gently: Where, I yell, are
the tablets for your heart, nitroglycerin or whatever they're
called? He doesn't answer. I leap to my feet: Tell me where
to run to, bastard, come on! His hand moves a bit, as if to
say, There's no need: it's too late! I rush to the telephone—
he had a special phone, instead of a dial you press buttons,
he taught me how to press them, and I used to phone the
speaking clock on 100, to find out the time, and the hour is
late, about one in the morning, and it's spring outside, a
moonlit night, I remember, he moves his hand, he snorts,
meaning, There's no need to phone, and it dawns on me: he
doesn't want to call an ambulance, he's worrying about his
reputation to his last breath. He lies naked, bruised, with a
bloody face. I say, Where are the tablets? and that we *have*
to phone. But he looks at me with an unloving gaze and doesn't
answer. He doesn't utter any last words after coming, and he
came like a young man—powerfully and hotly—only he
overstrained himself, and everything in him finally burst. I
look—his eyes are growing muddy, like a sparrow's, which
means finis, you know.

I run to phone the ambulance on 03. I explain incoherently, I can't explain clearly: I don't know the address, I never wrote him letters—What's your address? I say to him, but he's not in the mood for addresses, he no longer has an address, he's already like a sparrow, little muddy eyes. . . . I wouldn't wish such an experience on anyone, but they went on dragging explanations out of me: what and how? People kept arriving! As for the family: Zinaida Vasilievna is in Truskavets, treating her bladder, and Antoshka is away on a business trip. As soon as I had finished explaining over the telephone, I rush to him—and see he's died! I must hurry to get dressed before the doctors arrive. My clothes are torn; he's all battered up. The bell rings. I rush to the door, and a new obstacle: it won't unlock, damn it! I can't open it, the lock is complicated, like a railroad switch, long, with five turns. I never saw anything like it in my life. I yell through the door: I can't open it! They swear from the other side, run somewhere. They see that it's serious and start to knock down the door, but the door isn't ordinary either. While they are battering it, I tidy myself up as best I can, but I don't touch him again, he lies there and watches my fussing.

As soon as they break in, they run up to him, turn him and twist him, and begin to cover him with iodine, for some reason, and they come right at me with their complaints: "If only you'd unlocked the door in time!" But what can I do if I don't understand locks: Look, I say, look at the sort of lock it is, and they say: Why are you both so scratched and torn, like cats? Have you been fighting or what? I naturally say, "Excuse me, what do you mean, fighting? What are you in-sinuating?" Lord, I'm getting worked up all over again, just writing about it! Today there's a cold gusty wind on the street. Absolutely no desire whatsoever to go to the shops for grub!

I said to the doctors, "You'd better give me something to calm my nerves, an injection or something." "And," the doctors ask, "who exactly are you?" Except that these are no longer doctors. As if I'm stealing the family silver, and how can you explain everything to them? I love him! loved him! But they pursue their line: Why the bruises? Well, okay, I say, embarrassed, we were . . . playing games. "You have interesting games," they say, and they leaf through my passport carefully and sit in their trench coats till daybreak. They don't believe me, but in the morning they let me go all the same, saying that they'll call me in. Zinaida Vasilievna is flying up to Moscow, is being rushed in on a military plane, she'll soon be on the scene, the autopsy will find out everything; my head is in a muddle, but they let me go. I had been thinking: They won't release me. And when I reached home with a face all scratched by Leonardik, they question me again: "Weren't you the one who threw the oranges?" I was overjoyed: "Yes, it was me! me!" All of musical Moscow is in the know, but they say, What were you trying to get out of him? Big shots, you can tell from their bearing. They look at me agonizingly. I loved him, I repeat, leave me alone, this is my tragedy, I loved him, he promised to marry me, he hated that old fool Zinaida Vasilievna, he loved me for two years, he was planning to make a film about me, I've got the following presents from him: two gold rings with tiny cheap sapphires, the sign Virgo on a gold chain, endless perfumes, empty chocolate boxes, two pairs of shoes, don't touch me, don't insult a lady, how would you feel if something like this happened to you, someone dying on you at such an unsuitable moment! I was forced to reveal details that discredited him, but what else could I do? Go to jail for his fantasies? But Anton, the swine, also let me down, saying he didn't know me, and I say, How can that be? He was at the dacha in my presence. And then I remember, fortunately, Yegor the watchman. How they tore into Yegor too, perhaps they thought we were in cahoots, and they also tore into his wife, Lyusya, the maid and the drunkard, the lover of wine. And for saying they knew me, they were quickly tossed out of the dacha by Zinaida Vasilievna. But at this point everything finally came out about the oranges. They had played into my hands, witnesses were found, so that even if they weren't able to confirm love, at the very least the fact that he and I had sat together in the director's box at Britten was corroborated—and they sort of left me alone. And Grand-daddy returns with his spade, having dug up the vegetable garden, and as soon as he steps over the threshold announces, "Guess who's dead?"

# ELEVEN

A nd he holds out the paper. And in the paper there's a black forest of signatures, a black forest and a portrait with a black border, well dressed and severe, as if the photograph had been taken for this purpose; but in the depths of his face he's slightly bewildered and apologetic. I sit down with it in the warm water, in order to suppress my emotion; the gas water heater hums above me, threatening to explode momentarily, and I read it and reread it, and I'll confess: I was carried away with admiration!

I had known even before, of course, but I hadn't realized you were *so* famous, that you were *so* famous in everything. I had never guessed it. I loved you even more for your obituary, for the fact that you'd been a soldier and a husbandman, a tiller of the soil and a standard-bearer, such as no one will ever be again, and we had lost all this. But your legacy will always remain, a steel bayonet from a noble arsenal. I sat and wept, and the expressions you honored me with came to mind, your calling me a golden fish, our conversations about art, fascinating trips to the dacha, your embraces and your love. You were a giant. I was right to call you my Leonardik, and how you liked that! How accurately I had guessed! Because it was intuition. And I found it a joy to think that you died stretched out above me, that with your final cry you saluted our love, and that I will be the first to plod behind the coffin, in my mind's eye at least, the first to throw a lump of earth from the fashionable cemetery onto your coffin, where every grave resounds with the hard rumble of the paths of earthly glory and there are tunnels cut through to provide close con-tact among the deceased, who converse on their own tele-phone line; only it's sad there are no cypresses and their conversation is guarded at the eternally locked gate.

But I will not receive a pass into that valley of tears, I won't be given permission to visit dear *you*, piled with car-nations, to be accounted for later, and departmental wreaths; I won't be let into that hall where, surrounded by medals and the guard of honor, you will lie in your best suit, which will hide the scars and storms of love. You will be paraded before the public, the crowd of schoolchildren and soldiers (many soldiers), where, sorrowing and grieving, distinguished vet-erans and cultural secretaries will wipe their eyes, and where the smell of the flowers and the speeches overwhelm—no, I won't be let in there.

In a pathetic black dress, with my head uncovered, wearing no makeup, as if a total stranger to you, I shall come to say farewell along with the others, in my hands a bunch of white calla lilies. I shall lay my wreath, to a rustle of disapproval, inconspicuously make the sign of the cross over you, but you don't look like you, now that your dead face has become unpleasantly bloated, the poor victim of an unsuccessful at-tempt to bring you back from the dead. And some vulgar wit will hiss in my wake that instead of calla lilies I should have brought you five kilos of oranges. But Antonchik, with his summers in Madrid, will catch me with a well-aimed tearless glance, he who shouted about me as the genius of pure love and shook his cock before my tired eyelids in the forlorn hope that his affection would be returned—the wretched creature! Then some guys will come up to me silently and detain me —their faces will be fierce—not as if I'm seeing someone close off on his final journey but as if I'm after the family silver. They'll hold me by the arms, like a widow, and once more will lead me out in shame, and Antosha the spy will report back to his malevolent queen mother of spades, and she will swear to take her revenge on me, as if not I but she had heard his dying cries, as if he'd loved not me but her, and taken her to concerts, and dined her in secluded cafés on the outskirts of Moscow—as if I didn't have the right to this. And I shall start to get angry in the hairy hands of the guards, but holding my arms, they will lead me away and send me home, until all this alien public has paid him the last honors.

But you see, I had thought: We'll both be generous enough to burst out crying together at the grave of our joint husband. It wasn't money I wanted to share, not his estate, but a purely spiritual feeling, because I'd loved him, and he loved me, and he had wanted us to marry, only he was piously guarding his family hearth. He felt sorry for Zinaida, being not only a genius but a man of compassion. He gave all of himself, stepping out of the lilac mirage of television, all the while carrying melancholy within him, fear for the future, and this was why he hid his feelings, this was why he wrote, and made speeches, and demonstrated that one should not touch old wounds because they are purulent. And this is why the small fry are wrong, the mindless little people who are always discontented, because the current of history will overcome immature and undeveloped minds. And when Yegor, tossed out of the dacha, threw aside all restraint under the influence of wine and started to tell funny stories about him, about how he wasn't above behaving badly if someone depended on him, or how he would stamp his feet and appear before Lyusya, the obedient maid,

in surprising and even rude ways, shocking the maiden so
much that she was ashamed, even though it was hard to
embarrass Lyusya, since all she wanted was to get drunk on
wine and roll her eyes a bit, then I understood that no one,
including first and foremost his little family of monsters, was
able to understand the most important thing about him, only
to me did he reveal his essence: his endless compassion for
people's misery: he so wanted them to live better lives! But
Yegor, as soon as he had died, says, "He didn't want for
anything, the smart-assed bastard!" And he says: They'll forget
him after a day or two, they won't gather for the memorial
service forty days after his death, and if they do, it will only
be to fill up free of charge, because the deceased was a glutton.

That's true. He and I loved to stuff ourselves. Waiters
treated us reverently, understanding that this was no impe-
cunious man before them, this was Vladimir Sergeyevich himself, who took food very seriously. We gobbled up lots of
goodies. Who else could have rivaled him in the art of gorging?
And after all this plentiful rich food, taking a shit was such
a pleasure, it was like an epic poem!

No one understood him and no one forgave him; they all
just wanted to spit on the freshly dug grave, because it's not
true that we love the deceased in this country; instead we only
love the ones we didn't love when they were alive, but those
who were loved when alive are discarded after death. And if
Zinaida Vasilievna had invited me to the wake, I would have
forgiven everything! Everything! I would have been her prime
defender, her best friend. I would have remembered with her
the expression of his eyes, the quality of his thoughts, and his
hands, smelling of expensive foreign leather, and thus the
slanderers, not worth his little fingernail, would have been
publicly humiliated. But it turned out quite the other way,
and I became obliged to cross over into their camp, because

my endless patience came to an end, since they planned to throw me out, out of the hall where he was. They didn't allow me to bring as a modest gift my white-headed calla lilies. No, the base soul of Zinaida Vasilievna knew no compassion! And I had my memories, of his sobs when he had no one else to cry so hard and long to, muffling the telephone with a pillow, because he was always suspicious of the phone; and he had no one but me to share his ecstasy at the word I'd picked to describe him: dogshit. "Yes, I'm dogshit!" he exulted. "Dogshit! Dogshit!" Who else would dare talk about himself in such a way? Isn't this a Christian act? And now, as a daughter of the Russian Orthodox Church, I give witness, standing on the abyss of my decision to give birth to my fateful cherub: No one else has bad-mouthed himself like that! Yes, I've seen all sorts of bigwigs, ready to tear their hair out in acts of repentance forgotten for good two minutes later, but what were their words in comparison with the scourge of my Leonardik, who was a man of his time, though, not of the time when the arts blossomed around the ample Renaissance legs of the Mona Lisa, near the mansions of love and spring reveries? And his last idea, about the colonel who shot, like Tyutchev, his illicit lover? Surely here there is a muffled echo of catastrophe? Surely here lurks his melancholy?

Yes, it was me he loved. And regarding Zinaida Vasilievna, who finally lost her marbles, threatening suicide, though her stout body was incapable of it, he was simply a saint. Who else could have endured their creaking boat of a dacha, with all those parasites and spongers, those disloyalists? I found their presence repulsive, and it was no accident that they led me out of the stuffy hall, although I hadn't said anything and had infringed upon nothing whatever. I wanted to pass unnoticed, just as pure love passes unnoticed, but they got me by the arms and dragged me out, and on top of that they called me a guttersnipe. And Granddaddy, who had colluded with them, didn't say anything to me about this. Then why should I be sad if he has died, taking fright at me, as if I were infectious, and fleeing to the place where the footballer plays and time stands still? So go on then, die on your hospital bed, Tikhon Makarovich, although as a Christian I'm not against your being cured and continuing your trivial old fart's life, because I'm not a little girl and I'm not living in clover at all! I put on a pathetic dress, I didn't slap any makeup on, didn't do my hair, yet I was more beautiful than all of them on that mournful day when I was so humiliated! But they didn't give me the chance to savor my superiority. It's a small world. And already Viktor Kharitonych, my long-standing and devoted defender, has furrowed his goatlike face, ready for the nasty business of dealing with me once and for all. And Polina Nikanorovna has started to fidget, impatient to rip the bedspread off me, to poke her head under the sheets and breathe the air of my unhappy love. Polina Nikanorovna, the destroyer of illusions. She's sure to try and slander me, she's certain to delight in my tears, having set up my disgrace. Well, Kharitonych? What have you got to say, Kharitonych? With eyes downcast, he'll look away and start the meeting, and I, unprepared, in a gaudy summer dress, shall suddenly hear all sorts of new things about myself, they'll suddenly spread creeping rumors about me. And in the silence of humiliation the meeting will exclude me from the land of the living and herd me toward that place where the trains run empty, into the territory of my one-eyed daddy, who by now has entirely lost the gift of intelligent speech, into the territory of the rough-diamond father who has exchanged life for stagnation, a lifelong death sentence.

But the bird Ksyusha will fly in from Fontainebleau, open to the deepest joys and pleasurings and serious highs, and will offer me a way to escape, a courageous escapade, and I shall agree. And she'll phone X, who deviates from his noble passion for the men only for her, to ask him to grab his apparatus and rush to us, and she also said, "In X's peculiar sensitivity you'll find good fortune. He'll shoot everything in such a way that people will only be aware of art and you'll avoid vulgarity!" And she was right, my Ksyusha, and I have no regrets, although I had a feeling that I had stepped over that threshold where people understand people, and all because? Because my bergamot grove was so much more beautiful than most, and many had managed to enter it, and it was felt that too many were trampling it, and no one trusted anyone else, nor my sincerity. The garden was too beautiful, the fruits were too full of delights. So there was I, left with my fruits, bites taken from them, and they started to rot, first in one barrel and then in another, because life can be a bitch, you know, for a beauty amidst monsters! And when the handsome photographer X, an intimate of the Petersburg elite yet unresponsive to women, arrived, he intrigued me. Apart from Andryusha, on whom I could rely—and could even sleep with, like sleeping with a newborn baby—I don't trust these unresponsive men, seeing them as some sort of vague insult to my person. How can it be possible! And I didn't believe them, imagining that they simply weren't up to it, but it turned out they were up to it but just didn't want to, and they could see right through us and our womanly wiles. And X arrived with his modern equipment, with his almost remarkable apparatus, as if for underwater fishing, all in corduroy, oval nails, full of ancient tenderness toward our Ksyusha, despite his queer ways. And Ksyusha liked this. She didn't try to hide the sense of triumph it gave her, and Ksyusha says to him, "So like this and like this. Can you do it?" X thought and answered, "Let's give it a try!"

# TWELVE

**A** lover isn't just someone you sleep with but is someone you like waking up with in the morning. Viktor Kharitonych knew that and couldn't forgive me. So when Zinaida Vasilievna, dripping her widow's dew and making off with a fat pension, complained about me in order to whitewash her ruined spouse, who had lived with me for two years and a bit, and was happy as a pup, and died with a worthy cry—when Zinaida Vasilievna did her black deed, I was in a state of total ignorance. I was bewailing my loss and kept rereading the obituary to comfort myself. And Granddaddy, Tikhon Makarovich, lived the inconspicuous life of a Stakhanovite side by side with me and kept mum, as if he knew nothing about any of this. So when Viktor Kharitonych cordially, with fond intimations, invited me to pop into his office, not even a vague suspicion flashed through my mind. Rather, I thought he just couldn't calm down and, evidently, the hour had come to pay for my free-and-easy life; only he was misguided, I thought, in advertising our relations and being boastful about me before the eyes of the work force and Polina Nikanorovna, who always thought that a woman without a bra isn't really a woman at all but is the lowest thing in creation, since Polina Nikanorovna's bust has long since stopped obeying orders. She and I would never understand each other, even if we were to spend an eternity breaking bread at the same table during our tours of fairs and exhibitions, where men besiege the bus where we change into our costumes as if a load of meat has appeared in a shop. Natasha, God's little eater of raw greens, said, spinning the yarn of abstract words with quick hands, that the philosophy of meat rules the world and because of meat you can't see God properly or the questions of eternity. She, however, spurning meat, saw the composition of the air and smiled at it, and even saw microbes, and Veronika praised her while she fed her Timofei on meat, so that he would be strong and savage. But when Viktor Kharitonych, the old goat, invited me to a meeting, I immediately sensed that something was up. I have an excellent nose for such things and decided to turn down the invitation, but he kept insisting, and so eagerly and kindly that I decided he couldn't hold out any longer or perhaps that he'd heard something and wanted to worm out secrets. He loved me to tell him about men's virtues and hidden vices— that was his staple diet—and I entertained him with my stories: as that the minister of not quite heavy industry, but not light industry either, a man of amazing qualities, was angry with me because I sat cross-legged at a picnic for invited guests by the Moscow River, knees apart and ankles crossed. And I had already taken off my damp rag of a costume, given to me by that very same Ksyusha Mochulskaya who was critical of the philosophy of meat but, like the eater of green food, held forth angrily about how time lorded it over us, but it was just that I knew such an eternity where there was not only no depth but no grace, which is just total swamp, where trucks founder and the inquisitive boy next door, squatting a second ago, is swatted like a fly, and it burned me too, that cable, as it scratched my face. I don't need that depth, thank you

very much, but Ksyusha, brought up on choice cuts of meat
and girlish pranks, as a thin fifteen-year-old schoolgirl, not
yet starting the next-to-last grade, exchanged kisses with a
girlfriend, while my one-eyed daddy kept a very strict eye on
me and disciplined me harshly, not wholly out of altruism,
but I let it all fly past my ears. With reference to God,
who is, they say, poorly visible through meat, no, thanks!
But Viktor You-know-who, Kharitonych, used to get great
pleasure from hearing of the minister's naïveté, for he had
swallowed my story that I was a nursery school teacher, such
a worthy occupation. And Viktor Kharitonych used to laugh
his hoarse bass laugh, and as soon as I sat down cross-legged
in the middle of the picnickers, with my face to the Moscow
River, he was embarrassed, he thought it was a breach of
etiquette, because we were not alone but with a group of
people, who immediately choked on their kebabs, and that's
putting it mildly perhaps, but I didn't give a damn: I sit and
I'm enjoying myself, and the minister soon after this dies of
cancer, but before this he made his peace with me and even
introduced me to his aged mother. This, he says, is Ira, whom
I told you about, and he was, which was typical, a widower,
and his mother liked me very much. Only he died, eaten up
by illness. I actually took special food parcels to him in the
hospital. In his private room there was a color television, and
the doctor said to me, "Even if he manages to get back on
his feet, he still won't be a whole man," and I say, "Well, so
what—that isn't vital!" And the doctor says to me, "You are
a truly noble woman!"

That's what the doctor said to me, but the minister went
and died. He didn't get better, despite the hospital, and faded
away within a month, pure bad luck. But if he had been cured,
then Aleksandr Prokofievich would definitely have married
me, a remarkable and *brilliant* man, yet he was stern and could

never forgive me for sitting cross-legged and always asked in tormented tones, "But why did you sit cross-legged? What for?" and—the main thing—I had already been very properly introduced to his aged mother, and we dined, the three of us, on a white starched tablecloth, with crystal vases, and she liked me very much, the old woman. Viktor Kharitonych, who respected those of high rank, was happy for me and promised without fail to make me one of the queens onstage, but nothing turned out right; he wrote his little note to my protectors in which he said in his defense that I had left of my own free will, as it were, because of my great loss. Zinaida Vasilievna brushed away a tear and was left with nothing, because they made my love famous, proclaimed it publicly in obscure terms that those who need to will understand. But now he's summoning me in an ingratiating voice and doesn't warn me about anything, at eleven o'clock, so I go there nice and comfy, straight from bed, surprised by his warmth. I arrive and I look around: agitation, and everyone is staring in my direction, at my beads, I thought, I'd put on Latin American beads, amethyst, from Carlos, in order to attract the bastard, but his secretary leads me into the auditorium, where we do our shows, and a table is covered with green, except it's not for a banquet. Behind it sit Viktor Kharitonych and other representatives, and Nina Chizh. I knew Nina Chizh well. She loved cakes with artificial cream but didn't know exactly where she pissed from. When she had cystitis, she asked me, and I let her in on the secret, but otherwise we weren't very close. And Polina is also seated there, and looks at me in endless triumph, and Syoma Epshtein has popped up too. Viktor Kharitonych turns his eyes away and says that the need to discuss this has been coming for a long time, he says, and the moment has come, and he gives the word to Polina bitch Nikanorovna, who, as my direct boss, must, he says, express the general opinion, and Polina Nikanorovna jumps up from her seat and scurries onto the handmade platform to the microphone, as if to comment on my clothes, and they stare, whisper, gossip, and I still don't understand anything, but I'm thinking: Why are they all here? Even the stagehands in their sheepskin jackets and with hatpins in their teeth are poking their heads around the door, and seamstresses of various ages in semitransparent blouses—why have they all crawled out of their holes? There hadn't been so much commotion in our office since the time the personnel files caught fire, and I sit down and cross my legs, and Polina immediately yells at me that I shouldn't cross my legs, she says, and flaunt my beads like that, and someone unknown to me, whom, I see, Viktor Kharitonych is turning to and looking at with all his might, and whom he's trying very hard to imitate, also says that this is a violation of decency. So would you mind sitting properly, if it's not too much trouble! Well, I sit down, and Polina goes on about this and that, about discipline and the way I behave, both the external image and the internal one, my moral makeup. We've just seen the external image, she says, beads everywhere, and the inner is the same, if not worse. Consequently, it's interesting to ask, she says, what Tarakanova thinks, what she's hoping for, only it's already sort of late to ask, because we, she says, have asked on more than one occasion, have called her in many times and had a chat, both she and Viktor Kharitonych here, there had been discussions, she says, about my appearance, but things got no better and discipline was hopeless, and this had harmful reverberations, because the work was specialized, a person must be attentive at all times, and if someone's free time is characterized by disgraceful behavior, this influences everyone, so it is not simply a private matter. And indeed that's just the sort of behavior we have in this case. We received various hints, from all sides, and more than once I observed, during particularly exacting tours, there occurred impermissible incidents in the guise of men, and also alcohol, including pure alcohol, and all this attracted attention, particularly men, who literally swarmed around, like bees, but the honey, forgive the expression, was rancid! Not our brand! And the absence of discipline, which everyone knows about, and to which we drew attention, is nothing more than veiled parasitism, let's not mince words. And the unknown man, whom Viktor Kharitonych's nose is pointing to like a hunting dog, keeps nodding his support. And the hall, that is, my friends, are listening, and Polina states that their patience, one might say, has come to an end, and it's time, she says, to come to a decision, and beads won't help me, so there's no point in brandishing them, and your taste in clothes is well known. As for her own breasts living an independent life and hanging down when she goes bathing, she didn't touch upon that but shifted the blame for that onto me as well. But I keep on sitting there at a loss, still not quite awake, because, like Ksyusha, I don't neglect my sleep and don't like going without a good night's sleep. And at this point Nina Chizh, of the artificial cream cakes, goes red from the agitation of making a speech and babbles that it would be okay, she says, if it were only smoking and men, who were like bees, but there was something else too, and, she says, this is totally alien and incomprehensible to us, where on earth do such people come from? Syoma Epshtein, who had spoken earlier, states that he'd always had his doubts, but she was surrounded, he says, by an unhealthy climate of, how shall I put it, of admiration, yet look at what, he says, we were admiring, was it not an illusion? Because this climate was so unhealthy. It's as if he's casting stones at Viktor Kharitonych, only that one doesn't give a damn but sits there, exasperated, and chairs the meeting . . . and the cutters with hatpins in their teeth peep around the doors, and I sense things are taking a nasty turn! and suddenly, without rhyme or reason, Nina Chizh speaks out. Whom does she represent, eh? One expects it from Epshtein, he travels around the world and is the local legislator, but what's it got to do with Nina Chizh, the personification of a life that didn't work out, whom out of pity I took to a restaurant to see an orchestra—no one had ever invited her before—while we were traveling around the countryside north of Moscow? She for no rhyme or reason demands to know whether, if there were suddenly a war with the Chinese, Irina Tarakanova would join up as a volunteer and take off her beads. A serious question, especially in the light of events, and Polina hastens to add that given half a chance, Tarakanova would have signed up not as a volunteer but as one of the lovers of the notorious General Vlasov, and we'd have been left looking like fools, but we support her, and isn't it total blasphemy that she embodies our image and likeness, our deportment, and even, if you like, our hairstyle, and who is it, strictly speaking, that we're taking as a model? Epshtein shouts, "It certainly shouldn't be Poland!" And I think to myself: What are they hinting at, what Vlasov? That is, I knew—I'm no fool—but what's he got to do with it? My patriotism was aroused, and I yell, "Not true! This is too much!" But they answer me, it isn't too much, it's all correct, and it's about time for me to shut up and to stop shaking my beads, but I am shaking them and placing people in quandary, for which I will have to answer, they say, before the men and women gathered here, and I need say nothing, they say, on that count, because everything's perfectly clear, and Nina Chizh announces once more that it wouldn't be too bad if it were only men and alcohol, but if women are also mixed up in this, and not in the best way, to put it bluntly, then this shows a character that is both threatening and sinister, and

Syoma Epshtein says that there will be no mercy, and the unknown man, whose surname is Dugarin, actually flushed and looked at me with such feeling that I grew quiet and couldn't bring myself to deny the slander, and they say to me that it is in my own interest to listen, as if my actions aren't modest and pleasant enough, and anyway who are they to judge? But I keep silent and keep listening.

And then a whole row of them appeared, one more passionate than the other, and all of them try to point me out as one of the lovers of the notorious general and uncover in me more and more defects, and criticize, and even the cutters, with garments they haven't finished sewing, make speeches and extol their wares and ask that I not disgrace these by wearing them, though I wasn't all that eager—what do I want with such shit?—but all the same it's strange for me to hear this, and Viktor Kharitonych gets more and more agitated and looks away, and Polina Nikanorovna can't endure it and bursts out crying from the hatred that has built up inside her, she breaks down, and then Nina Chizh starts comforting her and offering cream cakes, and they start to eat them greedily in front of the whole gathering, as if they were in a bakery, but they don't even let me fiddle with my beads, they pounce on me, the pubic lice, but I sit and don't beat them off, I listen attentively. And Syoma Epshtein has already stopped sounding off, and the unknown man surnamed Dugarin has lost some of his uncontrollable anger, and he also offered some examples of my dangerous influence on the collective and said that you saw through her eyes and did not see through her, and even, perhaps, overpraised her, envying her looks and not paying enough attention to what was inside, and I thought that the business was drawing to a close, that the stormy debate was subsiding, but no such luck: my guardian angel flits out onto the stage, my defender of private interests, Stanislav

Albertovich Flavitsky, and speaks, with his slight burr, in a
sweet voice.

STANISLAV ALBERTOVICH: I may give the appearance of being
an outsider here, but my views on this case are very clear,
and I, my dear patients, on numerous occasions performed
abortions for Irina Vladimirovna. I don't try to work out
the number, because I've lost count and don't remember
an exact figure, although medical confidentiality isn't very
important when I talk to you, because you are carrying
out the will of the trade union that has sent you here.

VIKTOR KHARITONYCH: Without question.

POLINA NIKANOROVNA: (weeps) Boo-hoo!

NINA CHIZH: Boom-boom-boom!

DUGARIN: Continue!

STANISLAV ALBERTOVICH: (with animation) And every time I
was amazed!

VIKTOR KHARITONYCH: Quite right too.

STANISLAV ALBERTOVICH: I don't have anything in common
with Irina Vladimirovna, but I remember well her words
about her unwillingness to give birth to children in bondage, although as a doctor I don't wish her ill but wish for
her to think better of it.

POLINA NIKANOROVNA: She won't change her mind!

GENERAL VLASOV: She was in charge of my radio emissions
and liaisons.

SYOMA EPSHTEIN: Criminal! You should be branded!

STANISLAV ALBERTOVICH: We, the people in white coats,
    We angrily condemn the grandmother of Russian abortion.
    We, the people in white coats,
    We won't let the grandmother of Russian abortion into
    our homes!

POLINA NIKANOROVNA: I am Polina Nikanorovna.

STANISLAV ALBERTOVICH: I'm ineffably glad!

THE HALL: Friendship! Friendsheep!

THE CUTTERS: Hey, look, the general!

GENERAL VLASOV: (*in fetters, up to his ankles in water, surrounded by mice*) For all my criminal designs I am indebted to Irina Vladimirovna Tarakanova, an Italian con woman, Mussolini's mistress.

THE CUTTERS: (*weeping and singing*)
A cockroach and a spider
In our house reside.
Great minds that guide us,
A cockroach and a spider—
Pederasts!

NINA CHIZH: Boom-boom-boom!

POLINA NIKANOROVNA and STANISLAV ALBERTOVICH kiss before everyone's eyes.

VIKTOR KHARITONYCH: (*applauds fiercely*) Now that is something!

I: (*with a cry*) Et tu, Granddaddy!

GRANDDADDY, not stopping, walks past me, his glasses and his medals glinting. He used to clean his medals with toothpowder. He didn't believe in toothpaste because it was a harmful and dangerous innovation, leading the people astray. Granddaddy goes up onto the tribune.

GRANDDADDY'S SPEECH:

Dear comrades!

My very own granddaughter, Irina Vladimirovna Tarakanova . . . (*is silent*)

VIKTOR KHARITONYCH: Why are you silent?

GRANDDADDY: (*is silent*)

VIKTOR KHARITONYCH: You have a script.

GRANDDADDY: It must have fallen somewhere.

VIKTOR KHARITONYCH: (*conferring*) It's fallen somewhere.

GRANDDADDY: Can I just say it like this, without embellish-
ments?

DUGARIN: Speak, old Stakhanovite!

GRANDDADDY: Well, to begin with the fact that when she
leaves the house she never puts the light out and also
leaves the gas burning in the bathroom, and this could
well cause a fire and everything burn to hell, and I don't
want to lose all my possessions in a fire, I haven't lived,
you may say, for that, to end up losing all my possessions
in a fire in old age, and as for her strolling around the
apartment in a Japanese kimono–type dressing gown, I
don't mind that so much, seeing as she is shameless, but
when she suddenly leaps out of bed or out of a corner and
starts talking on the telephone, that (*to Dugarin*), my son,
is another matter, this shocks me as an ill person, and
people stay the night in her room, they laugh and splash
water everywhere, as if they owned the place, and the
water even flows out into the corridor, and in addition
she smokes in bed, and I worry and can't sleep, it would
nevertheless be galling to lose all my possessions in a fire
in my old age, or something else instead: once, I'm not
lying, I saw a whole pool of blood in her bed, I was about
to ask, but I'll say honestly, I was rather scared, after all
who knows what might have happened, but there was a
pool, and she goes around in a Japanese kimono–type
dressing gown—I have no complaints, because the dressing
gown is a good one, although an abomination as well, of
course . . .

VIKTOR KHARITONYCH: What conclusions do you draw from
all this, Tikhon Makarovich?

GRANDDADDY: (*sighs*) It all seems conclusive enough to me . . .

VIKTOR KHARITONYCH: But more specifically, with regard to
whether it is possible to live together?

GRANDDADDY: Oh, yes, that! Well, to begin with the fact that to live together in view of the threat of fire doesn't really suit me at all, as a respected man. And I don't need any care she can give me! To hell with it! (*stamps his feet*)

THE HALL: Oo-oo-oo-oo-ooh!

A shot is heard. It's General Vlasov, shooting himself.

CUTTERS: (*declaiming*) A holy hero! Holey hero! Holey hero!

A SEAMSTRESS IN A WHITE BLOUSE: Girls! Let's tear her hair out! Let's put out her eyes with pins!

GIRLS: Let's!

VIKTOR KHARITONYCH: (*sternly*) Hey, hey! No hooliganism!

NINA CHIZH: (*exultantly*) Boom-boom-boom!

SYOMA EPSHTEIN: Why did the corpse of General Vlasov shoot itself?

POLINA NIKANOROVNA: (*tenderly*) Who can tell?

THE CORPSE OF GENERAL VLASOV: (*with a southern Russian accent*) I didn't shoot myself. For all that is vile in me I am indebted to Irina Tarakanova!

VIKTOR KHARITONYCH: (*to me*) Well, then, what do you have to say for yourself? (*looks at me with hatred*)

I: (*standing on the tribune*) I never loved this (*in the direction of the corpse of General Vlasov*) person. I loved another. Very much! This is all because of him! I . . . I . . . (*I fall into a faint*)

As I lie unconscious, two familiar faces lean toward me. These are Viktor Kharitonych and his girlfriend, Polina Nikanorovna. The evening of that very same day is setting in.

VIKTOR KHARITONYCH: (*to Polina Nikanorovna, relenting*) Oh, you bitch!

POLINA NIKANOROVNA: Forgive me.

VIKTOR KHARITONYCH: Whore.

POLINA NIKANOROVNA: Well, so what?

VIKTOR KHARITONYCH: Nothing, you old prostitute!

POLINA NIKANOROVNA: Who, me?

VIKTOR KHARITONYCH: You.

POLINA NIKANOROVNA: Bastard!

VIKTOR KHARITONYCH: Forgive me.

POLINA NIKANOROVNA: Swine!

VIKTOR KHARITONYCH: Forgive me.

POLINA NIKANOROVNA: Scum.

VIKTOR KHARITONYCH: Forgive me.

POLINA NIKANOROVNA: I won't forgive you.

VIKTOR KHARITONYCH: Yes, you'll forgive me.

POLINA NIKANOROVNA: No.

VIKTOR KHARITONYCH: Bitch!

POLINA NIKANOROVNA: I won't forgive you.

VIKTOR KHARITONYCH: Whore!

POLINA NIKANOROVNA: Shut up! I'll . . . I'll fuck you with
my bristling tit to kingdom come!

VIKTOR KHARITONYCH: Such a thing's impossible.

POLINA NIKANOROVNA: It's possible.

VIKTOR KHARITONYCH: (*uncertainly*) Impossible.

POLINA NIKANOROVNA: (*making a threatening gesture*) It's
possible.

VIKTOR KHARITONYCH: Go away! I'll kill you!

POLINA NIKANOROVNA: Forgive me.

VIKTOR KHARITONYCH: I won't forgive you!

POLINA NIKANOROVNA: Vitya!

VIKTOR KHARITONYCH: What do you mean, Vitya?

POLINA NIKANOROVNA: Vitya . . .

VIKTOR KHARITONYCH: (*relenting*) Oh, you bitch!

And as they draw together, moving toward an intimate rap-
prochement, I stir on the director's couch, letting them know
that I've come around and am conscious during their verbal

defecation, and they fix their gaze upon me and see that I'm coming to life, and Polina Nikanorovna, pleased for her own reasons with my recovery, explains to Viktor Kharitonych that, she says, there had been no need for him to worry and they hadn't gone over the top at all but had acted according to plan. And Viktor Kharitonych takes himself in hand and starts to look a lot better, but I say in a weak voice that I want to go home, and they don't object and look at me joyfully, as at a fait accompli, and Viktor Kharitonych calms down completely and doesn't squabble with Polina any longer but chats with her gallantly and is very pleased with himself, because everything's going according to plan, no deviations or twists or turns. And I lick my dry lips and scowl at Polina and say that perhaps she'll leave us and that I would like to have a private word with Viktor Kharitonych, but Viktor Kharitonych is embarrassed by my request and, using the late hour as an excuse, suggests that they find a car for me and transport me to my place of residence, and he himself hides behind Polina, and Polina looks at me as at a squashed animal that's been run over, with a fastidious air, and I lie there, weak because I'd lost consciousness, and I'm slow on the uptake, although I know that Viktor Kharitonych is not *really* a bad man and that they'd pressured him, but I also know that she would have done it all on her own initiative, and even more! That is, she would even have killed me; but he's pleased too, because everything went smoothly. Well, I stood up, straightened my clothes, and, without saying a single unpleasant word to them, left to find a taxi, and outside there is warm rain, evening, people are out strolling, almost happy, and having looked around on all sides first, Stanislav Albertovich comes up to me stealthily—he'd been hiding somewhere in a shop or under an archway, where the stamp dealers had woven their nest—he comes up, shielding himself with a black umbrella, and suggests that we clarify our situation, and I remember vaguely that he had made compromising speeches about me and had even shaken his fist, which wasn't at all the sort of behavior you expect from a medical man: but he keeps asking me not so much to understand as to hear him out, and hints that he'd been waiting for me a long time, and that whatever I might think, it took courage to wait for me and to offer to take my hand and take me home when there was a cloud over me, and I feel ill, and I'm even swaying on my feet, but he explains that he'd fallen upon very hard times, exceptional circumstances, and asks me to understand, and if I can't understand, then at least to note his agitation. And I don't argue at all, only I'm not interested in him at the moment. I feel that crucial changes are setting in and, as Viktor Kharitonych said, fate-deciding days, and where will you advise me to go, not to Granddaddy's, I hope, who, however, has vanished in this rain, and where can I go and what can I do, and I don't listen to Stanislav Albertovich's conversation, but I get into a taxi and give my address, leaving Flavitsky beneath his black umbrella on the slippery slabs, in the middle of his confessions, and what are they to me—well, I'm not against them, but he won't help, and who will come forth to defend me? This was what was occupying me as I proceeded through the city, growing faint and coming back to life, now sweating, now shivering, because I don't remember how long I'd spent unconscious, and I find it difficult to say where it started, and indeed has it finished? Because it was the thought that they hated me which brought the loss of consciousness and memory crashing down on me, since to be hated was a new experience for me; no, of course there were previous occasions, but never anything like that, everyone clapping as I fell into a faint, and Nina Chizh handing vanilla puff pastries to everyone but not giving me one, except where am I going? But all the same I went home, because I wanted to have it out first with Granddaddy, Tikhon Makarovich, and find out where everything was heading, and only then to slam the door behind me, but I didn't feel like thinking for the moment, because I'd become very tired from the unexpectedness of it all, and my hands weren't obeying me, and there were ringing noises and strange cries inside my head, and I understand why they had called me to the meeting, but all the same they could have warned me. As it was, it turned out clumsy and unprepared—well, if Viktor Kharitonych had summoned me and said, We'll take you to task and dismiss you, and you weep a bit and suffer a bit in front of everyone, as is stipulated, I'd have done so with pleasure, I'm prepared, I would have wept and confessed immediately, but they didn't even want to hear me out but started yelling from all sides, and unknown people had their say, and even that general, as if I'd done business with him, but you see there wasn't anything of the sort. And he adored the submissive doggy-style pose, and if I could just explain the situation to him, if I could just make it home—and here I notice for the first time that everything somehow lacks solidity and is shaky, and it's impossible to distinguish the taxi from my feeling of grievance, or the whisper of the cutters from my own hands and hair, and I decide not to try to solve this serious matter, these fabrications like the one about the general, but I come home to Granddaddy's, unlock the door, and think: Now I'll really give it to him, and he stands in the kitchen, at the stove, wearing a red polka-dot apron, and fries cod, but as soon as he sees me he beams and comes toward me, but I answer him coolly that I don't understand these displays of affection, and he ought not to be quite so happy, because after all he is family. And he responds that he's got good reason for rejoicing, he's pleased to see me alive and well, which means that his forecasts

had been borne out and his wishes had come true, and just
when he was about to get quite depressed, because it was late
and I hadn't come home— But I say to him, Why did you
leave me, then? And what do you mean by forecasts? But he
answers me, Let's instead, Iruniya, have a celebratory drink,
and dives into the fridge and pulls out a half-liter bottle of
Kubanskaya vodka with a screw top and puts it on the table,
and on the table are appetizers—little cucumbers and tomatoes, sprats, cervelat smoked sausage, and the cod is sizzling
on the stove, and I say to him, Are you out of your mind,
you old bastard? What celebration? They're kicking me out
of here as hard as they can, and I'm flying ass-over-tit deep
into the interior to go cuckoo, cuckoo, and he says, Is it worth
getting upset about? Is that what happiness is all about? You
see, everything turned out all right! I say, You must be joking!
My dear, he answers, as if I don't know something about
life—but as if I don't know something about life! Only we
know it in different ways, and he radiates pessimism, looking
at me now anxiously, now respectfully, and hints that he is
up-to-date on all the latest events and that the underlying
cause of the obituary had been illuminated for him, and in
the light of such a revelation he found it strange to see me
sad, and I say, "Why should I be happy, when my granddaddy
is doing such a good job of denouncing me?" And he is amazed:
"You're saying that I informed on you, when I was shielding
you with my every word!" And I say to him, "So why, then,
you old scumbag, didn't you say anything to me in advance?
This morning, even, so that I could have been prepared and
dressed differently—no beads, at any rate, and not in Ksyusha's dress, but just any old way, like a nun," and he says, "It
had to be done that way!" "Who for?" "What do you mean,
who for?" I don't understand him, I go on trying to get the
truth out of him: why had he played such a low-down trick?

He doesn't understand, he says; with all his soul, right from the start, he'd demanded that I be shielded from any charges, that was the deal they'd agreed to and that was why he'd gone, that was why it had all ended so gloriously, although, he says, I have lost touch a bit with modern life and can't understand why they gave you so much license, and I didn't understand all the words, though I tried, and I say, "But why did you make that speech?" and he says, "And how could I not make a speech, if I'm a responsible member of society and want to live life a bit and don't wish you any ill, and as for my little speech," he says, "I chucked it into the john, how do you like that?" "I don't like it," I say. "Well, you're wrong to be like that," he answers, "for it was originally much harsher and more offensive, and I didn't like it. I thought and thought, you know, and threw it into the crapper this morning, and then I end up looking like a fool, a doddering old man, and I put on my medals and badges to impress them, so they'd know I was somebody too!" "They wanted to spit on your rusty medals!" I say. "You'd do better to explain why you went and spoke, without warning me." "Oh," he says, "you don't understand a thing; let's have a drink instead." Well, I think, if he has a drink he'll tell, but I'm wondering: He says he didn't denounce me, but look at what he said! "A pool of blood, eh? Isn't that denouncing?" He says, "I made it up about the blood because I was scared: They're all looking at me and waiting, but everything I'm saying concerns trivial private matters, and I worry that they'll lose their temper with me for breaking the agreement, and we'll both suffer. "But now," he says, "please come and visit when you want to; they'll keep an eye out for a year or two and then get fed up. I'll get used to having you around again, and as for their sacking you—" "What do you mean, sacking?" "Didn't you know?" "No," I say, "I don't know anything—I was fighting faintness and nausea." "Well, there you are," he says. "You're not well, but you still go off gallivanting and get involved in all sorts of escapades. I was right not to want to have you living here, but you swore on your parents' health, I knew then that all this would end badly, and so it has, although you, of course, flew high, if everything about Vladimir Sergeyevich is the truth, who, I will inform you, once shook my hand at a rally of shock workers, when I was still an uneducated person and didn't know how to take my temperature and crushed the thermometer in my bed. I'd ended up in the hospital from overfulfilling the plan, and when I recovered I learned that I'd fulfilled the quota of one hundred fifty Negro laborers on my own, and that's how I strained myself, and everyone made ecstatic noises, approving the Molotov-Ribbentrop pact, and when they started congratulating me, Vladimir Sergeyevich shook my hand as an honored guest, and now it transpires that you too knew him. . . ."

I downed half a glass of vodka, in order to get warm, but I didn't want to tell him anything, and indeed, he didn't insist; on the contrary, he became tipsy and launched into a story. He said he'd taken more care with himself for the rest of his career, and therefore stayed alive, because he'd always been satisfied with little and, thank God, had lived a life quite different from some, who soared high and fell painfully, but he'd lived, he hadn't worn his fingers to the bone and no one had ever done him dirt, and that while the paperwork from the hearing is still incomplete I can stay with him a few days longer, but after that, of course, I'll have to pack my bags and take myself off, that was their agreement, but for the moment sit and eat—look, have some pickled mushrooms, I opened them specially. He poured out some drink: Let's drink! He downed it and got cross-eyed drunk. "You're a bastard all the same," I said to him in a tired voice. "I'm a bastard?" Granddaddy said, livening up after the vodka. "They're the bastards, they, the darlings, they're the scoundrels, although it's not for us, sinners, to judge, but nevertheless bastards, oh, bastards, though not total bastards. . . . So they kicked you out of work! I, my dear, asked them right out: 'What are you planning to do with her?' This is what we intend, they answer: we'll sack her. That's as it should be, I answer, and then what? And they say, We don't have any other plans. What's that, I say, not really believing them, *only* sack her? Yes, they answer, but you must help us, so that there won't be sight or sound of her in Moscow! Well, then, I answer, I'll help; throw her out on her ear for the sake of the blessed memory of Vladimir Sergeyevich, who once shook my hand in the Hall of Columns and whom I've respected ever since, boot her out of work and out of Moscow, there's nothing for her in Moscow, get rid of her! But I think to myself: Just look what we've come to! A saboteur is made redundant." Granddaddy laughed drunkenly. "They sack her and don't touch her, like under Nikolai! This is what we've come to, I think, but all the same I can't believe it; I open the little mushrooms but think: Yet it's rather late . . ." "What do you mean by 'don't touch'!" I yell in a weak but vicious tone. "Some don't touch! Exiling me from Moscow!" "Stupid girl!" Granddaddy laughs, and his glasses flash merrily. "Can you really call that touching you? Iruniya, you're not being serious!" He waves a fork with an impaled mushroom in my direction. "I don't want to hear another word!"

We had another drink, and both of us were already nice and warm, both Granddaddy, flashing the lenses of his antediluvian horn-rimmed spectacles, and me, somewhat exhausted after this whole episode. But wait! I said to Granddaddy. I'll still show that Viktor Kharitonych! But Granddaddy wasn't listening, because he himself wanted to reminisce, and he always reminisced about the same old thing, how in one shift he fulfilled the quota of one hundred fifty Negro laborers, how he ended up in the hospital and didn't know where to put the thermometer and squashed it under the blanket in his great embarrassment, and he tried to catch the little puddles of mercury in his hands, and how he once put an ice cream in the pocket of his canvas trousers when he and Granny were at the zoo and how the chocolate ice had melted in his pocket and he hadn't noticed. "But how didn't you notice?" I always marveled. "I just didn't; I got carried away by the animals . . . and Granny swore at me afterwards. . . ." "Was she a real bitch, then?" I ask, because I always disliked women who are hysterical bitches, who are fussy about housework and get mad as hell when they do the washing and ironing. "There was some of that too," Granddaddy agrees evasively, but returns to the events in the Hall of Columns. "This is what I wanted to tell you," said Granddaddy. "I didn't like *your* Vladimir Sergeyevich when he shook my hand as an honored guest. I just didn't like him, and that's that! And I shook his hand without any pleasure, although he was, of course, an exceptional man and he held out his hand to me first." "Well, so you didn't like him, and good riddance!" I said pacifically. "That's fine!" I was weak, because we had knocked back a whole bottle of vodka, and I was recovering from my fainting fit, and I felt ill, and he and I drank to the earth becoming as soft as feathers so that Vladimir Sergeyevich might rest in peace. But I had seen many men, including Viktor Kharitonych, at their most defenseless, because I had entered history by the back door, and I always wondered what would have happened if I had suddenly shut my teeth on them, snap! But Granddaddy reckoned that they were all, these celebrities, inveterate drunkards and debauchees, for him even visiting a restaurant constituted debauchery, and he wanted me to agree with him about this, and I was slightly drunk and didn't argue, but all the same, he said, "I've lost touch with modern ways, and although I understood everything when they accused you, there was one thing I didn't get: *lesbian*. What sort of new label is this they're sticking on people?"

I didn't bother to explain, I brushed this aside, saying it's another pack of lies, and went to my room as quickly as possible. Granddaddy hadn't convinced me. I didn't want to leave Moscow. I adore Moscow! I toppled onto my bed and fell asleep.

# THIRTEEN

M y boy is beating under my heart. Pulsing away. I am getting used to him. N.B. I must think about disposable diapers, pacifiers, talcum powder, and, finally, a pram. A few days ago on Tverskoi Boulevard I saw a denim pram. I want one like that! Someday he'll crush you all with his little finger. I haven't got time to write. I'm knitting a little blanket.

The world isn't as small and cramped as it's said to be. Sometimes you stretch yourself, spread your arms—and living is possible. But after the meeting, everything of mine that could go to pieces did. Even Rituyla was somewhat afraid. By the way, where was she during the meeting? Ill or something? Rituyla said that she was put on the carpet because of me. She was summoned to see Viktor Kharitonych, and he frightened her. Round and round the garden, like a teddy bear. Ooo! Rituyla cried out, cowering in a corner. Polina started making barbed comments too, but Rituyla told me that she'll get married and stop working, because it's harmful for a woman to work.

Rituyla won't come to grief. She has licked her shameful wounds clean and is planning to bankrupt an Armenian called Hamlet. This is a pity, because if they all start calling themselves Hamlet, where is the real Hamlet? Rituyla will ruin him, that's certain; she's already started: I've seen a ruby ring. She'd been boasting and said that Hamlet is not against my being pregnant (Rituyla was now burning with curiosity); it's all the same to him.

My cunning granddaddy thought up a way to escape during the night. He checked himself into the hospital. I started phoning around then, just in case, because Viktor Kharito-nych had turned down a private talk. (You're the worst shit, Vitenka; as soon as you want me to give you head you call me, but when I need to have a heart-to-heart for the only time in my life, you just talk through your ass!) I started to phone, but they all held their tongues and did nothing, and everything I had went to pieces. Even Shokhrat, with whom I'd flown around the Muslim minarets in a YAK-40, such a pretty little plane, and it had all started because Shokhrat was staying in a neighboring room in Sochi, where we were on tour, and Rituyla was there too, and I had got into the habit of doing gymnastics on a spacious balcony, and Shokhrat ob-served me from his luxury suite and was dying to get into my room, overcome with anticipation at getting to know me, but a slit-eye is a slit-eye, he expects everything on the spot, he throws his money around and flings cognac on the table and sweet cantaloupes, because he's a rich landowner and impa-tient, and what do our little men have to offer?

And it was then that I thought: Why do they all look as though they're hypnotized? Why do they go around looking downcast and as if they've shat their pants, despite their moral superiority? Has someone put a spell on them? And Veronika says, "Have you ever had dreams about a rapist?" And I say, "My dear! I have dreams like that every night," and she says, "Well, then, listen to me," and Shokhrat answers in a voice from the other side, his words, "till better times," and he'd got wind of something, big-eared, big-lipped, big-nosed, slit-eyed, and hairy even on his back—I don't like that but some-times had to put up with it: a little wild boar—and then I phoned Gavleyev, and he said that he'd definitely call back as soon as he returned from his business trip, but he didn't return from his business trip, but how he loved the pose of doggy submissiveness! And I started to drag them all out of the dressing table and shook them out; they'd been reflected in the dressing-table mirror as if by a floodlight, one at a time and grouped variously, marked cards, a pack of jacks, aces, kings, but they all thought I was threatening them, though I was asking them for advice, that's all, and I didn't want to go to my father the cabinetmaker, and Viktor Kharitonych, with his sweaty face, said nothing and told Rituyla, "Don't be friends with her!" But as for sleeping with Rituyla—he didn't, or else they're both lying, I don't know, you can't fathom Rituyla, she's crafty, but all the same she didn't totally aban-don me, she used to visit in the evenings, she even shed a few tears, but in answer to the question What is to be done? she would just part her young hands in despair. According to her, I should go to my native village and be a sort of first lady there, shining with the charms of late summer, but I was the picture of health, a real classy chassis, full of the joys of spring, although, of course, my healthy curves had got somewhat tired, although as usual I resisted wearing a bra, I can't bear them, they're unpleasant, they're unnecessary. However, I had to put one on. Like a muzzle. I'm a pregnant woman, and if you don't like the thought of what it is I'm expecting, please don't imagine that I shall take any notice of your threats. I'll give birth to such a baby for you, hatch such a little egg—you'll break your teeth on it!

Oh, he's moving! . . . Get on with it! Get on with it!

(I'm knitting a little blanket.)

On the following day, Granddaddy went out into the front

garden, and I saw from behind the curtain how he was chatting with the old farts of the neighborhood and expressing amazement at the changes he'd encountered. "You'd hardly believe how times have changed!" he declared, staring closely at the domino players. "You'd hardly believe it!" And he became distressed and worked up, in his patriotic way. "If it continues in this vein, we'll go under at the next cataclysm! The things that are happening!"

He circled the domino players, perplexed and worried, but after lunch, pleading heart problems, he ordered an ambulance, he packed his pajamas, his worn-down slippers, his razor, his old-fashioned phrase "Yes, I hear you," and a package of his favorite Jubilee biscuits into his knapsack, and his face went haggard, he started to snort, the moment the white coats were glimpsed in the doorway, he really overacted, and they carted him off, to the howl of sirens, as if he were about to die; he didn't even wink at me as he left. I remained alone with the dressing-table mirror, and the telephone fell silent, as if it had been disconnected, and only Rituyla visited, but she's not much use, and I wasn't in any mood to think about caresses, and I didn't feel like listening to her about how Viktor Kharitonych was planning to rise rapidly in the world on the basis of the incident with me, because everything had worked out beautifully for him, and he was due for a reward, and Polina had been on the point of scheming against Kharitonych, hoping to battle the young cutters to take over his chair as director, but she had been caught with her fingers in the cookie jar, and it was simple for Viktor Kharitonych to straighten her out, and she—Rituyla choked with laughter— had groveled to him, but it made no difference to me at all, and I didn't even want to try to get reinstated in their vile company, although I hadn't heard anything from them, they didn't even send me a note saying I'd been sacked.

I've been sacked, that's final, and I need to sit and think

what my next move will be, but the telephone doesn't ring, and when I felt like relaxing a bit after recent events, Shokhrat had shelved me until better times, Carlos had been shot in the torture chambers, and Dato—well, what good is Dato: he spends eight months on tour, and as soon as he returns he's always busy, practices his instruments, doesn't utter a single tender word—there's a potential husband for you! I rejoiced that I didn't have such an unreliable man as a husband, who's never there when you need him. And as soon as they had taken Granddaddy away, I decided to tell Ksyusha my troubles, to describe my calamitous situation; I started to write her a letter, in which I described everything and lamented her absence, and before I had even started looking for her answer, my true friend calls from an international public telephone at Fontainebleau station, where there is a pear orchard and Napoleon, and tells me to hang in there, because she'll be with me soon, she loves me, and I must not get depressed, though of course that's impossible. And behold: she does arrive, full of grievances about life abroad, about expatriate Russians, with whom she's quarreled, and she's also quarreled with her Spaniard, the accountant, although in general she thinks highly of Spaniards, more highly indeed than of most, and she's dissatisfied with everything, but, she cuts herself short, enough about that, let's talk about you. And I start to explain to her all about Granddaddy and the mythical pool of blood, and she listened with the undivided attention of a loving girlfriend, having laid my desecrated head on her shoulder, and I complained to her in tears, which I washed down with Martini, like a humiliated child, but she kept trying to comfort me and once again recalled Koktebel, the luxuriant nights and bright days, and we sighed, like two bald menopausal women, but suddenly she looked at me with her intelligent eyes, such as you don't see every day, she looked (I'm writing, and on the radio they're playing "Rhapsody in Blue" by Gershwin) so attentively and merrily that I understood: She's thought of something, and so she had, only she didn't know whether I would agree, because while, of course, I had nothing to lose, there might still be some things to lose, and I said, I've got absolutely nothing to lose, and I don't want to return to my native dump because I know that all the dark storerooms there are full of sauerkraut with mold crawling over it, and she was overjoyed: "Let's kill ourselves together, at the same hour— you in your native town and I in the settlement, which you don't know, of Fontainebleau on the French railway, because Frenchmen are so arrogant and shitty, and they think that no one is better than them, but Spaniards, for example, are un-doubtedly better, even though I quarreled with my accountant just three hours before our trip together to Granada"—doesn't she get everywhere! but that's not the point. "Let's, Sunny, kill ourselves, for you see, I'm sick of putting up with that dentist of mine, my patience has completely run out, or else I'll poison him, I'm Madame Bovary! But if we don't poison ourselves with arsenic, then I have an idea that," she says, "may seem extreme to you." And she recalls the photo that my mother discovered in the bookcase, in the collected works of Jack London, when, after the restaurant in Ar-changelskoye—where it was, as always, rather noisy and tiring, and they served tough elk meat, and the place reeked of officers' messy debaucheries—I went as a guest to a stranger's apartment, and there a Polaroid captured me in interesting company, and when Mummy saw it, I thought she'd shout, What the hell is this? because to look at she's a typical cleaning woman with deep-set eyes and a frizzy perm and three-ruble earrings bought in a tobacconist's, but she didn't shout, she looked at it not exactly with approval but without horror and said, "Very interesting . . . ," and looked again, and I, of

course, got slightly embarrassed, and then Dato took the photo
with him to all his countries, so that I, you might say, have
traveled around the world in his wallet. Ksyusha asks, "What
if . . . ?" and suggests to me an intricate plan, because as it
is things are so bad, and I say, "We have to think this through
carefully, because the scandal," I say, "is very great already;
I've found that out to my own cost and I don't want a repeat,"
and Ksyusha says, "Do you want to return to your amazing
daddy? No. I thought not." I say, "But who needs me?" Although, I insist, I remain a beauty, my nerves are bad, coffee
makes me feverish, I'm tired, and my soul longs for ordered
family life, but where is it, this life? And Ksyusha says, "It's
up to you, but it's turned out that you're more widowed than
the real widow, Zinaida Vasilievna, because she has the dacha
and filthy Antosha, but you're left looking like a perfect fool,
and the years have flown by to no avail, and in addition people
are persecuting you, Sunny, that's not nice at all," and I
look—she's become a complete Frenchwoman, and this was
her final visit, because afterward they would call her, without
any justification whatsoever, a spy, and Sergei and Nikolai
Ivanovich, the two journalists, questioned me in great detail
about her: "Who," they say, "is this Ksenya Mochulskaya,
your best friend?" And I say, "She was a friend at one time,"
covering up like this, because it's all the same to Ksyusha, of
course, she's far away; in another world, she strolls around
the pear orchard, and birds sing over her head, but I'm with
the Ivanovich brothers, only they are fakes: one is towheaded,
with blemished skin, but the other is a very thoughtful type
and understands everything. I don't deny our friendship, but
I hurry to offer them something to drink, only suddenly the
pensive one agrees, the pensive Ivanovich, but the towheaded
one (it's they who wrote that totally obscure article about
love), this second one says, No, thank you, in a cold voice,

and they looked accusingly at each other, because they hadn't agreed what each was to say, and I say, "Forget this nonsense, boys! Have a drink," and at the same time I look over my shoulder and admire myself in the notorious little magazine; overcoming their embarrassment, I manage to look at what they have brought, and I'll say it straight: It came out well! I enjoyed it myself!

And so then it was that we started to think.

And Ksyusha had a friend who was a real professional, he had respected her very much even in Moscow and, to my mind, not without success, though he had different tendencies when it came to relationships. . . . Well, I have no bad feelings as far as that's concerned, they're almost one of us, only Ksyusha says, "You know what? There's no point in your being alone, now that you've suffered; there are plenty of people who will sympathize," but I say, "They've all deserted the sinking ship and are sitting in their corners, quiet as mice; there isn't even anyone to sleep with, and those that are left are really small fry, they don't count; and as for the ones who do count, this is the situation . . ." "Okay," she says, "you do have, then, such friends," and she asks me if I have seen Merzlyakov recently, with whom at one time a six-day love impetuously raised its head, only to finish in a tepid friendship, and we ended up screwing only once every six months, like old-time landowners. Well, there you are, says Ksyusha, that's good, and I had thought too that it would be possible to phone, and I started to, but he has a wife, and I don't like involving people, unlike Rituyla, who actually infected her Japanese wheeler-dealer, and he rushed right back to Japan, but before that there'd been various erotic binges, but I don't like getting people involved, Ksyusha knows, and I didn't involve Ksyusha either, the Ivanoviches worked out who Ksyusha was themselves, they racked their brains and worked it out. They ask me, "It was her, wasn't it?" And I say, "In any event, I've got nothing to do with it," and I say to them, "But what, strictly speaking, is all the fuss about?" I say, "Did I really reveal something that isn't mine to show for all to see, instead of something that's intimately close to my skin?" "No," they say, "it's beautiful, no denying it, you can tell at once that an expert took the photographs." I say, "I took them myself." They don't believe me. But I don't care. And Ksyusha's friend comes then, kind X, rippling folds of corduroy, and Ksyusha too, and on the eve of that day I'd phoned Vitasik, and he'd hinted that he'd look in somehow, and Ksyusha says to me, "Don't tell him everything at once, you should simply get friendly with him once more; she loved constructing all sorts of combinations. And how are things," she asks, "between you and Veronika?" "Okay, except she's a witch; she won't help me." "Why?" says Ksyusha, amazed. "it's quite conceivable that she can, only later." But for now let X come, X arrives, with his glorious foreign equipment, and Ksyusha says to me, "It's important to sustain the mood. What," she says, "is your mood?" "You yourself know," and she says, "that means something very mournful; that's always intriguing," and I tell her how I put on my black rags for my farewell to Leonardik. "Only," I worry, "won't it make me look irretrievably old?" "Really, Sunny," says Ksyusha, "you are an absolute fool, because you're still ooh-la-la!" And I say, "Very well," and I fetch the pathetic dress, and X circles as if nothing has happened and chatters chatters chatters, like a surgeon before an operation, and I'm not all bottled up inside, indeed I'm familiar with this line of business, I understand: a certain sad something has to be achieved, something lyrical without, adds Ksyusha, that parade of optimism which is obligatory in America, where they make fun of clever people and say to them: "If you're so clever, how come you're so poor?" X chortled.

"That's the type of saying," says Ksyusha joyfully, "which is current in America, and if they buy some little book or other and read it, then they quickly start putting on airs, like in the joke about the militiaman, and in addition," says Ksyusha, "they are very sweet and sincere, even generous—true, not all of them, but on the other hand very sincere: stupid, *excellent* people—" "Excellent!" echoes X in agreement, scrutinizing me gently. "A bit lower! Lower! Ex-cell-ent!" "—because in contrast to people with various complexes, they don't hide their stupidity—" "Just one more!" asks X. "Well," I say, "with us they don't hide them very deeply either, but what about in the realm of love?" "There," admits Ksyusha, "sincerity helps them." "And is it true," inquires X, "that they have male stripteases there?" Ksyusha is overcome with laughter. "Stop it," says X angrily. "You'll spoil the whole mood." Ksyusha stops at once. But whether sincerity is a virtue—she's not sure of that, "because at best—" "Open your mouth a little . . . that's it . . ." "Ksyusha, talk about something sad, about the danger of smoking or about cancer of the breast." "—because at best this is an adorning of virtue," and it seems to me that Ksyusha has become totally Frenchified: she goes into great detail over things, and she even enjoyed boarding her Air France plane to go back, it was as if she were already home, and René traveled to the States to give lectures and also despised them all there, but they said to him, "Know what? If you treat us with such contempt, then next time, when the need arises, we won't liberate your dear France; sit there in the shit," and he took offense and says, "They are complete boors here; get your things ready, *ma chatte,* we're going home." "But," she writes in a letter, "they treat Russians well on the whole, although they know zilch, because, as I said, they are very stupid people, but otherwise not bad; they know what's what in love, although they date in a strange

way: on a date they talk about science fiction books and go
to films about flying saucers, and they go wild over all sorts
of crap, and I'm not sure whether such a nation can grow any
wiser under the conditions of its stupid democracy, because,
my Sunny, Irina Vladimirovna, their democracy has numerous
defects, concerning which I shall inform you on another occasion, or not write at all, because you, most likely, couldn't
give a shit about their democracy." I answer, "In this, dear
Ksyusha, you're pretty close to the truth; I don't get involved
in politics not only because I don't understand anything about
it but also because I don't see any sense in it, just unpleas-
antness, actually my life is full of events as it is, but with
regard to the Americans I'm not in agreement with you, insofar
as a stupid nation can't put a man on the moon or print such
a beautiful magazine as *America*"—I have a subscription to
*America* thanks to my Viktor Kharitonych, who has a large
choice of utterly essential acquaintances, from a bathhouse
attendant to a jeweler, and in this way wins your favor, but
this was before his disgraceful behavior—"and as far as your
arguments about America are concerned, well now, when the
best women of that country have stood up for me . . ." "But
they don't remember, because every day they're supporting
someone else!" says Ksyusha sarcastically. "Not true!" I frown.
"They remember me very well indeed! And it wasn't for nothing that millions of Americans went into raptures over my
natural charms and beat their meat with my photos in front
of them, and so what if they don't read books, in contrast to
you or me, Ksyusha—let reading books be a Russian custom,
the only result of which is that one's head aches and years
pass—no, Ksyusha, while America is jerking off over me, over
my funeral accessories, I'm not planning to change my attitude
toward America, and you as a Frenchwoman live by your
ideals!" And at this point the photographer X says that he

likes our scam and that he won't permit any vulgarity but he'll do it all *comme il faut,* on a high artistic level, worthy, for example, of Renoir. "Oh, no you won't, thank you very much," I objected. "Those fat-assed and big-titted lumps, like defrosted Eskimos, leave them in the past. You take another approach and remember: my beauty is Russian!" And Ksyusha Mochulskaya, my Ksyusha, says, "Yours is truly, Sunny, a national beauty! But Americans," she adds, "are stupid nonetheless. Once in Chicago I watched a program on TV about how a polar bear was brought to a zoo, and they were all discussing the polar bear, discussed it for ages and ages, and still had lots to say." But the photographer X, born in the theatrical city of Leningrad, says, "Good, I know what I've got to do!" "Just don't be embarrassed," says Ksyusha, but why should I be embarrassed? my goods have never gathered dust on the shelf, and Ksyusha says, "And then we'll drink and have a good time," and the photographer says, "Definitely."

With his sleeves rolled up and his corduroy jacket thrown off, he arranged the lamps and placed the floodlights and illuminated my mature beauty and magnificence, and Ksyusha covered her gasps with her hand, amazed at the secret splendor, and the dispassionate professional is dumbfounded, as he composed the story of the true widow's loneliness, her bashful attempts to soothe her nerves in front of the dressing-table mirror, where the trophy perfumes stand jumbled with cans of hairspray, and my reflected background is the roaring gas water heater, which will amaze the masturbator over the seas with its radical construction, and I open up, and my black stockings rise sheer into the air, and I glance back in the half twilight, greeting the joyous reader, and I weep, and I lament, remembering my spouse, who passed on before his time, but look, my cheek has already blushed red from solitary torment, and my uneven breathing is getting faster and faster, and my inflamed eyes have half closed, eyes dimmed with tears and perfume, and the red-brown fox fur of my coat ignites in a mad blaze of color, and the gaping wound announces that I, a widow winged by a shot, remember too the kindness of my spouse and remain true to it, but life continues, despite the sad accessories, the jumble of outfits and the sickness of the green eyes, which suddenly become dove-gray, love-gray, lone-gray, and again the American customer is amazed, not understanding Russian transformations, and so on, until the humming gas heater takes me under its flammable protection, and the rivulets of water cascade off my woodland beauties: there the wild raspberry ripens alongside wild chervil, there the scent of pine needles, and there a hot silence, the meander of a river and a steep bank, grown over with pines, whose tenacious roots resemble the five fingers of a pianist, oh, my Dato! but the water heater hums and gives off a heat that will never replace for me the kindness of a spouse, who perished from the tremble of romantic days, seized by a passionate spasm as old and high as Russia's Valdai Hills—Russia, whose essence the Marquis de Custine in his travels of 1839 couldn't understand, no matter how hard he tried, but life goes on, water pours, and soap slips through the fingers, and the rickety stool dances, and if my melancholy yearning is not passing and won't pass, then nevertheless the pain is dying down, the swallowed pill dissolves from a bitter medicine into a sweet heat haze, no need to hide one's tears, let them flow in an even and radiant stream! And the black and sheer stockings, without lace trimming, stand like the black frame of an obituary notice, and through the fabric of the mourning rags shines a meandering light, a dusty and winding road, with the light of sunset, drowning in white sheets, black and white, white and black, and only my hair is on friendly terms with the red fox fur, and lifting my hair with the tips of my fingers, spreading and lifting, up, up, I mourn.

X twisted and turned in search of fleeing moments of
beauty. Ksyusha looked at me with such a surge of love that
it couldn't help imprinting itself as an ethereal patch of light
in the photographs. Ksyusha even flashed by in one of them
in the role of a comforting angel, flying down to earth to bring
tidings that my spouse had been delivered safe and sound, and
we embraced, and she buried her angelic face in my hair, and
only her breasts breathed, with their touching asymmetry, and
the brothers, pointing at the breasts, put the question: "Isn't
that Ksenya Mochulskaya, who has swapped citizenships? Irina
Vladimirovna! That, forgive us, hardly becomes you, although
we have no formal objections." "And since you don't have
them," I said, "then let's have a drink, boys," and the twins
drank some cognac and on the whole I liked them, good
fellows, and they were disposed to hear me out very attentively, only they got totally and irrevocably mad at Ksyusha,
but the photographer X was completely satisfied, and we
started to wait for the contact prints like schoolgirls, and I
sang Ksyusha new couplets about gypsies:


> Gypsies love vengefully
> Hard foreign currency . . .


and we cruised around in the pink car, frightening the passersby, and the prints were ready in time, and they were
magnificent, and we shouted for joy, these amazing pictures
were so beautiful, and Ksyusha demanded that X hand over
the negatives, and he parted with them regretfully and got a
fat sum, although he'd done it as a friend, but he put the
blame on his debts and uncertain circumstances, inasmuch as
he had just broken up with his wife on matters of principle,
but unexpectedly love for his family was returning to him,
love of small children, too late, however, and he, sorrowful,

set off for his historic city, taking the secret with him, begging us not to give him away, and no one would ever know.

I saw Ksyusha off on her journey too, and to the question "How did your beauty end up there?" I answered honestly, "I don't have a clue," because I can't begin to guess how, "but I was against this, because a beautiful woman, boys, is a national treasure, and not simply cheap trade for export—there are plenty of fans of such stuff here too," including Viktor Kharitonych, who had passed them to the West. And they say, "We need Russian beauties!" and I, laughing a bit: "I should say so!" and they look at me with interest, and I suggest, "Let's be friends!" They say, "Why not? And who is this?" And they finger Ksyusha, whose intelligent little face is in my hair, and I say, "What difference does it make? Just someone I know. . . ." But they say, "Isn't this Ksenya Mochulskaya, a shady lady?" "What? If you consider Ksyusha Mochulskaya a shady lady, then show me a sunny one!" And I also say, "If you really need to find the guilty party, who caused all this confusion, then have you heard of a certain Viktor Kharitonych?" In this way I set out to denounce him, not out of revenge, but because it was wrong to kick me when I was down and mock me when I lost consciousness and then afterward not even explain himself! And the reason was that he was afraid Polina—do you know Polina? —would expose him as my lover, only not everyone you sleep with is a lover, and, boys, I felt doubly insulted, because one shouldn't treat people like that, but they do.

Ksyusha quickly set the ball rolling in a big way (will I ever see you again, my one and only?), but friendship is friendship, though the Ivanoviches nevertheless put it very nicely: wouldn't it be better for me to catch my breath and abandon the struggle and go to my native region, far from the jeering crowds and the widow's wrath of Zinaida Vasilievna, who, they admit, is a tough cookie, but I say, "What next! On what grounds! I *loved* Vladimir Sergeyevich, and I'm not planning to suffer for love." They knitted their brows. "You say: 'for *love?*' " "What do you think?" And I also say that if I'm insulted, I can't guarantee how I'll react, and I hint that there are some other photographs, preserved in a safe locale, this time with both me and him, because, you know, he was full of ideas, as the autopsy revealed. Yes, we know, say the brothers, only you really shouldn't dangle in front of us, Irina Vladimirovna, something that has never existed. "Well," I say, "maybe for some it doesn't exist, but for others it can be found," in an icy voice, and I don't offer them more cognac, but they say eagerly, "There's no need to be like that, Irina Vladimirovna, but really, go back, go and have a rest, the town's no worse than many others, because even though Vladimir Sergeyevich is an important man, insinuations of that type would cause irreparable harm to his memory and all trace of him would quickly disappear, and do you really want to aid in such a thing? Far better that we *all* should remember him and honor his remarkable achievements. . . ." I see: the boys before me are not stupid, and I pour them each another glass.

In the meantime, Vitasik is introducing me to some new friends, almost all of them Jews, which disconcerted me, though several admitted warm respect for my daring, and I never feared anything, only Yura Fyodorov kept trying to badmouth me, despite the magazine, and Ksyusha had reached an agreement with them very quickly, so that their widely circulated magazine comes out, the delight of endless male readers, and pride of place and the centerfold is given to me, with all my photos—such a mournful composition—and some odd facts about me, including:

NAME—Irina Vladimirovna Tarakanova
BUST—36 [for some reason in inches; the statistics are
    false: Ksyusha took them off the top of her head]

WAIST—24
HIPS—36
HEIGHT—172 cm
WEIGHT—55 kg [now grown fatter]
SIGN OF THE ZODIAC—Virgo
PLACE OF BIRTH—USSR
IDEAL MAN—a rich creative personality
HOBBY—educating children of preschool age [prick!]

Well, now, let's get acquainted with IRINA TARAKA-
NOVA, or *Irochka* to her friends. She is sad, in mourning, and the reason is not a simple one: not every
young girl is fated to hold in her arms the aging, trembling body of a great (according to the criteria of *that*
despotic country) man, whom Irochka lovingly called
*Leonardik*—after the Italian artist, architect, sculptor,
engineer, and theoretician of the age of the Renaissance (1452–1519), the painter of the world-famous
Mona Lisa (Paris, Louvre, first floor, entrance from
courtyard)—but whether he's a genius or not, and a
genius in what, is a question of love. However, Irochka
has suffered varied problems [literally: inconveniences]
since his demise—as is admitted by her close friends,
some of whom informed us that she was forced to quit
her very well paid work [I received a *hundred* rubles a
month!], but enough introduction: now you can discover for yourself that *beauty conquers death!* [Magnif-
icently put!]

There was a sequel to the matter of the hundred rubles.
No sooner had the magazine appeared when I was visited by
an American and a Dutchman, another journalistic pair. The
American was about forty years old and good-looking: graying,

with a stylishly trimmed beard and languorous eyes. He kept
nodding, no matter what I said, and sometimes wrung his
hands helplessly and hit his knee with his fist. He arrived in
checked woolen trousers, blue and green. The Dutchman, in
contrast, looked like a bandit and obviously dyed his mustache
black. Disheveled and curly-haired, he flashed his glasses in
every direction and babbled away in Russian, because he'd
been born near Irkutsk, and he disappeared at least three times
into the bathroom to perform some lengthy incomprehensible
task (the damned light bulb had burned out!). I liked the
American; he didn't understand very well, but the bandit
helped him. They got out long, thin notebooks and stared at
me. I was in my kimono. They admired my courage, saying
I'd coped manfully. I chortled: You would have done better
expressing admiration for my femininity! They smiled, at a
loss: obviously they hadn't got it. For five minutes we all tried
to clear up what I meant: the Dutchman was the first to
understand and, brightening, explained as best he could to
his colleague, who eventually struck his knee appreciatively
and clenched his jaw, letting it be known that he too had
understood. I said that the magazine had misrepresented my
salary, and frankly, like a traitor, I shared the true sum with
them, and they said, That is, you mean, not per hour, but
per week? *No!* I said, impatiently. Not per week—per month!
After all, you were born near Irkutsk! "That was many moons
ago," said this strange Siberian Dutchman, raising his hands
despairingly. "And have you been living here long?" I asked
the American. "Oh, yes." He nodded. "Two and one halved
years." I think, however, I answered their questions politely,
and when the conversation turned to moral freedom, I stated
that I definitely didn't approve of all those Western things,
in particular their so-called sexual revolution, inasmuch as, I
say, it only spoils everything, since a thing of value is a thing

of value forever, but when it's mass marketed, you understand? That is, it turns against love—love, you understand? Love's a rarity, and it's worth a lot, not materially speaking, of course, but in the dimension of feelings, do you understand me? (They understand.) Well, that's good then, do you want coffee? (They don't want coffee.) They ask, So you are a Russophile or perhaps a liberal? I give a straight answer: "I am nobody, but I'm pro love, because"—I stress this in my interview— "this activity is divine. You are family men?" "Oh, yes!" (Yes, I thought so.) "But this cheapening, this inflation of love— do you understand?—causes irreversible harm to all mankind, even leading to, perhaps, the threat of war"—amazement— "Well, because there's nothing to spend one's energies on"— the American exclaims "sublimation!" and punches his knee—"Yes! and so both your revolution and all those dif- ferent types of obscenity you have there should really be re- moved. Write it like this"—I glance into their notebooks— "obscenities accessible to any Negro. Do you yourself subscribe to this magazine?" "My wife isn't too happy about it," said the handsome one (I did like him: a mixture of Redford and Newman!), but the Dutchman said, laughing, that if he buys a magazine, then he likes something a bit stronger to put in his pipe. Well, then, in general, love was best in an earlier age, say, the nineteenth century, because only then did real passions rage and were beautiful women loved—that is, beau- ties were valued, and no one would have dared insult them! Once, at a ball in Moscow, the czar was totally captivated by the fiery black eyes of the maiden Anna Lopukhina. She was soon made a lady-in-waiting and invited to Pavlovsk. A special residence was constructed for her, something like a dacha. The czar turned up there every evening, with purely platonic feelings of admiration. But the czar's barber and papa Lopukhin knew human nature better and foresaw an assured future. One

evening, when the czar was more convivial than usual, Lopukhina unexpectedly burst out crying, asked him to leave
her, confessing her love for Prince Gagarin. The czar was
shocked, but his chivalrous character and inborn nobility immediately made themselves felt. Orders were quickly dis-
patched to Suvorov to send Prince Gagarin, a very handsome
man, though small in size, back to Russia. The czar awarded
him a medal and himself took Gagarin to his beloved and was
sincerely happy and filled with pride at the knowledge of his
heroic self-sacrifice. There were no limits to his generosity:
he ordered three houses to be bought on the banks of the
Neva and made into a single palace, which he gave as a present
to Prince Gagarin. Papa Lopukhin was made a prince and
appointed procurator general of the Senate—a most important
post, resembling the post of First Lord of the Treasury in
England. The barber was made a count and an equerry of the
Order of Malta. He bought himself a house neighboring the
palace of the doe-eyed Princess Gagarina and put his lover to
live in it, the French actress Chevalier. The guards officers
in their bright-red greatcoats saw on more than one occasion
how the czar drove the barber there and would then come
and pick him up when he was returning from his lover. When
his majesty abandoned the old palace and moved with his
most august family to the Mikhailovsky Palace, Princess Gagarina, Anna Petrovna, left the house of her husband and was
accommodated in a new palace, beneath the very chamber of
the czar, which was connected by means of a secret staircase
with her rooms, and also with the residence of the above-
mentioned barber, who, being a Turk, had been captured in
Kutaisi. We may find an allusion to these sad circumstances
in an unjustly forgotten poem by Tyutchev. Who is he?
Tyutchev the Russian poet! Tyutchev! No, not like that—
the first letter's *T*, like *Tolya*; well, it doesn't matter—Fyodor

Ivanovich Tyutchev. ("Fyodor Ivanovich? It's such a shame you've done away with patronymics!" "What do you mean, done away with? When?" I said, horrified, shocked by the news. "I haven't been listening to the radio for a week. My batteries are dead!" The Dutchman said something in a language that was double Dutch to me. "Well, they're used so rarely now," the American said, not admitting his defeat. "I was convinced they'd been got rid of!") In a word, I concluded, men went wild at the rustle of a petticoat or the glimpse of a bare foot (I show my ankle: it doesn't arouse interest), as if they were all thirteen years old! And what happens now? (They're not interested.) Now, I say, go around in your birthday suit if you want to, as on your beaches, where men and women lie mixed together, and what do we observe, as my dear French girlfriend tells me? Zero attention! As if these are lumps of inedible meat! And is this, the question arises, beautiful? No, I say, I'm against equality and the dissolution of morals. I'm for tension and prohibitions, for under conditions of sexual equality no erotic apogee, gentlemen—quote my words—can be had! They scrawled a final flourish in their notebooks and continued their provocations: "Don't you want to come and live in our bailiwick?" And the Ivanoviches on their part show me the newspapers obligingly, and the photos are cropped, the Italians have even dressed me with black strips, embarrassed, and the Ivanoviches say, "Have a look, Irina Vladimirovna, at how your beauty has been used! Not according to its just deserts!" "Come on," I say, "give them here." And they thrust various clippings at me and translate: "RUSSIAN BEAUTY THROWS DOWN A CHALLENGE!" I'm doubtful: "Have you really translated this accurately?" They actually take offense. I say angrily, "This is garbage! What challenge? I didn't throw down any challenge, but as for the fact that they insulted me in the best feelings of love, that's true, and there is no circumstance under which it is forbidden to love a person, so what if he's older than you," and they say, "Look with pride: SHE DARED! That's the sarcastic sons of bitches the French, writing in their usual insidious way. Here's what the Swedes have cooked up: A RENDEZVOUS WITH LOVE AND DICTATORSHIP. And the fascists: TEN PHOTOGRAPHS THAT SHOOK THE WORLD." "Surely they didn't," I exult, "*shake* the world?" They smirk: "They didn't shake anyone; that's reactionary German crap, just to spice it up a bit. Still, Irina Vladimirovna, you're a fine one, we must say—well, is it really becoming," they say, "for one of *our* women to be tarred with the same airbrush as these types, enabling them to write all sorts of vile things about you? It would have been okay with flowers, for example, somewhere in a field, like in ancient Greece, that's acceptable, we don't have any objections to beauty; we ourselves could have put it on the pages of . . . a calendar for export," Nikolai Ivanovich agrees, "or even . . . we'd have found a place; we are also, you know, for daring . . . you think we don't understand? We ourselves battle the inertia in taste. . . . If it were to depend on us *alone* . . . you can't even imagine . . . they're afraid of everything! . . . But with flowers, what do you think? Eh? Somewhere on a hillock or next to a stream, in the rushes . . ." I think: That's just what's needed! That's what I had in mind too. . . . I'd even hang it in my own bathroom—(they laugh). "But with regard to the *hundred rubles*, you slipped up there, Irina Vladimirovna!" "Why? I don't understand." "Washing one's dirty linen in public. That was pretty shabby of you." "What, your wife wouldn't object if it were in the bathroom?" "Yours would, but mine's trendy. But all the same, some things are sacred. Sending up bereavement . . ." "Yes, that's out of order! And who put this idea in your head, Irina Vladimirovna? Everything you've got between your legs is, forgive us, open to view.

. . . That, Irina Vladimirovna, forgive us for our candor, is *unethical.* You are a woman after all. . . ." "Unethical?" I exploded. "And is it ethical to kick me out of work for love? That's ethical, in your books?" They shake their heads. "That wasn't us. We . . . here you are"—they show their badges, with quills on them—"we write . . . but one must also understand Zinaida Vasilievna. . . . We'll have to think . . . and oh, yes! If *they* hassle you again"—hiding their clippings in a briefcase—"kick them as far as you can, Irina Vladimirovna, okay?" I promise. "We'll sort it out without them," and no sooner had I seen them out when *they* ring: in broken Russian. Well, I, of course, can't not be hospitable: I meet them joyfully in my kimono, but our courtyard is modest, one could even say proletarian. . . . Oh, I can't stand it! He's kicking, the son of a bitch!

# FOURTEEN

S uddenly six of the most beautiful beauties in America—here are their names: Patti Y., Kim S. (Miss Arizona or Alaska), Nancy R. (a fourteen-year-old schoolgirl with a capricious mouth), Natasha V. (of Russian descent, who will later drown off the Florida coast), Karen C. (stunning hair), and the chocolate Beverly A. (I happened to see their group portrait, when they posed together at a New York swimming pool and spread themselves out by the edge of the emerald water in resolute and spontaneous poses reminiscent of James Bond's bellicose sisters-in-arms. Natasha V. even had binoculars in her hands, resting on a white handrail, and on Karen C.'s T-shirt one could see the silvery initials *I.T.*, and the chocolate Beverly bared her Creole teeth, in order to stiffen my resolve)—sent off a venomously polite protest, consisting of 222 words, in which they demanded that I not be insulted and indeed express their rapture for my Slavic daring and charm and warn that if Viktor Kharitonych and other phallocrats of his ilk continue in this vein, they'll mobilize all their friends and patrons (including three oil barons, thirty-five senators, seven Nobel laureates, various liberal American intellectuals, the dockers of the East Side, Canadian air traffic controllers, the brain trust of NASA, and the commanding officers of the Sixth Mediterranean Fleet) and ask them most firmly *not* to be friendly with my foes, and incidentally I find out that their beauty brings them an average income of three hundred dollars an hour (an hour!) and that they are therefore very rich, and Patti Y. is quite simply a millionaire. Rituyla phones me and, unable to resist, incautiously shouts into the mouthpiece that it's on the radio in the latest news bulletins, and I, in my kerchief and with my vacuum cleaner in my hands, gray-faced, rush to the old Spindola, with its broken knob, and indeed they're broadcasting it. Well, I think, now I'm really fucked!

Instead, however, the following morning Seryozha and Kolya Ivanovich pay me a visit, in beige Yugoslavian suits, exuding the impeccable smell of bitter eau de toilette; their boots shine and they are very polite, and they say that they haven't been spending their time in vain and have discovered a production error that, of course, it isn't very nice to reveal—that one ought to show only to someone near and dear—but I'd been treated unfairly, beyond the norm, and the blame is laid on Viktor Kharitonych, who had been carried away by excessive zeal, so he can take the rap, since he has been appointed to write a letter attacking the hot-tempered beauties, where he will have to say with full honesty—although it's none of their business, but inasmuch as they are already interested—that I left work of my own volition as a result of the trauma of the death; and they will do their part, they'll write an article, as long as I assist, although I don't have a choice. And I sit, like a widow, and pick at the fringe of the tablecloth, and I repeat, biting my nails, "He would have defended me. . . . He loved me so!" "We'll put that down," and they get their ballpoints out of their pockets and start writing away like the brothers Grimm, although I hadn't yet said anything, and they say suddenly, "Wouldn't you perhaps like to write a short note yourself to these fools, Irina Vladimirovna, say, Thank you for your concern, your flattery, only there's no need to worry, as you bathe in the swimming pool, because I'm fine and your information isn't accurate"? And in answer to this I say to Viktor Kharitonych, "Where are all these things, Vityok, that are just fine? You're mistaken." And he got all ruffled, and he says, "Okay, screw you, you see what you've done to me, I've never in my life written letters to America and moreover I hate writing letters, period, and you didn't save the old man, Granddaddy, from a heart attack," and I say to him, "Granddaddy is also on your conscience, Vityok; he got overagitated during his speech, when you frightened me with some dead general," and he says, "Okay, we won't talk about that, you don't know all the ramifications, so forget it." "And you," I say, "now that you've got involved, sit, don't be rude, don't whine," and he took a sheet of white paper, uncapped his pen, and, sighing, wrote out in his round hand: "Respected American Whores and Whorelets! As you have become aware . . . As we have become aware . . . Your letter has reached us . . . your letter . . . I must say . . . we find it unpleasant . . . unpleasant . . . At that time when our collective . . . I must say . . . Why? Why all this? Why are you interfering in other people's business? You are porn in a bigger game . . . For my part, I too am not a young man . . ." He started thinking, hopelessly. With revulsion he put aside his golden fountain pen. It wasn't his idea, he admitted, to set about persecuting me, but they had directed him to execute this villainy, and I said almost kindly, "Vityok, don't let's quarrel; write your letter instead, and I'm off," and he said to me, snorting like a bull, "Wait! I've missed you, I didn't find a replacement, I remained with my wife after all. . . ." "You liar! I know whom you've been spending your time with around the bars." "From Margarita perhaps?" and

I say, "What business is it of yours whether it was Rituyla who told me?" "Don't believe her, and my wife, as you know, is old and crumbling, she's like sand, don't rush, Ira." He lay down on the couch. "Aha!" I say. "On the couch where I was about to kick the bucket while you and Polina celebrated your humiliation of me? Screw you, you just finished yourself off!" But it went in one ear and out the other: "You are, doubtless, broke? Or did those tarts send you a million?" "They didn't send me anything, didn't even fork out for a sheepskin coat, but I won't take your filthy lucre—wipe your ass with it."

And he started to whimper, the old goat. "Don't worry," I say, "you'll manage somehow!" He feels offended, and I'm bitter and say with a laugh, "Will you give me my job back?" "Certainly," he answers, "only not right away. Be patient, let the fuss die down a bit, so they don't think it's the result of the pressure," and I say, "Well, I don't need it anyway; I can earn my hundred rubles just like that, don't worry," but he isn't worried: "You became famous because of me, but because of you I have to write this stupid letter"—he angrily and carelessly shoved the cap on his Parker—"and I appear an idiot." "You have only yourself to blame," I say. "Please understand, it was not my idea: we were advised. This," he says, "is the doing of the influential Zinaida Vasilievna, these are her intrigues; she's got it in for you because of the funeral, she wasn't even willing to share the tears with you—and I'm the one who has to take the shit! But do you remember . . ." I don't soften, and I say, "Darling, forget about that, don't get wound up—write your letter instead," and he says, "You could at least show me the magazine—I haven't even seen it." "What else?" "Come on," he says, "I won't tell anyone; I'll just have a quick look and give it back. You don't believe me?" "You'll just have to manage without it!" And I went

home, and Granddaddy is lying in the hospital: Kick the
bucket, you old fart! Traitor! No pity. And at this point,
incidentally, the article titled "Love" appears one Wednesday,
and I read with amazement that my insistent Ivanoviches have
actually written their article on love, from which, however,
it was impossible to gather anything, but nevertheless indirect
hints were made that love, it says, is a holy thing, a private
matter, and everything that takes place between two consenting adults mutually drawn to each other is beautiful and
enriches both parties, and people are wrong if they try to peep
through the keyhole, violating privacy and immunity, because
we are all intelligent people and are ready to answer for our
actions, and age, according to the traditional definition, is of
no significance, as is sometimes thought, but it also says that
from time to time people from across the ocean like to stick
their noses into other people's business, to impose a foreign
attitude, only love has ancient roots here and ancient traditions, take for example Yaroslavna's lament in Putivl from the
*Lay of Igor's Campaign* or Andrei Rublev's "Trinity," we'll sort
it out ourselves, so certain Peeping Thomasinas ought to watch
that they don't get their fingers caught in the door, despite
their flamboyant beauty, their predatory beauty, and their
ridiculous 222 words, inspired by a certain citizen of a third
country, a displaced person whose true profession is uncertain,
exploiting certain departmental miscalculations, and once
more the Ivanoviches come to call: "Well, how do you like
it?" "In my opinion, it's all there!" "And do you know someone named Carlos?" "What's that? Surely they haven't killed
him? Oh, no," I say, "that was a long time ago! Nobody was
talking Russian there, and I had a small amount to drink and
didn't know where I was and started to dance, and you know,
I dance really well! I can show you—oh, well, please yourselves. . . . No, I give you my word, I know nothing about

Carlos, what a subject to pick on!" "Well, okay. We hope, Irina Vladimirovna, that you will be a bit more modest, keep well, don't give yourself too many airs, look after the old man." "Thanks, boys, don't worry, I'll keep it in mind, well, see you," and they leave, and then Merzlyakov phones—Come over, he says, tomorrow evening, some people want to meet you—and I'd been starved for company, more and more alone, on my own and with my fate undecided, although I feel it will sort itself out, despite all the events coming at once or perhaps because of this, I'm at my wits' end, and I answer that I will definitely be there, when suddenly the doorbell rings at seven-thirty in the morning.

If I'm not mistaken, this heralds one of my provincial relatives. Only they are capable of bursting into my life without any warning, at a ridiculous hour, with a suitcase held together by clothesline. I still hadn't woken up, wasn't expecting anyone, and suddenly, the doorbell. Who's there? I put my eye to the peephole. A frizzy perm, and puffing like a steam train. What are you doing here? I say, as I open the door to her. Without a word, she throws herself on my neck and starts weeping loud enough to wake the whole staircase! "Daughter," she blubbers, "you're *still* alive? You're *still* safe and sound? I didn't expect to see you ever again. Golovnya, Ivan Niko-laevich, told me everything; in the evenings he sits in the pigeon coop and listens to the news broadcasts, and he runs up with a mad expression on his face: 'Antonina, disaster!' He told me, I sank down, I shook your father, listen, get up! A waste of time—I gave up and set off for Moscow." Her suitcase is black, impossible to lift; she hasn't by any chance come to stay for good? "And where's Grandfather?" "In the hospital." "Oh! Oh!" "Wait," I say, "you've used up your quota of ohs and ahs; tell me instead, why is your suitcase so heavy—did you fill it full of bricks or what? Well, come in,

now that you're here, don't weep on the stairs." She brought
the suitcase in. "You can strain your heart like that," I say.
"Have you gone totally off your rocker?" But she says, "Father
didn't understand anything, but old Vanya Golovnya, he runs
to us and shouts—that's the type he is—'Antonina, disaster!
I've just heard,' he says, 'about your daughter; they were broadcasting about Irina Tarakanova; she,' he says, 'was in the
magazine *America,* on the front page, in her birthday suit—
I didn't understand the rest: reception's bad nowadays, what
with the jamming, but they've either imprisoned her in the
Peter and Paul Fortress or sent her a lot further away, but forty
millionaires came together and put down a deposit for her,
and the main one, who had a Russian surname, Vladimir
Sergeyevich, they reported, shot himself in front of everyone,
and then they exchanged her at the border for five hundred
kilograms of wheat and one weather satellite, that's how it
was,' " and she drags her immovable case into the bedroom.
I took a closer look at her; I see some kind of defect in her
face; is that a bruise beneath her right eye? "Mama," I ask,
"who gave you that shiner?" "Ah!" she answers, sitting down
on a low pouf in front of the dressing table, so that it starts
cracking at the seams. "Ah! it's nothing," she says. "It's because I had a fight with the dining car attendant as soon as I
got on yesterday, I tore half her hair out because of the change,
she didn't give me all my change, you understand, I gave her
a five-ruble note, took some Northern Lights wafers, and she
says, 'What are you pulling, you gave me three rubles.' The
cook came out because of the noise, and kept watching us,
you know, and then he got fed up and says, 'I think I'll go
and eat some goulash instead, but you two just keep fighting.'
Then we began to feel ashamed and stopped, but we kept
swearing at each other for a long time, in order to calm down
a little, and near Moscow, she and I got a bottle of wine from

the buffet and celebrated that we'd stopped fighting, and on
the whole she's not a bad woman, Valentina Ignatievna, well,
simply Valya, you understand? Her son's started at the institute, the mechanical engineering one, such a marvelous boy,
he looks like her, true, I haven't yet seen him myself, and
the cook returns, having finished his goulash, he comes in
and says, 'Well, girls, have you stopped going for each other
like wildcats?' And we say to him, 'Beat it, you bald bastard!'
We laughed so much, I tell you, we laughed so much that we
almost missed the Moscow stop, and we said goodbye at the
station. Valentina Ignatievna went to her relatives, to the
Simferopol Boulevard, they have a two-room apartment, on
the ground floor, true, and you have to go through one room
to get to the other, but to make up for it there's a telephone,
but she says that she'll fork up to exchange apartments—well,
she's a thief, naturally!—and then again she has an acquaintance on the seventh floor, who works in the local regional
soviet, she's promised to help, perhaps you've heard of her:
Bessmertnaya? But the cook, the cook, the bald bastard, he's
now ensconced in Tushino, burning his scones. . . . We
laughed so much, and Valentina Ignatievna has invited me
to visit her, I'll be cross if you don't come, she says, I'll have
to go, but that cook: the bastard's gone to Tushino!"

    At this point my darling mommy almost wets her pants
laughing, but I cut her off in midsentence and ask, "Perhaps
you've decided to come live here for good?" and she answers,
"Just a little visit," but she's looking shifty, and one eye, I
see, has closed up completely. Look out, I say, you'll become
one-eyed, like Father. "Oh," she says, "don't remind me of
him! He's still alive," she says, "the cross-eyed Herod, he
can't do anything, he's a total alcoholic, it would be better if
he died, both of us would have peace, he can't pronounce
words properly, and the longer it goes on, the worse it gets,

I can't get a word out of him, for weeks he doesn't utter a word, sometimes you ask: Do you want something to eat? he just moos, meaning yes, he's always ready to stuff himself, he likes that, but does he say anything normal, no, he doesn't want to take on any work, and yet what a profession he had. You can rake the money in as a carpenter, live and enjoy yourself, but he just moos and asks for food—the sooner he drops dead the better. And now he's got a new routine: he calls me by a strange name; to begin with I didn't pay any attention, who knows what his reasons might be, but then I listen more carefully, I hear he's dignifying me with the name Vera! I say to him, Are you out of your mind, you old dog? I'm no Vera of yours, I've been called Tonya since the day I was born, do you hear? Tonya! I'm Antonina! Antonina Petrovna! Can you hear me? And maybe he's deaf, who knows, I'm wondering how I can drag him to the health center, except I'm ashamed to, how can I parade him before the doctors looking the way he does, and then, Golovnya runs up one evening, he's the one who listens to the radio, a neighbor, well, you remember, his pigeons shat all over him once, from head to toe, he runs in all agitated: 'I've just heard something about your daughter!' I didn't understand at first, I ran in and switched on that box of lies, and he explains, 'I myself didn't understand it properly, the reception's bad now, the clouds are low, but I get the feeling that she's gone to America in exchange for agricultural produce.' My legs just gave way: What do you mean, America! That's not possible! And he says, 'Everything's possible nowadays.' I burst out crying: when it comes to the crunch, she's my only daughter after all, and suddenly gone to America, without a word, and Golovnya swears it's true: 'That's definitely what I heard! She went to America and became a millionaire.' I say, 'Go try again, maybe they'll say something else,' and he says, 'No, let's go and ask

Polunov: he also listens in, when he's not drunk.' We went to Polunov; as soon as he saw me, he tried to shoo me away like I was an unclean spirit, and Golovnya asks him, 'Have you heard?' 'No,' answers Polunov, 'what's up?' 'You're lying,' says Golovnya, 'you've heard.' And Polunov answers, 'Leave me alone, and you,' he says, 'Tonya, consider yourself a goner.' I say, 'What's happened?' But he's mum. Well, I promised to give him a bottle, I had one put aside, I bring it, and he takes the bottle, shakes his head, and says, 'Your daughter, Tonya, is an enemy of the people, and at the very least they'll put her up against the wall!' Golovnya and I started to try to get everything out of him: Tell us—we push him—now that you've accepted the bottle and swallowed half of it! Well, he went and told us, Polunov . . . I had to sit down. And Golovnya, he knows what's what, says, 'So that's how things are, then!'

"Well, I packed my things, didn't say anything to your father, and anyway I know him, the one-eyed jack, he can look after himself, well, I just upped and came here. I think: Let's hope they haven't damaged my daughter beyond repair, she's my own flesh and blood when all's said and done. Well, during the journey I had a bit of a fight, only this is what I'll tell you: that Valentina Ignatievna, the one who didn't give me all my change, understand, I took some Northern Lights wafers, gave her five rubles, and she says to me that I gave her a three-ruble note, but there wasn't a three-ruble note in my purse, you know? How could I have given her a three-ruble note? And the fact that her son got into the mechanical engineering institute, it's because she's got contacts, she told me. I arrive, I mean, here, on the wings of mother love, and see: they haven't murdered my daughter! She's alive! My legs went out from under me in joy!" Mommy's laying it on with a trowel, but okay, I say, have a rest after your journey, then we'll chat.

From now on my beloved mother starts to buy endless
sticks of sausage, treats herself to plenty of cheese, and takes
a bath three times a day, *having a soak,* as she puts it. She
soaks herself so much that the walls sweat, and songs waft out
from the bathroom, and then she smears her armpits and other
parts of her aging body with my French perfumes. I don't
mind, but must she take them without asking? Well, she
continues, since they haven't murdered you, it means it's time
for you and me to start a new life. I, of course, say to my
mother, smelling of French perfume, "Mommy, what on earth
are you talking about—where are we supposed to go?" "What
do you mean, where? Israel, of course." "What are you talking
about, Mommy! What Israel? You and I aren't Jews, you
know!" "Why," she says, "do they really only let Jews go
there? What have they done to deserve special treatment? In
what ways are they better than us? They always do very nicely
for themselves, the fat-bellied Yids!" And then she thought
a bit and said, "Well, then, let's say that we are Jews!" And
my mommy looks like a Jew as much as I look like Mickey
Mouse, and with three-ruble earrings in her ears. I say, "Take
them off, don't disgrace yourself! In Israel," I say, "they'll
laugh at you. And then," I say, "can you imagine a country
where you can't spit without hitting a Jew?" "There can't be
such a country!" says Mommy, horrified. And I say, "That's
exactly the sort of country it is, that shitty Israel!" And I'm
thinking to myself: I won't go anywhere. But on all sides, my
new friends and even Kharitonych all ask, Why don't you
emigrate? Over there you're a celebrity, millions of people jerk
off over you, casting greedy eyes at your midnight-black stockings, and the Ivanoviches are also totally baffled. And why,
Irina Vladimirovna, did you get involved with those foreigners? What the hell did you need them for? You would have
done better, Irina Vladimirovna, to give them to *Ogonyok*
magazine; there you and your beauty would have got a whole

centerfold, through our good offices; of course, however, I have to say that no one seems to recall Vladimir Sergeyevich, they never say anything about him on TV, as if they were punishing this lost soul for my sins, and so a great man began to fade away slowly, and not half a year had passed. But abroad, Irina Vladimirovna, no one needs you. And I say, As if anyone needs me here! The telephone is silent, just as if it had been disconnected for nonpayment. . . . You're mistaken, Irina Vladimirovna, your beauty could still be useful for noble ends, for ethical education in the spirit of aesthetics, but what do those foreigners have? Just pure filth, that's what they have! And yet they also speculate: Why doesn't she leave? But I tell the twins, My dear boys, my tits are already sticking out in opposite directions like a nanny goat's udder, well, where could I go looking like that? No, I say, out of patriotic considerations I won't move from the spot, and I don't know any languages, only *chastushki*, and the Englishman neighed when I sang, having forgotten his wife, but she was worrying: they have two daughters, the family's on holiday, and suddenly such extraordinary goings-on! No, I say, I don't want to emigrate, not to any of the four corners of the earth, and instead let's be friends and not be angry with each other. Thus I spoke. Granddaddy was fretting too. "What's going on?" mumbled Granddaddy, strolling in the small front garden beneath our windows. "We give aid to everyone, we aid Greece and Canada, Iceland and Zanzibar. And what do they give us in return? Cuban cigars! All these cigars are good for is starting a fire! And I have no desire to lose everything in a fire in my twilight years!" His friends playing dominoes growl understandingly. At midday, when the sun blazed out from behind the chimney and the pensioners put on their panama hats, Granddaddy had a heart attack. They laid him on the table in the garden. Granddaddy lay amidst the dominoes. The doctors feared not so much for the life of the aged Stakhanovite as for his reason. Or rather, they weren't worried about anything at all. They walked around, ruddy and young, flashing their stethoscopes and joking with the seasoned nurses. Granddaddy lay neglected in his bed, from time to time moving his Adam's apple. He lay in his bed and didn't even know that, soon after, a car ran me over.

# FIFTEEN

Don't cry for me! You'll still have a good time at my wedding, I promise, I shall invite you all, but let us first return to that night, to that sticky asphalt with its oily patches, when I, given new wings by friendship, was returning home from my new friends. My new friends had greeted me triumphantly. In the room that held the books, where sad souls were imprisoned behind the glass of the book-cases in hard-veined, leathery embraces, a room that didn't seem to have been tidied, Vitasik introduced me: "This is our heroine!" They applauded. They looked at me with their deprived, eager eyes and kept saying, "You can't begin to appreciate what you've done! It's incredible! This isn't just a new Vera Zasulich! Only there's no Koni to win your case!" I kept modestly silent, with a knowing expression. "Aren't you afraid?" They thought I was afraid. I smiled. "Not at all; it's just that I don't want to leave Moscow; I adore it." They questioned me about the meeting, and one of them, a Jewish Hercules, getting on in years, with his stick at the horizontal, said, "No, admit it, it's terrifying! After all, you have nothing apart from your beauty!" I'm amazed: "Is that really so little?" Among my new friends, there is also Yura Fyodorov. He is jealous, like one possessed, because everyone is talking about

190

me, and they start to argue whether I'd acted correctly or not, and some say correctly and *beautifully*, and Vladimir Sergeyevich's former night watchman, the calf-eyed Yegor, says, "Let me kiss you!" But Yura Fyodorov says that behavior such as mine is a step away from destroying culture, by trampling on traditions, and that my act reflected the pernicious influence of European romanticism on an immature soul, and a man of Oriental appearance, with a putty face, winced fastidiously and said nothing. But still they were all delighted. And Merzlyakov—the Narcissus of our six-day love—was very proud of the fact that he knew me. But everyone knew me, and I told them how Polina had schemed hardest of all, the ugly bitch, and had me down as one of the traitor general's lovers, and that's untrue, because Vladimir Sergeyevich was planning to write a novella about me and had already prepared a libretto for the opera, and they all started buzzing together and clutched their brows, as if they themselves had been proclaimed the cutthroat's lovers—that's the sort of people they were, my new friends! Unlike Shokhrat, complete understanding and suede jackets, everything very decent and proper. But Boris Davydovich, the Hercules, looking at me as he would at his own daughter, says, "Do you know who she reminds me of?" And the women all around say, "Tell us!" There were women there too. They smoked a lot: the younger ones cigarettes, the older, cheap and nasty Belomors; they smoked a hell of a lot, and they had yellow fingers, ugly teeth, and mean faces, and when they smiled, they smiled with their lips alone, and after they laughed they would cough like men and brush away large tears; they were polite and very sad, and when you asked them, "How are things?" they always answered, "Bad!"

Boris Davydovich had been a young officer. "I am reminded of the time," he began, "when one German girl came up to me, in Germany, at the very end of the war, and asked, 'Mister Officer, would you like to come with me?' I was young and fearless; I answered, 'Well, okay then, let's go! But,' I say in German, 'you aren't infected, by any chance?' 'No,' she answers, 'how could you think such a thing?' Well, we set off. She took me by the hand and led me onward, we walked over the ruins and the graves, as Goethe wrote, to her place, into her clean little flat with great holes in its ceiling from military action. 'You don't mind,' she says, 'if I put out the light?' Well, a light here means a bourgeois antique candelabra. Well, so what, I don't object, strictly speaking, only why put out the light? As the French song goes, 'Marie-Hélène, don't blow out the candle . . .' " He looked at the female listeners slyly. They smiled. " 'Oh,' says my young Gretchen, 'I'm a good and honest girl, I only invited you because I'm so hungry. And for that reason'—she curtsies—'I'm embarrassed in the light.' Well, okay. 'Perhaps you'll have something to eat first?' I ask, holding some American canned corned beef in my hands and some bread. 'Because,' I say, 'it's against my principles to sleep with a hungry and honest girl, but it's been such a long time and I want you to understand me correctly.' 'I,' she says, helping me take my boots off, 'respect your need for pleasure.' Only a German woman could say that! Well, she and I are getting undressed in the darkness, and she starts getting very friendly indeed." At this point the women narrowed their eyes, waiting for the interesting bit. And I thought: The German's up to something, but I didn't say anything, I went on listening. "And," Boris Davydovich says, "I was filled with doubts; her expressions of affection are too much, I feel, and so I went and put the light on, and look: Hey! she's got a terrible rash all over those parts! So everything's clear now! I jumped up. And she says, 'Mister Officer, I was so hungry!' 'So,' I say, 'tell me, how many of our officers have you been with today?' 'You! only you!' she swears, with her arms folded over her breasts like an innocent child, and she can't be more than twenty, and her breasts, I tell you, are big and white. I stand there, you know, totally bare-ass, with my pistol in my hand, and smash her in the face! 'Tell me the truth!' I order her. 'You,' she says, 'are the tenth!' The tenth? I see. . . . I felt as if an electric shock had gone through me. 'Well,' I say, 'goodbye, you German bitch!' And I shot her right in the face, in that angelic little face, as I recall now. Then I bent over, looked once more at her terrible rash, spat, and got out of there, satisfied that I had punished the criminal. . . ."

"That's abominable!" yelled Akhmet Nazarovich furiously, contorting his putty face. "You should be ashamed! First you went after her, then you killed her! Killed a woman!" "All's fair in love and war," Boris Davydovich defended himself, throwing up his hands, grieving for his past crime. "But what a girl!" he exulted. "That's what you call a kamikaze! She took revenge for the rape of her Germany!" "I read a similar story somewhere," said a sullen Yura Fyodorov, who hadn't liked it either. "I don't know *what* you've read or where you've read it, young man," said Boris Davydovich, "but that was a story from my own life." "All war stories are similar," the watchman Yegor put in, trying to keep the peace. "Which Germany was this?" I inquired. "West Germany or the German Democratic Republic?" In answer, Yura Fyodorov started roaring with ostentatious uninhibited laughter and Akhmet Nazarovich announced triumphantly, "You see! You see!" He emphatically turned his back on me, and the women urged the men to be fair and just. "How can you say such a thing!" Boris Davydovich burst out angrily, and anger suited him, as it did Hercules. "She's just like that German!" "That's not true!" I protested. "I'm clean!" And I thought of Rituyla. "Clean?" snorted Akhmet Nazarovich. "Why, you can smell

her sin from the other end of the street!" But Yegor and
Merzlyakov leapt to my defense and said I was the weapon of
fate and revenge, and it was no coincidence that Vladimir
Sergeyevich had passed away, or that, brought to despair by
them, I had thrown down my challenge, but I protested that
I hadn't issued any challenge (they were all obsessed with this
challenge), but I didn't put too much emphasis on love, seeing
their monstrous attitude toward Leonardik.

At this point my pen dropped from my hand, and I didn't
write anything for three weeks: firstly, because I was finishing
the mohair blanket, and secondly, because I was sitting it out
with my belly not far from the town of Sukhumi. I'd been
kidnapped by the pianist Dato; he'd dragged me off to his
Georgian relatives. The noisy, untidy house, smelling of recent repairs, stood at the sea's edge. It rained a lot at first.
The family lived amidst constant noise. They seemed never
to stop quarreling and insulting one another, but it turned
out to be just their way of talking among themselves. They
even had their resident geriatric, a ninety-six-year-old woman,
a tiny bowlegged busybody (she has since died). "Do you
believe in God?" I asked politely. "Eh!" wheezed the gutsy
old thing, without taking her Cosmos cigarette out of her
mouth. "How could I not believe?" Dato played Schubert on
an out-of-tune piano. I visited him at night, forgetting my
fateful pregnancy, and he didn't even notice. He said, "You've
put on a bit of weight!" That's men for you, they don't see
what's staring them in the face. I did a great deal of thinking
about many things, staring at the autumn sea. We went to a
wedding nearby where there was suckling pig. The emcee
bellowed out the toasts. People danced, people fought. They'd
spent twenty-five thousand rubles on the wedding feast. Everyone chipped in. One young man had the end of his nose cut
off in a fight. Had it been planned? They argued a lot about

that the next day. It was at the height of the match crisis: the price of a box reached one ruble. Then—the Lithuanians.

They drove right through our village in a Moskvich—they were about thirty years old, very ordinary in appearance—and asked for something to drink. Auntie Venera (the names here are as luxuriant as the flora) took water out to them and treated them to some sweet purple grapes from the garden. We went to the beach with them, these Lithuanians. They were traveling to Batumi. Drop in on your way back, said Dato. They noted the address and sped off. The following morning a militiaman called. He'd found the address of our house in the Lithuanian's notebook. It turned out that they had been murdered. They had stopped for the night near a picturesque river. The man had been knifed and thrown into the water. His wife had been set on fire together with the car, gasoline having been poured over everything. "Why?" I asked. "Sadists," explained the militiaman. Georgian militiamen look more like criminals than militiamen. "Will you catch them?" I asked. "Definitely!" he said. He finished off his glass of champagne, wiped his brow, and went off with the lazy amble of a fat man in a hot climate. And Dato went upstairs, into the cool room, and started playing Schubert on his out-of-tune, out-of-sorts piano. The Lithuanian woman's name was, I think, Kristina. She sat on her husband's shoulders, and they walked slowly into the sea, while Dato and I sat on a large orange towel, involved in our card game.

I was leaving the house surrounded by persimmon and pomegranate trees. The mandarins were ripening. They were still green on the outside but were sweet within, pale yellow and perfectly edible. What significance does this have? During the nights, when the family had fallen into a heavy, joyless sleep—they sighed noisily, groaned, their bedsprings creaked, and they farted dolefully—I would creep in to Dato, but I

remained cold, dry, indifferent. For the first time I felt an
aversion to the sublime root. Dato was perplexed. I was a bit
perplexed too. "Your dick doesn't interest me at all." He
wanted to hit me, but the family was sleeping all around,
crystal vases glinting in the darkness, so he whispered, "Just
go away!" I went. At the Georgian wedding the bride's mother
was only thirty-five. I would be giving birth not to a son but
to a sort of instant grandson. Perhaps, asks Rituyla, you have
no money? And in fact I don't have money. I need maternity
jeans, but I can't be bothered to try and get hold of them.
Bastards everywhere. I don't feel like writing. I don't feel like
anything. I don't feel like dying either. And Ksyusha is a long
way away.

Back! Back! To those happy days when I looked forward
to eating and drinking, looked forward to everything, was able
to do everything. Back to the sweet vulgarity of existence,
when everything was interesting: when the instant a man looks
at you his snake is charmed upright in his trousers, when the
instant you step out to dance Carlos throws himself at you
and tears off your fur coat, that lively, progressive ambassador,
when Vladimir Sergeyevich, eyes half closed after dinner,
confides the latest political gossip, a genuine state secret, and
invites you, for want of anything better to do, to the opera.
I longed to visit Paris, Amsterdam, London, they didn't let
me go, I longed to touch the amazing Ukrainian breasts of
the political activist Nina Chizh! I longed for everything!

Back! Back! To those ancient times, almost the age of the
epic poets, when despite obstructions, obstacles, barricades,
and barriers I, like Hitler, forced my way to Moscow. I cast
my spell on Viktor Kharitonych, duped my clod of a granddaddy. . . .

Rituyla nags me again about her lousy Hamlet! This is
Rituyla's second month of living with him, and she's percep-

tibly richer. She says, "Are you game?" Now she's the nag. Finally, I got fed up and said, Okay, it's all the same to me, whereas earlier it wasn't like that. I don't even fear Leonardik much anymore, he'll enter and I'll say, "Bastard! This is your doing!" And whatever he is, he'll be embarrassed. And I will give birth whatever happens. No, not out of revenge or malice, not in order to see what he'll grow up to be, and not in the interests of science or religion, but because I don't have any option and I can't have. . . .

The Russian autumn is so beautiful! Pushkin is right. If I could write poems like him, I would write only about autumn, about the yellow leaves falling, how the sky is piled up with storm clouds, and when the weather clears, the sky is transparent like a soap bubble. And the sun? It's possible to stare at the sun without hurting your eyes—isn't that wonderful? But then winter draws nigh, and it will kill everything. I myself am like autumn, but all the others are like winter. Anyway, a car ran into me, when after a lot of arguing I was walking away from my new friends, ran into me and ran over me, when I, at about two o'clock in the morning, was walking away—it was then that Stepan halted me by wrapping his car around my thighs.

Many people say how intelligent I am and admire my intellect, and they're quite right, because, I won't deceive you, I never was a fool, and thus, having spent a few evenings running around with my new friends, I started to grasp what's what. When Dato found out where I was spending some of my time, he said, "Do you realize where you're heading?" "Oh, I hadn't realized you were a coward." And he said, "I just want to be able to work normally; that's not cowardice." And Ksyusha said to me, "From now on, for you in your country"—by now she'd become completely Frenchified, of course—"double-entry bookkeeping is just beginning, a dou-

ble life. This second account has only just been opened, and
it can only mean bad news, because this country of yours,"
says Ksyusha—no, this was Merzlyakov speaking, the Je-
suit—"is not a country but a departure lounge, and the main
question is," he mocked, "to be or not to be here." However,
he's still here, but all this is boring; I want to say something
else: Ksyusha affirmed that since a second account has been
opened, it is no longer clear what is, in the last analysis, *more
profitable*, and even if it doesn't come off, well, then, after
all, maybe nothing will come off in the first account either,
and one's whole life will turn out to be worthless and drab.
Her words were at first totally meaningless, and I didn't understand them at all, because Ksyusha talked in riddles on
occasions, and I simply thought: Well, she solved her problems
differently, didn't she, by marrying the dentist, but I'd also
learned a thing or two, and when I went in, to the question
"How are things?" I would announce, "Bad!" And I learned
how to narrow my eyes, and I couldn't see that they were
particularly poor: some of them even had cars. In short, they
tried to convince me that there had been a motive behind
Stepan's running me over, although I argued with them as
hard as I could: That's just not possible! But they laugh softly:
Don't you know their limousines are always followed by speeding ambulances, just in case they have to pick up all the
sluggish pedestrians who stand gawking and whom they knock
over like ninepins? What are you trying to say? That's dreadful!
And my new friends laugh softly and say: If they really wanted
to *you know what,* they would have used a truck or a bulldozer,
but they chose a Zaporozhets, which is subtly calculated to
disfigure you a bit, for what's the most important thing about
you? "Well, my looks!" "Exactly. Consequently, you need to
be relieved of your beauty, freed from its excessive burden,
and then you'll buzz off to your ancient town and expire there,
a freak!"

I started to think, my dear Ksyusha (because I'm writing for you), I became pensive and cautious, convinced by their logic, and they stood around my couch in a semicircle, having decided to make a house call to express their indignation.

I fell over. Stepan leapt out of the Zaporozhets and ran toward me, thinking he'd killed me. He bent over and prodded me. He was exceedingly drunk, and I said furiously, in spite of my pain, "Hey, you're drunk!" He was overjoyed that I could speak and immediately started offering money; he was trembling all over, agitated and anxious. There were no witnesses as he carried me into his Zaporozhets (up to that moment I had never ridden in a Zaporozhets), because everyone was asleep and not wandering through the dark secluded alleyways where drunk Stepans drive around. I sat in the cramped car, still not knowing what was going on, and he begged, "Don't ruin me!" He looked miserable, not like anyone from my circle. I ordered him to take me to the Sklifosovsky Hospital. Again he begged, "Don't ruin me!" "Give me one good reason why I should take pity on you," I asked, "you and your drunk driving!" He became totally demented and began babbling about his children. My thigh was deafeningly painful, my skirt was torn, and my head was spinning alarmingly. "I've got concussion," I said, "that's no joking matter. To Sklifosovsky!" "Try and understand, I've come from a birthday party," Stepan tried to explain. "I meant to leave the car there, but then I came out into the yard and saw it standing there. So I got in and drove off. . . . And anyway it's all your fault!" said Stepan, suddenly growing bold. "Shut up, you sneaky bastard!" I raised my voice, clutching my bruises one by one. "It's the devil's work!" Stepan repented. Neither of us spoke for a bit. "Oh, to hell with you!" I said. I'm all heart; that's my trouble. "Drive me home!" He was overjoyed and drove me home. On the way, my thigh began to hurt even more, and I got scared: suppose he's broken the bone? He drove me up to the main entrance and said, "How about if I carry you?" I live on the second floor. "Only don't drop me!" He picked me up. It was funny, he was carrying me over the threshold like a bride, only I was in no mood to laugh, because he nearly dropped me on the stairs, he stumbled, but it was all right. We made it. He laid me right on my bed. I threw him out of the room, got undressed, hobbled over to the dressing table, holding on to the furniture all the time: a stinker of a bruise, the size and shape of the Black Sea! I threw my dressing gown on—he's peeping in through the door, swaying there, grinning: "Some nooky each day keeps the doctor away!" Proletarian jokes! I go into the bathroom, treat the bruise with hydrogen peroxide, and when I return, he's in Granddaddy's room, asleep on the couch. I blow my top: "Get up!" Fat chance of waking a Stepan! He snores, whistling occasionally. I pull him by the ears, splash water in his face, slap him across the cheeks—no reaction! He slipped off the couch, stretched out on the floor, flung out his arms. I examined him closely. What are you? You look well fed. A cook? A shop assistant? An athlete? Are you a crook, or do you live an honest life? Are you happy with your life? His tie is crooked; he'd been having some fun. No answer. Probably he's happy enough, little lord of life. He reeks of classy port. I rummaged in the liquor cabinet, poured some cognac; after all, I'm not going to call the militia, am I? I drank half a glass; it helped. I drank another half glass: things were hurting a bit less. The hell with you! I switched off the light.

I wake up the next morning and hear movement in the next room. I go in: he's sitting on the floor, his tongue out, smacking his lips. His hair—a bird's nest. He stares at me. "Where on earth am I?" he asks hoarsely. "Visiting friends," I answer maliciously. "And where's Marfa Georgievna?" "And who's Marfa Georgievna?" "What do you mean, who? The birthday girl!" "Curiouser and curiouser! First you knock me down, and now you ask about some birthday girl!" "What do you mean," he says, astonished, "knocked you down? This is," says he, "Marfa Georgievna's apartment. We drank her health here yesterday. But I'm sorry, I don't remember seeing you before." "Wait a sec," I say, "I'll remind you." I lift up my dressing gown and show the bruise the size of the Black Sea, only I see he's not exactly staring out to sea. I say, "You bastard, what are you looking at? Look over here!" But he doesn't answer; he runs his tongue naughtily over his lips, and his eyes goggle. I cover myself and say, "Well, then, do you remember? Do you remember how you almost killed me in your idiotic excuse for a car?" "No," he persists, "I didn't go anywhere. Marfa Georgievna made me stay with her." "But you have children!" I remind him. "The children will under-stand," he says. His gaze sweeps over to the wall clock. "Hey!" he yells. "It's time for me to go to work!" I take him into the kitchen for some breakfast. Stepan behaves politely but refuses the cottage cheese point-blank. "I don't eat that stuff. You wouldn't have any hot soup?" I heat up some borscht for him. He sets about eating; he slurps noisily, chomps, fishes out the meat with his fingers. He actually sweats from the soup. He gets his breath back, wipes his brow: "Wow! That's better. . . ." I nag him again: "Well, then, have you remem-bered, Stepan?" To this he answers, "I'm trying to remember, but I can't. Just to be on the safe side . . . forgive me for disturbing you. . . . You don't know Marfa Georgievna, then? Your loss. She's a good woman. If you don't believe me, I can introduce you."

I didn't express any particular desire to meet her, and he, slightly offended, left. From the window I saw how Stepan, deep in thought, walking around his car, which was parked in the middle of the courtyard, scratched the back of his head and, revving up so the whole neighborhood could hear, drove away.

After lunch I received my new friends. They were led by Boris Davydovich, who was tapping his stick. Behind him were the women, with flowers and a fruitcake. Out of respect, they actually didn't smoke. I greeted them from my bed. Gathered at the foot, they expressed their sympathy. In a failing voice I started to tell them the story of the absentminded Stepan, but the further the story progressed, the more disbelieving their nice faces became. "We know all about these forgetful Stepans!" said Boris Davydovich finally, unable to contain himself any longer, sitting on the pouf near the dressing table. They all sighed: "Oh, we know them very well indeed!" and the women narrowed their eyes, as if they were taking aim. "Yes, they've really gone after you in a big way!" admitted Akhmet Nazarovich, as his putty face took on a suffering shape. In proof I showed them my brute of a bruise, but I showed it to them craftily. I had shown it to Stepan without thinking, in indignation, so that he would remember, but now I showed it disingenuously, I innocently drew back the blanket and lifted my nightshirt a little way, but I managed it so that not only the bruise was visible but the neighboring territory too; it was like Brother Benedict beholding beautiful borders, bespying bare Beatrice, that's how I did it, but most innocently, as if I were showing a doctor. So I put them— both the nonsmoking ladies and the men: Boris Davydovich, Akhmet Nazarovich, and the devoted Yegor—on the spot. They oughtn't to look, and yet it was sort of awkward to turn away when the subject of the conversation had been displayed, and my little shirt rode up so! The marvelous vista of the Bermuda triangle! And the instant I covered myself again, with the most innocent expression, I climaxed, the effect of my naughtiness. I came oh so quietly, without any telltale signs; I sometimes loved to amuse myself this way, and it was not without reason that Ksyusha, wagging an affectionate finger at me, accused me of an overgrown schoolgirl's exhibitionism, but how can one resist, when everyone was gazing at me, looking me up and down, whether I was wearing my bikini or my fur coat, just as they would a film star, except that time is passing, and our shelf life is no longer than that of hockey players, and I despise shameless aging women with their predatory glances, who try to turn back the clock— better to hang yourself. Only you, dear Ksyusha, still cause a sweet pain to rise inside me!

But my new friends gradually get over their unexpected and secret embarrassment (I remember from school: spell with two s's) and say, "Rubbish! He's no Stepan! What does he look like?" "He looks like a Stepan," I object without conviction, "and he stank of wine and spoke very warmly of Marfa Georgievna." "You didn't note the license number of the Zaporozhets, Irina Vladimirovna?" "It didn't occur to me!" "Silly child." "But they change the numbers like gloves!" exclaimed Akhmet Nazarovich, and they all agreed: like gloves; and I got to thinking: And what if they really do change them like gloves?

Except can it really be possible that he snored deliberately? and pissed himself in his sleep, which became clear in the morning to both eye and nose, which, incidentally, I did not mention previously, taking pity on the refined feelings of my guests, who were in a very militant mood and said, "Perhaps we ought to expose these so-called Stepans by jotting down the story of their perfidy and then informing the right people." I didn't quite understand whom we ought to inform, because in that world in which I lived, the right people my new friends meant were the complete opposite of the right people I knew

about, if one accepts their opinions, a risky path with unexpected twists, because, of course, I just let my jaw hit the floor
in astonishment at their revelations, and they wouldn't even
allow me to disagree, like a foolish virgin who has been punished for her beauty—Lucky for you it wasn't a truck—and
at that point I remembered Stepan's mad eyes looking at me
in the morning, and doubt seized me: What if they're right?

Ah, I thought, that's your game! And it's true, my Stepan
had overacted somewhat when he said he didn't remember
my bruise, played the fool and talked that rubbish about Marfa
Georgievna, but when I recall, on the other hand, how he
ate his borscht and picked out the bits of meat—once again
a new wave of doubts: he'd have to be a damned good actor!

Ksyusha! They made a total fool of me! Have you read
this? Have you read that? Where can one get hold of such
books, and also there isn't enough time for everything! They
stuffed me full with their erudition, confronted me, shamed
me, I listened to them, listened and got really mad! I got really
mad, fiercely mad, and if this hadn't happened, there would
never have been the battlefield, or my fatal running, there
wouldn't have been anything! But I got monstrously mad and
bad and said, "You won't get away with this!"

Yegor, Vladimir Sergeyevich's betrayer, got seriously
worked up: "Let me kiss you!" But the wise serpent, Boris
Davydovich, put me in my place: "Don't get overexcited!
Instead let's all think how to save you!" "Ah! Boris Davydovich," begged a stunted little madam in polyester trousers,
who just couldn't resist lighting up out of chagrin, "you need
to be saved yourself! After all, you're balancing on a tight-
rope!" "Well, I'm not such a daredevil!" Boris Davydovich
brushed this aside affectionately and smiled: "I didn't show
them my ass, unlike Irina Vladimirovna!" Well, let's suppose
that I didn't either. Firstly, I didn't show *them* and secondly,

it wasn't showing just my ass, but everything, even I was touched, because when all's said and done, it's beautiful and, of course, without any offense in the world, and rather from a pure heart and as an invitation, especially as I love doing it doggy style, like, by the way, everybody else, and according to Ksyusha's and my Mochulskaya-Tarakanova law, which revealed the various degrees of human intimacy, the palm goes to the god of love, the little anus, kiss its sweet lips, and everything else is a checkpoint on the way to the celestial city and a fallen idol, and once, with my back turned to Dato, I was on the phone, and Dato followed me with his eyes and couldn't stop himself: he swooped on me like a hawk, and Rituyla is always ready to talk on the phone for hours on end: "No, Rituyla! What do you mean, three times! Thirty-three!" "Come off it, don't lie!" says Rituyla, shrieking with delight. "That's impossible." "Not with me it isn't! Don't you remember how it was with Vitasik? My erotic blitzkrieg." But she says, "Please don't expect me to swallow that!" And at this point Dato pounces—I actually yelled into the receiver, I simply wasn't expecting this, and Rituyla doesn't hang up, she's all ears. "Keep on talking!" demands Dato, and we chat, and she says, "I'm getting turned on too!" But I was already in full flood, and begging for mercy, but there's no mercy— that's the way I lived, with Merzlyakov, with Dato, or all of us together, and life was passing, but then death began. Death began not because I'd forgotten about love or had my fill— you can never, my dear Ksyusha, have your fill of that—rather, death began because suddenly there was no one to love. And as soon as I understood that my new friends were right to have a second dimension (or, as you say, double-entry bookkeeping), then, having parted with them, I set to thinking, not because I wanted revenge against Stepan aka Janus, who so theatrically wet his government-issue trousers, but because an idea had entered my head, as if I had seen the light on the road to Moscow, and looking around me, I understood that far from everything being more or less all right, on the contrary there was much injustice and deceit, and that this was hanging over the tender earth, over the open spaces and in the ravines, like a yellow mist of snot, and falsehoods had accumulated in the rivulets, which had run dry, and in the hedgerows, and you could have knocked me over with a feather, and I got upset and felt so much pain, and it's all clear, but indeed, you see, my new friends were grieving in vain, searching for a liberation they could not conceive of because no conception will help here at all, for the life of me, even if you kill yourself trying, and they were killing themselves trying; however complex the convolutions of Jewish thought, it's all in vain—that is, it's actually amazing: why do they care more about our salvation than we do ourselves? This is how I reasoned, lying there with a huge bruise on my thigh and looking around me and thinking: what act of mine could make the yellow snotty mist disperse? but I looked around me and didn't discover much of interest, and my friends scuttled sideways like crabs and went away, chatting about Stepan and limousines that scatter people like ninepins. Yes.

And then I phoned Veronika and said, "Veronika darling, I must see you. There's something I want to discuss." She says, "Come over." By that time I had started to recover. I took a taxi and duly arrived. I tell Veronika all. I say, "I've noticed I possess a mysterious quality. I can absorb all the evil forces. What do *you* think?" She is silent for a while and then says, "Please tell me, do you have a recurring dream?" "Oh," I say, "and how—it comes back all the time!" And Timofei walks around me and sniffs me. He always sniffs me, like a bunch of flowers, when I come, and Veronika gets a bit jealous and isn't too pleased, but she restrains herself. Fair enough.

I'm jealous too. "Practically every night the same dream, if I haven't met a worthy man." Veronika winced: she didn't like men, but I didn't always remember this fact, I sometimes forgot, because it's so abnormal, but she didn't like them. She would say, "Just think, you fools, about the way they smell! They smell from their mouths and from everywhere." Ksyusha, the darling vixen, used to disagree with her, but I kept mum. "Female sweat is more penetrating, you can tell that from public transport." "No," said Veronika, stubbornly sinning against the truth, "no!" "Why do women use perfume?" asked Ksyusha, and answered her question herself: "Women don't trust their natural smell!" "Stop it before I throw up!" I begged. Veronika merely waved her hand dismissively. She preferred her Timofei to all others. Yes. One and the same dream. Night. The street. Not a soul to be seen. I'm walking in a wide yellow skirt. Suddenly he starts catching up with me, there's a hat on his head, it's as if it's glued to his skull, I rush terrified into the hallway, I run up and up the stairs, my heart is pounding, I'm on the top landing, and he's coming up, his jaws masticating, he's in no hurry, chewing his invisible cud, he walks confidently, he knows that I won't throw myself into the bottomless stairwell, and I know that I won't, and in despair I ring a doorbell. But no one answers. No dog barks, it's dead there, even though they're breathing and listening in there, and looking through the peephole, that's what I'm thinking about, he ascends, and now he's reached the top, he comes up to me, chewing his invisible cud, and, not saying a word, takes out, like an ax, his huge—I mean huge!—I mean *huge* weapon, Veronika! Well, I think, the little fool . . . My mascara runs. I would have agreed to it myself, myself, and with great pleasure! Right up to my midriff! Only you can't see his face. But Veronika, the witch, who dabbles in dangerous powers, she says, making a wry face, "But does he come?" I think, I don't have a ready answer. That is, I certainly come, but does he? I say, "I think he does. . . ." Veronika says with a sigh of relief, "Well, that's fine, then! But are you sure?" I tense up. I say uncertainly, "I'm sure!" and think to myself: He must come, surely? And then, without any doubt: "Yes! yes! I'm certain!" "But you've never seen his face?" "No," I answer, "he's always in a hat, which seems to be stuck to his skull, but the next time"—I smile—"I'll definitely ask him. When I wake up, I say to myself: I must ask him the next time, but then I forget from fear, and on top of that: what a huge tool! That"—I laugh—"is more than enough for me." But Veronika doesn't laugh. She says, "Do you know what, Ira?" "What?" I ask, astonished. "You can become a new Joan of Arc. That's how it is, Tarakanova!" she says. I grew quiet. "Do you want," she asks, "to become a new Joan of Arc?" "But wasn't she," I say, "burned at the stake?" "You don't run the risk of the stake," she says—a witch, all right, although she has an advanced technical degree—"but all the same you'll perish: you'll be immolated, Ira!" "What do you mean, immolated? Who will immolate me?" "The very same force that comes to you at night wearing the hat will immolate you!" "Oh," I say, "what horrors! No, thanks!" But she looks at me with her bright eyes and says, "But can you at least picture for yourself what you're going to suffer for?" "Well," I answer, "the general picture, yes . . . for justice!" "No," she says, "not only for that." "There's lots of injustice, but I'm scared of dying." "Fool!" she says. "Don't be scared! Only when you're dead will you learn *where* you've ended up. And all your sins and peccadilloes will be forgotten, *everything* will be forgotten, and angels will take off their halos before you, and you'll be czarina of the Russian universe!"

# SIXTEEN

hurried to my new friends. I rushed in—they didn't even look at me as if to ask: What's going on? Aren't you afraid to leave the house on your own? How could you take such risks? They merely said, "Shh!" and sat me down in a corner. Yegor looked at me with a moody artistic glance and plunged anew into his manuscript. . . . It suddenly and unexpectedly transpired that he was a playwright. There were a lot of people there, crammed on the couch, chairs, chair arms, and windowsills, and the younger ones, with feverish faces, sat against the walls. Tobacco fumes drifted out through the *fortochka*. The ladies, legs crossed, drew their chins toward their knees: they could think better that way. The play was called "The Bitch's Tit"; it was heavy going. The action unfolded in various places: in a vodka line or in a drying-out center; or in an abortion ward, or in the toilets at a railway station, or in a foul little room in a communal apartment. All the dramatis personae drank frequently and copiously of various alcoholic drinks, including the mysterious balsam "Flower of the Fern." As I entered, a tough conversation was taking place between two youths and an old woman cleaning the station toilet.

THE CLEANER: Monsters. That's the only word for them: monsters! They've covered the whole floor with puke.

PAVEL: Shut up, mother! I'm sick enough as it is. (*pukes again*)

PYOTR: Understand, mother, there was a reason. We beat the Czechs.

THE CLEANER: At hockey or what?

PAVEL: Oh, mother, what a game of hockey it was . . . ! (*waves his hand dismissively and pukes once more*)

The play's action shifts rapidly to the small room. A table. On the table are leftovers, empty tins, butts, grubby rags. Two young women are sitting at the table.

ZOYA: (*pouring herself half a glass of cheap vodka*) I'm no longer waiting for anyone.

LYUBA: Me neither. I chucked up the institute, left my parents' home, with its cream-colored curtains . . .

ZOYA: Liar. You're waiting for Petka.

LYUBA: No. The last abortion opened my eyes to him.

ZOYA: Liar. You're waiting for him.

LYUBA: (*pensively*) I'm waiting? (*angrily overturns the table with its debris and seizes Zoya by the hair*) Are you making fun of me? (*Zoya yells with pain*)

The play ends with the monologue of the old cleaner from the toilets, who just happens to be the neighbor of Zoya and Lyuba. Very drunk, she hurries into the room in response to Zoya's yells, parts the girls, and then does a repulsive boogie-woogie and expresses her credo as she dances:

THE CLEANER: (*continuing to dance, jerkily*) I don't remember. Some. Writer. Said. Man. Fu-u-u-ck. Sounds. Proud. I would. That writer. (*wields a floor cloth threateningly as she dances*) I would. (*shouts*) Bite on that, you bastard! Stitch that! (*exhausted, she sinks down in front of the footlights*) Humanism? I've had it up to here with your humanism! Today a young lad died in my arms (*she lifts her hands to her face and examines them closely*), choked on his own

vomit! . . . You know what you can do with your
humanism!

LYUBA: (*drawing herself up to her full height and going white as
a sheet*) Petya . . . my Petya.

CURTAIN

Yegor sighed, utterly exhausted, and, wiping his wet face,
took in all the listeners with a single anxious glance. The play
had made an impression: a nervous flush on the listeners' faces.
Boris Davydovich's wife went quietly to the kitchen to bring
in sandwiches prepared with the best sausage, at two rubles
ninety a kilo, and tea with sticks of toffee. "Yes"—Boris
Davydovich broke the long silence. "A powerful piece!" and
shook his statuesque head as if in reproach. Everyone milled
around, congratulating the playwright. "Well, you're really
something!" "An eye-opener!" "He knows life!" "From the
heart." "It all got too painful to keep inside." Yegor grew more
confident before our eyes and, as the author, was given the
biggest cup, with a rooster on it. All were unanimous in their
opinion that the play could never be performed; they expressed
some critical views too. Akhmet Nazarovich said that the play
could do with a bit more moral underpinning; no, he wasn't
opposed to what's called, in quotation marks, a bleak vista,
but it needs to be constructive in the highest sense! I remembered Vladimir Sergeyevich and said, "Of course! Art should
be constructive." "Dirty realism," muttered Yura Fyodorov.
"Lots of cheap allusions"—in his usual manner, smiling
mildly, my friend Merzlyakov dished the dirt. "Heartburn as
an aftereffect of the sixties." Everyone started shouting, but
in a friendly way. Merzlyakov was accused of aestheticism and
intellectualism. Nevertheless, Vitasik added calmly that he
hadn't liked the title, " 'The Bitch's Tit.' That's a *bad* name,"

he said. "Call it simply 'Puke.' " "I'll think about it," agreed the author. "You're wrong, Yegor, to be against humanism," said one female fan who was close to theatrical circles. "That's not me, that's the cleaner," objected Yegor. "Yegor, my pet, you don't need to tell me that!" said the lady, with a snake of a smile. "It's just that the swear words get in the way of your pithy demotic language," was the opinion of the pediatrician Vasily Arkadievich (I've written down his number—I'll get in touch after the birth). "Yes, you know, that shocked me a bit too," I confessed, smiling sweetly. "And in general"—I turned red, agitated at actually making a speech —"how is it possible? Not a single bright spot . . ." "Where am I supposed to find that bright spot of yours?" the dramatist suddenly exploded. "Make it up!" I suggested. "That's what being a writer's about!" "I don't make sweets out of shit," proclaimed Yegor, and covered his lips and nose with his night watchman's beard. "I'm not N.!" (He mentioned a fashionable film director.) "What's wrong with N.?" I said, amazed (I liked his films). "He, Irochka, is a notorious toady," Merzlyakov explained matter-of-factly. "At least he doesn't spread gloom." I shrugged my shoulders. Everyone was looking at me with interest, because I'm fashionable too and they've talked about me on the radio. "In Yegor Vasilievich's play there is indeed futility"—Boris Davydovich stood up for the author —"but it is a bitter futility, there's no complacency or cheap mannerism in it—and that's beautiful!" "But there's little point in art if it doesn't have designs on you," noted, for his part, Akhmet Nazarovich, my ally in the argument. "And in my opinion, there's not much use in art generally," I say, giving myself away. Everyone is thrown into confusion. They exchange glances and suppressed smiles. I raise my eyebrows indifferently. "You see, Ira," said Boris Davydovich, "when the times are out of joint, the word takes on some of the functions and responsibilities of activity. . . ." "There's the

word, and there's the Word," objected the former research
student Belokhvostov. "A word's a word—that is an empty
sound," I said, and fluttered my long eyelashes. "Why, of
course!" Yegor blew his top, putting his cup with its rooster
to the side. "She thinks it is better to display her asshole!"
"That's *not* what I think," I answered in the total silence that
followed this character assassination. "But I do know what *is*
better!"

Only a handful of the initiated are left. And I say, "Do
you have any champagne?" They say, "We think there's
some." I say, "Let's have a drink, and I'll tell you something
extremely important." They hurry to fetch it, pour me out a
goblet, and ask, "How are things?" "Bad!" They nod their
heads joyfully. I'm a good student, but I think: This is going
to make your jaws drop. You sit here and discuss things, you
listen to shitty plays, but time is passing, you moan and don't
understand why it all goes on and on with no sign of coming
to an end, there's no way out, you say, and people are all
tangled up in depression and misery, and all you do is tell
amusing anecdotes, but if someone asks you: What's to be
done? you're silent or else you think up such a cock-and-bull
story that everyone squirms with embarrassment. You expose
everything and get into a state, you all go around with gloomy
faces and listen to everything with your miserable mouths
hanging open, and you heave great sighs. You're marvelous
people, there's no denying it, conscientious, in shit up to your
ears but you still wage war on shit, you drink defiant toasts to
your hopeless cause and you bad-mouth the establishment,
you hoard your anger, you write satires on something that's
already a satire, but I happen to like the way things are
here—yes, I like it! I'm all for purity and order! That's what
I was thinking to myself, and I had the right, inasmuch as I
was preparing myself for death and not simply draping myself
in the colors of grief and mourning. And now ask me: Why

had I made up my mind to embrace death by rape? After all, didn't I know from bitter experience how bad it feels and how shitty it tastes? Yet having arrived home with someone moon-lighting as a cab driver, and not at all in a dream, I was about to enter the modest entrance hall of our building when an elegant man approaches me, well dressed and rather tall and says, "I've been waiting for you." So what, keep waiting! I should, fool that I am, have called back the cab driver, even though I didn't know him either—he still hadn't driven away from the courtyard—but instead I let him go and turn to address this unknown dark-haired man: "You've mistaken me for someone else, young man." But he says he isn't mistaken, and he's been waiting for me for a long time. This happened while Vladimir Sergeyevich was still alive, he doesn't know about this, and it is the dead of night and yes, it is autumn, and this isn't a dream. "No," he says solemnly, "I'm not mistaken. Now I'm going to rape you!" I start trembling throughout my body and answer, "You'll live to regret this!" and I make for the entrance, but he grabs me violently by the waist and flings me over to where the pensioners play dominoes in our garden, and I fly ass-over-tit and crumple up, and he rushes at me and starts strangling me. At first I beat him off, but then I see he seems serious about strangling me—that is, his hands are around my throat so that I can't breathe, and I panic and think I must let him know, okay, if that's how you want it, fuck me, you prick, otherwise he'll choke me to death, only how do I let him know, when he's pressing down on me with all his weight and is throttling me, I can't give any sign, and a horrible idea comes into my head, that he'll kill me and *then* rape me, and from this thought and from the lack of air—or perhaps lack of air caused this thought—I faint, that is, I lose consciousness, I switch off, goodbye, Ira! and I didn't expect to recover again, so when Vladimir Sergeyevich (or, at any rate, his image and likeness) turned up, I decided not to resist, I'd learned my lesson by then, and he says, "Well, it doesn't cost you anything anyway!" And Dato always reproached me that it didn't cost me anything, and he was always reproving me and swearing at me, until he started in, dying with passion, and I would say to him, laughing, "Watch out or I'll have your baby!" and he would grab me in his arms and would wash it out himself, in a sweat, as I gazed indifferently down on his premature bald patch: Do your best, fool, although I'm as barren as the Karakum desert! But that night things turned out differently: I came to and saw that he's on me and working away: well, I think, he didn't kill me, and I can feel from various signs that it's coming to an end, although I don't feel anything, as if his cock is totally nonexistent, as if he's fucking me with emptiness, and I realize he's pulled my skintight jeans down over my boots, the bastard, a real professional, I lie there, surely someone will come to my assistance, I weep, surely someone's heard my penetrating cries (and I was yelling!), that's people for you. . . . And now what? Now I'm supposed to save them? Those who heard me being tortured didn't even stick their heads out, didn't even phone for the militia! Now the question is: What do they really need? My new friends explain: freedom. Are they mad? That won't just mean robbery! That reeks of blood! He got up, brushed the dirt off his neatly pressed trousers, and said, "Well, let's go to your place." I answer from my trance: "You've raped me, and now I'm supposed to take you home?" He gives me a cigarette. We sit on the pensioners' bench and smoke. I say, "Why were you suffocating me? Another moment and I would have given up the ghost!" And he says, "You wouldn't have fucked me otherwise." Well, yes, right you are, there is some logic in this, but I think I must go, or else he might want it again and we won't be finished before morning, so I made myself scarce, ran out into the street, but my violator didn't pursue me, he headed off in the opposite direction, and I

rushed to Arkasha's, he doesn't live far away, and his family
is there, the wife opens the door, we hardly know each other.
"What's happened to you?" A stranger, she takes me into the
bathroom, she paints my scratches with iodine, as if I'm not
her husband's lover, not a lesbian! Arkasha came out at the
noise of water running, squinting like a rat at the light, and
I'm standing in the bathroom like an urchin, he got all agitated
and shouted, "I'll phone the militia!" But his quiet wife said,
"Stay with us." Tears actually came to my eyes. Like a sister,
"I'll never lay a finger on your husband again," I say. "Are
you a Christian, a Baptist perhaps?" But she doesn't answer.
An incomprehensible woman. And I say to him, "What, are
you off your rocker, Arkasha? It would just be another humiliation. All the cops will blow out their cheeks: 'Who'd
want to fuck this ancient hag?' "

And it all remained a secret, I didn't tell anyone, and as
for that imagined one, the one in my dream, he too disappeared for a long time, hid himself away, I even started to
miss him. And now I myself, you see, was trying to find a way
to ensure that my guts would be ripped up in some terrible
way and more to the point, look who I'd picked to screw me!
Well, it stands to reason: not my new friends, they couldn't
hurt a fly, they're all useless at fucking, you can see that with
the naked eye, all they want is to philosophize. Some of them
have the pathetic, whipped look of men who can't get it up;
others, like Akhmet Nazarovich, are live wires who twitch
around convulsively if briefly. No megakicks for me from that!
These people wave their hands about when they talk and are
as hysterical as women, while the former research student
Belokhvostov, who hung around with church people, drank
a hell of a lot and was poor, and I don't like poor people,
charity is not my middle name, and there wasn't a worthy
candidate among them, I don't include Merzlyakov, although

for a while now he too has been limp and become an ex again—that is, he's recently revealed himself as useless—but previously he was jolly, and I renounced all serious intentions and merely thought: If I become a new Joan of Arc, then we shall see! That is, I shall die, but to make up for that I'll become a saint, that's how it seemed to me, and it wasn't that I was intending to save Russia and all that kind of thing, but I felt like becoming a saint, sin is closer to sanctity than philistinism is, I now had the chance, Belokhvostov kept whispering to me of becoming a saint, for ever and ever, amen, and people will hymn my praises. Vitasik was against this, not because he didn't believe in miracles but because he felt sorry for me as a former lover, and I say to him, "Let's travel to the battlefield together," and he answers, "What's your purpose in going there? Fame?" Stupid Vitasik! What sort of fame is it when I'll be lying dead, immolated by the diabolic forces; fame only counts when you're alive; a dead woman is a dead woman, but a saint—that's something different, that's not fame, that's immortality, and then of course I was fed up. In other words, I wanted to save not Russia but myself. What does it mean to save Russia; I asked my new friends, what does it mean? Did I get a single intelligent answer from them? I did not. Akhmet Nazarovich, half Russian, half a member of a national minority, answered my question thus: "It will be great when goodness and concord spread over the Russian land and everyone will love everyone else and work diligently." "Bullshit," I say. "There'll never be anything like that!" "Yes there will! Yes there will!" they persuade me. "Oh, give up your silly dreams!" I said to them harshly: I was going to meet my death! They understood this and listened to me, though they were dubious: "But won't this, Irina Vladimirovna, be terrorism? Won't it be ecologically harmful?" "No," I say, "it won't harm anything, and no human blood will be spilled." "So what will be spilled?" Everyone knows what: the semen, stinking like pus, of Russia's great foe, the voluptuous flesh-devouring demon, usurper, and autocrat. And once it is spilled, he will rapidly droop, grow wrinkled and weak, and then justice will prevail, the sorcery's endless spell will be broken, because the only explanation for all this is witchcraft.

They listened very attentively, that is, they didn't interrupt or object, struck dumb by my message and forgetting Yegor's play. "Where did you get all this from, Irina Vladimirovna?" *"I heard a voice."* And it's true. There was a voice. It was the voice that sent me to Veronika. And what did the voice say? The voice said, "Your cunt has sucked in a large quantity of the most varied corrosive sperm, Irina Vladimirovna, you've really reached a dead end, darling, it's time to call it a day." That's what the voice said. So at breakneck speed I ran to Veronika, who understood everything and asks: "But have you ever had any dreams about being raped?" I confess the sins committed in my sleep: I often had these dreams, and then, having made a wry face and not wanting to be involved, she blesses me with the sign of a true witch and dispatches me to my death: "Go and perish!" And I say to my new friends, "I possess an exceptional quality. I can suck all evil forces into me, I can. Just explain to me, for Christ's sake, what will happen then, what magical new city, what El Dorado will appear, so that my enthusiasm may ripen inside me and I won't have to do it cold, like a fool."

They fell to thinking and said, "It will be a great holiday for the state, the nation will be reborn, those powers held captive will come to the surface, like spring torrents, skills and science will develop, pineapples will ripen near Perm, and peasants will build themselves two-story stone houses with hot and cold running water and garages and swimming pools and hothouses, raise fat cattle, and sing happy anthems.

You've no idea, Irina Vladimirovna, what it will be like! Our land is mighty, Irina, mighty and original, only it's lying idle, rotting without work (that's what the foe's voice sang to me), no one's heart is in the work, everywhere shortfalls, loafing, ungathered harvests, labor is perverted, a worker is ashamed to be a worker, a waiter gives you filthy food and feels sick himself, everyone is making money on the side and botching goods at work, everyone's got lazy, become alcoholics, grown disfigured—in a word: mudslingers! The end of a great people is approaching, it has already begun, help them, Irina Vladimirovna!"

I listened to all this in a heavy state, but their cheeks were burning, and their women at this late hour had actually started to look prettier, despite their frigid aspects. "Let's assume," I said, very coolly, not going along with their enthusiasm and their unfounded generalizations, regretting the fact that Vladimir Sergeyevich was no longer with me, "let's assume that everything will indeed be as you say it will. But where's the guarantee that the appointed hour hasn't passed already? Is there anyone left to be saved? Won't I be taking on an unnecessary sacrifice, and won't I perish in vain?"

I'll be honest: the opinions of those present were divided. Some, for example, Boris Davydovich—he's their main man, deal with the organ-grinder, not the monkey—were convinced that although things had gone on for so long that it was almost too late and it would have been better, of course, to have worked on this a bit earlier, three or four hundred years ago, if not earlier, before we had been force-fed with barbaric Asiatic ways and when the landscapes of Kiev were in no way inferior to Claude Lorraine's sunsets, still he trusts the primordial qualities of the indigenous population, trusts its passive resistance to capitalism and the inhuman exploitation of man by man, and this position is right because the ideas are right. But others were actually disillusioned by such words and populist nineteenth-century "back to the people and back to the earth" views, because you can't put a brake on the development of capitalism, but you should use it for your own ends, and accused him of indulging in fantasies with no firm foundation; in short, they were of little faith. Vitasik was the first to express his doubts, but no one took much notice of him and they didn't give him the floor, but I looked at him, daydreaming about the six lightning days of our love, when, without ever getting out of bed, we lived only on overwhelming passion, and Merzlyakov gasped that he had nothing left to come with, but he came all the same: blood. There you have it: then he was coming blood, but now he was exuding pessimism. "Permit me," he says, "to be heard. I love Ira not only as a symbol of courage and not only because, as you put it, she allowed her ass to grace millions of magazines—no, there's simply no point in a young girl's perishing in vain!" "Cassandra! Cassandra!" they start hissing at him, my new friends, and one of them, in sad spectacles, expresses his doubts as to whether Vitasik is a Russian. Merzlyakov was, however, completely Russian, despite the smoothness of his slow speech and his manicured fingernails and his face, which, I confess, I found sweet once upon a time, and I took umbrage for him and said, "Let him have his say!" and Vitasik spoke. He said that in his opinion, there was no surgical operation, even of the most mystical nature, that could assist rebirth, that sort of development must come from within, and a people chosen for a religious mission should be left to its own devices, and we aren't its physicians. "Who are we, then?" "What do you mean?" said Vitasik, surprised. "Self-styled advocates." The women were scandalized, but Vitasik continued, because that's how I wanted it: "Irochka, there isn't anything for you to save, but you can save someone—yourself—and forget about everything else, get it out of your head." "Why? Why?" they shouted in unison. The dramatist Yegor said, "As far as drunkenness is concerned, they won't give up drinking. Vitasik is right there. I do not presume to judge about the rest." But Yura Fyodorov disagreed with them both. "Drunkenness," he said, "is not the greatest sin, if it is indeed a sin at all. It is, if you like, a form of universal repentance, now that the church has been marginalized and is in a state of stagnation. It is repentance, and this means that the moral powers of the people are far from spent. For, Irina Vladimirovna," he said, just as if he had never tormented Ksyusha with his cloak-and-dagger insinuations about her paralyzed little sister, "for, Irina Vladimirovna, know that the more they drink, the more they themselves are tormented. When they get drunk they melt into tears, and thus they don't drink because they are swine, as Merzlyakov here affirms—" At this point Vitasik leapt up and yelled, "Swine? I didn't call them swine! But it's not my fault that they're wood from the neck up!" "I beg you, stop it!" Our host could contain himself no longer. "Do you understand what you're saying?" Vitasik turned crimson. "I have only one regret, Boris Davydovich: I should never have brought her here." "Listen, Merzlyakov," said Boris Davydovich, "we are all clever people here, yes? Okay, we don't like the same things. Why can't we come to some sort of agreement?" "Because"—Vitasik wasn't calming down—"we have here before us the historic paradox of free will. The people don't want what they ought to want, and do want what they ought not to want." "An irresponsible play on words!" declared Akhmet Nazarovich disgustedly. "They want to live well," said Yegor. "Nonsense!" said Vitasik with an airy wave of his hand. "Let's look at the facts. They have never lived as well as they do now." "What?" "You leave the church alone!" commanded the former research student Belokhvostov. "The church will still prove its worth." "It won't prove anything!" "Will!" "You'd be better off looking at how they live." "You don't know life!" "And of course *you* know it!" "Shut up, both of you!" "How dare you?" "I'm obviously the daring type!" "That's enough! *Enough!* Belokhvostov, hands off Merzlyakov! Just let him fuck off! I'm telling you in plain Russian—put that bottle down!"

"I think I'll be off, then," I said, getting to my feet. Everyone felt a collective shame. My head was whirling. And I said to my now quiet friends: "My dear ones! It's as clear as day that nothing is clear. And inasmuch as *that* at least is clear, then let's give it a try! And then we'll see how it goes." "Oh, yes, as always," mumbled Merzlyakov, "do it first, and then see." "Take it easy," I said. "I'm not a priceless objet d'art; so what if I do conk out. I wouldn't be the first corpse!" My argument was irrefutable. I saw tears in the eyes of the masculine women, the girlfriends of my new friends, and Akhmet Nazarovich came up to me and embraced me like his own daughter. Yegor too kissed me: he believed in demons, despite his own devilish cunning. They started thinking about how to do it. A plot was hatched. I explained.

We need a field, a field where innocent and righteous blood has been spilled. Someone, I don't remember who, noted that blood has been spilled everywhere, so we shouldn't have to spend too long looking. Vitasik, true to form, said somberly, "Ah, but was it innocent and righteous?" Akhmet Nazarovich nominated Borodino. He had no respect for Frenchmen, he considered France a nation without a head on its shoulders and thought that the battle of Borodino marked the precise moment when a shield against debauchery and easy decadence was erected. The young Belokhvostov suggested Kolyma, in all seriousness. This enjoys wide popularity nowadays, and he

called on everyone to fly out there immediately, he's willing
to organize the seats on the plane and everything, he'll provide
living quarters, he has a friend there, a gold digger—as long
as his friend's still free, of course. Unexpectedly, all of them
agreed, unanimously, to fly: both the men and women, and
Boris Davydovich with his stick, they said that there, of
course, would be best of all, only it's a bit far. To their amazement, I flatly refused. I said I wouldn't fly to any Kolyma
because the dim Chukchi Eskimos and reindeer live there, let
them have it, and as for the fact that Russians froze there,
well, there aren't many places where they haven't frozen, poor
souls! "Perhaps, then, where the Russians met the Tatars,"
Yegor suggested timidly. He was, in my view, right. This
covers both the faith and one's primordial land. But I won't
go to Kolyma. "It's too cold for running there, I'll catch my
death of cold," I said. "And though it's close, I consider it
shameful to go to Borodino," said the pediatrician Vasily Arkadievich (an attractive appearance, mustache, manners).
"At Borodino lie the bones of an enlightened nation! There
lie the bones of people who were superior to us in every respect!
Just take a look at their children nowadays. Even the infants
are miracles of serenity, upbringing, culture. They don't howl,
they don't act up, they don't pester their parents, they always
play sensible games! They are liberals from the cradle, and
liberalism is the highest form of human existence, but ours
only rush about and wail, and chew their mothers' breasts to
shreds! It's a shame that they lost their heads in the smoke
of the Moscow fires!" "Yes, a full hundred years ago one of
the brothers Karamazov complained about that," noted the
encyclopedic Boris Davydovich. "All the better!" said the
pediatrician. "Smerdyakov," elaborated Boris Davydovich.
"That doesn't prove anything!" said the pediatrician, unper-
turbed. "No, it proves something!" Akhmet Nazarovich, who

had been quiet, went on the attack. "What sort of enlightened people are these Frenchmen of yours, if their history and their whole life is one everlasting Munich!" "Ha ha ha!" Vasily Arkadievich burst into an ostensibly natural laugh. "Ha ha ha! So in your opinion they should all have died for your sakes. They didn't give a damn about you! Just as you and I don't give a damn about the Chinese!" "It's not true," noted Akhmet Nazarovich with dignity, "that I don't give a damn about the Chinese! Indeed, I'm not in the habit of damning anyone at all." "Oh, yes you are!" said the children's doctor, flying into a rage (neither mustache nor manners). "I vividly remember how fifteen years ago you talked about dropping something nasty and heavy on the Chinese, out of fear, I remember." Akhmet Nazarovich went red as a beet and said, "And I, Vasily Arkadievich, remember how you dashed off a little letter to the medical journal, when you had had your wrist slapped ever so gently, and in it you sang the praises of everything, yes, absolutely everything!" "Gentlemen!" shouted Boris Davydovich. "None of us is free from former sins. I, for example, killed a young and innocent German girl at the end of the war. But you see we are expiating them and we shall expiate them, my good friends!" "Borya," said Boris Davydovich's wife. "Remember your weak heart!" "But I, for example, am free of sin," asserted the young Belokhvostov joyfully. "I haven't licked anyone's ass." "Well, what a shame," I said, feeling sorry for him, remembering the won-drous law of Mochulskaya-Tarakanova. "You don't know what you've missed!"

I understood at once that the young research student didn't know much about women, and I didn't much fancy being in bed with him. I imagined him: the face of a gopher, all emotion and sickly sweetness, nylon underpants—no, thanks! So I resisted the temptation and, naturally, didn't tell them about our law. In the end they chose a battlefield, and then the question of transport arose. Vasily Arkadievich gallantly offered his Zaporozhets. I refused point-blank. Unpleasant associations. The bruised thigh. And then it's not suitable to set off on such risky adventures in a Zaporozhets. It would be mockery. Yura Fyodorov offered his services. It turned out he had a Zhiguli. You have a Zhiguli? Well, who'll go with Irochka? Will you go, Vitasik? Vitasik said he wouldn't go. His wife has an allergy of the internal organs. A very useful diplomatic tool, that illness. He was the only one against. They all looked at him as if he was a renegade, and I actually started to feel sorry for him and said, "I know why he's against it." "I know too," said Belokhvostov, who had by this time drunk some vodka. "He's not a fan of Russia. But I'll go!" "No!" I said. "You're not going, you'll get drunk." He was humiliated, as Merzlyakov observed with a nasty smirk, "Now shut up. You won't be here in six months time, for all your love of Russia!" "That's no argument," said Belokhvostov. "That's *no* argument, and even if it is, then do you know the logic of it?" It seems there was no love lost between them and Merzlyakov. "No, do tell me," inquired Merzlyakov politely. Belokhvostov started to laugh evilly. Yegor intervened as a go-between, the former lackey, everybody's favorite. They chose a Tatar battlefield, despite Akhmet Nazarovich's reminding them of the former strong ties between Russia and the Tatars. "One mustn't oversimplify!" he said angrily. Yegor volunteered to go with me too. He was a master of telling stories, and to entertain me during our journey he told me, apropos the Tatars, that a certain Kazan sculptor had been chiseling away at Zinaida Vasilievna and that she would cry out during lovemaking, "Ride me, Tatar!" "But did Vladimir Sergeyevich know?" "No," answered Yegor, all innocence. "Why on earth didn't you tell me earlier!" I said regretfully. "Perhaps then I wouldn't have had to run over this damned field. . . ."

# SEVENTEEN

A and so the field. The tragedy of my absurd life. It was a warm September day. More accurately, it was early morning and not yet warm—you know the sort of morning frosts we get in September, the transparent breath of autumn—but the sun was rising, the leaves were turning golden, promising mild weather. Five or six hours of fast driving to the field ahead of us. They arrived and honked to me from the yard. The final stroke of the eyebrow pencil, one last inspection in the mirror, that's everything! I'm ready! I ran downstairs, holding a wide wicker basket with food in it, like going off for a picnic: a watermelon, bought from a Kalmyk, ham-and-cheese sandwiches, chicken with thin crunchy skin in foil, a loaf of white bread for twenty-two kopecks, a bottle of dry wine, raspberry-colored tomatoes, napkins, a saltshaker the size of a thimble, and a thermos of strong coffee. "Hello, boys!" I smiled. I didn't want to be sad that day. I had sandy-colored jeans on, very hip, and hardly worn, a short suede jacket the same color as the skin of the fried chicken, and a scarf of red, white, and navy around my neck. All dolled up. "The national colors," Yura said approvingly of the scarf. Yegor kissed my hand, tickling me with his mustache and beard. "Well, Godspeed!" I said, slamming the car door and making the sign of the cross, although I wasn't baptized. "God-speed," said Yegor staidly. "Don't slam the doors too hard," the owner grumbled at us both. We set off. The seriousness of the moment was tangible. In a few hours (in the evening, at twilight) two fates were to be decided: Russia's and mine.

A pleasure jaunt. The breeze in one's hair. A few odd clouds, very like cotton balls for removing makeup. At full speed we rushed toward the southeast, into the depths, toward my field. The clean, tarted-up Moscow suburbs greeted us with flippant copses, around which hung apples and golden spheres coming at the end of their blossoming—dahlias, chrysanthemums of all different colors. I can't stand chrysanthemums. Why? Once, at a funeral . . . okay, I'll tell you some other time. In the villages, schoolgirls in tiny chocolate-colored dresses were carrying huge satchels, and out of their morning drowsiness, unafraid and curious, the workers stared at us through the back windows of buses.

You don't have to go far outside Moscow to notice how quickly life becomes more simple, how the pace slows, and how the influence of fashion grows weaker, how even forty kilometers away people are only starting to wear out what has already been worn out in Moscow, how faces are weaker, even though many of them have the veneer of an anger peculiar to the outskirts of Moscow, that belt of gangs and evening hooliganism encircling the capital, dance floors behind fences, social clubs built of wood, hatred of people who own dachas and a contemptuous envy of the inhabitants of the capital; the strong wave from the city, spreading out in circles, as if a stone's been hurled—and the Kremlin is this stone—clashes with an answering powerful wave, rushing in from the suburbs, and everything becomes mixed: women's sleeveless working jackets, gray and padded, together with smart shoes; bagels with bad tobacco: here they try to overtake but fail to catch

up, and here they remain with a criminal smile. We travel
farther, to where the suburban bus routes end, where suburban
trains stand puffed out, dying at each platform, still built of
concrete, though the seedlings of country life are growing
stronger, mud on boots, feet becoming rooted to the ground,
hens and the chipped classical porticoes of postwar buildings,
and after the awkward industrial town with its multicolored
slogans, a new leap, last year's fashions give way to ancient
fashions, memories of youth, the twist in school, miniskirts,
fringes, flared trousers, long-haired Beatles fans, and the whistling of transistors; time is exchanged for distance, as if there
is a bank in Russia operating according to an exchange rate
established from time immemorial, and, traded for kilometers,
time thickens in the air, is conserved, like condensed milk,
and settles, viscous, the decades shuffled; just now over there
a woman came out wearing the heels of our childhood, while
there in the field a soldier's blouse from our parents' youth
has flashed past, and over there we have eternity already,
which nests among the old women, who are more stable than
the Swiss franc and who as if by decree left the Komsomol to
become parishioners, because the ancestors' blood in their
veins is stronger than obstinate atheism, but the capital still
asserts its rights, there are cars of many colors in the front
gardens, although among them one sees more and more antediluvian models, Moskviches with homemade brakes and
pregnant-looking Pobedas; but now the metropolitan province
ends, the fields grow broader, the terrain humps up and gets
hilly, not ironed out by civilization, the distances between
villages get long, villages that more and more acquire the
appearance of being deserted, water pipes are replaced by water
pumps, the boys' shirts become multicolored, their faces are
freckled, but this motley also fades away to nothing, and the
face is freed from anxiety, for on the edge of time a face can't
be bothered with anxiety, and before it has had time to say

goodbye to youth, with the sound of the wedding celebrations still echoing, the face petrifies, and what is eternity if not the equilibrium between life and death?

It is always like that when you leave Moscow. Looking out of the train window or driving to the south with Ksyusha, to the Crimea, you see life hesitate for many kilometers, and the chimneys smoking in the distance seem to be cardboard cutouts, but suddenly, halfway through the journey, hardly noticeable at first, a new tide of life begins, having nothing in common with the breakers from the big city: this is the splashing of a wave from southern, Ukrainian life. In the fields, many-headed sunflowers grow fat and fertile, sweet corn, the joke of past years, gets stronger, there the body knows the sun's kisses, and when you go outside, your cheek is sensitive to its caresses, and then, in some roadside eating establishment, where the borscht is no longer guaranteed to cause stomach upsets, you'll be asked, "Where are you from? From the north?" And they'll tell you what mild winters they have there—but we're not going there today, that's not the road, that's not the route, we shall stop halfway there, having fled the capital's gravity but without traveling as far as that lazy southern shamelessness, where the women don't wear underwear, love to eat, and manage to have a nap after lunch. Today we shall stop halfway there, on the boundary line of peace, where emptiness reigns in the shops and surprises no one, where peasants walk beside the road in black jackets that they wear year in, year out and in black caps that once upon a time they placed on their heads and then forgot. Well, how's things, eh? Nothing special! And this is the sum total of the conversation, and the peasant women rinse the clothes in the ponds, raising their lilac, rosy, sky-blue, and green bottoms, they rinse the washed, darned, patched laundry and don't bear grudges against anyone.

And only the drivers make a racket. Their noisy loads

rattle. Risky overtaking. Yura holds the wheel tighter. Driving
from a position of strength. Fyodorov gives way. Swears.
Chances hitchhikers. From Vladimir to Kursk, from Voronezh
to Pskov. Well, how's things? Nothing special! Moscow has
everything. The girls put out for everyone. We feed everyone.
There's no order. That'll be three rubles.

And a beauty is transported free of charge.

And we were traveling in a fashionable little car, well
polished by Yura, like Romanian furniture, on the cassette
player hits that we were fed up with and Vysotsky for the
hundredth time, he nodded to me after *Hamlet,* a saxophone
like a concertina: the landscape of forthcoming autumn, the
fields expanded, the forests spread their crowns, tractors
crawled over the fields, and from death I was expecting immortality; isn't it about time to have some breakfast, I said to
Yura, isn't it time to build up our strength with some food,
let's lay out a magic carpet, look, there's a cheerful dappled
forest over there, moreover everyone wants to pee, but Yura
was a stubborn driver, he didn't want the trucks he'd overtaken
to catch up with him, and he refused, while good-humored
Yegor, who had fallen asleep on the back seat, was dreaming,
like a tomcat, of ham. On his knees lay a useless map, he
didn't have a clue about route-finding, even though he'd traveled half the country, from Karelia to Dushanbe, and why did
you travel? Dushanbe, it transpires, means Monday in their
language, until he'd got the job as Vladimir Sergeyevich's
boilerman he'd traveled for want of anything better to do, and
I was delighted and said, Then Tashkent is Tuesday, Kiev
Wednesday, Tallinn Thursday, and Moscow—definitely Sunday! And I told the lads how from childhood I'd dreamed
about becoming Katya Furtseva, minister of culture, and how
under my direction theaters and music halls throughout the
country would have flourished from Monday to Sunday, how

wonderful it would have been, and how everyone would have
loved me. The lads laughed at me and forgot about the
purpose of our journey, and I forgot about it too, and I would
have appointed Yurka my deputy—no, Mother, you would
have undermined all culture!—and I wanted to travel on and
on just like this, with endless jazz and the sky above; but I
also wanted to eat and to pee, and I rebelled, and Yura gave
way, and we spread out the tablecloth and started digging in,
because we were starving, and when we had eaten and had a
smoke we felt totally content and I didn't really want to travel
any further, I crashed out in the grass, how good it was to lie
like this, everything so marvelously good. But Yura was tapping his watch. The road soon became a real mess, with deep
potholes; Yura drove in low gear. We were traveling through
a Russia that had grown quiet, and I became sad: we have
different roles. My escorts treated me deferentially, lit my
cigarettes, patted me on the shoulder, and Yegor took a candy
out of his pocket; I smiled at Yegor with a tear, but a feeling
of confusion caught up with me: are they really so selfless?
they're transporting me to give me away, no, what am I saying,
I volunteered for this, but what are they thinking to themselves
and in what ways is this deference better than the type one
meets in restaurants? I was the cause of that deference, I had
fixed rules: when you get down to business with a cock, you
check that it isn't dripping like a leaking roof, and conquest
for them is more important than pleasure, they puff and strut
in front of me, they whistle victory marches, and I would run
to wash it all out and off, victors! they didn't love loving,
they loved conquering, and came without growing weary, and
now, like a fool, I'd got all teary on seeing a candy; whereas
I knew the true worth of restaurant deference, I knew it but
forgave it, this was all I could expect, so let it be paid for in
gold, and not in poor kopecks! I despised men who had no

money, didn't actually consider them men, but now, after all, this was voluntary, why was I so unlucky? I'd wanted so little, my own home and coziness: where were they taking me? They were taking me to hand me over, like when the Finns, after having captured some pathetic refugee, accompany him with honor to the river, to the border, chewing gum, cigarettes, a cup of coffee, polite and pleasant, hanging their heads, another cigarette? I'd been told about such things, but more was wanted from me, why had I agreed? gentle as with a woman condemned to death, what do I know about death except that it's painful? and no one, no one had felt sorry for me, well, just Vitasik, but can this really be called being sorry? for he could have come the evening before, when I was frying a chicken, I was alone, no, he stayed with his wife, with her allergy, he didn't even telephone! A friend indeed, while these two, why were they so pitiless? for the sake of what? And they're frightened that suddenly it will all go wrong, they won't get me there, and they wink to each other in the mirror, or had I become paranoid? I had got all gloomy, and they too were anxious, Yegor stopped his jolly stories in midstream, Yura only half laughed, silence hung in the air. I started to sob. They didn't say a word. And what could they say to comfort me?

We drove into a dusty muddled town with no real beginning or end, hands cold, like a frog, the years contracted, can't make sense of it, I'd lived so little! and my tipsy father smirked in my face. I said, Do you know what I want? I want some fried sunflower seeds! To the market! They set about questioning the passersby, and became very cheerful. The passersby answered in coarse but tuneful voices. They were very detailed with their instructions about the names of streets and landmarks, after the pharmacy you'll see a hardware, turn left, and inquisitive, looking in my direction. Along unpaved

lanes, reminding me of a certain old town, we made our way
to the market. By this time there were few people there and
they weren't doing much business, the sellers yawned and
suffered, and there were puddles, although there hadn't been
any puddles on the way, we walked across rickety bridges,
there was a broken-down horse tethered to a post, and dogs,
but there were sunflower seeds and apples too, all spots and
bruises, all speckled, little apples, looking like people's faces,
and sitting on sacks of onions or perhaps potatoes, the peasants
were downing beer, weak beer with flakes of sediment, the
dogs cringed submissively, and they had only to sniff the sacks
for the peasants to drive them away, scaring them off with a
rotten onion, they pricked up their ears and tails and ran off
without taking offense. The peasants were offering various
rags for sale, a red-faced mushroom collector in a long raincoat
was selling chanterelles, half squashed in a sack, in another
aisle were odd pieces of hardware: screws, nuts, pipe joints; a
little old man, a locksmith, was drinking away his profits,
smoking and coughing all the while, and alongside the pipes
a pair of baby shoes, cornflower blue, with scuffed toes. My
boys moved away toward a younger, more energetic tradesman.
With some pride he displayed on his counter piles of journals,
booklets, plastic handbags, and brightly daubed portraits: kittens with bows, cute little dogs, the poet Esenin with a pipe.
Yegor flicked through Gogol's "epic" *Dead Souls* and asked the
price. Yura, who had been picking his way with more care
than any of us, got himself muddy.

And, having looked around the market, I thought this
was just the place for me to ask the people what it was they
lacked and what I must run for. Everything revealed itself
unambiguously. There we were. Moscow parrots, with our
studied nonchalance, loitering around, and there they were,
the possessors of the earth, the preservers of the whole, the

capitalists of eternity. They lived, we existed. We were splashing in time like little silvery fish.

The difference between us turned out to be amazingly simple: their life is full of uncomprehended sense and meaninglessness. It appears that consciousness is acquired in exchange for the loss of meaning. It is much later that one starts the pursuit of this lost meaning. Later still comes the moment of triumph when one convinces oneself that meaning is reached and achieved; however, there's a little-noticed misunderstanding in the fact that the newly achieved meaning turns out not to be the equal of the one that was lost. Comprehended meaning is deprived of the innocent freshness of original meaning.

This possession of meaning is not due to their own merits; they possess meaning the way a cow possesses milk. However, it must be admitted that milk is necessary for life. Our chief crime is in our attitude toward meaning, but we often project our guilt onto the natural possessors of meaning, and in this way we shift the qualities of meaning onto their shoulders. Such an aberration formed and continues to form a significant part of our national being.

Why should one hide this? For I too was once *they*. I was indistinguishable from my school friends, I was like my mommy, who has remained *they*, despite the way she raves on about her desire to move to Judaic Palestine, but in me there was an abundance of life, and in this thoughtless and cheerful superfluity my unhappiness was engendered. Consequently, consciousness is a luxury, and like any luxury, it brings with it a sense of guilt and, in the last analysis, punishment. It is the loss of meaning itself that is our traditional punishment.

And that's all there is to it. But at that time this didn't occur to me, and I pestered Yegor, nodding at the yokels and smiling from afar at the mediocrities: Yegor, I badgered him, explain to me, for God's sake, in what way are *they* better than us? And Yegor, who had also once been *they*, said, I haven't a clue, they aren't better than us in any way. Then I put a trickier question: Yegor, that means *they* are worse? And at this point Yegor starts to have doubts and doesn't want to admit that *they* are worse. But *they are* worse, I insist. Stop it! answers Yegor, but Yurochka, a hereditary intellectual, whose conscience had become fixed firmly in place, says, No, in some way *they* are better. . . . And since they are better, I say excitedly, then let us seek their advice, boys! Let's tell them without more ado where we're going and why, how I'm going to run over the field, attracting the great usurper (but is he a usurper?), and how he will immolate me, and how the scales will fall from everyone's eyes (but will they fall?). Boys, let's ask them, let's! Don't let's try to be clever, we can be clever later, for the moment let's come out into the open: in what ways are *they* better than us and in what ways worse? I don't know! Let's hear the answer! The reason *they* are better than us, Yurochka said without hesitation, is that *they* don't ask us whether we are better than them or not, but we ask them! Well, is that really such a great advantage, if their brains work at the speed of a broken watch? No. I don't want to run blind; I want to ask. And my escorts, my cavaliers, can't do anything with me, and I go up to the peasant women and say:

"Listen, women! Stop your trading for a moment! Do you know who I am?"

The women merely cast sidelong glances at me and tried to conceal their goods, all those clothes and tights, as if I were a government inspector or garbage, and some of them ran toward the exit, to get out of harm's way. I see that I've scared them, they'll run off in all directions and it'll be impossible to gather them together again, and so I went and climbed onto the counter, my hand clutching the pillar supporting the roof above the market alley, and yelled:

"Stop! Listen! Hey, all of you here! Stop! Today I am going to accept death so that all of you, without exception, may live better and more beautifully, I'm not kidding, I shall accept it, as in her time did Joan of Arc! I shall run over a Tatar battlefield, which is not far away from you, do you hear? Stop, women! Don't run away! And you, men! Stop drinking! I'm asking your advice, not trying to trick you. Explain to me at last, good people, what you want, how you want to live, so that my sufferings for you may not be in vain, so that I may go to my death for the sake of happiness and for the sake of your lives!"

I shouted all this because I was no coward, and what's more I was only asking them for advice, indeed I was only asking them to stop and listen, it was after all something miraculous, so they ought to, if only out of curiosity, but Yegor and Yurochka panicked and tried to get me down from the counter, though I fought them off, while the women—the women were fleeing without any attempt to hide what they were doing, bolting, and a peasant sitting on a sack of onions was twisting his finger against his temple and looking at me with an open grin: either drunk or else from a nuthouse. . . . While Yurochka and Yegor were pulling me down from the counter, the local arm of the law appears, he condescends to investigate the shouting, he creeps up on me. "You," he says to me, using the polite form, looking up at me from below, "why have you climbed up there in the market alley, where trading is going on? Citizen, why are you disturbing public order? Show me your papers." At this point the women, I see, are peeking out from around the counters and, of course, are glad, and the men are also looking, taking swigs of beer.

I leap down from the counter, I look, the militiaman is a really shabby specimen, a humble fellow with no stars or stripes on his shoulders, the lowliest of the low-rankers. I say to him, "I won't show you my papers! I don't feel like it." At this point, I see, Yurochka pulls him to one side and whispers something. He's saying: a Moscow actress, we're just passing through, capricious, you can see that yourself, and our passports are in the car, let's go, I'll show you, we parked in the square, and your weather is marvelous, no rain for a long time? Do you smoke? They lit up, and in this way we would have got to the square, but I say, "Now that we're here, you could at least buy me some sunflower seeds!" "There, you can see for yourself—" Yurochka laughs, and the cop laughs and looks around the market in a lordly way: Well, who's selling seeds? Yegor bought me some, we set off for the car, with the cop at our heels: "Boys, won't you sell me your jeans?" And Yurochka, a hereditary intellectual, he naturally says, in an oily voice, "We'd love to; it's just that we've left Moscow for a short while only, we haven't got any spare trousers, you understand. . . ." The cop understands: you can't go back to Moscow without any trousers, "And you," he says to me in parting, but a bit bashfully, "don't you go stirring up the people anymore . . ." "It's not easy," I say, "to stir them up, you wear yourself out just trying. First of all they run away in all directions, only the drunks remain, and even that bunch will crawl away on all fours. . . ." The militiaman smiles. The actress is joking. But all the same the thought has lodged in his head: Why did she climb on the counter of that stall in the market alley in those interesting boots of hers? And so he remains with this thought and follows us with his eyes and keeps on living with this thought: Why? What for? Thus he lives and remembers me, and the memory aches sweetly, and before he goes to sleep he says to his wife, Nina, "But I still don't understand why it was necessary for that Moscow actress to climb up onto the stalls, hey, Nin?" and Nina, having thought, answers, "Maybe she was rehearsing a part." And the militiaman answers, "Yes, that must be it, Nin, most probably rehearsing . . . yes indeed, Nin, why didn't I think of that before, that she was rehearsing a part—?" And his wife, Nina, will say to him reproachfully, "You're slow on the uptake, you are, Ivan, oh, you're so slow-witted. . . ." And then they'll be silent for a long time, silent for a lifetime, and when they rouse themselves and look, she is a rough old woman, and he's retired, was a sergeant when he left, with medals, and it's time to die, and we are dying.

As soon as we had driven out of the market town, Yu- rochka turns on me, he expresses his displeasure, he reproaches me for my caprices, but I crack the sunflower seeds, spit out the husks, and stare through the window at the absence of anything of interest. They are silent for a while and leave me in peace, my warmhearted escorts, and they start to argue between themselves about why so many of the trucks we meet, particularly after leaving the metropolitan province, have in the window a portrait of Stalin in his marshal's uniform. Upset, Yegor said that the people respect him for the war, but Yu- rochka retorts that the people are merely protesting against the chaos all around and there's no hidden agenda here, be- cause they don't want any violent reprisals, it's simply nos- talgia. They display old Mustachio Joe, says Yurochka, because they don't remember anything, they don't know and they don't want to know; and then they had a long argument about whether the people know or want to know about the massa- cres, and there was just no way they could figure out whether they know *or* forgive, are prepared to forgive everything so long as there's order, and I listen and listen and say, "Why don't we ask them?" And they say, "You sit quiet. You've asked once already, and we had to run for our lives." In fact, no one had even touched us! And they began to argue further: Would the nation have held up if there had been no Stalin, or would it have gone to pieces, and although they decide it wouldn't have collapsed, it is obvious to me that it would have collapsed and Hitler wouldn't have been defeated, and I ask them, "In your opinion, did any woman go down on Stalin or not?" They thought about it. "It's impossible to know. Everyone says that Beria used to be sucked off, it was written all over his face. . . . But anyway," they say, "what difference does it make?" And I say, "There *is* a difference, because if no one gave him head, that's why he went around being such a beast, after everyone's head." They started roaring with laughter, said this was nonsense, and started up a learned conversation, which became very boring and uninteresting for me. Because I have, perhaps, a specifically female perspective on this issue.

Whether he killed innocent people, as some assert, or not, that doesn't matter now, it's unimportant, perhaps he had his reasons for killing them, because they didn't believe he wanted to do good for people and they were getting in his way and he got angry with them and murdered them like a great man insulted and angered. But Yegor dug his heels in and said Stalin wasn't great but was a sadist and a bloodsucker, a butcher and a monster. So I say, "Hey, what are you getting so worked up about? Good riddance to him, that Stalin, I'm fed up with it all: let's talk about something else." But Yegor says, "You can't be a real Joan of Arc if you approve of Stalin," and I say, "What's all this about me approving—what do I want with this Georgian gorilla? Most likely he simply enjoyed being in command, and after all, one is hardly going to shed tears over killing foreigners!" "But he killed Georgians too!" Yurochka says indignantly. "And you say that he was unfair!"

I trump them. "And incidentally," I say, "Vladimir Sergeyevich used to tell me—he'd met Stalin on several occasions
—that Stalin could see right through anyone, to his very guts,
yet you say he isn't great. . . ."

I watch them: they're not very pleased with my speeches
and say, "You'd be better off remembering how that car almost
crushed you, think about that, even though it's chicken feed,"
they say, "compared with Kolyma. Yes," they say, "if they'd
sent you to Kolyma, so that every guard could commit assaults
against your beauty, then you'd be singing a different tune."
But I answer that Kolyma would have had nothing to offer
me, and consequently, on the contrary, I would have been
with Vladimir Sergeyevich at Stalin's receptions, the greatest
beauty there, and I would have smiled, full of elation, into
the cameras. "Don't let's quarrel, boys! It's ridiculous to quarrel
because of Stalin; perhaps we'll quarrel about someone else
too, the emperor Paul perhaps?" And they say, "So why are
you going to run around the field, then?"

Well, that's different. It has nothing to do with politics.
It has to do with what is called sorcery. So many degenerates
are reared today, they drink cheap booze, they mumble in-
distinctly, but as soon as I start running, it will become clear
who's right, who's to blame, "and just," I say, "leave me alone;
I could have married a Latin American ambassador and lived
in Panama and washed my hands of everything." "And why
didn't you get married?" "I just didn't, I don't know why
myself. And so many times it's been like this: fate is on the
point, just on the point, of smiling on me and, it seems, is
just about to bear me away to happiness (and do I need much?),
but no! some puny pygmies and sexless sluts get lucky, though
they offer nothing of what you want. . . ." They exchange
glances and say, "Fair enough, Irochka, let's not talk about
that," but the way they're needling me burns me up, I'm as

stubborn as a mule, you don't know me, when I dig in my heels you'll never shift me. Sometimes some man or other will be burning red hot with passion, he's just about to mount me, when I suddenly say, "No! I don't want to!" "What? why? what's happened?" He's shaking all over, he just has to, but I say, "No! I said no! I don't feel like it any longer." And I watch with pleasure how he goes all limp. So that he shouldn't think too highly of himself. Who does he think he is after all . . . and it's the same here. Oh, I think, my dear, dear friends! Just wait! Go on, exchange glances! What's the point, they're saying, of arguing with her, let her run around the field first, let her strain herself and perish, let her be torn in half by the hostile semen—it's not important: she'll die, but we'll be left to live our lives, above us the sun will rise every day, while she can be food for worms!

They had already turned off the main road, they are looking at the map, not far to go, soon that Tatar battlefield will turn up, they don't have to suffer with me or put up with my caprices much longer! I say, "I've come to a decision: I'm not going to run at all; you have ruined my heroic mood once and for all." I look: Yegor is turning red, very soon now, like a grenade, his bearded face will explode, but Yurochka, he understands that the critical moment has come, he's cunning, he says, both sadly and radiantly, "Irochka, you aren't running for our sakes, and it wasn't us who suggested this run to you. You are running because you heard a voice from above, and we are simply accompanying you, that's all, and if you're not going to run because of us, then that's just the pretext you've found. Say honestly that you've got cold feet, and we'll head home, to Moscow." I say, "Let's have a smoke! My nerves are really . . ." I light up a Marlboro, they're the only brand I smoke, a certain restaurant manager gets them for me, he's almost an official millionaire, that is, he doesn't even hide the fact! But his restaurant: pah! a real joint. . . . I say, "Fair enough, boys I've become so worried that I've actually got a stomachache; it's terrifying. And I do understand my, so to speak, mission is perhaps, greater than me, I daresay Joan of Arc didn't understand everything with her little fifteen-year-old virgin's mind, I daresay she too was paralyzed with fear, particularly when she was tied to the stake."

And I'll say in all honesty: my condition was a strange one, even before we arrived at the field, the sort of state where you don't belong to yourself. If I had completely belonged to myself I naturally wouldn't have run, I wouldn't have done such a stupid thing, but I would have forgiven both that Stepan who ran into me and all of them in turn, and if the worst had come to the worst, I would have slipped away quietly to the place where the little magazine was conceived, with my little photographs, but, I say in all honesty, I was in a strange state: on the one hand, half of me is dying from fright and believing that the catastrophe will really and truly occur—that is, my running around the field won't be in vain, will be for real, no fooling, the sort of foreboding that makes one's blood freeze and one's legs grow numb—but my other half feels that I will run come what may, no matter how much I cling to the boys, this half in the end outweighs the other, and all this is happening as if it's bypassing me, occurring without my consent and agreement, and not even because I wanted to become a saint, for some reason I'd stopped thinking about that, but it's just that I had the feeling there was no way back for me. And if I could explain and convey exactly what all this was like, then I would be a genius, but how could I! For me, an aging beauty, having decided to make a last parade of my fading attractions, the theme of mourning was double-edged, not only mourning for Leonardik, not so much for his untimely end, but for me! for me! for me! I felt old then, once and for all, and nothing beyond that was of interest.

And at this moment the field appeared right on cue, leaping out from behind a bend in the road, an ordinary sort of
field, covered with clover, and in the distance a small river
shone beyond the alders on its banks, well, says Yurochka, I
think we've arrived. We climbed out of the car and saw how
the land lay. Yegor did some exercises, stretching his limbs.
I spluttered with laughter. A bearded man shouldn't do gymnastics. I say, "But are you sure that this is *the* field?" They
say, "But there's no one here, no one to ask." "Okay," I say,
"what do you say we make a campfire; there's still a long time
till dusk. . . ." We set off for a tiny grove, gathered brushwood,
found wild mushrooms. I sat down on the ground. It was cold.
"Oh," I say, "I'll catch a cold." Then I started laughing: "No,
I won't have time. . . ." And I look: my escorts' faces have
flinched; somehow it's also gotten through to them that I won't
have time, maybe some sort of feeling visited them too, I don't
know. . . . I say, "Well, why don't you say something; are
we going to stay silent like this until evening? Tell me some
story or other. You, Yegor," I say, "are a pen pusher after all.
I daresay you'll describe all this in a short story? The clover,
which, you'll say, is on the field . . ." "No." Yegor shakes his
head. "If I do portray it, then it will not be a short story, but
I don't know what; well, like the Gospels maybe. . . ." "For
some reason," I say, "I keep smoking and smoking, I'll find
running difficult, I'll be gasping for breath," and I threw away
my cigarette. Well, what else can one say about the field? A
field just like any other field, slightly uneven, there are so
many like it, it would have been possible to find one nearer
Moscow, you always think that there should be something
particularly special, as if white bones ought to be lying around
amidst the clover, and skulls, side by side with arrows, lances,
and I don't know what else, like those pictures of famous
battles and heroic warriors, and also there must definitely be
carrion crows, and the carrion crows have to be cawing, but

in fact the field is peaceful and empty, the copse edges it, it is turning autumn gold. We start to eat the watermelon, but for some reason without any appetite, even though it is sweet, the Kalmyk hadn't tricked me, you won't regret buying it, he said, you'll come back for a second, and I also tell them a joke, the watermelon has brought it to mind. "Do you know," I say, "why Vasily Ivanovich wanted to cross a watermelon with a cockroach? So that when you cut it, all the seeds will scurry away. . . . Funny?" And I can see that it's not funny, but what else can I think up, when all sorts of nonsense is hammering away inside my skull.

# EIGHTEEN

And so our wait for the sunset came to an end, the west showed red with a haughty, murky light, the sunset stood like a wall, foreshadowing the impending cold, but we sat by the bonfire and picked away at the watermelon—the conversation had been sluggish for a long time—and now and then, to prevent our freezing to the spot, Yegor would stand up and, snapping branches against his knee, silently throw them on the fire.

The darker it grew, the harsher and more triumphant became the faces of my escort-friends, keeping their silence, each thinking to himself about the lofty and the impossible, because on this occasion the impossible was possible. As for me, looking into the fire, my thoughts had become displaced, and out of the blue I remembered school hiking trips around my native region, tents, pots over the campfire, cleaning mushrooms and potatoes, and the obligatory dances to the transistor, gurgling and staticky, and as soon as you get into dancing they interrupt with the latest news bulletin, and boys make awkward advances, the sweaty palms of pimpled youths, and the same chill breeze toward evening, and even a similar solemnity before sleep in the country, only we weren't drinking anything, and their kisses were unsophisticated, and when it

had become totally dark, when the colors of the sunset had
run and it had rolled itself up, and the forest had changed
from gold to black and moved aside, and we were sitting at
the forest's edge, something jogged me, something nudged me
in the side, and I understood: It was time. Time!

I won't hide behind deceit and playacting, won't be cunning or pretend: I was horribly afraid, I didn't want to die, I
had been dying all day long, dozens of times, and I hadn't got
used to dying, not one bit, I thought about Grandfather's
empty apartment, where under the pillow my embroidered
cambric nightshirt was waiting for me, waiting in vain, and
I felt sorry for it, that it wouldn't be needed by me anymore,
and someone else, no one knows who, would put it on and
defile it just by doing so, and it could have been so different,
if not for my enemies, who had multiplied around me like
rabbits, large, gray, red-eyed creatures, and I said, "It's time!"
I wanted to ask what they would do then, what would happen
to me, to my body, would they take it back or would they
bury it here, and I thought that in the car trunk I'd seen a
spade wrapped in rags . . . but I couldn't ask. They, most
probably, were also thinking something like that, because
suddenly Yegor, clearing his throat, said in a low voice, "Now
they display Stalin in the windshields of their Kamaz trucks,
but in the future they will display you." But Yurochka said,
"Lord, is it really possible that it will happen? Is it possible
that this bad dream we've been cursed with will dissipate? I'm
trembling all over and crying at the thought of this, and I
bow down before you," he added with tears in his eyes. And
I answered them hoarsely, my face sweating: "Boys . . . something's nudging me in the side and is saying, It's time!"

They shivered in unison and looked at me timidly and
helplessly, like children regarding their mother when her labor
pains have started, looked helplessly and with trembling, com-

muning with the obscure secret. "Yes," I said, "this is indeed
*the* field: I feel its restless emanations. . . . I'm terrified,
Yegorushka!"

Yegor rushed to me, clasped my shoulders with his strong
shaking hands, and then, leaning over, left a worried fraternal
kiss on my cheek. As for Yurochka, he simply pressed himself
to my palm and didn't say anything. I lit up a final cigarette
and didn't even have time for a proper drag before I burned
my fingers. I threw the butt into the fire and picked myself
up, and started to undo the zipper of my boots slowly, my
little Dutch boots, bought with the checks for use in restricted
shops, checks earned by my dear artist-on-tour Dato. You little
fool, I thought, in what Paraguay are you now playing your
violin concerto, your requiem for your Irochka? I took off my
boots and thought about what to do with them. Throw them
into the bonfire? I won't need them now. To hell with them!
But suddenly I felt embarrassed about making melodramatic
gestures, for theatricality would be an insult to the mystery,
at that moment I was starting to live a different, final life,
and I mustn't make unnecessary movements, everything
should be serene, Ira, no fuss. I took off my boots. I threw
them to the side. My painted toenails—I had beautiful toes,
almost as musical, indeed, as my fingers, and not stumps, such
as the majority of humankind has, all deformed from cheap
footwear and lack of care—I looked at my toes and said to
myself: No one was able to appreciate these toes at their true
worth, not one person . . . and in fact no one appreciated
me at my true worth, they just looked at me as if I were a
piece of succulent pink meat, and their trousers stood up when
I entered a room: ministers' trousers and poets' trousers. And
the trousers of my own dear daddy.

Oh, Ksyusha! At that moment I wanted to embrace you,
to bequeath to you my last words and kisses! Deep in thought

about you, about our life together, I took off my sand-colored jeans—they were also a present, a present from Vladimir Sergeyevich from his last business trip before his death, to Copenhagen, where he had gone to battle, as was his wont, for the cause of détente and from where, after a week's battling, he had brought back these jeans, a pack of playing cards, and a rare weariness. He was so bored with traveling to one place or another and with battling that he didn't even pretend anymore, he used to resist trips or he would travel reluctantly. Leonardik, take me with you. Take me as your secretary or unofficially, please, just this once, Leonardik! You didn't miss anything there, honestly. Who'd want those hotels, restaurant cooking, protocols, and meetings. Or the perpetual draft in the halls from their air conditioners!

I silently took off my sand-colored jeans—in order to keep me happy he had brought back three pairs, khaki-colored, beige, and sandy, but I had fallen in love with the sandy ones, sold the others—I took them off and put them too aside, and as soon as I had taken them off I felt the dampness and chill of the autumn evening.

I slipped off my tights and they rolled into a little ball and lay there, like a mouse, on my palm; my legs had kept their tan, a quick-fading northern suntan, the tan of Serebryany Bor and Nikolina Hill; this year I hadn't gone anywhere, this year they'd made my life a misery, I was constantly frightened that if I went away they'd come and grab the flat and seal it up.

Having taken off my ash-gray tights, I knelt down, pulled off my suede jacket and, after it, over my head, my sweater, made from very pure, soft Scottish wool, and after the sweater—I was a bit disheveled, and I instinctively wanted to tidy my hair with a brush—after the sweater my white sports shirt with my initials on the front, I.T.: the American girls had managed to get something to me after all; and now my breasts and I were already in the power of the evening chill and dampness, now to hurl myself into the river and— a minute later—into the embraces of a fluffy blanket, a glass of cognac, and home home home. And I was in the unsteady power of the bonfire.

My clothes are neatly folded and placed to the side.

The boys, understanding that this farewell disrobing was intended not for them, fixed their eyes upon the bonfire, but even then it seemed to me beside the bonfire that I could feel a distant, alien, and excited gaze upon me, as if someone in a far-off window had aimed his binoculars at me; he trembles, kneeling on the windowsill, and prays to God that I not put out the light immediately but walk aimlessly around the room a bit, flaunt myself before the dressing-table mirror—this is how it seemed to me, or else that I should comb my hair, but I didn't say anything about this to the boys, who were burying their noses in their knees.

I stood up once more. I rose above the bonfire, pulled off with that strange shame that had remained with me since childhood my skimpy white cotton pants—I can't stand flow-ery pants or, even worse, striped ones, I love the white color of purity and I always removed my pants with shame, and men would immediately die, and I'll tell you that a woman who takes off her pants without showing shame knows zilch about love.

I pulled off my pants, stepped out of them, and firmly pressing my breasts between my arms, as if plucking up cour-age, *making up my mind,* I said with a smile . . .

I am well aware of this smile of mine. It is sort of guilty, it is a very Russian smile. Foreign girls aren't able to smile in this guilty way, they can't feel this guilt, or perhaps their guilt never rises to the surface, does not reach the eyes or the skin.

I was apologizing not for something in particular but for everything. Thus, when saying farewell to guests, a hostess, particularly a provincial one, will smile this smile and say, "Please forgive me if anything wasn't *quite* as it should have been. . . ."

And I was leaving life with this sort of smile, I felt it on my face. Forgive me if anything wasn't quite as it should have been. But I said something different.

Boys . . . well, all right . . . I'm off . . . and give my things to the poor. . . . Well, what else? Don't cry for me. There's no need. And no mausoleums at all. Let everything remain between us. But don't waste a single minute; when the scales fall, don't linger, don't wait for the wrinkled flesh to become tight and elastic again. Ring, sound the bells! Let it be a holiday, not a wake!

Thus I spoke or thus spoke someone quite different on my behalf, through me, and painfully squeezing my breasts between my arms, I prophesied as something egged me on. They bowed shamefacedly, my boys, and I strode into the darkness but, suddenly, turned around and added, I added the following, though I didn't understand the meaning of these words: And don't shed blood, there's been enough blood shed already. And be kind to the Chinese. Don't offend the Chinese! . . . See you.

Fair enough about the blood, but the Chinese! Where did the Chinese come from? I'd never thought about them. This remained shrouded in mystery.

Was there a moon? Yes. It hung low above the forest, but the clouds kept covering it. It was not bright and not full. I felt the sharpness of the earth, her unevenness from the plow. I was no longer looking back at the bonfire, I started to seek a direction in which to run, and somewhere through the dark a patch of trees was visible, facing me, rotting alders, growing alongside the river, and I decided to run in their direction.

I started running, I ran, my tender soles flinching, the earth was pricking so painfully, as if I was running over thorns, but I felt this only for the first few steps, and my breasts leapt and bobbed, and soon I didn't feel any of this, I ran, and the farther I ran, the thicker and more impenetrable became the autumn air, which had been so rarefied to begin with, with every step the air became heavier and more difficult to run through, and I ran on, as if I were running not across a field but in water up to my neck, so labored was my running, yet at the same time I ran quite fast, my tangle of hair fluttered, I soon felt very hot, and this heavy water in which I was running grew thicker, concentrating itself into a ray; that is, the ray grew thicker, directed on me from somewhere on high, but not from the farthest heights, not somewhere from the stars, but lower, as if from the clouds that were hanging over the field, and I felt that I was running in this ray, but this wasn't the ray of a searchlight or a lighthouse, not a pillar of light, no, it bore no relation whatsoever to either light or darkness, it had a different, lusterless composition, something viscously honeylike, something like jam, and it was sticking to me more and more, and, sticking to me, it would sometimes lift me up a bit, it seemed, in such a way that I was hanging without any support, my legs flailing in its thickness, then it would let me down again, and I would feel the grass on my soles, it played with me in this way, this ray, one minute it would crash down and crush me with its jammy viscous mass, the next it would release me and follow me as I ran, and I would run farther, and then it would lift me up again, and once more I would flail my legs untidily, but I was moving somewhere, I wasn't staying in one spot, and, whether from this persecution or from something else instead, the earth wasn't standing still either, but started to heave, now up, now down, first up and then down, swinging high and low, halfway

up, then down again, and then right up, and once again down,
but the invisible jam enveloped all my body: legs, stomach,
breast, throat, head eventually, and the earth started to push
up at me, make me stumble, fall to the grass, but I resisted
this with all my strength, because I realized that as soon as I
fell, the earth, heaving beneath me, leaping like a wave, would
drag me across the hummocks farther and farther, and I would
be scratched all over, battered, tortured, but I didn't want to
give in, I didn't want to surrender, I had no intention of giving
in, I felt that *it* was stronger than I, but this gave me the
strength of desperation, no, you won't stun me, you'll take
me alive, and not as carrion, that is, I wasn't thinking of
saving myself, but I didn't want to reconcile myself to defeat
sooner than I had to: just like someone drowning in the sea
at night, a long way from the shore, and you feel you can't
make it, and you thrash your arms, and you are carried farther
and farther out to sea, farther and farther, but despite this you
swim toward shore, for indeed while there is still strength left
you won't sink to the bottom, even though it's useless, this
is what I was like, I struggled too, even though I was gripped
by terror, that is, I understood—when the earth started to
throw me up in the air, to grow mad beneath me—I understood that the pillar of viscous material was the very thing
that had to enter me and tear me up, and this, I will tell you,
was no longer like my rapist, the dream one nor the real,
who, of course, were giants in the size and strength of their
erection but all the same were human, fitted into some sort
of human boundaries and actually caused mixed feelings of
pain and rapture, that's how that was; but here by contrast
there were no boundaries, no limits, I don't even know what
to compare it with, with something totally out of bounds,
well, as if I were three years old and he was a monster and a
weirdo, a three-year-old tot who doesn't even guess what's

awaiting her, but sees only that mister isn't joking, that this is far beyond human limits, at such a thing people yell with their whole being and tear their hair out by the roots, and I too, it seems, cried out, at any rate my mouth had opened in such a way that a cramp seized my cheekbones, and I yelled something or other there, at any rate I wanted to shout simple basic words: mama! mama! mommy!—though I wasn't thinking at that moment about my mommy with her earrings and perm, I wasn't calling her, I was calling some other mother, everybody's mother. And you know, I'll tell you: God forbid that you should have to undergo such a thing! I wouldn't wish it upon my worst enemy. . . . But then, having turned somersaults beneath heaven and earth, I started to feel that the force of this ray or column, I don't even know what to call it, it started to grow weak, that is, it was as if for a minute *he* had been distracted, and then, when he started up again, and he did set about it again, then it was as if there was less ardor, more indifferent eccentricities, waning passion, and suddenly it was sort of: snap! and he turned away, in a different direction, and it was as if I had flown into emptiness, and I look: I'm running with as much strength as I can muster through the rarefied autumn air, despite my utter weariness, in short, he'd released me, that is, he hadn't behaved like a normal man, who gets more and more worked up, gets so excited that until he comes he won't let you go, he's very likely to beat you if you don't give it to him, although I sometimes took such a risk, out of malice or else so as to be even more valuable for him: as if to say, I'm not the type of person who can be had that easily—but here *he* had gone cold toward *me*, as if he'd got a good hard-on from me at first and then his mood had changed, he'd stopped wanting it, he'd stopped liking me perhaps, and even though I perfectly well understood that his embrace would cost me no less than my life, I nevertheless took offense, and I even looked all around me, stupidly, as if to say, Where has he disappeared to, my torturer! I must also say that his torturing was not sweet in a human way, that is, I want to say that it is sometimes the case that they smack you in the face and you really enjoy it, well, masochism, although I don't really fit into this category, only on rare occasions, there's Dato, for example, but otherwise I am more likely to bash someone myself, and Leonardik even begged me to do so, but here there was absolutely no pleasure, that is, one sensed that there was no man there but just this kind of sticky living jam, and perhaps once upon a time there were some women who would come as they were impaled on the stake—I don't know, but my pleasure didn't rise to such heights, and I can honestly say that this jam didn't make me cream my jeans.

In sum, I had run practically to the river, all in a lather and a sweat, I can't get my breath back, I'm thinking: Now I'll throw myself into the water, and I'll steam like a red-hot poker, and the water will boil around me—this is how hot I was! But I didn't throw myself in the water to cool off, but instead I wandered back, to the bonfire. . . . I don't know how far I walked, but I got there, emerged on them out of the dark, and my appearance made them think I was no longer of this world, they leapt to their feet, their eyes open wide, and I say, falling on my knees next to the bonfire: Boys, beat the retreat. They say to me: What? How? I explain. *He's* there, that's clear as day, he tortured me, tortured me, played with me like a doll, and then went and turned away . . . as if to other, sweeter tortures. Yegor, shaking his beard, says, Take this, drink it. You should recover a bit. Lord, what horrors! But I waved away the glass of vodka: There's no need, Yegor. I, I say, will get my breath back a bit now and then I'll run again: for you see, now it's certain that *he's* there!

It turns out that the voice was correct. . . . The voice! The speaking cock! The brothers Ivanovich will later offer this vulgarism as their contribution. Whew! I actually got a tickle in my throat as I thought about this. What jolly fellows. Shortsighted materialists. But I bet you're superstitious. Black cats? Broken mirrors? Dreaming about blood? What? Go on, say something. They are silent. They weren't *there*. But Yurochka says, Surely you're not going to go running again? And Yegor, You shouted so loud that the whole countryside could hear you! But I sit down beside them, like that painting Luncheon on the Grass, crouching, while tremors shake my body, and Yegor puts his jacket around my shoulders, like a country suitor, and offers me some vodka, but I refuse, and I don't feel like smoking, but something's tugging at me—I pull myself away, you won't believe it, rush back to the field, bargaining myself away, explain it how you like, and not even for the sake of something grand, this was already understood, but perdition beckons me, beckons me, I had moved into a new state of being and was no longer a dweller on this earth. I will tell you frankly, it's not that I wasn't afraid of death, no, I was afraid, but I had split into layers—I and not I, one is shivering, the other flaps its little wings. And of course, no one can live like that, I myself know this better than anyone, I write and I know this, and one must not write about these things, it is *forbidden*, except that this isn't the prohibition the Ivanoviches will afterward place on me, that's for sure! This is a different type of prohibition, of a more subtle force, I shouldn't be writing, I should be praying, praying, but I write, I flap my little wings, and this writing summons me, summons, I can't stop writing, fool, and it is as though I am again running through the field, the same shivers and fever, and the fateful child howls in my womb, orders me from the womb not to write, threatens a miscarriage, but I can't not tell, and indeed in any event I'm done for, such now is my fate, Ksyushechka. And so I write. I write how I ran, and I ran as I write. . . .

And here's what I want to say to you all. After I had got my breath back, recovered, even though there was still noise in my head, this hadn't passed, it went on, I stand up, throw off Yegor's jacket, and once again step out into the dark. And as a parting shot I say to them, If it doesn't work out now I'll run a third time. I won't give up. And as I leave they look at me as if they're looking at Joan of Arc, and they're weeping. Can it really be that this smoke will not clear before the Second Coming? And if I made a shitty Joan of Arc, perhaps you'll make a better one. And I also thought: Inasmuch as he can smell my sin and bergamot from afar—until I got pregnant, when the smell was extinguished, and this is also an omen! —since I smell like *this*, then how can *he* resist me? He has nowhere else to go! It will gush, his poisonous semen cannot but gush, his festering flow! With these thoughts I start running once more.

And once more, before I had run forty meters, the earth started to turn and spin beneath me, and the ray became focused and grew taut, becoming jam and pus, the earth fell back beneath me, and went to fly on the swings, and that column which was jutting out of the clouds stuck to me and started torturing my soul and breaking my body, everything burned in me, my innards groaned, burst, and I shouted in a voice not my own, and called a mother not my own: Mama! Mommy!! *Oh!* And this time the force seized me and was in no mood for joking, so I know that even if it doesn't fuck me, it will still torment the life out of me, I feel—on the edge of my reason—that I am becoming more and more irresistible and beautiful to him, the monster, he grasps my breasts in a clutch from which there is no escape, aiming to tear them out by the roots, so as to lick and suck the blood from the gaping holes, and then chop off my legs and arms and fit the stump onto himself, like a marionette, well, I was certain: right now! He'd been sizing me up for a long time, playing around, and I no longer knew whether I was running or flying upside down into the sky and clouds or whether I was crawling along the earth on all fours, my tears fall, I howl and shake my head, my breasts ripped out, my side torn off, whether I was lying dead, or something else again, that is, I'd lost all points of reference, as if my sense of balance had collapsed, like a clock from the wall, and smashed into smithereens, that was the state I was in, close to total madness, and it was with good reason that afterward the Ivanoviches looked in my eyes, found primordial chaos in them, and asked sympathetically: had I not *gone nuts* after the field? Wouldn't it perhaps be a good idea to get some treatment? No, it wouldn't, no need. And I hadn't gone off my rocker, only gone crazy for a time, but then on the field I had no thoughts of the Ivanoviches, they would both have fitted into the palm of my hand, and I had already said goodbye to everyone and to you, Ksyusha, in particular, but again—dammit!—it had gone wrong! My impression was that he'd been distracted again. Hey, what are you trying to say! Well, you know, as with a frigid woman, the wave is almost ready to roll over her, and suddenly it goes past, and however much you lick her there, play with her— past! past! past! Do you understand, Ksyusha? Remember what a hard time we had with Natashka? A tricky case . . . The same here. Only a million times more terrifying and, if you like, more hurtful. For you see, I'd agreed to this. For you see, not everyone would endure this. You, for example, Ksyusha, couldn't have stood it, you're frightened of any sort of pain, you're even frightened to have your teeth treated by René, and he is after all your husband, he won't hurt you deliberately, and in addition he's French, a delicate man, but I endured! I wanted it! I had spread my tail like a peahen: here! take me! kill! But just come, at last, come with your stink and stench! He didn't take me. He didn't kill me. He didn't come.

And once again I returned to the bonfire, to my guards, to Yegor and Yurochka.

They are sitting there green, like cockroaches, twitching and shaking so violently that their faces, cheeks, noses go in different directions. I see that they too have felt something evil. I crouched by them, said nothing. And what could be said? Even without words it was all clear. And at this point Yurochka begged, Don't run, Irina, for a third time, he says. God knows what will come of it, nature might ask for it doggy style, and instead of being better it will be even worse for us all! And his teeth were chattering: Don't run a third time, Irochka, I entreat you! But I say, Don't talk rubbish. It won't be worse. . . . And Yegor, he hurries to agree with Yurochka: What do you mean, it won't? What if it is worse? And he expands: You see now it's still okay, bearable, oh, you're nauseated, of course, but being sick isn't the same as being a stiff; we'll manage. . . . Let's go back to Moscow in our warm car!

In short, the escorts have lost their nerve, observing my runs from a distance, and they don't even cover me with a jacket, they show no concern or respect for me, on account of their own terror. At this point I pull on my Scottish sweater, pick a blade of grass, I sit and chew at the stalk, rest and do not believe in their fears, it won't be worse, and this devilish field summons me to it, to run over the bones of fallen fellow countrymen, over the bones of the infidel and horses' bones, to fly upside down into the heavens, and I have got used to the taste of death, and there is no way back to my former life for me. And there is darkness and silence on the field, and the field just lies there in total peace, and the moon, appearing occasionally, illuminates the milky mist, and this is all very deceptive, and I feel like running some more.

Well, I get up, throw my sweater aside, I'm off, boys, I say. They sit huddled up together, unhappy about what I'm doing but unable to bring themselves to oppose me, while the bonfire has expired without their care and attention. Well, I get up, go out into the field, my heart beating from new premonitions, I take a deep breath of the sweet clover air, brush my hair back behind my ears, and, quickening my pace, start racing over the hummocks.

I run. Run, run, run, run.

And for the third time the evil spirit grows thick around me and once more begins to play with me, flying and making me lose my bearings, but the thing is I'd got almost accustomed to these jokes, I move my legs unconcernedly, moving at full speed through this jam. And suddenly in the silence of the field I hear: some voices are singing. They start up discordantly, and uncertainly, but soon there are more and more of them, well, a whole choir, and they sing something like a burial service, they sing as at funerals. I can't make out the words, even though they have grown louder, and now it's as if the whole field has started singing, and the dark forest over there is singing, and all the blades of grass beneath my feet, and the storm clouds, and even the river, everything, everywhere. . . . And the singing is so sorrowful, so valedictory and funereal, that you just find it physically impossible to run with the singing going on, especially when you are naked, and you want to stop and cover yourself with your hands, while around you everything sings. My movements slow down, and I try to work out whose requiem they are singing, mine perhaps, and it seems to me that it is mine, but it also seems that it is not only mine, that they are singing an anthem for everything around: the sky, and the storm clouds, and even the river, they are singing a requiem for themselves, and for me, and for everything at once, and I stop and listen as these forces, alive and incomprehensible, sing a sorrowful song, they surround me and sing, and they sing not in reproof, as if to say your plan is in vain and your running worthless, but rather they sing mournfully and prophesy my death, and place me in a white coffin and nail me up, a mortal woman, God's servant, Irina Vladimirovna. And so I stopped in confusion and thought: Let me fall on my knees, tumble facedown into the clover, with my bum in the air, and bury myself in the tangle of my bergamot hairs, and let come what may, since they're bearing me out in a white coffin anyway, and they're singing, singing ceaselessly. Let come what may! He'll do what he thinks best! If he fucks me, then he fucks me; if he buries me, then he buries me; everyone has to face the funeral music sooner or later. . . . So here I am on my knees, in the middle of the singing field, which is overflowing with these totally Russian voices, and the evil spirit, the chief and unclean one, pinches me from time to time on my thighs and buttocks. I remain like that for a while, weeping in vain, and then I raise my head and, boy, how I shout with a voice not my own, appealing to the storm clouds and the dim moon: So are you going to fuck me or what?

And in a flash the field fell silent, and an audible silence reigned, and the choir of incomprehensible forces froze in expectation of an answer, everything concealed itself, and the white coffin did not stir. But after this pause of expectation, this pause of bitterness and last hope—suddenly how it thundered! how it thundered over the field! But it wasn't the thunder of thunder, it wasn't lightning, it wasn't a thunderstorm that had broken, hammering on the coffin lid in taut drops, and it wasn't the rustling of a rotten alder disturbed by the wind, and it wasn't the carrion crows leaping up, no, it wasn't thunder that had clapped, just a shudder that ran through the field, like along the skin, and at first I thought: Well, hold on, Irina, your hour has come, but it wasn't a death sentence that had thundered in the clouds, even though I was thinking: Well, now he'll ram me, oh, God, he'll immolate me! But no, I sense it isn't that, that's not the right sound for thunder, not the right rumble, that's a different noise, and the milky mist became dyed with a yellow color, and the stench of this huge fart slithered down from the heavens onto the grass, and there was no more air to breathe, and I choked. . . .

Well, I got up, reeling, clutching my temples, like an old woman, and no one was singing around me any longer, and I thought: Fuck you, you prick! Farts are *so* rude, *so* funny! And I set off; to the accompaniment of chuckles, sniggers, screams, I plodded my way over the gray field.

And when I reach the campfire, my weary arms hanging by my sides like ropes, and come upon my friends-acquaintances, the men sitting there are no longer green, they're flushed red and are actually laughing a bit, pouring wine, and the fire is blazing merrily. What's the reason for such gaiety? I say, "God, I'm exhausted!" "Well, sit down, have a rest." "Did you hear anything?" "What sort of thing do you mean?" "Did you hear how the choir sang with sorrowful voices?" "Choir? What choir?" "There was a choir there." They say, "If you say so." But I say, "What's up with you—drunk or what? I was putting myself at risk," I say wearily, "and you've been getting pissed?" "No," answers Yurochka, "we're not pissed, I don't drink when I'm driving," but he goes on pouring wine down his throat. And Yegor says, "If you're alluding to me, well, I had a teeny-weeny drop to drink, because everything's turned out so well." "What the fuck do you mean, turned out well?" "Just that," he says. "Here you are, alive and well, in all your fair beauty, like a bouquet of flowers, so my friend and I had a little drop to drink. Sit down here with us." And he gives me a significant look. "But didn't you hear anything else?" "What is there to hear when there's nothing but silence? We could make you out from a long way off. You were gleaming white, like a banner. . . ." "Look away," I say. But Yurochka says, "Thank God that it didn't turn out worse, because you see, it wouldn't have got better, that's why we were sitting like cockroaches and clutching each other, fearing even worse times. Yegor, be a pal, go to the car and bring us another bottle of vodka, come on, let's have a drink!" But Yegor puts his hands on his hips and answers assertively, "I won't go to the car for vodka; I want Ira to kiss me first, like a brother." And he plunks himself down on my pile of clothes. I say, "Get off my clothes first and then you can call yourself a brother." They exchange glances, like a pair of educated bandits, and say nothing. "And you," they say, "don't be in such a hurry to get dressed, we're part of the family, we understand everything." "*What* do you understand?" They are silent, exchanging winks, smoking little cigarettes. I then went up to Yegor gingerly, not hiding my nakedness. "Give me your cheek for a kiss." He offered it. I hit him with what little strength I had left. He toppled backward. "God, both of you are shit!" I said. He got up, protecting his bearded face, and he was funny, but repulsive too. I dressed in total silence, and Yurochka waited patiently, but once I was dressed and was crouching by the fire to warm my hands, he hissed, "Don't give yourself too many airs; who do you think you are? I'll give you Joan of Arc!" At this I say to him, "Do you remember Ksyusha? Remember how you hassled and nagged and mocked her? You got on her nerves so much that she slept with you, but she slept with you out of pure hatred, from utter revulsion and contempt." "And do you want it in the face too?"

Yurochka inquired, smiling politely. And I'd gone through so much that day, and more, that I couldn't even be bothered to tangle with him, I say, "Go on, then, hit me! Hit me, coward! Hit me, liberator of the people! Hit me, you filthy swine!" And I hit him in the face. And during his moment of hesitation—and he, I knew, was no Yegor, he is all arrogance and conceit, he's a maniac—I leapt up and ran away from them. Oh, I think, fuck them both! I had been expecting more from them, hoping for better. . . . I ran away into the darkness, not into the field this time but toward the road, and vanished in the gloom. I sat down. I thought: What do I do next? Where do I go? Are there any real people living around here?

The others are silent for a little while, and then I hear Yegor yelling, "Ira! Irka-a-a-a! Whe-e-e-ere are yo-o-o-ou?" I'm silent, I don't respond, let him shout. Then I hear them crawl into the car, start to honk, honk for all they're worth, and switch on their headlights. Honk honk, my little geese . . . But I'm thinking: Surely I won't go back to them? And I answer my own question: Well, of course you'll go back; what else is there to do? You'll go back all sweetness and light. And they're saying much the same sort of thing to each other. After all, she's not going to sit there all night freezing, enjoying the autumn, is she? As soon as she starts to shiver, the campfire will smoke her out. . . .

You're tired, you ran until you dropped, you're pooped, Irochka, you've really run a lot today, you've run enough for a lifetime, Sunny. . . .

And I hear: Yura's also yelling. "Ira, come back! Come back! Let's go to Moscow! Come back!"

And I, fool, know perfectly well that I ought to stand up and return, their headlights burn and call that I must return, stand up and respond, because after all where can I go, with dark night all around, and then I'd left my watch by the campfire, a gold watch with a gold bracelet, Swiss, a little present from Carlos, but I didn't get up, and I didn't go. "Ira-a-a-a!" the boys shouted in a duet. "We've got to leave! Don't fool around! It was momentary madness! Please forgive us!" And once more they honk, once more luring me into the light of the headlights, into the car warm and soft, like a pillow, and under the pillow the cambric nightshirt, and I'll sleep on the back seat the whole way back, curled up like a dormouse, and I won't see either the villages or the blinding lights of the few oncoming cars, I will sleep, sleep, sleep, and of course I should get up and go, only I have no strength, only I can't lift my eyelids, can't open my eyes, and I thought: I'm not long for this world anyway, and the moment I thought this, I switched off. Timber! I crashed. And that's that.

# NINETEEN

When I got back I phoned that brotherly pair the Ivanoviches and without further ado, over the phone, capitulated. And they came straight over, glum, angry, rustling their trench coats. "Oh, why, why did you run over the field, Irina Vladimirovna?" they both exclaimed the minute they saw me. "What was the need? We'd already reached agreements about everything. We'd smoothed everything out. They were taking you back into the collective. And we'd convinced Viktor Kharitonych too, despite his strong resistance to readmitting you. But now? Rumors have started. The gossips have started to stir and whisper in literary circles: 'Joan of Arc! Joan of Arc!' What were you trying to prove, and to whom? *Why did you have to do this?* Oh, Ira, Ira, you've ruined everything. And don't ask us to take our coats off! You should have consulted us first. For if you're going to run around a battlefield, then you should at least have a well-defined mission! But you! And you've gone and dumped Vladimir Sergeyevich in it too. Because of you he'll become a total persona non grata; nothing connected with him is shown on television anymore. You have drained the last reserves of his reputation. Drained to the dregs! Oh, how he would have told you off! How he'd have chewed you out!"

And they left me to worry about my fate. Gavleyev! Of course! of course! Naturally I remember. A connoisseur of plump round bottoms and intriguing couplings . . . Of course! of course! And I had forgotten. . . .

I greeted the brothers with a cough, with sniffles, a piercing earache, and I answer in the hoarse voice of a stranger: "And you? You're fine ones to talk. For what purpose, for the sake of what strategy, did you set Stepan on me with his midnight armored car?" "And who might this Stepan be?" "Oh, spare me!" "No, you tell us what you want to say in a way that makes sense." "Oh"—I flinch—"as if you don't know. The Stepan who meant to cripple me just a bit, to spoil my beauty for me, and when he had failed to carry through his commission he pretended to be drunk and wet himself, right here, here on the rug near the couch, smell if you don't believe me, he spent the whole night here, and in the morning concocted something incoherent about Marfa Georgievna and a non-existent birthday party."

Sergei and Nikolai exchange glances. High-ranking journalists. But I explain to them in a hoarse, offended tone, like a rusty pipe organ, "Oh, spare me, please! There's still a bruise on my thigh equal to a sixth of my whole body surface; spare me, I'm not a child." And suddenly they start oohing and aahing and spread their hands helplessly! "Well, Irina Vladimirovna, this bears the traces of foreign aid. It can only be Boris *Davydovich* who's put his mark of Cain here, no other!" "Indeed," I answer, "and my humble thanks to this clever man. I'm a weak woman, and I didn't pick up on it at first." "Oh!" The brothers draw their breath in sharply. "Irina Vladimirovna! You're turning into a Jew," they say. I say to this, "There you are. Everyone's insulting me, deceiving me." And I let a tear creep down my cheek. They throw off their trench coats, hang them up, wipe their feet. "And you too," I complain. "Who am I to believe? Sit down." They sit at the table. "Okay," say Nikolai and Sergei. "With reference to the Tatar-Mongol field, which is situated so many kilometers away from Moscow [I don't remember how many, I'm no good at remembering figures], he must have put you up to this too, this Boris Davydovich? Hey, calm down . . . calm down . . . calm down." "How am I supposed to calm down?" I whine pathetically, twisting the damp handkerchief in my hands. "My gold w-w-watch . . . Swiss . . . I l-l-lost it there, with a g-g-gold bracelet." "Then it was him *again?*" "No," I answer truthfully, "not him; I heard a voice." They prick up their ears even more. "Okay, what sort of voice? Tell us. It's in your interests." "Oh," I say, "there's nothing to tell. It's not the sort of thing you'd ever understand." "???" "You," I say, "are shortsighted materialists." "Did you know, Irina Vladimirovna, that *creative* materialism can tolerate various natural and physical enigmas? Our Sergei here, for example, writes pieces on parapsychology." "And do you believe in signs?" "Well," answers Sergei evasively, "neither no nor yes nor anybody's guess." I blow my nose. "Let's," I say, "be friends again!" "Be friends!" The brothers grin mistrustfully. "We keep trying to be friends with you, and then you go and run around a field behind our backs!" "I've been punished enough as it is," I complain. "See, I've got tonsillitis, my temperature's a hundred and two, I'm all on fire," and the Ivanoviches burn together with me in a blue flame. "Well, Irina Vladimirovna, we didn't expect this from you, to be honest! You are a Russian woman after all!" "Russian," I answer, "what else?" "Well, surely this is sacrilege," they say, amazed, "is it not? To trample on a national shrine with your bare feet, to run all over it in the buff? You misled us. And the editor in chief Gavleyev is beside himself with anger, because he printed an article that whitewashed you." "Oh, okay, boys," I apologize, "okay! I

ran without thinking what I was doing; I won't do it again, I
promise," but I'm thinking: Oh, to hell with her, this Russia,
let someone else worry about her, I've had enough! I want to
live. "You're pragmatists, right? Right. Then we can come to
an agreement?" But they keep on their own tack: "But suppose
the national equilibrium had been disturbed—what would
have happened then? And Gavleyev, he's losing his faith in
human nature; he believed in you too." I say, "Inform your
boss, Gavleyev, that no violations of the equilibrium took
place, nor can they take place, inasmuch as," I say, "I learned
the lesson the hard way and now I'm quite satisfied that this
equilibrium of yours is just what's needed! Put your boss's mind
at rest." And I suddenly remembered those women in the
distant market who understood the equilibrium better than I
did. "Well, women," I said, clambering up onto the trading
counter, "ask for what you want, and whatever you ask shall
be!" They huddled into a bunch and answered hesitantly, "We
don't want anything, we're fine as it is." "But are things really
that good?" I say. "And why," they answer, "should we complain, annoy God without good reason; there's no war." But
I say, "Well, is there anything you want?" "Well," says one,
"you buy some of my sunflower seeds, buy some, daughter,
we'll let you have them cheap." "I don't want," I answer,
"those awful seeds of yours; all you get from them is indiges-
tion. . . ." The brothers departed, actually slightly relieved,
went off to report to Gavleyev. "Only, Irina Vladimirovna,
take care not to spread rumors about those runs of yours too
much, particularly to foreigners; they'll tell a pack of lies and
interpret it all wrongly." "How could I?" I assured them.
"Never in my life! And don't you insult me either," and I
told them about Yegor, about Yurochka, about their stupid
quarrels and how they sat on the grass green like cockroaches,
but I kept silent about the evil forces, because that's *mine*,

and the Ivanoviches say, "Smart boys!" But I thought: You're all smart boys! On that we parted; but at this point a human stump shuffles into the market, Uncle Misha, lacking three of his limbs, holding a glass full of vodka in his hand. Help it down with a cucumber, Uncle Misha! But Uncle Misha is of a different opinion. Having downed half the glass, he answers, "What's the point of drinking if you dilute it with food?" And his spit showers. Women shove spotted apples into his pockets. The women bite the husks off the seeds, crack and clean them. The sun sits in the puddles. Uncle Misha finishes his vodka. He never gets drunk, Uncle Misha, he never gets sober. He crawls around the market, scrabbling with his single claw. He scuttles into the waiting room, his cheeks burn; I spent many hours in the waiting room. There was a rubber plant growing out of a bed of cigarette butts. The station boss took pity on me and sold me a ticket that had not been claimed. There are portraits on the walls between the windows. Green and brown tones predominate. Like film actresses, the subjects look forty years younger than they really are. They've lasted well, but they probably simply hadn't had time to age: they had overworked, there had been no time, and their consciously noble expressions breathed the festive air of yesterday's victories. Sitting on the yellow Ministry of Transport bench, I gave them a thorough examination. I liked them all. Neither they nor I was rushing anywhere. My legs were protesting. The stump crawled around. The draft portended tonsillitis. The train pulled in when day was breaking. People suddenly appeared from God knows where, flooded in with their knapsacks, with their suitcases. Embarkation. Lifting their feet as high as they can, they climb into the cars. The conductors, sleepy women muffling themselves up in their overcoats, were shouting out orders. . . . What an extraordinary meeting!

In a dimly lit third-class coach, they sat playing cards with a vengeance, guffaws and sweet-smelling breath.

They were all there: Tanka with her clap, and the gentle tall Larisa, and Nina Chizh, who had forgiven me, and Andryusha, my queer little one, and sitting with her back to me she turned around: Irka! Rituyla! Hugs and smacking kisses. Fancy meeting you here! Where have you all come from? From a fair. We've been putting on a *show*. Andryusha, as always, *so* elegant, and his gestures always hesitant. Only with Andryusha did I feel like a *real* human being. After parties he would help clear up, wash the dishes wearing my apron, and carry the rubbish out into the yard. Then we would call it a day, and after we'd gone to bed and talked a load of nonsense, gossiping and giggling to our hearts' content, we would fall asleep, our backs cuddled together and the *fortochka* open. How well we slept! We would wake up full of life. We would romp in bed. Andryusha, I would say, How beautiful you are! You are Apollo! How lovely! Permit me, let me kiss you, oh, let me, Andryusha!

But he would get all embarrassed and say, "Irisha! My angel! Let's agree not to profane our friendship with all that sort of thing! Look through the *fortochka*: snow on the trees. It's white, Ira. . . ."

We drank coffee. We once even managed to drag ourselves out of the city, to go skiing. Oh, why are there so few pure men like Andryusha in the world! If there were more of them, then what a burden would fall from fragile female shoulders! How gloriously everything would resolve itself!

"But where have you been, Irishka? Why are you looking like that? Your face is burning. Has anything happened?" "Perish the thought, girls! I was simply visiting the country. The car broke down. My admirer stayed behind to sunbathe." "Do you want a drink?" "Oh, cognac! And where's Polina?"

"She went by bus. Have another swig." "Oh, heavenly! Rituyla, is that you? How are you, dear?" "I miss you. You've
got new friends." "Oh, I wish they'd all drop dead! I'm fed
up to here with them!" "And I, most probably . . ." "Who're
you going to marry? Hamlet?" "So?" "No, that's fine!" "He
gave me this." "Five grand?" "More!" "Take care they don't
rip it off, together with your finger! Andryusha dear! How I
miss you, and all you girls too." "And we miss you! We miss
you! When will you return?" "How do I know!" "Come back.
Or are you going to *fly off* to warmer climes?" "No, Ninulya,
I can't . . . it's too late." "But do you know, Marishka's upped
and left?" "Oh, really?" "Gone to Holland." "Well, soon there
won't be any young birds left at all. Only old crows." "Even
the old crows are leaving. And the old cows." "That's true.
Ugh, what's that?"

Everyone looked. I won't say what we saw. "They're the
absolute pits!" I said. "Let's go and have a smoke."

Andryusha accompanied me and Tanka to the platform at
the end of the corridor. "Are you cured, then?" "Ages ago!"
"And you?" "What do you mean?" "Well, weren't you . . . ?"
"No, that was Rituyla." "That woman's no fool," enthused
Andryusha, who had never even smoked in his life. "She did
the right thing. Shoved the boot right in front of him. As if
to say: fill it to the brim if you want." Everyone laughed. That
is, those who weren't sleeping, although the majority were
asleep and weren't laughing. "But how will he put them on
in the morning?" "Just as they are." "They're the pits!" I said.
I was heading for Moscow. I've been heading there all my life.
At the doorway, some men were showing off about who had
been where and how many times. Suddenly someone clutched
my shoulders with his paws. "Was it *you* who said that we
were the pits?" Andryusha, punctilious as ever, said to the
man, "I assure you, you've mistaken her for someone else."

"Beat it! Hey, boys! She said that we're the pits!" These heroes of the drying-out center weren't too upset, and everything would have turned out all right if it hadn't been for Tanya—she's *another* headstrong one—who said, "Well, what are you, then?" grinding her cigarette under her heel. "You bitch!" yelled the man. "You gobble every cock in sight, and you call *us* the pits!" "Oh, okay." I waved him aside dismissively, trying to reduce everything to a joke. "What girl doesn't like a gobble nowadays?" With his paw he pulled me around to face him. A typical male face. A pig's face. "Why did you say we're the pits?" "I didn't say a thing. Leave me alone." "No, you said it! Boys, she said we're the pits!" Andryusha, mildly: "Well, shall we be off, girls? You've had your smoke, so let's go." There was nowhere to go. They were standing and looking at us. Andryusha got excited. The guy was blocking the door with his body. Knocking from the other side of the door. A butt in his mouth. He took out his butt and tried to jab me in the face with it, but I knocked his shaky hand aside, and he hit Tanka in the cheek with the lit end. Only Tanka can yell like that. She can outyell a factory siren. The guys stood and watched her. She was taller than them; I was too. And we were wearing heels. Then a second man suddenly goes purple and says, "What was all that about?" And the first one says, "She called us the pits." "So what?" "Nothing, that's what." They started wrestling clumsily, and there was no room for anyone else. Tanka and I opened the door and hurled ourselves into the coach, colliding with the conductor: she'd come out to separate the men. Everyone was asleep. Feet—women's, old men's, soldiers'—were sticking out into the aisle. A typical railway car smell. I know, believe me: at this hour the cleanest air is in the toilet. The window's slightly ajar there. I locked myself in and went to the window.

They've burned Tanka's cheek. . . . Oh, well, it'll hurt a

bit, but it'll pass. I breathed the fresh predawn air. I wasn't thinking about anything much. They're enjoying themselves, I thought, remembering the travelers' amusement as they watched a man throwing up into his own boots. How they'd enjoyed that! And even his wife, frowning at first, finally smiled as if to say: There's a fool for you! . . . After all the anxiety and commotion of getting on the train, they've sat down, had a bit to drink, the train's started, they've cheered up. Isn't it funny? How will he put them on tomorrow? What a laugh! But I didn't laugh. And then a man with a typical male face came up and took offense, because I didn't, you see, find it funny. . . . But perhaps I'm really not right? And did you really not, Irina Vladimirovna, with your pa and ma, with such a life history, getting spliced twice and the endless scandals, did you really not have the sense to realize that they are to be pitied, pitied, pitied? Why did you enter into this criminal agreement? Why did you want to get involved in this? It isn't really necessary to save anyone: save them *from whom*? From themselves? So what is to be done? What do you mean, what? Do nothing. And very likely, my dear Ksyusha, it's time for me to put a period to my stormy life, it's time to see reason. I wasn't thinking about anything.

Andryusha! Andryusha, you're good, you gave me your place, you climbed up onto the cramped third-tier bunk, you're nice, marry me! You and I will sleep together, our backs cuddled together, we shall listen to beautiful music, and your little ways—no problem! They don't worry me. I shall be *true* to you, Andryusha, and should you want a baby, a dear little teeny-weeny baby who will look like you, listen, Andryusha, I'll give birth to one for you. . . .

Return to your roots, Irina! Take a whiff of the striped socks! Take a closer sniff of this smell, Irina! It is *your* smell, child! Everything else is a snare of the devil. *They* are *you*—

you are *they*—and don't fuck about; otherwise there is nothing left for you to do on this earth. Remember, Irina . . .

I cautiously sniffed the air.

I glanced up at the top bunk. He was lying there with his eyes open. "Andryusha!" I said. "They're not to blame. I know that *for sure.*" "What's that to me?" said Andryusha. "To blame or not to blame . . . why should I bother to go on living in all this shit?" "Andryusha," I said, "there is a way out: marry me. . . ." The wheels were rolling toward Moscow. They would pause, stop, and roll on. Mail trains stop at every station. Andryusha was silent. I was hurt. "Why are you si- lent?" I whispered. "Don't you believe me?" "But is that really a way out?" answered Andryusha. "Is that really, my dear, a *way out?*"

So why should I care? I've forgiven far worse than that. I covered my head with the bedclothes and forgave him.

# TWENTY

W hen I got back I phoned the brotherly Ivanoviches and capitulated. But all these things are trivial, and I omit them. And then night fell. In other words, something had certainly become displaced after all, had freed itself and given itself full scope in the natural world and beyond, *higher*, because night fell, and it fell on *me*.

Lord! Give me the strength to describe it!

Tonsillitis hit me. I burned, tossed in my bed, wore myself out, fussed and fidgeted. My throat was ablaze, a burning inferno! It got so red hot that the room seemed illuminated, a dry claret color. . . . Everything became repugnant to me: the sheets, the ticking of the clock, books, wallpaper, perfumes, records. Even my pillow bothered me, and from time to time, raising myself an inch or two, I hammered it with my fist in blind despair. My temperature crept up, foul weather outside, boughs glimpsed fleetingly. My mind revolved people and fruit juices, what would be good to drink, who might look after a sick girl, the drinks and the people blended into one another: pineapple juice was too sweet, it contained a diluted, stringy Viktor Kharitonych, and I spurned it, together with its pulp; the cloying mango called from the depths of my

memory a face seen in passing on a grubby meadow on Nikolina Hill, without a body, without a name, and in reflecting
sunglasses; orange juice was *too* acid, not to mention grape-
fruit, and the mere thought of it tormented and irritated the
mucous membrane, but the grape, healing and viscous, took
me to the syrupy coast of Sukhumi, and Dato smiled a heavy
smile at me. The tomato reminded me of the sediment from
belching and, suddenly, of my best girlfriend, who, like tomato
pulp, clung to the roof of the mouth, and the amusing pastime
of youth, a Bloody Mary, flowed down a knife, and having
gone through them all in my mind and having chosen none
of them, I settled on boiled water from the kettle in the
kitchen, which tasted of Rituyla but was colorless and empty
all the same. For a long time I debated whether I should get
up or not, that is, whether even to sit up in bed, pulling down
my crumpled nightdress, which had crept up again, the true
companion of my illnesses, usually I don't wear it, let the body
breathe, but it crawls up anyway, useless, and then I put on
a jacket as well, a scarecrow look, and little dark-blue woolen
socks—a most excellent appearance, this scarecrow look—
and my throat like a feather from the Firebird, and I thought:
That's my punishment for the field, I was tricking myself,
clinging to my illness, I'd got off lightly, with only this trivial
illness, and it's good, I thought firmly, that while I ran I didn't
cut myself on glass or on an open can with jagged edges, and
I remembered how, that first evening at Leonardik's, before
Leonardik's time, I had cut myself and, lying there wounded,
wasn't clear who it was coming from behind, apart from Ksyusha and Antonchik, because there had been no one else, that
Antonchik who had opened my mouth that morning to that
life-giving champagne, which appeared as if by magic, and
congratulated me on my lush beauty, but even champagne
wouldn't have done me any good now, and I couldn't help

grimacing as I betrayed my love for it at this distant memory, but I remembered how I'd woken up with a pain in the sole of my foot, but my memory fails me as to how I cut it, only Ksyusha stirred, pronouncing inaudible words with swollen sticky lips, and in fact I'm frightened of sleeping alone: the creak of floorboards, door hinges, oarlocks—the river—the slam of the *fortochka*—the photograph—a spring—the girl with a pitcher. . . . I reached for the night-light in the form of an owl—don't drink, you'll turn into a frog! don't drink—I reached out and, ill and innocent, switched on the light—and wasn't even able to cry out.

On the small narrow couch, to the right as you enter the bedroom, next to the door—the bed is on the left—sat Leonardik.

He sat hunched up, his head lowered, and, with a rather sad, even guilty gaze, as if apologizing for the intrusion, was peering at me from under his brows.

I pressed my hands to my breast and stared at him in sheer horror.

He was not looking completely his old self. Not only was he stooped, he looked exhausted too, like after a long march lasting many days, with sunken pale cheeks and light-blue, bloodless streaks for lips; his nose seemed much more aquiline and aggressive, his high forehead more prominent, and his grayish hair had gone slightly curly, there was more of it than before, and the difference gradually dawned on me: the man here was younger than the one it had been my fate to know, the one whom I had met at the dacha and I'd spun around on the icy tennis court with a happy rosy face, he was younger, tougher, and the oily light no longer streamed from his face, and the black blazer with its silvery buttons was also new to me. Well shaved, with bags of tiredness under his eyes and with two deep bitter furrows going from his nostrils to the corners of his mouth, he looked more like a punch-drunk white guard than a successful representative of culture.

Looking at me, he said in an even, precise voice, "You are ill. I've come to look after you. You need a drink."

I wanted to scream, but instead my cowardly teeth chattered. "Bring me some boiled water."

He got up eagerly, delighted to do me a favor. The light flashed on in the hallway. In the kitchen, the kettle lid tinkled. The spout knocked against the glass. And he reappeared smoothly, with a glass of water, and smoothly stretched out his arm, coming closer to the bed. I took a sip, trying to grasp the glass's rim with my unsteady lips, and cast a sidelong glance at his fingernails: they were deformed and twisted, cutting into the soft flesh of his fingers. He was embarrassed by my glance, and moving off to the couch, he hid his hands behind his back.

"Don't be afraid," he begged.

I shrugged my shoulders weakly: an impossible request.

"It was cold on the field," he announced, in what was half a question, as if he were trying to strike up a polite conversation.

"Cold," I whispered.

"September," he found the answer.

"Now I'm really screwed," I whispered.

"Oh, and why?" he said with gentle doubt.

"You've come."

"I've come because you're ill."

"You shouldn't have put yourself out. . . . You're dead after all."

"Yes," he agreed obediently, and added with a stale smile, "with a little help from you."

"Not true." I shook my head slowly. "You did it yourself. From ecstasy."

"Don't misunderstand me! I don't regret it."

I glanced at him with weary, almost indifferent suspicion.

"Don't you believe me? Why should I lie?"

"I didn't kill you . . . it was you. . . ." I shook my head.

"Oh, what does it matter?" he exclaimed impatiently.

"For you, perhaps, nothing matters anymore, but I live here, where *everything* matters."

"Well, and how's life?"

"You can see for yourself . . . wonderful."

We were silent awhile.

"And are you planning to live like *this* much longer?"

"Oh, no, I've had it up to here!" I answered with animation. "I'm fed up! At last I'll get myself some sort of family, have a child. . . ."

He gazed at me with deep sympathy, with such compassion . . . I couldn't stand it! So I said, "Please don't look at me like that. In fact, you'd better leave. Go back where you came from. I still want to live."

He shook his head. "You'll find it impossible to live here."

"What do you mean? Will you start shadowing me?"

"Why don't you understand?" he said, amazed. "I'm grateful to you. You freed me from my shameful life."

"One shouldn't go round doing that," I said.

"You lightened my burden."

"Oh, forget it!" I said, my shoulders shaking. "God grant everyone the good fortune to live as badly as that!"

"I'm ashamed . . . ashamed . . . ashamed," Leonardik muttered, like a madman.

"I understand." I grinned. "Had a good life, played around, now's the time to confess and repent. . . ."

"And I will repent!" he yelled, spraying saliva.

"Is it really possible that you'll be a roaring success in *that* field too?" I said, astonished.

We were silent.

"You're cruel," he said at last.

"And you?"

He stood up and started walking back and forth across the room, agitated, as if still alive.

"You and I," he announced, "are bound together far more strongly than you think. We are tied not just by my blood—"

"Harping on that again!" I made a wry face. "But who tricked me? Golden fish! Who promised to marry me? Did you marry me? Well, then, leave me alone. I'll sort it all out myself."

He halted in the middle of the room and said very quietly, "I want to marry you."

"What!" I was dumbfounded. "You should have thought about that sooner! A lot sooner! Now it's simply *ridiculous!* Bridegroom!" I snorted, hurling him a look that could kill. "No way! What kind of fool do you take me for?"

He hung his head at my words but continued at a leisurely pace, taking his time: "Since I became free—"

"Oh, so you're free!" I interrupted him. "Well, naturally! Now you're free to appear to me, though formerly you wouldn't have dared set foot here. Now you're free of *your* Zinaida Vasilievna. . . ."

At the mention of Zinaida Vasilievna he simply waved his hand dismissively. "I lived with emptiness."

"Now you yourself are emptiness!" I exploded. "Go and repent somewhere else. Clear off to your dacha, to Zinaida! She'll be *overjoyed* to see you!"

"I don't need anyone but you. Try to understand—"

"I don't want to understand anything! Perhaps it's slipped your mind, but that sort of thing just isn't done here. Marriages like this don't get registered. This sort of thing just doesn't happen; don't try and pull the wool over my eyes!"

"But you see, it wouldn't necessarily . . . wouldn't necessarily have to be *here,*" he said with excessive timidity.

"Ah, that's it!" I got it now. "That's what you're offering me! Leaving for another country, a new home. Except it'll be a little farther away than the one mama wants to go to . . ."

"All the same, you'll find it impossible to live here."

"Hey, stop trying to scare me! I won't suffer, don't worry! I am no longer, for your information, a needle lost in a haystack. Six American girls supported me. Perhaps you've heard about it? It was on the radio."

"Just listen to yourself!" He clasped his hands then immediately hid them behind his back. "Or rather, listen to me. . . ."

"For God's sake don't tell me that over there it's better. Just don't try and persuade me. . . . I *will* be fine here!"

"Yes, you'll be *really* fine here!" Leonardik narrowed his eyes mockingly.

"Shut up!" I yelled. "What's 'over there' got to offer?"

"There you'll be with me. We shall come together as one in love. Light will once more flow upon us. . . ."

"*What* light?" I groaned. As it was, the light was blinding me.

"In this circle of existence we turned out to be defeatists, we set our sights too low. Both of us. But you nevertheless recognized me and *called* me. But I was so blind, life had sealed my eyes so completely . . . that was catastrophic. I stumbled like a donkey after a carrot. Where pleasure is like a carrot dangling before your eyes, it eclipses everything, you tremble at it. I trembled so . . . trembled *so* . . . I didn't even recognize you." He was silent for a while, taking a breather. "That *running* of yours was so beautiful. I was lost in admiration. And your willingness to embrace death! And for the sake of what?"

"And instead of death I embraced shame!" I exclaimed, dissolving into bitter tears.

"It was beyond your powers." Leonardik shook his head affectionately. "No matter how you ran, you were doomed to be defeated. When you cry, you're divine," he whispered.

"I wanted what was best," I said.

"I believe you! But for this country"—he knocked on the dressing table with his frightful fingernail—"for her, the spell that binds her actually preserves her. So *that* act couldn't make you a savior; what you were doing was destructive, it would undo the charm: you were running *against* Russia, although you ran beautifully. . . ."

"How is that, against Russia?" I said, offended.

"Because sorcery casts a spell against bloodshed; it's like cement: it holds together the centrifugal forces. I'd suspected something of the kind while I was alive, but I did everything in my power to ensure that no one would believe me. . . . Oh, the shame!"

"There you go again!"

"No!" Leonardik said, rousing himself. "It's like a bad dream you're cursed with and can't stop thinking about! It's not just the living: those who have died too, the *former* fellow citizens, can't control their obsession. As if there were no other problems!"

"One sixth of the world's land surface, for all that!" I stood up for my fellow citizens.

"But you see, *only* one sixth!" Leonardik cried.

"And where is the capital of the place you come from?" I inquired.

He directed a significant look at the ceiling and then smiled cunningly. "You always wanted the bright lights. . . . Why delay?"

"If you love me, you'll wait," I answered, being equally cunning and resourceful.

"I can't wait," muttered Leonardik. "I've been miserable without you."

I distracted him: "This is what you can tell me instead!" and suddenly I felt genuinely happy. "If you've appeared, well, since you've appeared, it means, therefore, He exists? He exists, yes?"

"It means, therefore, *I* exist." Leonardik grinned sorrowfully.

"No, wait a moment! What about Him?"

Leonardik remained stubbornly silent.

"Is it really possible that you don't sense Him there?" I said, astounded.

"No, why do you think that?" uttered Leonardik without the slightest enthusiasm. "I feel Him. I feel Him and I repent, I burn with shame. But I can't help myself. You attract me more."

He gazed at me from the couch, a beast at bay.

"You and I have to satisfy this passion in order to return to Him."

"Then He exists!" I rejoiced.

"What are you getting so happy about?"

"What do you mean, what? Eternal life, that's what!"

Leonardik curled his libertine's lip.

"That's nothing to be happy about. . . . To attain it, you have to cleanse yourself of yourself, become separated from your own dear 'I,' which, hoping for infinite continuation, is in fact doomed to perish and be resmelted. . . . The laws of matter are as grave as the moist earth." He sighed.

"To listen to you, it's as if there is no difference whether He exists or not!"

"I'm talking about the gravity of matter. *His* rays hardly warm the earth. You might think that the difference between a believer, whose way is clear, and the unbeliever, who is dust and a fool, ought to be much greater than the difference between a man and an amoeba, but in fact the difference is microscopic."

"People really do live as if He doesn't exist, but the reason they live is because He is."

"Oh, you do turn a phrase neatly!" approved Leonardik, surprised.

"What else were you expecting?" I smiled, flattered.

"All the same," said Leonardik wanly, "it doesn't matter which example you pick. Pride in successful reasoning very often weighs more than the value of the argument. And this forms part of culture as an inevitable adulterated mixture, which never allows culture to reach high truthfulness. . . . Damned gravity!" He sighed again.

"Surely something will remain of us?"

"Here, bones; there, a vague memory of former incarnations—a whole pack of incarnations. A pretty crappy hand, frankly . . . We are nothing more than masks over a clot of life, but while we love . . ."

"He's not very nice, this God of yours!" I said with a shiver. "Perhaps you haven't understood Him properly? Perhaps *this* is your punishment?"

He went pale, although he hadn't been exactly rosy-cheeked to start with.

"Perhaps . . . ," he muttered.

"And yet despite this you still call me to you!" I said indignantly. "What exactly can you offer me, apart from this melancholy and coldness?"

"Love will warm us both. The artist and the heroine. Talent and will. We *must* become one!"

I was beginning to feel more at ease in conversation with him, because it was interesting and wide-ranging, and I looked at him with curiosity. I'd heard a lot about *them*, I'd always been afraid, I was unable to pass a cemetery at night without trembling, because even when I was a child I'd felt that something was not right there, there's something there that frightens you in spite of yourself, so even if I planned to be brave, walking past the graveyard and telling myself not to be scared, I would get scared in spite of myself, so I knew that evil forces were at work there, it's not that I was frightened of going *there*, into the earth, that's a different terror, but of them calling out to me, perhaps because I attracted them more than other people, though other people complained too, and I'm not easily scared. But he sat like modesty itself, in gray flannel trousers and in a black blazer with silver buttons, only very sad, and he said very sad things, though I wanted him to comfort me with a kind word, because I was pretty ill and I was going through a bad time, but instead he just laid the sadness on even thicker, but at last we were quits, that is, he had *forgiven* me, and I took a stealthy breath, because I thought that was why he had come, to tell me he didn't bear a grudge against me, although I, of course, hadn't killed him, but it might have seemed like that to him, because I'd been present at his death, but as soon as he saw that my fear was subsiding, then, it must be said, he became more familiar, too familiar even, and this put me on my guard.

"Irochka . . . ," he said. "I call you Irochka automatically, though this name doesn't suit you very well—"

"What name does suit me, then?"

"The one with which you ran around the field, tearing my soul inside out."

"I wasn't running for you."

"I know. That's what turned my soul inside out."

"Perhaps you would have preferred a cross-country run in your honor?"

"Did you love me once?"

"I *loved* you," I answered with conviction.

"And now?"

"What choice do I have, now you're dead?"

"But I've fallen in love with you again, and much more so. The only thing I think about is you. . . . I was so weary with desire that I kept longing to come to you, yet I was afraid of scaring you, but when you ran around the field I thought that you were fearless, and I allowed myself . . ."

"Yes," I sighed, "it would have been better if I hadn't run!"

"How beautifully you ran! I can no longer go on without you!"

"What passion!" I giggled uneasily. "A lovelorn ghost!"

"Irochka! Don't you see? I'm pining for you, I want you!"

"So that's it!" I said, distressed. "There we were, having a philosophical conversation about metaphysics and things like that, and what's the result? Everything ends in this vulgarity and banality."

He bit his lip.

"But if it's stronger than me!" he exclaimed. "Irochka! I beseech you in the name of our earthly love: give yourself to me! Please, even if only this once . . ."

I went apeshit. I say, "Are you off your rocker? What am I supposed to give myself to? You see, to be honest, you don't even *exist*. Merely a fiction . . ."

He objects, speaking with a tremble, not a voice: "My intentions are serious. I'm ready to marry you. You are mine! I didn't understand this before, but now it is as clear as daylight. Until I have my way with you, until I satisfy my passion, I am doomed to linger, moping and moaning like a nonentity, a useless figure of suffering. Oh, please . . ."

I say, "Very interesting. And how do you envisage all this? Forgive me, but I don't take part in activities like this. What is it exactly? I think it's called necrophilia, yes? I don't sleep with corpses!"

He says, "But I'm no corpse!"

"Well, it's all the same. You're not alive, not real!"

"In fact," he says, offended, "I am in some ways more real than you are!"

"Then," I say, "go back there, to those who are more real, and do with them what you will, and don't touch me!"

"Is this how things stand, then? You prepared yourself to be *serviced*, ungirded yourself in the field, but you turn me down, your cavalier and victim?"

"Just listen to me! Stop hassling me! Leave me alone! This is all too ridiculous for words! Do you want me to die from a heart attack?"

"I'll be gentle," whispered Leonardik.

"Screw your gentleness!"

All my composure had left me. I was horribly afraid. What should I do? Cry out? But I feel in my guts a treacherous lack of will. I know it's better not to resist. Otherwise he'll give me such a fright that I really will die. Wouldn't it be better to give in, voluntarily, since matters would be worse if I resisted? I know that from experience, but what help is experience here? Ksyusha dearest, can you imagine it? I'd never known anything like this!

But he, damn him, looks at me and, of course, reads me like a book. "You can't escape it," he says. "You're mine all the same." And he gets up from the couch, aroused and trembling.

I say, "Remember God!"

But he shuffles silently toward me.

"Stop it. . . . I've had enough of this. . . . Halt!"

But he is approaching. I snatch a glass from the bedside table and hurl it straight at his head, and I don't understand what happened, but I hit the mirror. Crash! The mirror is in smithereens. A black hole, a star. I start to shake.

"Look, I've broken the mirror because of you!" I say.

But he keeps harping on the same old thing: "Whom were you planning to give yourself to on the field? You weren't afraid then. So why be afraid now?"

"On the field," I say, almost weeping, "I was running for something sacred, but what have we got here? Just some post-humous lust of yours . . ."

"Fool! I'll marry you!"

"And what then?"

"We'll never part!"

"Don't come any closer! Not a step farther!"

But he sits down on the edge of the bed, at my feet, and says, "Do you really think you'll have a bad time with me?"

"Shall I tell you something? Everything is wrong about your philosophy: you're spreading gloom in the hope of making me so miserable that I'll leap into anybody's arms, even *yours*, like into a noose!"

"Untrue . . . I want you," he raves.

"Okay, okay, get in line!"

"You and I are an inseparable whole, Joan of Arc, Zhanna d'Arc!"

"What's this? What do you mean, Zhanna? Nonsense! Now I'm Zhanna and God knows who else, but as soon as you've screwed me you'll treat me like shit again! I know! Not on your life!"

But he declares, "If you put up a fight, I'll smother you with a pillow. I'm strong."

I look at him. He is indeed strong. Much stronger than he was during his lifetime. So muscular . . . He really is capable, I think, of smothering me. What's to be done?

I say, "You ought to be ashamed of yourself. You've come to a sick woman. You promised to look after her . . . my throat hurts . . ."

"Zhanna, beloved! I shall love you so much that you'll forget all about your throat!"

"Aren't you," I ask on a note of caution, "exaggerating your abilities somewhat?"

"You'll see," he promises, unbuttoning his blazer.

"Wait, wait! Don't be in such a hurry! Don't you try and seduce me, understand? You won't succeed! I'm scared of you, do you understand? Scared!"

He lays his hand with its repulsive fingernails on the blanket and starts stroking my leg, he strokes and strokes, my eyes almost pop out of their sockets, but his hand moves higher, higher, higher. I see that he's already starting on my mound.

"You won't turn me on. I don't sleep with the dead!"

But he caresses me and answers, "I'm no corpse, I repeat, I'm a warm-blooded creature. Feel my hand."

And he stretches out his sinewy hand to me. Automatically I recoil.

"No way! Touch your hand! Why is it you're warm? Perhaps you've come to life again, eh?"

He answered enigmatically: "Perhaps . . ."

He's hiding something! Yet I can still tell that he's not a man but something else, even with those warm hands.

"But why are your nails like that?" I put the insidious question.

"Forgive me," he says. "I can't do anything about them."

And so, it follows, he's not a real man!

"Hey, Leonardik, are you planning to rape me or what? Don't you dare touch me!"

And he says, "You killed me!"

And I say, "But you've already forgiven me for that! You're rather inconsistent!"

"I'm bursting with desire," he answers, "and you're talking about consistency!"

Well, what's to be done? I see that I can't handle him. I'm even afraid to push him away. . . .

He sat there quietly. And then he was on top of me! He

pressed himself to my face, clung to my lips, shoved his foul tongue between my teeth, and gripped my neck with his hands, as if embracing me. I started to twitch violently, my legs flailing everywhere, all over the bed, my socks flew off, he's already thrown off the blanket and is rolling my nightshirt up, he plucks at my breasts, grabs me by the legs. So there's nothing to be done, I slide away like a grass snake, better to be taken from behind, I think, so as not to see, I lie facedown and don't press my legs together, otherwise, I'm thinking, he'll tear me completely to bits down there and I'll be all cut up, and I mutter, "What are you doing, Leonardik? What are you doing! You're mad! You're dead!"

This is what I'm muttering, and I spread my legs just to be on the safe side, if it's got to happen, and I whisper, "Only don't kill me! I still want to live a tiny bit more! . . . Aah!"

When he was alive, Leonardik was never much of a swords-man, and I often spent a lot of time and effort fiddling with him, fanning the fire that had gone out, oh, you'd blow and blow for hours, literally hours, and all to no avail, until a tiny spark . . . oh, the boredom! But now, I can tell, things are taking a very different course. He pressed into me, squeezed my breasts with his hands, not like before, driveling, passive, but firmly, even perhaps a bit more firmly than was quite necessary, that is, just what the doctor ordered—he straight-ened himself and charged. Off he went! Back and forth, com-ing and going inside me! I thought: Okay, here it comes. Okay, one second more! However, nothing of the sort. And I even started to find it interesting. Well, I thought, what a transformation! Who would have thought it! And in addition he mutters something along the lines of: You're my little girl, beloved Zhannochka—that is, he'd really got into the part, was fantasizing about heaven knows what, and this made him even more passionate. He's really banging away hard. Lord,

I think, what a surprise! First he occupied me with intellectual conversations about God, and then, blowing his cover, got down to business . . . Aah! More, oh, more, Leonardik! Oh, yes, yes . . . how sweet! A-a-ah! a-a-ah . . . how delicious! My dear . . . ooh! a-a-ah! God! *Ooh*, a-a-a-a-ah!

I bury myself in the pillow, get my teeth into it, I yell. I come once, come again, and yet once more the waves seize me, the orgasms come in waves, one runs into another, my body's jumping out of its skin. Oh, my God! He doesn't give me time to collect myself, and as for his— Well, you couldn't ask for anything better! And I start to scream and bite, my whole body's bursting, I bite the pillow, and then, in order not to lose myself completely, I stick my thumb in my mouth, and suck, suck, suck. . . .

God, give me strength! . . . But he goes marching on and on and on, he gathers more and more momentum, he goes faster and faster and tears along, nowhere to turn, no mercy, I'm dying! Ooh-aah! stop! no more! no, more!

This is *something else!*

I come time after time, I no longer understand anything, no longer know what's happening to me, I'm all ablaze like the Firebird, there's no me anymore, I'm completely in this other world of passion, and he's with me, and he exults, and moves inside me with some intricate unendurable vibrations only Carlos knew, and even then not quite like this, despite his Parisian chic, only I feel: Soon! soon! Ooh! I yell out: Mommy dearest! Oh, fuck! fuck! Oh! But he is getting closer and closer all the time, and in another second both of us will disappear—Leonardik! Zhannochka!—in shudders and tears —I'm in flood—I'm in flood—my final shudders! And *it came to pass*.

# TWENTY-ONE

I am woken by the twittering of birds. The warmth of an Indian summer, the white net curtains undulating. I lie across the bed, on my stomach, embracing the pillow. There are brown stains, feathers are escaping from the pillow, my thumb is swollen and bitten half off. And the birds sing. The blanket's on the floor, my nightshirt is ripped. I raise myself slightly and look around. . . . The mirror—a black star; my combs and creams are full of splinters.

I wiped my forehead. I'd forgotten my illness, but now I guessed that my temperature had fallen. I cleared my throat, and it didn't seem to be stinging anymore. But this didn't concern me much: I checked that I was still alive. Well, I got up, out of habit made for the bathroom, but suddenly, walking through the hall, where the light still burned, suddenly everything came back to me! I collapsed against the wall, gave a groan, sweat broke out, I felt weak, I stood there, stood there awhile, then I dragged myself into the bathroom.

The water heater was humming. I squeezed out the toothpaste, opened my mouth, and the whole absurdity of this morning toilet appeared starkly before my eyes. Barefoot, disheveled, tousled, with a toothbrush in my hand, I *understood* Katyusha Minkova, my friend from school in the back of beyond, who, tormented by her plainness, had confessed to me, in the strictest confidence, that she dreamed of having a zipper on her side and being able one day to unzip it and step out of herself, and then everything would be different.

But why, I thought, putting down my toothbrush, why do I feel so unutterably ill at ease? And then it dawned on me: my smell's changed! How can I put it? Well, as if my bergamot orchard had been ravaged and my bergamots had been snatched and were rotting . . . a very distinct feeling indeed.

Ksyusha! Ksyusha!

Except there's no Ksyusha, she's sitting tight in her Fontainebleau, like a prodigal daughter. Well, whom can I phone? Surely not my two escorts? But the weather's warm outside. I thought and thought. I dial Merzlyakov's number; he and I are friends after all. His wife answers the phone, her voice reserved and unfriendly. I know that I should, but I don't hang up. "Hello!" I say. "Could I speak to Vitasik?" He comes to the phone: "Yes?" But what should I say to him? I say, "Vitasik! Come over as quickly as you can! I'm in trouble!" He is silent for a while and answers, "Then the article's ready? Good, I'll come over and pick it up. Thanks, Marina Lvovna!" I am appalled by his lack of invention. I'm at death's door, and he says, "Marina Lvovna." I actually wanted to call him again and tell him not to bother, but he turns up two hours later, and all this time I was waiting, terrified, and I threw the window wide open, just in case, to let in the bustle of the street, although of course they oughtn't to put in an appearance during daylight, but then again, hell only knows what they might get up to, since they screw so fiercely! Thinking about this, I go mad with fear. But at this point, thank God, he arrives, with the happy face of someone who has managed to escape from his family on his day off; he gives me a smack on my cheek and starts complaining amicably. "How dare you," he says, "phone me at home?" "Vitasik dear, please forgive me: an emergency and not a caprice—my world's turned upside down, and I'm a wreck." He looked closely at me. "What's the matter with you?" He already knew that I'd run on the field and the only result had been our quarrel. "The boys looked for you all night. Where did you get to?" "They're lying, they didn't look for me! They drove away," I say. "I was sitting by the road. . . . Doesn't matter. . . . I made it home. . . . No, no, I'm almost well again. . . . It's just that they became complete pigs after I ran for the third time, but to hell with them! That's not important now. See over there?" He looks: a broken mirror. "Yes. How did it happen?" "I chucked something. I was aiming for his skull." "Whose?" "*His.*" "Whose precisely?" "Well, his, Leonardik's. That is, Vladimir Sergeyevich's . . . I had a visit from him."

Vitasik has to sit down on the couch. He's unnerved. This doesn't surprise me. His gaze is distrustful and wild. It alternates between me and the mirror. "What, did he appear in the mirror?" "What are you talking about! He was sitting where you are!" Vitasik jumps up from the couch. . . .

Vitasik, hero of the six-day love. You could at least have taken off your nice jacket! He left it on. He asked, "Did he threaten you?" "What do you think! He said if anyone finds out that he visited me, then that person'll be in for it—" My hand flew to my mouth. "Well, thanks very much!" said Vitasik. "I've got nobody but you," I said defensively. But Merzlyakov is cunning, he has a shrewd mind: "But perhaps he was tricking you, to stop you from gossiping?" I cheered up. "Of course, a trick! But what if he does come again?" "Did he make a promise?" "He's drawn to me. He said that God is not at all like we imagine Him, and that although He exists, this is in principle of no importance. . . ." "So what *is* of importance?" said Vitasik, on his guard. "I didn't understand,"

I confessed frankly. "But on the whole he spoke about how important it is to preserve nature, not to pollute the forests and the sources of water. . . ." "Hmm," said Vitasik, "and what about healing the sick, kindness to animals, respect for one's elders, obeying the authorities . . . did he enlarge on those themes too?" "Why do you ask?" " 'Oh, yes, and through it all, you didn't change, you did it yoour-r way' "—Vitasik started to sing the old song cheerily and out of tune. "You're wrong," I said, disagreeing. "He has changed. He's repenting. He said that he'd understood much, but he still approves of and supports the idea of universal communism as an idea." "And did he feel awkward about making advances to a live young girl?" "But he confessed his love for me first!" I took umbrage on Leonardik's behalf. "Moreover, surely he's right? Surely one should heal the sick and plant trees?" "What a touching and humane phenomenon!" said Vitasik, much moved. "I would have asked him for his autograph." "He's renounced all his books," I said. "Surely not?" Vitasik didn't believe it. "He was calling *everything* into question. He said that culture has been emasculated on all sides, that only a new revelation is capable of bringing it back to life." Vitasik knitted his brow. "Wait a sec—what sort of new revelation did he have in mind?"

I can't stand men whose minds work on a different plane: they are always using abstract words and chat for hours in smoke-filled rooms!

"I couldn't give a shit about that revelation!" I lost my temper. "I'd far rather you told me what I ought to do!" "But what do *you* want?" "For him to leave me alone!" "I wonder, was it a ghost or an apparition?" Vitasik became pensive. "What's the difference! The main thing is that he had me." "And what about you?" "What about me?" "Did you like it!" "Are you mad!" I exclaimed. "Like it! He smothered me with a pillow!" "And how many times did you come?" "I don't remember." "Well, that's cleared up, then." "Nothing's clear!" I protested. "I'm frightened that he'll get into the habit of screwing me. Vitasik! I won't be able to endure it! It could kill me!" Vitasik was silent for a while. "Do you know," he said, "that Yegor and Yura were called in yesterday? What have you been telling people about those two?" "I didn't say anything about them! It's simply two journalists came to see me, you know, the ones who wrote the incomprehensible piece about me." "Did they come on their own initiative?" "Why, yes, of course! They already know about everything." "What will they be up to next!" Vitasik said sourly, startled. "Perhaps they know about him too?" he conjectured. You can never tell with Merzlyakov whether he's joking or telling the truth. "Why don't you go down to the station and tell them that you've been raped? After all, he did rape you, didn't he?" "Want to know something?" I said furiously. "What?" asked Vitasik, somewhat impudently. "Come here!" I ordered. "Lean over!" "Yes . . . ," muttered Vitasik guiltily, having made sure for himself. "It smells just like a corpse!" I said. Vitasik shook his head. The smell had disconcerted him. "But you're clever," I said. "you know everything; tell me, have such things ever happened before anywhere in the world? You know, far from human eyes . . . Perhaps witches slept with *them?*" Vitasik lifted his hands helplessly. He'd never heard of anything like it. "But what am I to do?" I asked, and told him the story of Katyusha Minkova and the zipper on her side. "There's only one thing to do," said Vitasik after some thought. "Get dressed! Off we go!" "Where are we going?" He looked at me strangely. "Where do you think? To church."

While I wrapped myself up, protecting myself against the return of the illness that had vanished in my panic, Vitasik strolled around and studied the objects in the bedroom he

knew so well. He had once been at the top, but then he had
gone to pieces and come down in the world, and we had
become friends. "Irochka, tell me, please, all these ideas of
yours about the field, and the meeting with 'Leonardik'—
where did all this come from? You were always a down-to-
earth girl. You didn't accidentally fall into the hands of some
psychic or mystic . . . ?" I denied this firmly. "I suppose trousers
aren't suitable for church? What about this tartan skirt—too
colorful?" "It will do," approved Vitasik. "I don't sleep with
anyone at all now," I explained, "and indeed, since your time,
darling, I've lost most of my enthusiasm." "You always did
have lovely manners!" Vitasik bowed. "No, it's the truth!" "I
too have slept with no one since you, apart from my wife."
My friend smiled. "But do you believe in God?" I asked. "You
know, I still can't make up my mind, try as I may," he said,
stumbling a bit. "I know that it's necessary and very useful,
but perhaps because I know all this," he told me on our way
to the church, "I just hang around, you understand, and keep
waiting, waiting for something. . . ." "Well, and after what's
happened to me?" Vitasik cast a sidelong glance at me. "In
any event, it's inspiring. . . ." And it still isn't clear whether
he's joking or teasing, but I am friends with him after all.

And we set off for the countryside, as if there were no
churches to be found in Moscow, but he says that the outskirts
of Moscow are somehow more easygoing, and so we drove off,
and once more I'm traveling through an autumn landscape,
past yellow trees and ponds falling asleep, like fish, and shortly
afterward we flew up a steep hill, past a boneyard of faded
wreaths and fences and crosses, uneven like children's scrib-
bles, and suddenly—there's the church, burning and shining
like a bronze samovar. We've arrived. And it was a Sunday,
and the service had just finished, and the people were gradually
dispersing, they came out onto the porch and made the sign

of the cross, looking back at the samovar, and I threw on a triangular head scarf. We enter, we push our way against the current, they're still selling candles, I wanted to buy some, the air, warm and stifling from their breath and filled with tar, has a thickness I can't fathom, and I stand last in the line for candles, an alien lanky figure—a beanpole, with my model proportions, my slender ankles betraying my noble line, whereas believers are the little people, stunted, you very rarely meet a tall person in church, and if you do you automatically turn to look—but we lingered over the candles, weren't paying proper attention, and as we were about to make for the iconostasis, the cleaners stopped us, you can't, we're about to wash the floors, they say, that's it, come on, come on, place your candles and leave, don't outstay your welcome, but Vitasik tries to win them over with his charm, he smiles at the cleaners with his well-oiled, generous smile: "Please let us pass, we have some urgent business to attend to, it is absolutely essential that we pray," but they, naturally, don't let us pass, they couldn't care less, you should have come earlier if you've got it in your heads to pray, instead of being in the land of Nod until midday, and they don't let us past, as if it's the lunch hour, but Vitasik insists and actually, losing his smile, starts to lose his temper, have you no shame, we won't, he says, prevent you from washing the floors, but they wouldn't budge, and even pushed us, that is, tried to herd us out, but suddenly they let us through, please, come on in, I saw from Vitasik's face that here, too, one could reach an agreement that leaves everyone satisfied, and we walked past, and they started washing the floor and didn't pay any attention to us, even though only a moment before they were nasty and obstinate.

We walked up to the icons. Emptiness. Candles flickered all around, burning down. What should I do? I turned to look at Vitasik. He whispered, "Get on your knees." Well, I was ready to kneel with all my heart, although I'd never been on my knees before; on the other hand, Vladimir Sergeyevich had never visited me like that before. And so I knelt. And Vitasik knelt alongside me. I put my fingers together and hesitantly made the sign of the cross, and I didn't do it wrong, I made the sign as one is supposed to. And he made the sign of the cross after I did. He crossed himself and turned red; he was embarrassed, as he told me afterward, in the country restaurant, because, he said, two very different things embarrassed him in life: religious rites and male homosexuality, that is, his childhood upbringing had sort of drawn a line, and with his adult mind he understands that this line is imaginary, but it's been there since childhood, well, take for instance Andryusha: one can say it's natural, and there is no dividing line, but when you're trying to cross this line, because you've reached the limit, argued my Vitasik, then, despite your genuine interest, you just can't stop worrying about whether what you're doing is right or not and whether you're not just deceiving yourself. "So what if you are deceiving yourself?" I asked Vitasik, having drunk a bit of vodka, because this line was less clear to me and I didn't understand what the problem was, strictly speaking—what if some man does caress his cock? You're silly, really you are, Vitasik! But we were both unbaptized. We kneel like two fools. "Well," he whispers, "come on, Ira, start praying." "How?" "Well, tell Him what's happened to you, state your attitude to it, and ask passionately for it never to happen again—there you have it, in a nutshell. . . . Now pray, or else they'll ask us to leave. Pray, and I'll pray for you, and for myself too, such a strange event, and if it doesn't work, then we'll put the blame on psychotherapy, nothing terrible about doing that, so as not to look like fools. Only," he says, "why talk of psychotherapy,

when he tells you how much he loves you and wants to carry
you off." But I'm thinking: I really do need to pray, it can't
make things worse, only I don't know how, and all the icons
are kind of strange, I'm not accustomed to all this, that is, I
always wear a crucifix around my neck—crystal, with a thin
rim of gold—and icons, I know, are treasures, people seek
them out and are proud of them, and another name for them
is *images,* and people deal in them and get put in prison because
of them . . . I understand all this, passions and beauty, but
it's alien to me, like buggery in Vitasik's case, but I start to
pray as best I can, and words begin to form on my lips, and
I address God for the first time in my life, with the following
words:

Lord! I kneel before You for the first time and for the first
time utter Your name not because I'm having a good time,
like when I sigh sweetly and my lips whisper Your name, which
goes well with pleasure, and I used it all the time—please
forgive me, I didn't mean to offend You: merely habit and a
lack of understanding. But times have changed, and You know
everything about me. You even know the simplehearted prayer
I am addressing to You, and I'm not trying to find the right
words, since the right words could be a sort of craftiness, and
You know what will happen to me after this prayer, and tomorrow, and the day after tomorrow, and many days after
tomorrow, and You know the day when I'll die, just as all
people die, but You perhaps will change Your mind if I repent,
except will I repent? You already know this too, and I can't
put one over on You. And so what then am I to do, if everything wasn't quite as I told Vitasik, and indeed, who knows
what it was really like, apart from You, because there's much
I don't understand, and Ksyusha's right in saying that my
beaver's bigger than my brainbox, and that, You must admit,
is as it should be for a woman, and so, what do I want to say?

what do I want to ask for? This is what I want to ask for . . .

   And suddenly it all came gushing out, and I started to pray; one's first prayer is like one's first love: you forget everything, and tears flow. Because there's no justice in the world! Women far uglier and commoner than I live beautifully, even magnificently, and people make a fuss over them, whereas I . . . I, of course, am not without sin, but what have I done to deserve this punishment, which is beyond my strength? Because Leonardik died with my help? Okay. Let's examine the facts. By the way, he himself broke his promise: he didn't marry me, and okay, my prayer does contain the husks of everyday life, but then again all of our life here is, forgive me, husks, and nothing else, except that some of them are multicolored. He didn't marry me, although I'd lost two years, and the years were passing, and my hopes were fading, especially since Carlos had left and nothing was as it should have been and all that. And how do things stand now? Where can I go? I ran on the battlefield, yes! But I didn't run for my own sake. You will say that my reason was that I had a good chance of becoming a saint or simply a national idol. But I did risk my life! And what greater risk could I have taken? The reason someone's a saint, the reason someone's an idol, is that he places his life below the interests of the people, and if he thinks about himself when he takes this risk, because he can't help thinking about this, and if the saint is being crafty, deceitful—well, that's his business! And perhaps I went to meet certain death, and I heard a voice, because I felt: I shall be found worthy. Except that even the best, sweetest little whore can't cast a spell strong enough for our Russian sorcery. The bait here is, most probably, sweeter still. . . . I don't know, I haven't thought about what it might be, and I don't want to think about it. As it is, I covered myself with shame and—pardon the expression—shit. And now this new calamity. He came, he fucked me. . . . What for? one asks. He wants to get married. But can you marry a dead man? He says we're kindred souls in our own way and that although we lived at the same point in time, our paths didn't cross because of circumstances beyond our control, but at last they did cross. Only we didn't understand at first what was what, and we missed each other once again, and he suddenly realized what had happened only when he was dead, and he had started to pine, doing his posthumous time in the celestial bathhouse changing room set aside by You, from which, evidently, there is still a return route, and he came back for me, before any terminal transformations set in, citing his love for me, which after his death had flared up even more strongly. That's what he said. Okay. But now tell me what to do. It's not the fact that he fucked me which is awful, although that's awful too, but the fact that he's asking me to go away with him, and I'm full of doubts. . . . Vitasik, who is kneeling right here next to me, he said, while we were on the way to the church, that *all* roads lead to God, all, only very few follow the first sum- mons they receive, they stop after the first step as if they're rooted to the ground and don't go any farther, and this is how they live out their lives, but you, Irisha, have gone farther than many, and I disagree: I've gone *a hell of a long way!* But You will ask me, of course, what I *do* want. Carlos as a husband or something like that? Will You be satisfied then? And if I say yes, then You'll say, Well, what do you know, a fine one she is, she wanted to become a *saint,* but now give her Carlos or a cosmonaut and she's happy. No, a cosmonaut doesn't suit me. Let him fly to his heart's content, without my tears and participation.

So what is it you want, Ira?

I'm all mixed up, Lord! I gave a man a helping hand toward death's door, and now I'm complaining about his coming to see me. . . .

Well, so what are we to do?

Lord, I believe in You so shakily that one moment I'll write your name with a capital letter and the next with a small one. Lord, this girl is in a dreadful muddle, and grant me some time! Let me try to make sense of You and me!

You won't make any sense of it, Ira.

Why won't I make any sense of it?

Because it is not given to you to make sense of it.

And what is given to me, Lord?

That you should go among people and throw light on all their filthiness and ugliness from below.

Lord! *How much longer* do I have to peer at people doggy style, looking back and bearing witness to their base features? Yes, I know quite a few people from that angle, and I'll tell You that they are ugly and deformed and have been a total disappointment. But is it really my fate to observe only vileness? For You, Lord, look at them differently; after all, You increase and multiply their lives, You don't brand everybody. Or perhaps I don't belong to You? No, I belong to You. To You! Don't give me to anyone else! I beg You . . . give me new eyes! Lift me up from my hands and knees!

No, Ira.

Lord! Surely it isn't right to deprive someone of all hope.

But as soon as you fulfill your purpose, you will come to Me, and I shall wash you clean. The time is drawing nigh, because your beauty is waning. . . .

But I haven't even been a mother yet, Lord! Grant me that at least!

Vitasik was shaking me by the shoulder. "Stop it! Where do you think you are! Shouting like that in a place of worship!" The cleaners, kilting up their skirts and tucking them into their belts, were approaching, threat written all over their faces. Vitasik stood up to meet them. A little priest poked his head out of a side door, looked at me, and vanished: Father

Veniamin, as it became clear later. Vitasik quickly and quietly tried to explain to the cleaners. They shook their heads; they were not to be budged. Vitasik dragged me toward the doors, the women's curses following us. "Vitasik," I said, finding myself outside. "Vitasik . . ." I burst out crying. He helped me into the car. "Why did you bring me here? You're all conspiring against me! I don't want to look at your ugly mug!" I kicked and pushed. I shoved him out of the car. "Calm down." He grabbed me by the arm, painfully. I wept. "Surely it's wrong to deprive someone of all hope? I don't believe in this filthy little godlet. We live in a godless state, after all! What have they taught us since childhood? The opium of the people! How true! How true! What was the point of building all these churches! Idiots! Why couldn't they have torn them *all* down, roots and all!" It's just that my nerves were upset. I have a problem with my nerves. I need a break. I need to calm down. I need to spend an autumn season on the Caucasian Riviera. I wiped away my tears. The narcotic mist was clearing. "Vitasik, darling," I said. "Forgive me. Forgive me for everything. I won't set foot in here again! . . . Vitasik, have you still got some time? Vitasik darling, let's go to a restaurant, okay? I've got money." "Money? I've got money too!" Vitasik growled, delighted that the hysterics were over. I smiled at him, my eyes red and without makeup. "God, I could eat a horse!" I said, squinting.

And so we embarked on our return journey, as on a dance, overtaking the traffic and making up for lost time and space, delighted with the tangible substance of life, which rises like dough out of a pan, beyond measure, over the brim! Let it flow! Oh, how I want to eat! On, on, across the bridge, up the hillside, where in a country inn cooks we know are clattering their knives, their shiny faces melting above the stove, where chicken tabak sputters and fat spurts out, where beefsteaks chuckle, where sturgeon glows on a spit, while beef is stewing away in little pots! On, on, where on intricately decorated trays, their arms outstretched, my waiter friends serve vodka so cold that the glasses steam up and red wine that has lost its chill. Hurry on, on, where footsie is played under the tables and the stuffed aubergines drop broad hints!

We draw up. And pushing past the timid line of people who had collected on the porch in the downcast attitude of preprandial waiting, we march straight up to the door and knock: "Open up!" And in answer to the authoritative knock, one of our friends springs onto the porch, such a darling, Fyodor Mikhailovich, in his waiter's uniform, with a smile and a stripe down the side of his trousers, he hisses at everyone else but beckons us and admits us immediately and locks the heavy bolt behind us. Now we'll break our fast! Now we'll get some serious drinking in! And inside, we are greeted warmly by the courteous Leonid Pavlovich, who without trying, just by looking at someone's eyes, is able to establish straight off the worth of a customer, calculate his moral makeup, his financial resources, his official position and his family circumstances, and so on: whether he's ever been convicted, when, how often, and for what crimes, whether he has traveled abroad or is just someone who claims to have, and if a foreigner, then from what country and what has brought him to our part of the world, Leonid Pavlovich, my friend, highly recommended, and he leads us into a private room with thick curtains, and there the table's already laid—especially for us —and the hors d'oeuvres are already served: salted saffron milk-cap mushrooms, *satsivi*, Georgian cabbage and sauerkraut with red whortleberry, *lobio*, all sorts of greens, hot *lavash*, salmon with slices of lemon and curly-haired parsley, meat and fish in aspic with horseradish, crab salad with mayonnaise, Tambov ham with a lump of jelly, cured fillet of sturgeon, oh, yes, and a little caviar, and so on—in short, a gastronomic collation designed to defeat melancholia, neurasthenia, black

magic, hard times, depression, totalitarianism, Critical Realism, and all other sorts of -isms. Then—rubbing my hands,
to the ringing chimes of bracelets—then let's start with the
vodka. Take a mushroom with the vodka, the king of mushrooms, that's right, spread yellow butter on the hot *lavash*,
spread a thick, thick layer of caviar on the butter, and let's
have another drink, and forget about the absurdities, in the
final analysis, the next generation is right, which—try some
fish—in the guise of my Rituyla asserts that it's *stupid* to struggle and suffer, life is for living, because when you struggle,
firstly, you strain yourself and waste your energy, secondly,
you waste time, thirdly—some more vodka!—you might get
your teeth smashed in: what you've fought for you'll get caught
for, as in my case! fourthly, bear in mind, you have to settle
accounts with—I clench my fists to show who's meant—and
that's tiresome as well as unworthy of us, and fifthly—what's
fifth?—fifthly, you should clink glasses and live as though
everything's beautiful, because then everything will immediately become beautiful and no need to fuss—oh!—and what
you remember as infrequently as possible will vanish of its own
accord, be wiped out in time—exactly!—just mind *one's own*
business, or, in fact, do nada—that's another good way of
spending one's time!—and don't struggle against anything,
don't get involved—yes, yes—don't run on battlefields but
*run away*, spend money, if one has money, and if not, then
not, but I used to worry, and Great-grandmother would look
down from the wall at my vanity, and her look was full of
condemnation, but we belong to the generation that worried
and sang ambiguous risqué songs: that's not what's needed—
we don't need ambiguity—that's where our misfortune and
captivity come from! from ambiguity—it has destroyed us: thus
argued Merzlyakov, having a slug of vodka, and I agreed with
him, and thus argued I, and he agreed with me, and we drank
vodka and agreed with each other, and we were both extremely

merry, because they'd treated us to delicious fresh cabbage
soup, and then we ate two shashliks each with a burning-hot
sauce, and then we ordered another bottle of vodka, and, it
goes without saying, we soon polished it off. And we were
amazed, sitting opposite each other, at how many stupidities
we'd managed to commit while teasing the silly geese who
rule the roost here, and we knew that we'd developed a taste
for it, and it was difficult for us to stop teasing them, to let
sleeping geese lie, because that's just the way we were, and
in addition a goose is gruesome, it's a foul fowl, and its nip is
painful. And although Vitasik had in his time brandished his
fists, his punches had a far shorter reach than mine; he had
merely admired me from a distance when I threw the oranges
at the British orchestra and when I flaunted my beauty in the
splendid magazine—he lacked true grit, but all the same I
liked him, because I was fed up with trash, and he's not trash,
we said no to cognac and took more vodka and then had
chocolate ice cream sundaes, with wafers, as if I had never
had even a trace of tonsillitis, and I *really* felt like ice cream,
and had some, and we were both of the opinion that there
was no need to tease the geese ensconced in our capital and
make them turn nasty, and the biggest daddy goose of all—
he's up there! I said, meaning the filthy godlet who had given
me a lecture, despite the fact that he had been abolished a
long time ago, once and for all, and a good thing too! And
Leonid Pavlovich, despite being busy and despite the other
customers, looked in on us several times, paid compliments
and made polite jokes, and when Vitasik stepped out for a
minute, Leonid Pavlovich noted that my admirer was from a
*good* Russian family, and I informed him that there had been
a moment of the loftiest love between us, because I like boys
with skin that's smooth and clean from being well fed with
food from the markets, because his trousers are pressed and
his nannies used to take him for walks in the park of culture

and leisure, because he knows several languages and from his earliest years possessed effortlessly what other people would sell their grannies to get, and I love people to whom everything comes easily, with no sweat, and Leonid Pavlovich approved of me, and Vitasik had liked me too, and we had fallen in love with each other that very same evening, and now we have met up once again—and at this point Vitasik came back and we started talking again, and of course we sat there until closing time, and bankrupted ourselves, handed over all our money, and Leonid Pavlovich advised us to get a taxi and even lent us money for the fare. And we took a taxi, and by midnight we'd reached my place, and when we had got up to my apartment to drink some tea, Vitasik noted in passing that it was midnight and he'd promised to be home for lunch, but I tried to persuade him to stay the night, not because I wanted to seduce him or anything, but because, when we got home and I saw the apartment—the broken glass and the light in the hall—although I had both had something to drink and stopped believing in God completely, I suddenly felt unwell, and I said he must phone home and say he was with me, because he himself said, Why all this ambiguity? but he started to object that you mustn't cause pain to someone close to you, that is, his wife, and I said that his wife must put herself in my position, because what if *he* comes again, disregarding the fact that I'm slightly tight, and, for argument's sake, kills me, because he wants to revenge himself on me—what for?—for no reason, and kills me, and I die in my sleep, without ever waking up, but if you're with me then he definitely won't come, and even if he does come, then you can have boys' talk in the kitchen about the new revelation, which you want to ask him about; but Vitasik says that while, of course, he's not against a male conversation about a new revelation, it's time for him to go home, because his wife, an interpreter, has been expecting him for the past ten hours, if not more, and will be worried, because the thing is, she trusts him, because he could have had an accident in the car, but he'd left his own car by the river when we had driven away from the country restaurant, obeying Leonid Pavlovich's request, who had in addition presented me with a bunch of white carnations, here, give them to your wife, as I took them out of the vase, and Vitasik told him that he would return the money the next day, because he had to come back for the car in any case, and leave the money with Fyodor Mikhailovich, seeing as Leonid Pavlovich doesn't go anywhere near work on Mondays, and I said, "Lie down next to me, take your clothes off and lie down, here's *our* bed, here's the somewhat smashed mirror— and to hell with it!—and here's the pouf—remember? we used to sit on it, face-to-face, and I—you remember!—would put my fur coat on, and you said, laughing loudly, What sickening kitsch! and for some reason this excited you, and you couldn't tear yourself away from me." "I just can't stay!" He extended his arms despairingly! "And therefore . . ." "Okay, then, phone your wife!" "Phone? It's one o'clock!" "What do you mean, one? It's still eleven!" "It's always eleven with you!" "But I plopped my watch down on the field and left it there. . . . Vitasik, tell me: why didn't you want me to run?" "Because I wanted you to stay safe and sound." "And do you know, when I was running, I was thinking: He'll flood me in a minute! immolate me! but instead Leonardik came here without even knocking." "And what about in the church?" "What do you mean, in the church?" "Why were you yelling?" "Because, you fool, try to understand, one mustn't deprive a person of all hope! But just to be on the safe side, I'm cunning, I'll get baptized, understand? Stay with me—come on, lie down, take off your pants!—please, at least until the first cock!" "I can't!" "Oh, come on, I beg you. If you like, I'll go down on my knees for you." He leapt up: "Are you mad!" "I'm Princess Tarakanova, I'm seizing and kissing a man's hands for the first time in my life! Oh, do stay!" "I have to go home!" "Are you frightened that he'll come?" "He won't, so go to sleep. I'm off. Goodbye." "Don't go! You know, I want you, don't you see, come on, you can cure me, I'll drown out the smell with perfume, you know what people say: a fuck a day . . ." "What are you babbling about!" "Aha . . . I know. You're scared of catching it!" "Leave it out!" "Yes! Yes! You bastard!" "Ira!" "This is the first time I've ever *asked* a man." "Ira! Irisha darling!" "I left Carlos because of you! You ruined my life! You turd! Go away! I don't want to see you again! Go away! And don't ever come back! I'll get christened and I won't be afraid, but you—you reptile! you lecherous bastard! How many lovers have you got? I'll tell your educated wife everything; so she trusts you, eh?" "Irisha!" "You're pathetic; you can't even get it up!" "There you go . . ." "What do you mean, there you go? You ruined my life! I hate you! No, don't be in such a hurry to leave, shithead, mommy's dear little sucker boy! So you want to stay prim and pure? It won't work. Coward! But I'm not afraid of *anyone*! But why does everyone go on living, while I perish? Vitasik, answer me—no, answer me: do you love me?"

Toward morning he fled; I think I socked him in the kisser toward morning. Or was there something else as well? I just don't know.

He fled at cockcrow. My neighbor on the ground floor had reared some chickens and two roosters. Our local cop came to see her and forbade her to keep them, but she still keeps them, we even sent a collective letter of protest denouncing her to the Moscow City Council, all the residents signed it, I also put my name to it, but in spite of this she keeps them, and they crow.

# TWENTY-TWO

W ell, that's it. I've fallen! I've *fallen!* No, I don't
mean that I've fallen because I agreed to Rituyla's
entreaties and, suffering from enforced poverty,
gave in, *or* because the thunderer Gavleyev still hadn't sent
his weighty word crashing down, hadn't welcomed me into
his team—and what do I need his team for?—*or* because Rituyla had insisted and begged me, and, in my delicate condition, I said, "Okay! Have it your way," and Hamlet was
delighted, we met at Rituyla's place, and the remuneration
was a hundred rubles more than he had promised, I was satisfied, and Hamlet was too. He orbited my globe and kept
saying, "I'm really happy! really happy! you'll be a good
mother," with his Armenian accent, I took a look in passing
at his cock, it was the cock of an uninteresting, semiliterate
person planning to marry a little fool, my Rituyla, and he got
all tense when, according to the script, we were supposed to
perform together, I understood then that it would end in blind
jealousy, Romanian furniture, a house in Yerevan—Oh, do
come and visit us!—and in the meantime the Armenian was
stroking my stomach from time to time, enraptured by the
propitious bulge, and asking, "But won't we disturb *him?*" So
thoughtful of him, you know! "No, of course not! Go for it!"

But alongside us is dear Rituyla, whom he's actually forgotten in his greedy passion for fresh meat, he goes into raptures over both of us, but falsely, they'll both have to pay dearly for this, but what business is it of mine? I know my business, even though this Hamlet's cock is a short one, and I thought: I wonder what Shakespeare's Hamlet's cock was like? How many inches long and thick? Why don't historians paint this vital detail for us? Why does all this totally pass them by, as though everything didn't revolve around this, or so it seems to me, or rather, to be more precise: that's how it seemed to me before, because now that I have other, more pressing concerns, I don't think like that anymore, and I thought, when he was being too gentle with me, saying, "Won't we disturb his peace: you could just pull him out, like with a corkscrew, yes?" I thought and said, "What a shame, dear Hamlet, my man from Yerevan, that your cock doesn't screw like a corkscrew!" And they, eastern people, are hairy and shaggy, I like this, by the way, sleeping with Dato is like sleeping with a bear cub, but they have their shortcomings: they are easily offended. His eyes get all bloodshot, but I'm not afraid, no offense, Hamlet, but Rituyla goes: "Ha ha ha!" Later she'll shed tears over that laugh, with diamonds in her ears, the little fool, but she says, Why shouldn't I try to hang on to a man like this? I looked into his pockets; the smallest bill you'll find there is twenty-five rubles, and they're all crumpled up in such an offhand way, as if they're three-ruble notes, and I'm an undemanding girl, I want to get married, and he believes that he was the first—aha, they're stupid, that's good!—but he asks her, Listen, bring me together with your girlfriend, but as soon as we got together, he went on his guard, at once, particularly when I stretched out toward her, because I'd missed her, well, I think, another time, then, but he swooped on the fresh meat, with its round belly, he became inflamed with passion, but

I'm already bored, and then we drink champagne, my brut! I had said, But there has to be brut! I insisted on this, and he spent two days in a taxi going around Moscow, looking, I said, "You have to know where to look, my man from Yerevan!" He took offense, they're so touchy, words can't describe how touchy they are! "You," he says, "why are you talking like that?" What's it to me, I say what I like, but we sit in peace and quiet, we drink champagne, and Rituyla, my former acolyte, asks, "Well, has everything turned out okay for you?" And she wants to hear that it's all sorted itself out, all the fuss has died down, but she doesn't know anything about the field, there had been no fuss, Yegor and Yurochka had lost their tongues. *They* had put the screws on the boys and quite right too. They'd started sounding off, getting cocky, but as soon as *they* put the shit up them they went white about the gills, and I, pandering to her, say, "It turned out okay," and she says, "So life goes on? Yippee!" and clinks her champagne glass, and Hamlet, she explains, liked the magazine very much, a rarity and a *curiosity*, he paid a lot to get hold of it, Hamlet nods blissfully, well done, I say, spare no expense, he's staying in the Hotel Berlin. "I," says Hamlet, "when I saw such beauty, I was stunned," and Rituyla says, "Just imagine, that's my best friend!" and so this is how I picked up my honorarium, my royalties for a night with Hamlet, the sole benefit from it, the rest was harmful, well, so be it, but he says, "You really are as beautiful as a foreigner; I have some photographs where there is even . . ." "I know! I know! I congratulate you," I say. "I'll run to the bathroom this minute," a joke, he twists his head, in his pigeon heart he senses I'm taking a piss, but he doesn't understand, and Rituyla takes offense on his behalf, as if she's already his wife, in advance, just to be on the safe side. Rituyla paces up and down without any clothes on, you're pretty, my sweet, pretty, and she's fingering me, well, she's got her finger on the button, Hamlet grew all tense, he'll smash her face in, oh, I can see it all now, I've got foresight, I can read foreskins: "Let me tell your fortune from your German helmet!" And he says, "You're not serious?" Rituyla can't contain herself: she cracks up, but I say, "I'm not joking, I only have to look out of the corner of my eye and I can tell right away who your parents are, what color Volga you drive, how long you're going to live." I look: his eyes are insincere—a swindler. I find it unbearably amusing, but he is annoyed, it's so easy to upset a man, Ksyusha is a master at that, and Veronika rubs her hands with glee as she listens to how some man made a total prick of himself, and I say, "And why is it that all your Armenian women are so ugly," and Hamlet takes offense all over again. "No," he counters, "they are beautiful!" "So if they're so beautiful," I say, "then why did you come to Moscow to look for a bride?" And he says, "They're very proud!" "Ah, we know these proud types: the uglier, the prouder! Of no interest whatsoever."

There, I think, my time too is drawing to its close. But just wait a little while: I'll give birth to something for you all in the end. There is plenty to worry about, though. Stanislav Albertovich has started to smell something fishy too, something's wrong, he glances nervously at my face during our consultations and no longer congratulates me, he's not so ready with the kisses, my Dr. Flavitsky has cooled off. "Why such lack of interest, Doctor?" "Work," he complains, "is a pain, and do you know what, I'm being taken to court, one of my female patients, a snotty little seventeen-year-old!" "Well, that takes the cake! What nerve!" I say, "Will it be a boy or a girl?" "Seems like a boy. But no guarantee." I say, "He's really up to mischief in there!" Flavitsky says sadly, "Well, then, everything's in order so far." I say, "Are there any abnormalities? The smell isn't too much like a corpse?" "Yes, child, there is certainly something of a smell; I can't think where it comes from." I joke, "That's me decomposing while I'm still alive." And I was seized with doubts. About giving birth. But it's too late for an abortion. . . . And so I fell!

First, about Veronika. She's a witch, but after the field she and I aren't getting on; I phoned her, but you have to drag words from her, and I don't understand why. She sent me to certain death, and now she can't even be bothered to ask how I am. And as for my new friends, it's as if they've all died—oh, what the hell, I wouldn't want them even if you paid me. Rituyla doesn't count, and Ksyusha's in America again, I couldn't hold out, I phoned her in Fontainebleau, spoke to the dentist in English, she's acquired a Czech film director there, in America, she hinted as much to me, and flew across the ocean. Ksyushenka, you have forgotten me completely, and they didn't give her a visa for Moscow, since she's a spy and a saboteur. She said crossly, "I'll get by somehow." Except it makes no difference to me: she's my love. And Gavleyev is silent. Well, stay silent, then. The French dentist says in English, "She is at New York," and I say to him, "*Merci*, goodbye," and hang up, and think: Where can I turn for advice? I phoned Merzlyakov: he's grumbling. "I'm in trouble too," he tells me. What wouldn't I give for your troubles! And Dato's on tour, I phoned, his family loves me, but they answered evasively. And Veronika? What a bitch! Why? I don't understand. Perhaps her Timofei has kicked the bucket? No, he's alive and well. . . . And I fell. That is, it would have been okay to have sought any other advice, but instead I turned to Katerina Maksimovna.

I go in to meet her, she's sitting there, drinking her evening tea, with bagels. A little one-room apartment, all crammed with furniture and rugs. She lives in Chertanovo, in the settlements almost on the heath, a hellishly long way from the

center. "I've been expecting you," she says. "Sit down, we'll
have tea." And she takes a teapot out from underneath a large
padded Matryoshka tea cozy, pours me a strong bitter brew,
undiluted, no, that's too strong for me, "When," she asks, "is
the baby due?" and looks at my stomach. "When? In two
months time." We both fall silent. She sits there, doesn't ask
any idle questions, has a sip of tea, dunks her bagel, and fixes
her gaze on the television. I say, "Katerina Maksimovna, I
have a favor to ask of you." She is silent, listens further. I
say, "I am going to have a baby, but my fiancé," I say, "abandoned me, he doesn't call, he's vanished from the face of the
earth, he doesn't even know," I say, "that we're going to have
a baby. Can't you summon him? I need to speak with him."
"Why," she says, surprised, "did he leave you? or has he got
himself another girlfriend and gone to live with her?" "I don't
know," I answer. "I don't know anything, where he is, what
he's doing—I don't have a clue, but I do know that this has
nothing to do with another girlfriend, I'm his girlfriend, it's
just that he's stopped coming to see me, something, evidently,
is stopping him, but I have to see him without fail!" "That
means," argues Katerina Maksimovna, "that we ought to
charm him back to you with a spell." "Oh, yes," I say eagerly,
"something like that, bewitch him, so that he'll come to
discuss the baby." She says, "Have you got a photograph of
him?" "There's one at home." "Next time bring the photograph and one hundred rubles, I need ten candles at ten rubles
each for this task, have you got that?" I answer, "Here's one
hundred rubles for you," and hand over my Armenian money,
"take them for the candles, and I'll go and get the photograph,
I'll be back in a flash," and I simply can't wait, I rush for a
taxi, fly home right through Moscow, through a blizzard and
knee-deep snow, the Kremlin burns in the middle like a flying
saucer. I grab the photograph and hurry back, I shake the
snow off in the passage and ask for some house slippers so as

not to leave stains, and take the photograph out of my handbag oh so casually, as if nothing were wrong, but my heart is beating so fast. I'm scared that she'll say no. She takes the photograph in her hands, peers at it, then places it gingerly on the table, and looks at me. "Do you realize *what it is* you're asking?" I say, "I do." She is silent, her face is displeased. I light a cigarette and say, "Katerina Maksimovna, don't you worry about me, he's already come to me once, he sat down on the couch, the picture of manners, we had a chat, and he left." "When he came to you that time did he look like he did before he died?" she asks. "Very much so," I say, "just a bit sadder than in life, and about five years younger, just like in the photograph, I picked it specially, he gave me a few." "No," she says, "this is something I cannot undertake." "Why, Katerina Maksimovna? Oh, please, my darling! Look, there's some more money!" I dig in my handbag. She stops me. "Wait," she says, "there's something you've got to tell me: Is this baby of yours by him?" And she looks at me expectantly. I say, "Would that be wrong? What do you think? That's basically why I'm asking him to come, to clarify that point. . . . But he doesn't come, or he doesn't exist anymore, they've transferred him somewhere, you know, like in the army . . . perhaps he's already far away, so far away that he'll never return." I flick ashes into a dark-blue saucer and lean back on the couch. "He offered to marry me!" I exclaim. "And what answer did you give him?" "Well, you could hardly expect me to answer him just like that, Katerina Maksimovna! I thought that he'd come again, but there's no sign of him, no sign at all. Or perhaps he's had second thoughts. But as for me, I'm keeping the child. . . ."

Katerina Maksimovna stood up and said, "Come tomorrow evening, my beauty. I shall use a book to cast my spells." I leapt up. "Thank you!" "You can show your gratitude later." I say, "I can give you checks for the special shops, if you'll

take them; I think they'd be fine." She says, "Later! Later!
Go!" She actually got strict with me. I was afraid that she
might change her mind and made a sharp exit.

I was exhausted by the waiting. The next evening I arrive
again. She is smoking a cheap cigarette. The television howls
and blasts: the war. I ask cautiously, "How did things go?"
But she shakes her head. "No," she says, "nothing's working
out; I spent all night casting spells with my book. Without
success. It means that he doesn't want to come to you." I say,
"What do you mean, doesn't want to? Why?" And she says,
"He can't come to you. You've got the evil spell of corruption
on you, the *evil eye*." I am amazed. "What evil eye? After all,
he came once before." "But now," she says, "he won't come."
I say, "But why?" And she says, "Try to remember what you
did after he left." "What did I do? I went to stay at my
girlfriend's, at Rituyla's, because, of course, I'd been scared
out of my wits, and I lived with her, and if he was jealous of
my attachment to her, then that was stupid, and then again
he always knew that about me, and consequently he shouldn't
have been jealous. And what else did I do? I really don't
know. Well, once, after this happened, Merzlyakov, Vitasik,
visited me, I told him everything, he's a friend, I don't remember, I got drunk that time." Katerina Maksimovna made
a wry face and said, "Dear, I'm not asking you about that.
You're sure you don't remember anything else?" "Well," I say,
"Dato dropped in to see me briefly, before his tour, only I
already knew that I was pregnant, but I didn't tell him, or
else he would have killed me, and then, yes, I wanted to have
an abortion, because the smell embarrassed me, and Dato says,
'You smelly bitch, why haven't you washed?' And I say, 'But
you sometimes like me smelly, Dato.' 'Yes,' he says, 'but this
is going too far!' And I got ashamed of doing it with other
men, although all sorts of shallow types tried to invite themselves in, and then just one Armenian a few days ago . . .

But that," I continue, "doesn't count at all. What a fool, even though he's a Hamlet! That is, I don't understand one bit what basis Vladimir Sergeyevich has for being annoyed at me!" "But," says Katerina Maksimovna, "don't you feel guilty in some other way?" "No," I say. "Think carefully," she says. . . . I thought. "I don't know," I say. "Where else did you go?" she asks. "What do you mean, where? Well, I ran over the field, only that was *before*, he knew about that, that was the reason he came, he said as much." "I am not asking about the *field*," says Katerina Maksimovna, the owner of a one-room apartment in Chertanovo, almost on the heath. "Rather, where did you go after you'd seen him, your fiancé?" And she looked at the photograph. And there he is, lying on the table. Lying there and smiling at us. "I don't remember," I say, and I really had forgotten, but she says, "How about a church, standing on a little knoll, in the middle of a cemetery, a church, yes, is that how it was?" "Oh, yes!" I say. "Of course, and a boneyard of wreaths, in autumn, oh, yes, on the following day. That was Merzlyakov's idea: to go there at once. And we went." "And what happened next?" asks Katerina Maksimovna, lowering her eyes, as if at this point it was necessary to describe the sort of intimate details that are shared only between lovers but that she had to know because it was part of her job, like a matchmaker. Does your precious daughter have any flaws? A birthmark the size of a lampshade, for example, on her buttock? No? "I prayed," I say, "clumsily, for the first time in my life." "About what?" Katerina Maksimovna lowers her gaze even more, running her cigarette over the surface of a crystal ashtray. "That I didn't want him to come anymore," I confess, blushing all over. She was getting on my nerves. "And then?" she asks. "And then," I say, "I returned to this church, somehow or other I got there by suburban electric train, and found the priest who had heard my heartrending cry, a young priest, and I say to him, 'Baptize

me!' First of all he was amazed, but I told him everything—
only I didn't say anything about *him*," I said, pointing at the
photograph, "so that he wouldn't be scared, but even what I
did tell him was enough for him to baptize me, he was so
overjoyed. 'You,' he says, 'are Maria the Egyptian, that's who
you are, yes!' He doesn't know about the field either, he
doesn't need to know that! 'Do you understand,' he says, 'that
your salvation alone is worth more than a legion of God-
fearing, just men? You,' he says, 'are a most welcome soul for
Him,' and he baptized me there and then, without any god-
parents, and an old woman held open my elastic and poured
holy water into my underpants, putting out my shame! . . .
Aah!" It finally dawned on me, and I looked at Katerina
Maksimovna in dismay. She silently ran the hot tip of her
cigarette over the crystal ashtray. "I see," I said. "Well, then,
now that you see, be off, and may God go with you," Katerina
Maksimovna said to me timidly. I've known her a long time.
Ksyusha and I and the other girls used to go and visit her.
She used to read palms marvelously. We would listen for hours.
Everything jibed. We gaped in astonishment. But now she
seems to have taken a vow of silence! I say, "Katerina Maksimovna, don't make me leave!" And I look at her: she's
disgusting, her hair is thin and straight, a straggly bun at the
back of her head, there are loads of women like this in the
shops as soon as they open, they argue in the lines, only her
eyes stand out, cherry-colored and watchful. I say, "Don't kick
me out!" "No," she says, "leave, my dear!" But again, there's
no firmness, and I see she's leaving something unsaid. She's
throwing me out, but not on my ear, she's throwing me out,
but she doesn't open the door, so how am I supposed to leave?
I light a cigarette and am silent. I look at her. She looks at
me. Conspirators. While the television howls and blasts. And
my favorite little priest, Father Veniamin, he also has special

eyes, they sparkle . . . but he's still young, rather silly, and silly people's eyes often sparkle, and his bright eyes make my insides moan, "My sweet . . . my little one . . . my sugar . . ."

All these memories flooded in, and now, when I write, I'm remembering them now, yes. And red ants are creeping over the table, I write and squash them under my fingers, they've spread all over the house, and they're worse than cockroaches, they're dreadful: as soon as I die they'll crawl all over me, worse than worms, they won't even leave any bones, they'll grind everything into dust, but for the time being I squash them with my fingers and write. . . . There's another one crawling over the table. . . . I say, "Katerina Maksimovna, oh, please do what you can for me!" But she lifts up her cherry-colored eyes and says in an even voice, "Go tomorrow early in the morning to a health food shop and buy," she says, "as fresh an egg as possible, it's essential that it should be as fresh as possible, and then, just before you go to bed tomorrow night, take your clothes off and roll this egg over you from top to bottom, from your head to your toes, you must do this twenty times, and when you've rolled it all over yourself twenty times, then put the egg at the head of your bed and sleep with it next to you till morning, and then in the morning come and see me."

I almost fell at her feet, saying, "Thank you, I'll do everything just as you ordered, so then, twenty times?" "Yes," she says, "twenty times," and I flew home. The next morning I went out to buy an egg, I went into the market, visiting the shops selling dairy produce, am shoved to and fro among all the old ladies, the pensioners, I squeeze my way to the counter, show me the freshest egg you've got, I look to see what date's shown, and I make my selection, while the clerks—real tarts—look at me as if I'm sick, get bitchy, show their astonishment, as though I'm trying to steal their eggs or I've gone off my rocker. "Give me one egg!" I say. And they all think: She's off her head! Well, I bought it, I went home, and as soon as evening set in I lay down, my belly sticking out—the froglet is turning somersaults in there—and I started rolling the egg from tip to toe, I rolled it twenty times, got exhausted because of my belly, and then placed it at the head of the bed but just couldn't get to sleep from thinking about the future. And in the morning I turned up at Katerina Maksimovna's.

She places the egg on a saucer. Let's, she suggests, have a cup of tea first. We drink our tea, but in silence; I'm waiting. She says, "Did you do everything just as I instructed? . . . That's good." She stood up, took a patterned rag from a chest of drawers, wrapped the egg up in it, and then started to hit the rag with a small hammer. She hit it and hit it, but the egg didn't break. I went cold: it's a bad omen! She hit it again, but the egg didn't break, and then—in a flash—it smashed. . . . She undoes the rag, looks inside, she looks and looks, and then raises her cherry eyes, her bad eyes, to me and utters with the very ends of her lips, "Well, you're in luck! The *evil eye* has left you!" And she shows me: a little black vein, like a worm, is beating inside the egg, trembling. . . . "Well," she says, "you're in luck!"

While I think: God, how far I've fallen!

But I don't say anything to her, I merely say, "Thank you so much, Katerina Maksimovna, I am very much in your debt." And she says that nothing else depends on her or indeed on anyone, but the doors, she says, of my home are open to my fiancé, but I can't say when your fiancé will come, I don't know, and as far as payment is concerned, then why shouldn't she accept it, if it is owed to her, all right, I'll take it, since the *evil eye* has left you, and she asks for another hundred. And so the second Armenian hundred went as payment to Katerina Maksimovna, and Leonardik looks at us from the photograph and smiles.

# TWENTY-THREE

## ANNOUNCEMENT

I, Tarakanova Irina Vladimirovna, also known as Joan of Arc, Maid of Orleans, also occasionally known as Maria the Egyptian, Russian, pregnant, not a Party member but deeply sympathetic, divorced, first husband—don't remember, second—a football player—a princess, a patriot, a sponger against my will, resident in the Union of Soviet Socialist Republics since birth, who at 23 years of age returned to my historical motherland, to Moscow, address 3 Adriano-polskaya Street, building 2, flat 16, *consent* to enter into matrimony with my cherished fiancé, Leonardo da Vinci, formerly an Italian artist, now a nameless and lost BODY.

The wedding will take place at my apartment at the stated time.

[Signed] Irina Tarakanova

My beloved Anastasiya Petrovna!

Just a quick note. No, it isn't a rumor, I really am getting married. Yes, just imagine it, to a foreigner. He is a Renaissance artist. We'll live at his place. I beseech you, prepare my old folks. Even if they don't give their blessing, then *at least* let them not curse it! Mommy! Daddy! Forgive me! I know not what I do! Anastasiya Petrovna, I want to invite you to the wedding, but I know that you won't be able to come, well, of course, your family, little Olya . . . Anastasiya Petrovna, don't worry, I won't take offense. In answer to your question, may you swallow it, my answer is: you *must*, my sweet! You can hardly spit it out after all! Here everyone swallows. But sensibly. Don't choke yourself on emotions! Well, that's all. I must run.

I embrace you and kiss you.

Yours till death us do part,<br>Ira

# TWENTY-FOUR

And then I thought: Erect a monument to her, and the people will be overjoyed, the revels will begin, but I, suffering from prenatal breathing difficulties, shall lie down for a while, dream awhile, why not! it's still a long way till night, I'll gather my thoughts together, or else he, he, my froglet, he'll take revenge for me, so that you'll groan under the weight and die sorry deaths! Let it be! I welcome this grave new world of mass death and grant my permission, be bold, my froglet, the worse the better—crush them with your tail! But all the same I'm not evil, no, and doubts seized me. And I waited to consult with him: to exterminate or have mercy, or perhaps to content myself with their tears of suffering alone, but there were doubts, because I'd gone too deep into the sphere of that life hidden underfoot and had forgotten the divine, and when I remembered, it turned out that I wasn't on the lists, and the subject was closed, and I said, having given up on it—what the hell, I'm not vindictive—"All of you, live." Let them all die when their time comes. And what can you expect from them if you squeeze them, it's not a lancing, with pus coming out, that's their guts, and how are they to blame, apart from the fact that they're to blame for everything, and inasmuch as it is so, I'm not going to sentence

them and won't condemn them to slavery. Sleep, my froglet,
a deep, deep sleep from which no one wakes. I won't let you
loose, I'm not a destroyer, not a monster, not a troublemaker.
I don't need anything from you at all, and as for myself, don't
you worry, I'll look after myself, I'm fed up with all of you, I
am inviting you to the wedding, this isn't hysterics, I'm ready,
I lie here and breathe and I start to live again, that is, I'm
not going through with the birth of my son, and I'm awaiting
a dear visitor, not with excitement exactly but because he is
my only adviser, and if on this occasion he and I, as was the
case once before, didn't come together as one but to make up
for it were close to each other, but we fell in love, we didn't
meet, but we exchanged fire, and I guessed who and what he
was in the end, but he just spent his time howling ecstatically
. . . Yes, he turned out to be blind, but he'd led a glorious
life, that is, he triumphed, he found himself, he did everything
correctly: they are of shallow draft, but he was a deep-water
vessel, even deeper than before, because there was no need
to understand, what's the point of understanding when it's
clear that if you do understand, then life will be lost, so you
just sit there to your heart's content on the veranda, when
the heat of the day is dying down, as I never once had the
chance to sit, and be pure, and sip white wine, but that track
has been closed to me, I have a different destination and can't
change trains, that's for you, not for me, I ran, but you didn't
make a single move, merely oohed and aahed. They're not
worth my little finger, even broken, and it doesn't matter,
but I ran, I ran my race, I lie here, feeling lonely, in expectation of several feeble questions, when the air gets animated,
and the mirror with the hole, which still remains as it was,
from laziness, but I call you: come as guests, if it takes place,
if it doesn't take place, come anyway, we're not cut out to be
parents, and what can we do with him?

I was ready, I wasn't even worrying, because I'd come out on the other side of suffering, and I'll finish the rest of my sufferings later, I have no regrets, and the highest treason has painted my daily grind in pastel tones, I lay and looked at the dusty trophies, at the cups and prizes—not a bad old horse there, and I'd been right to love horses, although I knew nothing about them, but I loved riding, and once on the beach, toward me, under harness, but we won't, mistress mine, roam away from our story, let us gaze at the blank sheet of paper and say to ourselves: in our mind-fogging idleness we have something to talk about, now that at the end we have come closer to the original, if only from the other side, yes, I'm a fool, and even though I know I won't see it, and I myself shall not be able to make sense of the main thing, and that's why I'm waiting, and this waiting is in vain, the running ended with a choir, lop-eared rabbits on the field, that's important for an accurate account, and if they sang, then at least they weren't dressed up in winding sheets, there was none of that, and as for my not being among you, my dreams prompted me to that, but closer! closer to the business! concentrate, Irina, Irina Vladimirovna, your wedding is at hand, and your groom is late, that is sad and adds an element of unnecessary anxiety, you can't hurry him, but perhaps he's changed his mind, got tired? Oh, no, rubbish, we can't go anywhere without each other, empty talk, but nevertheless why do we have to swallow all this shit, what final joy are we manuring and with what aim? Here I started thinking, pen in mouth, have I missed anything in my account, you yourself used to say about life: STICK IT OUT. We have stuck it out—out of our minds. Hysteria is beautiful, like a fountain, but I have managed to scratch something down in time, like a spider covered in ink, forgive my handwriting, and I even composed a will: Give my cunt to the poor, give her to the invalids, the cripples, the workers in lowly positions, the little men, bad students, to masturbators, old men, parasites, street urchins, butchers, to anyone. They'll find a use for her, but don't demand explanations of them, that's their affair, but I ask you not to consider her something cheap; though she has seen much wear and tear, she is magnificent in all her dimensions, narrow and muscular, wise and enigmatic, romantic and aromatic—full of love by anyone's calculations, however she is very delicate and fears the slightest violence, which can lead to the most painful fissures, concerning which the good doctor Flavitsky will offer consultations to the owner, he is the one who keeps an eye on her. But in the last analysis, if you collect money for a monument to her, don't put it in the middle of a busy square, that's tasteless, don't put it facing Saint Basil's, for it is unbecoming for the Blessed Basil to behold her every day, and also don't put her on Manezh Square, like a Christmas tree! There are in Moscow far cozier corners, the meeting places of lovers and thieves, beggars and jerkoffs. And I beg you, not in the Sadunov baths: it's slippery there. Put up a monument to her . . . but wait a minute, don't make it excessively big, it should not shoot up into the sky like a space hero or a rocket, it should not crush the earth underfoot like the tribune Mayakovsky next to the Chinese hotel, all this is a *male*, alien principle, not suited to me and not befitting her, no, sweeter by far for her would be a bashful monument, covered by a shawl or an overcoat, I don't remember, somewhere in a small courtyard, where that writer, with no roof to call his own, lived with his friend, humiliated and misunderstood, just as she was too, let this be just such a quiet monument, along the base of which should be set out scenes from the life of love: see the photographs of the keeper of archives Gavleyev, for he is the main consultant, he will be the one to cut the ribbon, but where? The Patriarch Ponds, possibly, but there already, above the children, sprawls the idle idol Krylov in military boots, there are the little squares next to the theaters, Aquarium and Hermitage—but she isn't an actress!—and then there is one other, but Marx is there, all the places are occupied. There is, it is true, space in the parkland of Serebryany Bor, but I don't want to be at the back of beyond, the devil knows where, like the usual statue of the girl with an oar, not out of pride, but out of sympathy with people; it's a long way from the metro, you have to go by trolleybus, I'm frightened people will get crushed in the rush, no, the Aleksandrovsky Garden under the Kremlin wall suits me down to the ground, with its Dutch flora and militia fauna, I always felt respect and a restrained affection for militiamen, but then again the monument will be to her, not to me, this time round I haven't deserved either a gilded monument in Paris or an equestrian one, or even an infantryman one—in this country I haven't earned it, this time it's for her, and let it be like a rose, without any excessive fantasies, like a rose —and plant flowers around it, many flowers, and lilac, that's the least utilitarian gesture you can make, and so be it, as a counterweight to glory in battle, glory to love at the other end, and flowers, flowers, flowers. . . . I can't foresee any objections, and we shall dedicate it not to my person but to a round historical date: the year 2000 of a new era. It will be necessary to obtain permission, I know: bureaucracy, don't get angry with me, because I meant no harm, and I don't mean any now, even though it is strange that you still know how to converse, my father is so much more consistent, he has given up the gift of speech, and as for his calling my mama Vera, well, that is actually symbolic, I must tell her, when she arrives at the wedding. Yes, by the way, I give my consent. And I'm not cross with Daddy, he's also a prince, and most probably, therefore, not a Jew, and most probably he couldn't give a shit about Russia, because he himself is Russia. In your country, Ksyusha, you can do what you want to, but we, ever so quietly, in our family fashion will just sit in the kitchen, we won't provide new plates for each course, we'll sit and drink a bit, and grow prettier as color comes to our cheeks, and strike up a song, and one of us will even dance, and then we'll lie down to sleep, and if there isn't room for someone we'll make up a bed on the floor: we'll lie together like brothers in arms—brother with brother, friend with friend, daddy with mommy, we're not proud people, we're happy with both the stick and the carrot. But enough, consider it a request: not one word more! You can put up the monument, but if you don't, others will, if, of course, they hit upon the idea, but all the same, think less and love more. But I hasten to invite everyone to the wedding, and bring presents, expensive ones, or even better, simply money. This will go to the monument, except don't make it a very large one, and definitely red granite, that's how I want it and it will suit her. Okay, let's move on to private life: in the last analysis, my novel doesn't have any abstract content but is about the family, my novel is a family romance, I always respected the family, and bringing up children in particular, but nevertheless I weep only for Ksyusha, I don't need anyone else, only her, but she was wrong to be angry with Leonardik and bad-mouth him, but to make up for it she had no equal in another area and will never have: no one could so quickly and involuntarily go into frenzied orgasms as she, no one came with such a rare gift of joy, and she even used to go a bit pale from the fullness of life, I used to take lessons from her, that is, from my very first sight of her, a woman doesn't look at another woman in that way, and I really couldn't stand intolerance, let them all live, I didn't mind, that's why I'm waiting for advice, and my admirer responded to my call—he rolled up, but I am lying and I take my belly for a walk, and my belly button has popped out, well, totally, just like a third eye, and the mirror has a laceration, I didn't get new glass, and a wind blows from there, but there was no nonsense: his appearance was elegant enough, and he took up his place in my modest life, making himself comfortable on the couch, and I said, "My master! I have grown exhausted waiting for you, what a son of a bitch you are," but in reply he said, "Stop swearing like a gangster, I didn't come to listen to such shit!" and he fell silent, just like a king, but I took exception to this: "You're a bastard, Leonardik, a total, fat, and greasy bastard, honest to God, if you don't want to believe it, don't, but you're a bastard, you made a mistake in rejecting me, but I washed you clean and saved you, with your filthy blood pouring over me, shut up! just listen to the rest: I am much more noble than you, both by breeding and by upbringing. Who are you?" I say. "You played up to everyone and jumped when ordered, but I lived and breathed the steppe air of a Russian town. Meeting you cost me so much: my daddy, two husbands who have gone to seed, and also a hundred other cocks, at a rough count, without going into details, but I fulfilled my purpose, it was a glorious attempt, why has it been so long since your last visit?" He is ashamed and rather transparent, slightly more transparent than on the previous occasion, aha, I say, you're dissolving, and want me to do so too? "It was difficult," he says, "for me to come to you." "Well," I say, "get lost, then!" I look: the guy isn't there, he's in a huff, Ksyusha, all guys are the same, even when they're half transparent, he's not even interested in touching me now, but once again I lie and stroke my belly, discussing the trivia of life, and I've got loads of time, it's spring outside, the season of vitamin deficiencies, but buying pomegranates and vegetables at the market, I eat for two, but a ram butted me, I'm walking away from the metro, I've got a long way to go, I couldn't get on the bus, and there's a herd there, cows, calves; I went past, despite the horns, but farther on were the rams; I thought: Small livestock, and wasn't afraid, but one ram flew at me from behind and caught me—it was painful! sweat poured out, I recovered, sat down, I jot it down, but he comes and says, "Hey, that's enough! Let's be serious." "Let's." "Are you going to have the baby?" "It would be interesting to know what the baby's father thinks about that." He says, "Why do we need him?" I say, "What? Why couldn't you have said that earlier?" "You yourself didn't want me to visit you." "That's true. Okay, let's forgive the old bastards!" "Please, watch your language, I've come to marry you." And I say, "A marriage on paper only?" He understood the hint and fell silent. "But here," I say, "they've forgotten you completely, there are too many living ones, perhaps I should stay, to keep your memory alive?" "That's not a very good idea." "So what is a *good* idea?" He says, "To be honest . . ." He's silent. "How best to put this?" "Well, of course," I say, "I'm so dense . . ." He says, "But when you've got *nothing* to measure things against, how can you explain?" And he falls silent once more. He's not telling the whole story. I say, "Why aren't you telling me everything? Pardon me if I get hysterics." "You," he says, "are a past master at that." I say, "Leave me alone; perhaps I can live a bit more." He says, "And what about me?" in an extremely egotistical way. "Okay. Only please, don't try to influence my choice. I know myself. And this" —I point at the froglet—"is a little present for them all." He says, "Don't exaggerate. . . . Everything's like water off a duck's back for them. And don't try educating them." "Well, all right. Do you love me?" He says that love isn't the word, he worships me, he frets, sits, the little paleface, but accessible to me, while I sit on the bed, with my big belly, full of life and stinking, I sit, panting. "It's terrifying," I say, "for you

see, I know what I did, that is, concerning Katerina Maksimovna, won't they punish me for that?" "So you," he says,
"want to know everything in advance and find out the price
of everything beforehand? Don't you like surprises? Everyone
else does. I do," he says, "for example." "Well, then," I say,
"should I make a dress or what?" "Make one," he says. "Or
how about giving birth first and then getting married?" He
shrugs his shoulders. "As you wish . . ." "And don't you feel
sorry for them? For he'll be a real monster for all that." "If
it's not the devil, then it's the deep blue sea." "Yes! But at
least not my doing!" And I dream of marrying him: he's so
delicate, I get up, walk over to him, stroke his hair, his hair's
silky like a baby's. . . . "When?" I say submissively. "Today."
"What do you mean, today!" "Why put off till tomorrow . . . ?"
"Just let it not be hot air!" I cried out. "Leonardik, what's
best?" We started to consider the various options. I was
squeamishly hard to please: cutting my wrists, jumping from
a height, are unsuitable, pills are unreliable, they make you
nauseous as well, all the other ways are painful. "And can't
you do it for me?" He knitted his brow. "Oh, puh-lease . . ."
And then I look, he isn't there. Leonardik, where have you
got to? He's gone to get an ax. . . . I ran out onto the street,
in six weeks the sticky little leaves will appear, and I, a married
woman, will rush to my son, in joyful agitation, I'll send for
Mommy, she'll be, the bitch, a grandmother! And I'll have
a nanny, and my better half, Viktor Kharitonych, taking time
off from state business, will start phoning home to bill and
coo, to make the ornamental secretaries jealous on the telephone: "Well, how's our wee one doing? has he eaten all his
food? is his tummy hurting? does he look like me this morning?
or like you? or doesn't he look like anyone?" My joy, how
could he not be like you, if you loved me, pretending to be
the very figure of a ghost, having forgotten all about the affairs

of state, and despising your middle-aged wife, whom you
haven't cuddled for quite a while. Oh, Carlos! Oh, my Latin
American ambassador, admirer of Neruda and foe of juntas
and other fascist experiments, drive your little Zhiguli out of
the garage, with its little pajama flag, invite ministers and
kings, all you have to do is spit once and they'll come running!
No, Carlos, your Mercedes is not longer than my Leonardik's
passion wagon, we also knows how to when we wants to,
forgive me the stupid joke, but know: my sonny is beautiful,
like the god of your country, I knew in advance. Everything
will end in peace, you are mine, you are my husband, but
there is Babel in the yard already, and a black hundred of
cocks has lined up, ready for presents and hors d'oeuvres, ready
for forgiveness, enjoy yourselves, my dears, I'll be with you
yet, for the last time, and you, little brothers Ivanovich, come,
come here, we shall take our leave of you, thank you for the
article, we'll settle accounts later, and you, special correspon-
dents of the world's press, you have popped up here—hi,
bandits! See, I am receiving guests, numbering all told a black
hundred, and also their wives, neighbors, relatives, loafers,
and lovers, and Antoshka, how could one forget Antoshka?
We are on friendly terms once more, and please, call me
"Mama," and this is your unborn little brother, the little black
worm, say hello, hey, why have you turned away, be bolder,
don't be afraid! and kiss Mama on the cheek and don't dare
tell anyone, hey, that's just not done! you bastard! Further:
Dato, he'll play for us, here's the Steinway, Mendelssohn
obviously, only not too loud, or else it'll make my head ache,
yes, Dato, today I am going to marry you, Dato Vissarionovich,
and your father, Vissarion, knows me as an out-and-out
beauty, like a goddess, and Antoshka whispers in my ear:
"Mama, you are my genius of pure beauty, Mommy dear," and
over there are Yegor and Yura Fyodorov, the pair of scared

guards, armed with gladioli. I'm getting married today, and here's another pair: my former spouses, now run wild—hi! I don't remember the face of one, but there's something vaguely familiar about him, on account of the headlong flight from my parents' home, the second is wearing a baggy suit from the local department store, he doesn't drink, doesn't smoke, doesn't play with his ball, how is this? Surely you haven't died, my little boy? You were the one who whetted my passion! You! So forget your provincial complexes, the whole black hundred of cocks was your doing after all! Hey, all of you! Well, okay, then, I'm not going to shout—no, I *will* shout: just give me a little bit longer! Mommy, you stand by the entrance, at six-thirty you will open the door, but get yourself dressed up a bit, here's a necklace for you, here's some bracelets and clothes, wear them to your heart's content, take the perfumes, these too, take everything, I don't need them, don't cry, it's a present, hey, hey, I'm happy, Mommy, don't cry, but as far as *your* fate is concerned, it worries me less and less: if you eat everything that's left and beat everyone to death, if you put each other away in the prisons and camps, if you forbid people to have a shit under pain of death, if you ration drinking water, I shall exclaim: Obviously that's how it must be! I *approve!* I bless you, that's all, enough for today, ah, Vitasik, the six-day hero, you too have favored me with your presence, and Merzlyakov is very crafty, he is always watching: Just who is it she's marrying? and isn't there some dirty trick here? and why is it that the guests who have gathered, instead of going into the apartment, are standing up to their knees in the March snow higgledy-piggledy with diplomatic representatives, ambulances, and with the raven-black Marias produced here in the fatherland? Why? Vitasik strains in thought—why is she thrusting herself toward us through the *fortochka,* holding her kimono none too tightly and teasing us with the chance of glimpsing her breasts? Could it be that she's trying to pull the wool over our eyes, this pregnant whore? thinks Merzlyakov tensely, lost and drowning in the March snow, which will soon melt, and in fact what we could really do with here is a little picture of nature: the rooks have taken wing and arrived, the crows' woody nests are on the birch trees, in the last analysis we have a right to beauty guaranteed by the Slavic soul, for you see after all we're not misers, not skinflints, not Danes—what? even at this stage you're still not acquainted? Here's my Dane, he came and went, but all the same he's here with us today, from the International Exhibition of Medical Equipment, he *doesn't* have blond hair, he sent a lackey from the National Hotel with a present of two boxes of grub and a watch with a bracelet, not expensive, of course, but pretty good going for a single cum, he came and went, but Viktor Kharitonych—he's with us forever, he's one of us, from Vologda, oh, how beautiful he is with his ugly mug, let us describe it after all: and so, wearing glasses, beneath the little piggy eyes, an attempt at a beard, a face as if it's rotted away from being overcooked, his skin is glossy and porous, like a steaming cowpat, his lips are damp, his penis is pointed like a sharpened pencil, he sits in his office and draws lines to keep his mind active, but all the same he's my future husband, he's been promoted since that time, soon he'll start giving all the orders; however, he protected me in whatever ways he could; however, he came to an arrangement with them and, so the rumors go, is getting married to the rich widow Zinaida Vasilievna, when she was in mourning and arrived with her white lace handkerchief to complain about me, like in El Greco's painting, I was always a cultured woman, I wore a kimono, in which Igoryok—ah, you too, it seems, are not acquainted? there wasn't enough paper for everyone, he drove off in my kimono, at night, as soon as we had gone to bed, his car started to howl in the wind, a fault of the hidden alarm system, because the Italian car alarm started howling from the wind and the cold, thinking that the frost was trying to steal it, and then the neighbor who lived above me, who had once dropped in on me with wine to make my acquaintance, I had apologized, using the excuse that I was busy, the neighbor had made off with his tail between his legs and harbored a grudge, and now the car screams, Igor, grabbing the kimono, rushes out into the yard, and the neighbor, throwing open the window, bawls, "Seeing as you're with a whore, you ought to come quietly!" From fright Igor drove off, still wearing my kimono, and vanished forever, although he was beautiful, rich, in my presence he phoned from bed to give his underlings in the motor transport depot a roasting, and got very excited from swearing at them, and demanded that I touch him at the same time, and then the kimono arrives by parcel post together with the bedroom slippers, well, I invited the neighbor to the wedding too, and even that Stepan who had knocked me over, just doing his job, I couldn't resist, I invited him, he came with Marfa Georgievna, they got married recently, and my new friends came, under the leadership of Boris Davydovich, his stick tapped in the echoing entrance hall, his stick with its handle in the form of a bearded prophet's head: for some, Lev Tolstoy; for some, Solzhenitsyn; for his own kind, Moses. My new friends came, in the twilight of their recent glory, their ranks thinner, Belokhvostov is already in Pennsylvania, he's not doing the work he's qualified for, he's content, and with them women with snipers' squints and cigarettes from the Yava tobacco factory, they came and squinted their eyes, and Leonardik is already flying around, ready to make a scene: "What are they doing here? Why are there so many foreigners? Lovers everywhere you look . . ." "But what can I do: I made friends with men with all my heart." And Leonardik said then, going crazy and flabbergasted by this: "And what's more, you're still too intimate with them." And only you, my most beloved friend in life, were not there in this squalid yard. A spy and a terrorist, you flew only as far as the gates of the capital's airport, and there you were mercilessly deprived of the visa that had been issued to you due to someone's absentmindedness, and you were thrown out of the country and flew back in tears, with a landing at Warsaw, and Leonardik said, "Thank God they've kicked her out, she would have been the last straw!" But Rituyla came, and Hamlet. Hamlet was very excited, he had fallen so much in love with me in that short period that he wouldn't part with the magazine, and Rituyla had hacked up the little magazine with her manicure scissors and burned the scraps on a rubbish pile, Hamlet wept on hearing of the loss, but Mommy stood in front of the door at her post, like a centurion and a beast, Granddaddy the Stakhanovite died a year later, missing his granddaughter, Daddy the furniture maker had refused to come to Moscow, he had fallen victim to a new rare disorder: trolleybusphobia; he considered them inventions of the devil, despite all the entreaties; however, on the appointed day, having put on a white shirt and a tie, he drank a full glass of wine in front of the mirror and remembered my childhood, concerning which I had written to him in a letter: My Dear Daddy, know this too, life will pass by, I'll pass by and go away forever, but the only man who was ever really dear to me, really close, really loved, with whom I felt better than with anyone else—please turn over to the bouquet of peonies—yes, know: it was you! Your daughter who loves you, Ira. He took the postcard, creased by the years, out of his jacket and burst out crying. He was forgiven. Mother was holding back the intrigued guests, looking askance at one another in a dilemma and already separating into hostile parties, not offering one another their hands. I waved to them from the window. Leonardik, however, was sprawled on the couch in the pose of a satisfied fiancé. He said, "Oh, how happy I am to be marrying you, my beauty!" I said, "Perhaps the turkey's burning, idiot?" I was eaten up with worries, looking after so many things. I was very concerned about the turkey. The tables were laid in both rooms, the mirror's shame had been draped, I still have to put myself in order, but Nina Chizh, leaning against a silver birch, wept from envy. Leonardik, of course, wasn't there. It's not exactly that he was late, but simply that we had agreed that he should arrive a bit later. Damn him! He still bore a grudge against me, when he came for the third time, and the tenth time, and the hundredth time, he flashed in and out, appearing and disappearing like a shoal of fish, as if he'd lost patience, day and night, but during the day he was inclined to be lackluster and indecisive, at night on the other hand he moralized and preached how I didn't understand what was taking place and that I was no Joan of Arc. "Stop nagging me," I would say, "and just who are you exactly? Here you are, read some of this." And I would take one of his masterpieces down from the shelf and select a page at random. He would curse and spit and scream. "Aha!" I would say. "How's that, then; hardly classics, I'm afraid, so stop nagging me." I felt sorry for all of them there chilled to the marrow in the snow and vileness of the yard, I wanted to tender each one of them some tenderness, but my present was meant for all of them, like an appeal. The novel was ending with a wedding.

It's time to finish! It's necessary to curtain off the dressing-table mirror with a slept-on sheet, but for the moment, having sat down on the pouf and been reflected in the glass, I look, seized by worry and weariness, at my belly, make up my eyes, start thinking, become pensive. Irisha, the guests are waiting!

The tables were fragrant with meat, fish, and vegetable pies. My dowry: crystal and silver plate, nothing to be ashamed of. I slapped my stomach: Well, how are you, froglet? He grew quiet. Your mommy has got to the marrying age. And once more to the window, and through the *fortochka* to gaze at the crowd that had been invited: and Katerina Maksimovna had come, and Veronika with Timofei, who is rushing around the yard like one possessed. "Hey, get ready, Ira!" Leonardik, sprawling in the triumphant pose of a lord and master who has had his fill, hurries me along, they never are able to conceal their bestial triumph, I sing artlessly, do my hair, glide along the parquet floor, what can I think about, I put thoughts aside, although I catch myself thinking when, then, *will* I have time to think, if not now, the clock has struck six, well, I've still got half the time on the clock in order to remember everything or to spend some time in prayer: Father Veniamin, my sugary little priest, was also among the guests, but he was not in uniform, I saw him in plain clothes for the first time, that was why he seemed more alluring, and that's why my hands were fumbling at the buttons and zipper in order to grab hold of it—oh, this fair moment!—already impatiently, dully dribbling, but, Ira, this is no time for that! You must say something to them! Why *must* I? It's absurdly funny. And what am I to say to them? We're not in Rouen. Where are the English? My entire Britain is made up of the routed orchestra with the Yalta bastard at its head, broken loose from his leash, with a rope around his neck, while his wife, the mother of tiny daughters, languishes in the foreign-currency bar, in despair, distressed by their visit to this barbaric great power, where ideas of what's right and proper don't coincide with the Greenwich mean. We're not in Rouen. But nevertheless have your say. Irina Vladimirovna is playing truant. Irina Vladimirovna has stolen a sweet. She's gobbling it down. His legs comfortably crossed, Leonardik sits, with a carnation in his button-hole, in one of his countless appearances. Well, good.

Walk slowly, watch your step, in this country we have a bad, ugly stance. I was an exception. Develop your walk, I've got nothing else to write about, I grieve over all that I have done, I ask you to take into account my broken life, I was always on the edge, was not in control of myself, I was too shy, I didn't believe that anyone could desire me. Soon, soon the stream of guests will flow into these cheerless rooms, soon they will yell out, "Bitter! Bitter! Kiss the bride to make what's bitter sweet inside!" A mountain of a feast. "What are you dawdling over?" growls Leonardik. It's usual for a groom to worry. I am getting married for the last time, but I'm not getting worked up, I am simply happy to live and work in this country, amidst such a marvelous people, and if I wasn't to someone's liking, then I apologize. And you, Viktor Khari-tonych, don't be too harsh! What else do you expect from a woman! But such a beautiful one . . . And my most dear Stanislav Albertovich is wrong to say that I'm the grandmother of Russian abortion. That's offensive. And, as I embraced lifelong girlfriends or specialists in the one-minute stand, who among them did not think about me at that moment, who did not think: With her, only with her did I feel myself a king, she is unforgettable? And I decided to keep things look-ing at their best, I grant you peace, and carry my corpse with care from the basement of the police morgue: I loved you all. I got up and went into the bathroom, I'll take this highway, there is noise on the other side of the door, and poor Mommy holds the siege in check with difficulty. Mother dearest! You were a terrible fool, but I like the way you shout! Shout, don't be shy! Leonardik, give me my bedroom slippers. . . . Where am I going? To you, my dearly beloved, my darling, I'm coming to you. Till we meet! I know that beyond this door there's emptiness and in the yard there's March slush, that the air is damp, muggy, rotten, that the tables are groaning under the weight of victuals, and I don't say anything, so wouldn't it perhaps be better to go into the bathroom and take a warm shower, let my neck, in the grip of old age, relax! Let the wedding wind down. Beat it! I composed you in order to compose myself, but when I discompose you I shall dissolve myself as a person, but before this dissolution I shall note totally irrelevantly: The landscape of early spring in Moscow is too orphaned without brut, and so drink champagne! I bought three crates for you—there, take it from the balcony, if the frost hasn't caused the bottles to burst during the night, oh, Leonardik, and what if it has? What sort of wedding would it be without champagne? I had a drink and a bite of salmon, you will find the bones in my stomach. Departing for my groom, I shall say that I've got nothing to say to you. That's right, and you, captivating American beauties, go on, write your next protest. It will contain the bitterness of your inability to comprehend fish soup made from sterlet or our red whortleberry preserves, it will say how the brotherhood of women knows no bounds, united in the agony of having their cunts ripped. What I have done today means that instead of the Bermuda Triangle you will discover a hairy loving little heart. Vitasik, you know: I was always slightly sentimental. I walked in your white sweater around your rich apartment and waited for a miracle. It occurred: you fell in love with me forever. But circumstances are more powerful than we are and far above us and everything else, on high, today we are uttering endearments to each other like at a railway station, the only thing missing is the guard, and so it's time, goodbye, or else they'll make it in time. I clamber up onto the soapy stool, toward the ceiling, the stool I used for washing clothes, and the soap has caked. I climb up, and Leonardik enters.

"Zhanna," he says, "you're choosing *this* method this time?"
"Yes," I answer. "Oh, well, I suppose it's suitably vulgar."
"Yes, my lord," I agree. "Yes, my unearthly bridegroom."
"Shall we kiss?" We kiss. "Shall we make up?" We make up.
Life is difficult. I take a step toward him. I throw myself into
his embrace. Tighter! Hold me tighter, my dear! Enter, enter
me, my prince! Oh, how good! Oh, God, how the walls and
towels are spinning! Aah, how unexpected! More . . . Yes,
come on, more . . . squeeze harder! yes, harder! Yes, yes, keep
on. Let me come sweetly! You're totally choking me, beloved
. . . Oh, no! Don't! That hurts, idiot! I don't w-a-a-a-a-a-
a-a-nnn-nna . . . wa . . . w . . . wa . . .

Light! I see light! It widens. It grows. One bound and I
am free. I hear soothing voices. They egg me on approvingly.
The gas water heater drones. I see her: she is swinging evenly.
And such a generous belly. Goodbye, froglet! Don't jerk, hurry
up, fall asleep, sleep, hush-a-bye baby, froglet! I look at her:
she has fallen silent. Awash with happy tears. Mommy opens
the doors. The guests flood in. The wedding! The wedding!
But where's the bride? And here comes the bride! Good to
see you!